Between Thorns and Glory

A Novel

Kimberly Frost Pinkney

MW01171370

Between Thorns and Glory
The Way Publishing

Copyright © 2022 by Kimberly Frost Pinkney. All rights reserved.
No part of this book may be reproduced, scanned, or distributed in any printed or electronic form without permission. Please do not participate in or encourage piracy of copyrighted materials in violation of the author's rights. Thank you for respecting the hard work of this author.

This is a work of fiction. Names, characters, places, and incidents either are the product of the author's imagination or are used fictitiously, and any resemblance to locales, events, business establishments, or actual persons—living or dead—is entirely coincidental.

Dedication

To my mom, Patsy Frost

Mom told me daily that I could accomplish anything I wanted then, by example, taught me to believe it. She became the first woman postmaster in our little town of Loco Hills, New Mexico, which she called a "blink 'em city" because if you blinked, you missed it. People loved talking with her at the post office. She often counseled them and gave moral support and love. When she was thanked for helping someone through a hard time, she would say, "I didn't do anything. I just listened."

Often, I came home from school to the aroma of freshly baked bread or cake that she had made for a friend, neighbor, or relative. She enjoyed visiting people and lavished her bottomless love and cheer on the sick and the sad.

She supported me when I wanted to start my own business at sixteen and drove me to my appointments so I could do my homework on the way.

She always understood me and knew what I needed even though it took me decades to understand some of what she was talking about. She taught me to be my own person with my own mind. Her encouragement and legendary joyful laughter are anchored in my memory and my heart.

Chapter One

Allison struggled to find her festive spirit in between her joyful heart's desire, the path of achievement she'd devoted herself to, and the stifling match her mother had chosen. Taking a deep breath, she summoned her courage to release Professor Mort Hebert's hand.

Allowing her sparkle to come through her composed and polished persona, Allison gracefully grabbed her sister by both hands, and they swirled in a circle in the middle of the dance floor. Madeleine's wedding gown and Allison's emerald maid of honor dress flowed out in a whimsical white-and-green cloud of taffeta, lace, and tulle.

"Oh, Maddie, everything is just perfect! So magical," Allison said. She spoke with so much joy, she hoped the whole wedding crowd could hear her over the band playing a fast bluesy rock tune.

"Allison, I've missed you so much. I can't wait until you're back home for good." She stopped swirling and hugged her sister.

Allison could feel the discord and the distance that had been between them melting quickly. "Almost there. One more semester to graduate. But you better stop being mushy, or we'll mess up our makeup. Our every move is being recorded." Allison beamed her signature broad smile at her little sister. "So, are you ready for your wedding night? Or do we need to have the talk?" Allison smiled with a mock-serious look.

"Seriously? I'm not puritanical like you. I know I'm a sinner. But I'm proud of you for waiting until you're married. Very admirable.

You better watch out for Dr. Death, though. I heard Europeans have a different take on the matter than we do."

"I wish you wouldn't call him that. Mort is a perfect gentleman. Besides, he blessed the sacrament the first day I met him. He would never do anything to jeopardize his faith or his job, for that matter. Besides, I trust him completely."

"Oh, good. That is reassuring." Maddie rolled her eyes. "But are you sure about him? I mean, what about Jonathan? You just don't seem all that..."

Allison felt her joyful expression fading into defensiveness.

"Oh, never mind. I'm probably just jealous that he gets more time with you than we do these days." Maddie kissed her sister on the cheek.

Allison looked down and tried to recover her happy face. She felt horrible that she had missed all the wedding planning, but every time she'd tried to come home, somehow Mort needed her there for this event or that. She had felt isolated from her friends and sister for the past six months. She didn't know how to make everyone happy. She didn't know how she was going to do it, but she would just have to figure it out. Her own happiness depended on it.

"Maddie, I feel like I've missed so much being gone these three and a half years."

"I know it's been hard around here without you. Losing Grandma Emma and Grampa John both and having you gone. That just leaves Jonathan and Luke and me against Busy Bea. You were always the buffer."

"You know how to deal with her, Maddie. Actually, better than me. I just do what she wants, but I'm not really sure that's the best thing to do."

"Yeah, probably not. I know it's selfish, but while you're doing what she wants, she doesn't pay much attention to the rest of us.

With you gone, she's trying to micromanage Emma's Flower Shop and Nursery, and she doesn't know a thing about it."

"Don't worry. She's still micromanaging my life from afar. Why do you think I started dating Mort in the first place?"

"She thinks she has to run this perfect family to impress Grandmother Scott."

"Yeah, and that's impossible. Grandmother Scott has a permanent sourpuss face. Do you think she made that face when she was a kid and it stuck?" Allison said with all seriousness.

They both looked over at the table where Grandmother Scott was talking crossly to her daughter-in-law, Bea. Allison and Madeleine's father, Spencer, sat next to his mother, wearing his quiet smug look. When Grandmother Scott stopped talking, she realigned the edges of her mouth with the bottom of her chin.

Allison and Maddie broke out in laughter.

"How does she even do that?" Maddie asked, gasping for air in between giggles. Allison hadn't laughed like that with her little sister in what seemed years although it was only just before her mother had practically ordered her to date Mort.

Luke and Jonathan set their drinks down on the head table and made their way through the crowded dance floor.

"Allison, she's *mine* now," Luke said.

Allison offered Madeleine's hand to her new husband and bowed as though she were a gentleman excusing himself from a lady. She found it very amusing to pretend to be proper since Southern California had a such a casual atmosphere.

Allison watched Luke swirl his bride around the dance floor while holding her tightly.

"Wanna dance?" Jonathan asked.

"Absolutely!" Allison gazed up into Jonathan's shining obsidian eyes. She marveled once again at how such a bright light could come from such dark eyes.

Not everyone considered Jonathan to be good-looking, but Allison had always thought he was the most beautiful man she'd ever seen. His skin was deep brown like the center of a black-eyed Susan. He wore a closely trimmed beard that was soft and scratchy at the same time. His tightly curled black hair was cut close, almost military style, and his head seemed to have a permanent dent around it where his cap usually sat.

"I think this is the first time in all these years that I've actually seen your head, Jonathan."

"It probably is." He gave her his sideways grin.

"Is that old hat you always wear the same one Grampa gave you on your first day at Emma's?"

He chuckled. "Yep. I never saw the need for another one." He changed to a low, serious tone. "Just like you, Allison. Once I saw you, I never saw another."

"Jonathan, please. Don't bring this up again. We're having such a good time."

Allison tore her gaze from Jonathan's obsidian eyes. She forced her focus on the twinkling lights interspersed among hundreds of flowers that draped over the dance floor.

"You know I'll always love you. The preacher is still here. The place is still decorated. You and Maddie can trade dresses." He gave her that gorgeous toothy grin she loved.

"Oh, Jonathan." Allison looked down from the lights and followed the happy bride being twirled around the dance floor by her beloved groom. "You know that I'll always love you too, but you know how things are. We can't. I..."

"Alli, when are you going to start making *yourself* happy for once?"

"Making others happy makes me happy."

"But you can't be responsible for other people's happiness, especially someone like Busy Bea. She isn't even in charge of her own happiness. Being perfect won't control how she treats you."

Allison looked around the room and spotted her mother. Jonathan must have sensed it because he twirled her away.

"Honestly, Jonathan. I know you and Grampa John have both told me that a million times, but I just don't understand what you mean. I don't want to control anyone."

She looked up into his eyes, hoping to convince him once and for all, but she could see that she hadn't.

"I really hope you get it soon because I'm afraid that if you don't you'll really lose yourself to that Dr. Death. There's definitely something fishy about that guy."

Allison felt her whole demeanor sinking into the floor. "But he..."

Jonathan let her off the hook by interrupting her. "How long is Busy Bea going to make us wear these monkey suits anyway?" Jonathan fidgeted inside his tuxedo without letting go of Allison.

She was grateful for the change of subject. "If it were up to her, forever. Oh, speak of the devil—here she comes."

"Jonathan, the band is having a problem with the power or something. I thought you said they were set up," Bea said as she grabbed Allison away from him.

"Mom, we're dancing. The band sounds fine to me. Jonathan—"

"It's okay, I'll go see what they need." Jonathan smiled as he interrupted Allison.

She marveled at how Jonathan never lost his joy no matter what her mother threw at him. "Mom, I wish you wouldn't treat Jonathan like a servant. Grampa left him an equal share of Emma's as he left me and Maddie."

Allison wished her mother would accept Jonathan and stop thinking of him as that poor African American kid from the wrong side of the tracks. She thought that maybe her mother would accept him if he belonged to their church. Allison felt guilty that she'd failed at her attempt to convince Jonathan to join her church. But he was stubborn, just like Grampa, and although he believed in Jesus, he chose to steer clear of traditional organized religion.

"Allison, you're forgetting your manners. You have left your beau alone for far too long."

"Mom, he's occupied." Allison looked around the reception area for Professor Mort Hebert and found him deep in a discussion with a group of professors. She dutifully approached the group.

"Ah, Allison. At long last," Mort said in his distinctive French accent. "You know Professor Bluff and—"

"Of course, I've known them my whole life. How are you? It is so good to see you all again." She smiled at the group of researchers and professors.

"Your grandpa would have loved this night. He was so proud of his two granddaughters. I know Maddie is a talented administrator like your grandmother. But you, Allison, he always saw you stepping in to take his place in the research side of the business. And don't you worry—we all know you had the equivalent of a PhD before you went for your bachelor's. You'll do great things in this field."

"Thank you so much, Professor Bluff. It's always been my dream to return to Emma's Nursery and Flower Shop to continue Grampa's legacy and his research contracts with you and all the other professors. Jonathan will do innovative things as well. He's done a great job running Emma's, don't you think?"

The professors and their spouses looked around at the expansive tree section of the nursery covered in millions of lights and red roses lushly decorated for the reception.

"Yes, indeed," Professor Bluff answered. "Jonathan outdid himself and anyone else on this wedding."

"I heard he started a Bible group for youth here at Emma's," said Professor Sloan, dean over religious studies at the Christian college where they all taught. "Let's see... What did they call it? Seeds?"

"Sprouts," Allison said.

"Yes, of course, Sprouts. What a clever name."

"Yes, he's training teen boys the way Grampa taught him. They listen to the Bible while working with plants. Grampa always said that boys weren't meant to sit in a room all dressed up. The land is theirs to toil, and that's where they'll find their connection with the Creator."

"Well, your family, and the community, are extremely lucky to have Jonathan. How did your grandfather find him?"

"He was a friend of Luke's. The two of them came to Emma's one day when Luke and Jonathan and I were about fifteen to pick up an order for Luke's dad, Bobby. Grampa saw something in Jonathan, and he hired him that same day. He's been here ever since."

Jonathan and Luke suddenly appeared one on either side of Professor Hebert. "Enjoying yourself, Professor He Burt?" Luke slapped him on the back just as he had taken a drink, nearly spilling it on his suit.

"It is *Eh-bear*," Professor Hebert said, emphasizing the French pronunciation of his name. He gave a small cough and inspected his suit for spilled punch.

"Where is a bear?" Jonathan looked around, acting innocent.

"No, my name is pronounced *eh-bear*, not *he-burt*." Professor Hebert was visibly perturbed.

"Oh, don't worry about it. We'll just call you Dr. Death, Mort," Luke said dragging out his name and popping the *T* while simultaneously slapping him on the back again.

Allison came to his rescue. "Don't mind them. They're just a couple of jokers."

She grabbed him by the hand and led him to the dance floor. They could hear the group of professors laughing with Luke and Jonathan. Allison knew that everyone was watching Professor Hebert dance her around the floor. She felt like a sparkling jewel in her green taffeta maid of honor dress, dancing with an elegant and brilliant man. Allison was so happy.

She looked up into Mort's face and saw a man out of his element, a Frenchman in an uncouth society. She thought how wonderful it would be to be married to such a sophisticated, prestigious man, a graduate of the University of Paris, a professor at a Christian college, and a leader in the church. Even her mother and father approved.

She was happy to have their approval, for once. She was used to bending to her mother's will. She didn't have any other choice. In fact, as she danced with him, it reminded her of how he'd looked that night at the gala, when her mother had insisted she go out with him. He'd been asking her out for months. She hadn't really been able to figure out why. She didn't think they had any chemistry together, but he was relentless in his pursuit.

He was good looking in an exotic European kind of way and so-phisticated. Maybe too sophisticated for her. She was a dirt girl, born to be a nurturer of flora, and he was a man of letters on the subject of horticulture. Her only problem was that she couldn't picture him here at Emma's Nursery and Flower Shop. Hopefully, he would get a position at one of the local colleges if they were to marry.

"Allison, my dear, you look lovely tonight. Most women begin to lose their polish as the night wears on, but somehow, you become even more radiant," Mort said.

"Thank you, Prof... Mort." Even though they'd been dating now for six months, she still hadn't settled in on what to call him. A for-mal distance between them kept her off balance. She wondered if it was from her or him. He said all the right things—things that Jonathan and Luke would have found corny but women loved to hear. Her stubborn anxiety would not subside. He was so aristocratic, and she was so American. Her mother was excited about him and told her that it would come in time. Her father was a stiff kind of guy, and her mother adjusted. So Allison had decided to adjust. But she didn't want to think of anything like that tonight. Her life-long friend had just married her little sister, and they were so happy. Settling for contentment, she could dance here with Professor Mort all night.

"Allison, darling, why do you not give the tour of your family's grounds?"

"Sure, I can show you around. Let's go." She led him out of the reception to a small footbridge over a slow-running brook and into the perennial area, which had been set up for the wedding. The nearly endless selection of colorful flowers had been placed around the perimeter in an impressive design. An elaborate arch of roses of various shades of red stood empty and dark at the front of the rows of white wooden folding chairs. The automatic misters hissed, sending sparkling drops over the various colorful blossoms of impatiens and dianthus. The farmhouse-style building that housed the offices and flower shop was also lit up with lights on the outside but was dark on the inside. Fresh potted flowers decorated the wraparound porch in a beautifully rustic display.

"That's the flower shop. Plus it has the offices that Maddie uses to keep the books and where Jonathan manages the orders and contracts."

"Is that where your grandfather kept his research notes and logs?" Mort asked.

"Yes. He called his office 'the crow's nest.'"

The office was set off from the rest of the building. It had three walls with huge windows overlooking Emma's property. Two rows of greenhouses, the barn, the outdoor display area, and the tree section could be seen from there. The office was separated from the inside display area and floral workshop by a wall-sized plate glass window.

"He said he could see the whole operation from right there at this desk."

She stepped into the dark display area. Her footsteps echoed across the empty shop as she led Mort to the crow's nest. Taking a deep breath, Allison savored the mixture of soil, flowers, and ink that flooded her senses as she stepped into the office.

"It's just as he left it when he passed over a year ago. He was so organized, there was no need to move anything." She lovingly glided her hand over a neat row of log books on a built-in counter. Mort did not seem to be listening. Instead, he fingered the file cabinet, opening and closing each one softly.

"In fact, Jonathan records the research results in these log books just like Grampa used to." Allison was eager to redirect Mort's attention back to herself. "But he waits for me to come home on break to write up the reports. I've been helping Grampa write reports since I was about twelve. Grampa John and Grandma Emma passing within days of each other has left a huge hole."

"That is a lot of trust your grandfather had in you," Mort said.

She smiled proudly. "Yes, I guess he did."

"Do you trust me, my dear?"

"Of course. Why wouldn't I?" Allison had no reason not to trust him. She wondered why he would ask that. Couldn't he see that she did? She would try harder in the future to show her trust. She respected and admired him, and she loved him in an awestruck way as though she were dating the horticulture version of a rock star. He was well into his life at age twenty-eight, while she had yet to reach her twenty-first birthday. He had completed his PhD and post-doc programs in record time and had become one of the youngest tenured professors ever at her college. Although at times she wondered why he hadn't pursued a more prestigious college rather than settling for a Christian university, she assumed he had chosen this path out of religious fervor.

"In fact, Maddie had always wanted to get married at Grandma Emma's cottage, but no one could bear to move their stuff around, so they opted for the nursery. Come on, let's get back to the reception."

"Not just yet, my dear." He romantically scooped her up by the waist. "I want you all to myself." He guided her out of the office and shop, back into the night lit with thousands of twinkling lights.

They walked arm in arm past the beautifully decorated wrap-around porch of the farmhouse converted to offices, display area and floral workshop.

"Back here are the greenhouses. This is where all the real work happens, like growing all the flowers and the research we're contract-ed for."

He held her snugly to him as they walked between the two long rows of a half dozen greenhouses on each side. He felt stiff in his Eu-ropean tailored suit. It made Allison feel rigid on the inside.

When they arrived at the last greenhouse, Allison pointed to a big old-fashioned red barn. "There's the barn where the mower re-pair shop is and all our equipment and supplies are stored. Upstairs is Jonathan's apartment."

"He lives here? In the mechanic's garage? Tsk." He gave a motion of his hand in an arrogant gesture of disapproval.

Allison glossed over his disrespect. She wasn't in the habit of tak-ing up for anyone, not even herself. She tried to muster a matter-of-fact tone. "Yes, he has since he was sixteen. Grampa had an apart-ment built for him in there."

Professor Hebert opened the door of the last greenhouse and ushered Allison inside.

She could hear the faint music in the background. "We better get back. We're going to miss the party."

"You know how much I like to have you to myself," Mort said.

The greenhouse filled with tropical greenery and rare roses was warm and humid, and Allison started feeling uncomfortable in her taffeta dress. She was trying to hang on to the mood she had accomplished earlier when dancing, but it was fading quickly. Professor Mort seemed to have a morose effect on her frame of mind.

"Look, I almost blend right in to the vegetation in here." Allison giggled with forced delight. She twirled around, and when she came back to face the professor, he was down on one knee.

He held out his hand to her. "Will you marry me, Allison Louise Scott of Emma's Nursery and Flower Shop?" He popped the *p* of *shop*, mocking the American accent.

At first, she thought he was joking. She laughed. "Oh, do get up. You will soil your trousers," she said, imitating his formality.

"Well, will you?" The simple words sounded flowery in his French accent.

She thought about if she should answer in French, but she feared his criticism of her pronunciation. She didn't want to ruin the moment. She knew she shouldn't take so long to answer. He would get the idea that she didn't want to. She wondered if she did want to or if she really had a choice.

Suddenly, her promise to Jonathan to come back to Emma's flooded over her. She put the thought aside. She would sort it out later.

After all, the professor was her perfect match. Everyone said so. Well, her mother, father, and Grandmother Scott did. Maddie, Luke, and Jonathan couldn't stand him.

She didn't believe that she would ever love someone like she loved Jonathan, and if she couldn't have him, then the rest didn't matter. If her happiness didn't matter to her mother, she wondered why it should matter to her. It would just be easier to do what her mother wanted. That would make her so happy. If her mother was happy, Allison believed that she would be too.

"Yes." She looked down at Mort with a forced smile and solemn eyes.

He sprang to his feet, kissed her, and swung around off her feet.

"Wait. No ring?" She released him and backed away into the workbench. She looked at him with her arms crossed with the illusion of power.

Mort walked slowly toward her with a look of intensity and impatience. His attitude changed so abruptly that Allison was confused.

"You are overdressed for the greenhouse, my dear," he said with a sinister twist of his mouth. His eyes gleamed with something she didn't recognize.

Second-guessing herself, she convinced herself it was his look of passion, but she was suddenly afraid of him. She side-stepped, trying for the door. But he was too fast. He blocked her and pinned her up against a table of thorny rosebushes.

"Ouch," she said. "Thorns."

She could feel blood from the thorny prick trickling down her left arm. But he didn't let go of her. Somehow, he had both of her hands in his left hand, above her head. With his right hand, he picked her up by the waist and placed her back in front of the workbench. He kissed her passionately. She didn't know how to handle such aggressiveness. She reluctantly went along with him and returned his affection. Finally, she started to relax and trust him again. But then he tightened his grip on her hands and forcefully pulled her dress up. The rough wood table splintered into her backside. She was shocked at what was happening.

"Stop. No. I'm waiting for marriage. Stop!" Allison yelled.

He stopped kissing her but didn't release his grip. "We are going to do this like in the Old Testament. They sent the bride into the tent, and when she came out, they were married."

"No, stop. I'm a virgin. Not like this. Not here. I want to wait until we're married." She was breathless and crying.

"If you scream, you will ruin your sister's wedding. Is that what you want?" he said in a menacing whisper.

She stared at him in disbelief. He had calculated this like a chess move and chosen the perfect time.

"Well, are you going to answer me or not?"

"No. I don't want to ruin my sister's wedding. But please, please stop."

Allison panicked. She didn't know what to do. He had her. She didn't want to ruin Maddie and Luke's wedding. She doubted they would hear her anyway. If she tried to fight him with all her might, he already had her hands and she was pinned to the table.

"Thisss is your fault. You are the one that wantsss thisss." His words sounded like hissing. He suddenly no longer looked like the prize catch but the devil himself.

Then he forced himself on her. He was powerful and experienced in taking what was not given. She cried and begged, but she couldn't move. She had never known how strong a man could be. She was powerless. She had believed that her love for him would have to grow, but at least she had trusted and respected him as an honorable leader in the church.

Two marriage proposals in one night. How stupid could she be? She'd picked the wrong one.

He took his time while she strained every muscle to free herself. She could hardly breathe through her sobs. Then came the piercing pain. She was in shock at the horror of the moment, but she never stopped fighting to get away. Finally, after he had fulfilled his desire, he released her. She tried for the door once again, and he grabbed her by the neck.

He looked at her with disgust. "You little liar. You said you were a virgin." His grip on her tightened. "Listen to me carefully. You will fix yourself up and go back to the reception. You will not say a word. What goes on between a man and his wife is to be kept private. Do you understand?"

He released her, and she collected her torn panties from the floor, shaking uncontrollably. It was over. She had already begun mourning the loss of her innocence.

He laughed at her broken state. Then he got close to her without touching her, and in her right ear, he whispered, "You are ruined now. No good little Christian boy will ever love you."

Chapter Two

Thirteen Years Later

In one hand, Saren twirled a dandelion blossom, launching small parachutes to the wind with each revolution. Her other hand rested on her precious little best friend. Frost, also known as the Frostie Dog, had been named by Saren's father, Luke. He'd chosen it after his mom's family, the Frosts. The individuals of the Frost clan were smart, tough, and independent, and they knew no fear. Even though Frost appeared fluffy and sweet, he'd had those characteristics even from the beginning. When Luke's mom, Dina Jo, first met Frost as a puppy, she'd exclaimed, "Oh, the Frostie Dog!" The nickname had stuck.

Nothing in the world was more fun for Saren and Frost than their daily "walky walk walk." Frost couldn't contain himself when Saren picked up his leash. Even without a leash, he followed her everywhere and was never more than ten feet from Saren at any given time. When she went to school, he waited at the door for her to return, not eating or drinking. He was completely devoted to her and her alone. The fluffy white dog was eminently cheerful as he trotted along with his tail held high and his ears alert.

Despite her youthful age of twelve years and eleven days, Saren took exceptional care of Frost. She carefully brushed his curls, and he always looked like he could win a dog contest like the ones on the sports channels.

Frost sported a wide royal-blue satin ribbon tied into a voluminous bow. Luke often commented that Frost was a boy and had no business wearing a bow. She held the position that men wore bows around their necks when they got married, so Frost could wear one every day. To Frost, every day was as exciting as a celebration.

She wasn't trying to turn Frost into a girl. Even if she'd wanted to, Frost was far too manly to succumb to that. But he did love it when she dressed him up in his blue ribbon. He wore the ribbon proudly, as if it symbolized that he was the number one dog in the world.

That very special afternoon, Saren's long chestnut hair cascaded in the cool breeze of late spring. The sun sparkled through the holes in Saren's straw hat. It almost felt like the tiny sunrays were tickling her nose. Saren always wore a hat. Her fair skin was too sensitive for direct sun. However, Saren loved being outside, so each cheek constantly had a warm rose glow on it.

Saren was, of course, not perfect. She did not always do her chores on time and frequently daydreamed while in school, but she knew who she was. She loved life and, most of all, adventure. Her only problem was that she had never had one. She was on the constant search for a mystery to solve.

"Come on, Frost, it's time to head back. Mom will be wondering where we are by now. This was supposed to be a short walk."

Instead of turning around, the Frostie Dog pulled Saren deeper into the forest.

"Okay, I'm with you. Let's walk a little farther. We haven't been this far down the forest road before. Maybe we'll see something exciting." She didn't know why, but she felt like something extraordinary was going to happen today.

They passed dried-up wild daffodils that gave way to budding irises that hadn't yet reached their full glory. Passing the last house on the road, she could see only forest and flowers ahead.

"These flowers must have been planted by the pioneers or something," Saren said. "I wonder where the gardenias are blooming.

What a sweet perfume God put in the air. Is there anything He didn't think of?"

Saren treated flowers and plants as her friends and knew most of their names, having grown up around her family's business, Emma's Nursery and Flower Shop.

Frost found something on the side of the dirt road worth investigating. Saren stopped to wait for him. Looking around, she admired the beautiful mountains full of old live oak trees all around her. The rosebushes were already sprouting their first leaves.

They passed over a small brook. "I can't wait until it gets hot. It will be fun running through the stream."

"Hey, Frost, what are those workmen doing over there? Let's go see."

Luckily, it wasn't hot enough for the snakes to be out just yet, so she figured it was safe to cross the field of yellow grass and poppies. Together, they bounced and bounded through the tall grass toward the men. As they got near, she heard the distinct buzz of a chainsaw. Saren was careful to stay just far enough away to not attract the attention of the workmen.

"Whoa, Frost, it looks like they're cutting down that dead oak tree. One more victory for the dreaded bark beetle." Sadly, the bark beetle had killed a large portion of the forest the previous year. So many trees had died that a huge forest fire had engulfed an entire mountain town a few miles from where Saren lived. The county had taken up the task of cutting down all the dead trees to prevent more fires. The workmen were cutting certain branches off the old oak in preparation.

"Let's watch, Frost. I've never seen a real tree felling before. We can help them shout *timberrr*!" She looked around and found a nice flat granite boulder to sit on.

Saren decided to read a little while she waited. She was never without a book and her journal. She looked forward to writing about the tree felling after she saw it. They didn't seem to be doing anything interesting enough to write about, so she picked up her book and began to read. It was another Nancy Drew because she couldn't get enough of mysteries.

"Too bad we don't have any mysteries around here, Frost. We would be good at figuring them out, especially with the help of my assistant. Right, my dear Frost?" She addressed him as if he were Watson, Sherlock Holmes's sidekick.

Frost lounged lazily at Saren's feet on the warm grass mixed with yellow and orange poppy blossoms. The hum of the bees added harmony to the buzz of the chainsaw in the background. Saren was so engrossed in Nancy Drew that she almost forgot what she was waiting for.

Right then, the buzz ceased, only to be replaced by a deep squeak. The sound was unearthly, as if the bowels of the world were being ripped out. As the tree started to fall, the workman yelled, "Timberrr!" and so did Saren. Caught up in all the excitement, Frost barked as though he were hollering "Timber" in doggy language.

The tree was down. The quiet chorus of the humming bees and chirping birds returned to the mountain valley. Saren put her book back into her pack and retrieved her journal to record the excitement. As she picked up her pen, she looked back at the fallen tree. The workmen were taking a well-earned coffee break before taking on the arduous task of cutting up the tree for transport. The limbs of the tree were still bouncing from the impact.

"Wait... What is that?" Through the forest on the other side of the great fallen oak, she could barely make out the shadows of what looked like... *A house... A cabin... A cottage.*

Saren shifted her hat so her green eyes could adjust from the bright midday sun to the shadows of the deep forest. It couldn't be a house. Saren knew everyone in the small mountain town. How could there be a house she didn't know about? But, nevertheless, there it was, behind the dead oak, deep in the forest's shadow at the end of the valley.

"If anyone lived there, I would know them." She reasoned that it must be an old abandoned house from long ago, and decided to take a closer look. "Well, if we want to get close, we'll have to go way around to avoid those workmen."

Maybe a thirteen-year-old would have more patience, she thought. Being only twelve, she couldn't wait until tomorrow to get a closer look. So off she went, with Frost following, across the small valley and over a grassy hill into the forest surrounding the cottage. The boughs above completely blocked the sky, and the forest was dark and cool. Leathery dried leaves from the live oaks carpeted the forest floor. They gave out a kind of squeak rather than a crunch beneath Saren's soles. Chittering squirrels took notice of their arrival, and she did not feel welcome.

Frost hesitated and tried to go back, but once Saren's determination was established, she would only go forward. Frost, having lost that tug of war, bounded over bushes to lead the way. His ears were perked and his tail high. He was on full alert for danger. He stopped and sniffed the air. He gave a small warning whine to Saren.

"Come on, Frost. Don't be a chicken. Go on."

Even though Saren couldn't see the cottage through the thick forest, she kept as straight as she could toward where she knew it was. The way was rough, and in places, the oak chaparral was nearly impassable. Finally, she came to a clearing of short yellow grass and the occasional sage bush. There it was. Most of the house lay hidden behind a tall hedge of rose vines. Being across a small meadow from the cottage, she could only see a round tower breaking the ceiling of vegetation and trees shrouding the cottage.

As she contemplated how to get a better view, Frost let out a low warning growl. This was extremely rare behavior for him, so Saren took it seriously. She paused and looked around. All at once, the sage bushes seemed to storm the Frostie Dog from every direction. He was blocked in, and large sage leaves and twigs smashed into his fluffy white fur. The foxtails grew right out of rock into his underbelly and poked him in the paws. Frost yelped in pain.

"Oh, my goodness," Saren yelled and jumped over the sage that hadn't been there a few seconds before. She reached down into the bushes that had suddenly engulfed Frost and plucked him out. With a loud yelp, Frost popped free of the green tentacles, completely covered in rough and prickly foliage and foxtails. Holding Frost in her arms, she looked around for the best escape. She spotted a dirt road on the other side of the cottage, past another clearing. As she neared the cottage, the guardian briars and rosebushes seemed to tighten and grow denser, blocking her view of the cottage. The thorns and vines snagged her clothes and tried to grab her. She freed herself from all the vegetation entanglements and successfully negotiated the briars. As soon as she reached the clearing, she ran with all her might across it toward a dirt road. It was just a wide path through the dense forest of oak chaparral, live oaks and pine really, maybe just an ATV trail, but it was away from the thorn bushes.

She sat Frost down to catch her breath. She examined him. He was so tangled with spiky twigs, sage, and foxtails that he couldn't even walk. He just stood there frozen, afraid to move for fear of being stuck in a million places on his small body.

"I have to get you home, Frostie Dog." She picked him up and jogged down the path in the direction she believed led home. Suddenly, a large vulture appeared out of the darkness of the forest. It swooped into the shielded inner yard of the cottage and reemerged with something hanging from its feet.

"Look, Frost, that vulture is carrying something. What does he have in his claws?" Saren stopped to watch the curious sight.

The vulture swooped down right over the top of Saren and Frost and dropped a large black snake on top of them.

In spite of all his prickles, Frost jumped out of Saren's arms, giving her the chance to fling the snake from her shoulder. Once on the ground, the snake began to slither away. Frost positioned himself between the snake and Saren. Just as Saren squatted to pick up Frost, the snake turned toward them and lifted half its body into the air to come eye-to-eye with Saren. It gave her a sinister stare with bright-yellow eyes. Saren rose with Frost and slowly backed away. As soon as she was a safe distance away, she turned and ran down the path with all her might.

After about a quarter of a mile, she came to the back entrance of the red barn at Emma's Nursery and Flower Shop. She was greeted by Ol' Blue, her Uncle Jonathan's dog, who was half Australian shepherd and half blue heeler.

"Wow, look where we are." She picked up her pace as she passed the barn and in between the two long rows of greenhouses to the shop. Saren ran to the Crow's Nest to find her Uncle Jonathan, but the shop was closed. His pickup truck was gone, and all the displays he normally took into the refrigerator at night were still outside.

"Oh, no, he's out looking for us." She ran almost the whole seven blocks to her house with the Frostie Dog in her arms. She didn't want Frost to be in his current state of discomfort for any longer than necessary. She ran out of breath on the last block and walked as fast as she could. She knew she was going to be in big trouble. She had stayed out way too late. Twilight had faded into a clear night with no moon and lots of stars. Her mom and dad and Uncle Jonathan were going to be mad. However, that didn't trouble her.

"Frost, we have had an adventure."

He looked up at her with a patient and excited look even though he saved his wagging for a less foxtailed tail.

"Not only did we have an adventure, but now we have a mystery. We must find out who lives in that cottage and why it has its own magical forest protecting it. Yep, we have our work cut out for us, my dear Frostie Dog. I wonder what could be inside that cottage. Maybe it has treasure in it. It could house an old hermit lady with twenty cats. Maybe a witch or a beautiful princess is locked in the tower. Perhaps it's haunted. It could be a vampire's house or a werewolf's lair. Maybe mad scientists like Dr. Frankenstein lived and worked in there. Possibly we have watched too many black-and-white horror movies."

Whatever was there, she couldn't wait to find out. She had a feeling it was someone special—and her adventure had only just begun.

Chapter Three

Saren's arms, shoulders and back ached from carrying the Frostie Dog's twelve and a half pounds all the way from the cottage in the woods. As Saren rounded the corner onto her street, she saw her mom looking down the street the other direction, talking on their portable house phone.

Her dad was about to close the tailgate on his pickup truck when he seemed to feel her presence and looked up. "Maddie, look," he said, leaving the tailgate down as he took off toward Saren and Frost.

Before Maddie could end the call and put the phone down, Luke had already sprinted the half block to meet his daughter. As he took Frost from her arms, he asked, "Are you okay?"

"Yeah, Dad, we found a cottage in the woods."

"What happened to Frost?"

"He was attacked by some hostile sage bushes," Saren said, watching her dad's expression. She loved how her dad always humored her vivid imagination.

"Well, I can see that. But what happened?" Luke sounded serious, but Saren could see the gleam of amusement twinkling in his hazel eyes even though it was dark.

She quickly relayed the story exactly as it had happened. Her mother was closing in on them at a jog.

"Saren, I know you love to exaggerate, but I need to know what really happened today. Okay? Your mom won't be as patient—" He didn't get a chance to finish his sentence before Saren's very concerned mother caught up to them.

"Saren, where have you been? We were worried sick. Your Uncle Jonathan is combing the streets for you right now." Madeleine paused, out of breath.

Saren looked from her father to her mother. "Mom, we finally have a mystery!"

"Fine, but even private eyes have business hours. Yours end specifically before the streetlights come on. Is that clear, young lady?"

"Sure, Mom," Saren said. She tried to sound as obedient as she could sound.

"Don't 'sure' me. Is that yes or no?"

"Yes, my business hours end when the streetlights come on," she said with too much excitement. Once Saren was focused on something, nothing else could bother her—and now she had a mystery to solve.

They rounded the corner into the driveway.

Saren's seven-year-old brother, J.D., came hopping down the steps of the front porch with a toy car in his hand. "Ooooh, you're in troouubllle," he taunted.

"Son," Luke said, "go back in the house and bring us Frost's brush and his scissors."

Luke put Frost on the tailgate of his pickup and patted it, signaling for Saren to sit. He looked at his wife with a calming expression. "So, Saren, tell us what happened tonight."

As Saren relayed the story to her parents without the magical elements, she pulled foxtails out of Frost's paws while her dad brushed his fur and cut loose sage leaves and twigs. Her parents repeatedly exchanged mysterious glances with one another.

"Saren, I don't want you going to that house again," Madeleine said sternly. "I mean it, and I don't want to hear another word about it."

Saren was shocked by her mother's attitude. Normally, her mom was easygoing and enjoyed talking about everything with her, but she shut down the conversation quickly. Then she headed into the house.

"That was weird," Saren said to her dad. "Was she really that worried?"

"Saren, there are some things that you'll understand when you're older. Go ahead and take Frost in for his bath."

"Bathy-bath-bath, Frostie Dog!"

Frost's ears sank as he tried to get away.

"Not this time, Frost. I already gotcha." Saren giggled as Frost gave her the hopeless forlorn look of bath-time dread.

Saren took Frost into the sunroom off the kitchen to the large utility sink. She could hear her mom and dad. They were sitting on the landing at the top of the stairs. The open floor plan of their house allowed sound to carry, and her young ears could pick up every word, even over the flow of the water into the sink.

"Maddie, be reasonable. There's no real harm in it," Luke pleaded with his wife.

"Honey, I know you may not think that the weird stuff that goes on at the cottage is bad, but I do. I think Jonathan does too. He just won't admit it. It's dangerous. What goes on around there isn't normal. You saw the Frostie Dog. He could never have gotten that mangled on his own."

"Okay, I admit there's an element of the unknown. But, Maddie, what if this works? Nothing else we've tried has. None of the doctors or any of the research we've done has helped. What if we let Saren 'investigate'? Maybe she'll happen upon something none of us saw. *She* is the key—I feel it."

"Luke, no. I won't risk her. I've already lost one..." She couldn't say the words. "No, I won't risk her. No way. I don't even want to talk about it anymore. There's a sinister spirit out there, and I won't have Saren exposed to it."

"Maddie, what if it's a good spirit? Have you thought of that? Just... Maddie, I need this to be over. I want my wife back. The way you used to be. Full of joy and love and hope. You were never fearful and protective like this."

"Exactly. If I had been, maybe none of this would ever have happened."

"Don't blame yourself. You had nothing to do with this."

"We don't know that for sure."

"We do." He patted his wife's leg. "But okay. I'll have a talk with Saren. Neither of us will bring it up again."

"Thank you." Maddie blew her nose, and they headed down the stairs.

An old-sounding pickup truck pulled up into the driveway. Saren recognized it immediately as Uncle Jonathan's.

Saren loved her "uncle." He had always been in her life and such close friends with the family that he had become family. He always wore a tattered ball cap with Emma's Nursery embroidered on it. Her earliest memories were of hanging on to that old hat while he walked around Emma's with her on his shoulders.

He constantly walked fast, giving the impression that he was a thoroughbred jumping around inside the starting gate that never opened. He was perpetually waiting for something so he could run free, as fast as he or anyone could run. Saren often wondered what he was waiting for. He had a strange kind of sadness behind his kind eyes, but a sadness that still had hope and light.

Before Maddie and Luke made it to the bottom of the stairs, Uncle Jonathan was inside the front foyer, closing the door behind him. Seeing them and without saying a word, he headed toward the sound of the water running. With a wide stride, he passed the dining room through the kitchen and into the sunroom.

Finding what he was looking for, Uncle Jonathan leaned up against a pillar. He crossed his arms, putting one foot across the other, and looked at Saren without saying a word.

"Hi, Uncle Jonathan." Saren loved how he smelled like leather and sweet alyssum with a dash of cinnamon gum.

"That's what you say? 'Hi, Uncle Jonathan.'"

Saren chose not to dwell on the mishaps or misfortunes. She figured going forward was far more interesting than talking about the past. She was, however, curious about the odd events that had happened in the forest. Most kids would feel bad or defensive and afraid of getting into trouble, but to her, blame didn't lead to anything, especially answers. She took full responsibility for her actions and let others take theirs.

"Frost and I found an old cottage out in the woods. Did you know it's on a road that leads right to the red barn? Who lives there? Do you know them? How come I've never seen it before? Did you know the forest around the cottage is magical?" Saren sounded like a rapid-fire machine gun to herself.

He didn't answer. He turned to watch Luke's approach. Maddie stayed in the kitchen, and Saren assumed she was making dinner. That was weird. Saren wondered why was she letting the men handle the situation. Her mom was always in the middle of things.

Ooooh, she was really onto something. She had stumbled onto a big secret. Why else would Uncle Jonathan just stand there quiet like that? He was never quiet. He always entered the house with a loud holler announcing his arrival. She had never seen him and her dad be so quiet and serious for so long. Now her inquisitiveness burned even hotter.

"All done?" Luke asked. Saren was drying Frost with a big fluffy towel. "Your mother doesn't like it when you use her good towels for drying Frost."

"He's a member of this family too. Plus, he's a hero, remember, he was brave and stood between me and that evil eye snake."

"Okay, let's take your hero outside before he dribbles hero juice all over the house," Luke said.

Once outside, Saren set Frost down on a patch of grass. She leaned against the faded Emma's Nursery and Flower Shop sign on the side of her Uncle Jonathan's pickup.

Luke and Jonathan stood, forming a triangle with Saren.

"You're a young lady now," Luke said. "You'll need to treat time like an adult, be on time. This shows that you have respect for the time of those waiting for you. Okay?"

Most kids would have made an excuse, but Saren took her father's words as instruction, not criticism. She smiled reassuringly. "Got it, Dad."

"Your mother doesn't want to hear any more about that cottage. So you'll have to tell all your new information, questions, and ramblings to your dad and your Uncle Jonathan. I know we're not as fun or as pretty, but we'll have to do."

Saren stood straight up and beamed at them. "You mean, I can..."

"Sshhh. Not so loud," Jonathan said.

Saren lowered her voice to a whisper. "You mean I get to investigate?"

"I need a helper after school." Jonathan gave her a nod and gestured for her to go along.

"How many days, Uncle Jonathan?" Saren asked, dragging out the question to show that she understood the game.

"Every day, from after school until precisely one hour before sundown. You'll be home in time for dinner. Bring the mail home to your mom. That way she can work from *home* and won't have to come to the shop." Saren was glad it was spring and the days were getting longer.

"You have a helper, Uncle Jonathan." Saren reached out her right hand to shake on the business deal.

"When you're out on the grounds of Emma's and take Frost for a walk, make sure you keep a lookout for snakes. Report to me or Uncle Jonathan exactly what you see or hear on your walks," Luke said. "Got it?" He moved his eyes toward the window without moving his head.

Saren understood that the firm look he gave her was for the benefit of her mom, who was watching them from the kitchen window. Saren put on a serious, dejected expression as though she were being scolded. She would have to work hard to contain her excitement around her mom. She hated hiding things from her mother, but Saren had seen how upset she had been. Saren knew that whatever she and her dad and Uncle Jonathan were up to, it was for her mother's benefit.

"Saren, head on into the house and help your mother finish dinner," Luke said.

"Good night, Uncle Jonathan." She gave him her usual warm hug. "Thank you. I will be the best helper ever!"

"I have no doubt about it." He looked deep into her eyes.

She bounced and hopped back into the house with a clean and very tired Frostie Dog. She could smell spaghetti coming from the kitchen. "Yeah, I'm starved."

She jumped up and down with excitement. She tried to pretend to be excited about the spaghetti, but really, she just could no longer contain her anticipation of the new adventures that awaited her. How would she ever fall asleep tonight?

Chapter Four

Jonathan watched Saren bounce into the house. "How can she have that much energy after carrying a twelve-pound dog at a jog for—what? At least two miles?"

"Well, you know what drives her. She's excited about her mystery," Luke said.

Jonathan looked up at the night sky as if to search the heavens for a sign. "Fog is rolling in. It usually doesn't make it this far inland." He looked over at his friend. "Are you sure about this, Luke? Maybe we should just tell her and give her access to the cottage."

"No, we can't betray Maddie's trust like that," Luke said. "This way, Saren discovers the cottage and its mysteries on her own, just as she already has. We just don't stop her. You heard the story—it was obvious she was meant to find it. I believe she's the key. She'll see what we can't."

"Okay, I'm in. It will definitely be believable that she cracked the code on her own. Remember the time she found that diamond ring at the nursery?"

"Yeah, she explored every avenue until she found those people and returned that ring. She has not gotten less determined in the last two years." Luke adjusted his hat.

"Hey," Jonathan said, "did you or Maddie tell her to call it 'the cottage'?"

The family had always called the old house Grandma Emma's cottage. When they first married, Grandma Emma told Grampa John that she wanted a cottage in the forest. When he purchased property that included the nursery, the farmhouse, barn and a stately old Victorian mansion, Grandma had joked that Grampa was an overachiever and proudly referred to her Victorian mansion as her cottage.

Luke took a step back in astonishment. "No, we didn't tell her. I didn't catch that at all. We are all so used to calling it 'the cottage.'"

"Weird. Do you think she thought of it herself?"

"For some reason, her calling it a cottage makes me feel like she's being watched over and protected." Luke looked up at the night sky. "I hope we are making the right decision, but I believe she'll be safe."

"Me, too, and don't forget—she has her trusty sidekick, Frost." Jonathan chuckled.

"Yeah, but he's prone to getting saged." They both laughed.

Jonathan hopped in his pickup. Luke tapped the hood twice to signal that his path to back out was clear of children and dogs.

Jonathan sped quickly back to Emma's to finish closing up. Ol' Blue met him in front of the shop. She seemed more excited than usual, and he patted her on the head. "I know. You had a visitor tonight. Good dog."

He finished his duties quickly then headed out to his apartment in the barn to shower and change. He felt refreshed from more than just from being clean. He had a renewed faith that things were changing. He called for Ol' Blue. She jumped into his utility task vehicle. With Ol' Blue riding shotgun, Jonathan headed down the narrow path behind the barn into the forest.

Chapter Five

After school, Saren ran straight home. Practically crashing through the screen door, she called for Frost. She grabbed his leash off the peg by the door and was back out again in one blurry swoop.

Madeleine hollered, "Hi, honey. How was your day? Mine was great..."

As she ran down the porch steps with Frost, Saren could hear her mom carrying on a mock conversation with herself.

Focused on her adventure, Saren trotted down the sidewalk and headed down the lane toward Emma's Nursery and Flower Shop and the mysterious cottage. The Frostie Dog seemed to sense her excitement, because he kept pace with her instead of stopping at his usual sniffing spots.

"Hi, Uncle Jonathan!" Saren yelled as she let the door close behind her, ringing the bells hanging from it. Two young men around age fifteen carried large bags of potting soil into the back of the shop and set them on the worktable behind the front counter.

"Right on time, young one," Jonathan announced. "We have a mystery to solve."

"Oh, goodie." Saren suddenly remembered that she sounded very much like a twelve-year-old when the two teen boys looked over at her and snickered. Thirteen-year-olds apparently didn't say "goodie."

"Who are they?" she asked.

"A couple of boys from the Sprouts program. This is Logan and Oliver."

She gave them a friendly smile. "Hi."

The boys nodded and mumbled, "Hi." Then they occupied themselves, trying to look busy.

"So, Saren, your mystery. How many carnations, roses, and orchids are we going to need for prom coming up at the end of the month?" Jonathan asked.

"What?" Saren tried to hold back her disappointment.

"We have to *cover up* the seeds so they can have a chance to grow. Otherwise, the seed gets eaten or smashed, but in any case, stopped. So, we have to show some progress here at Emma's. Investigation takes training and skill. So, back to our mystery, sometimes we can't ask the person who knows. We must follow clues. What if the only person that knows the answers can't tell you? What if you're the only person that can know and you don't know? Then what do you do?"

"Oh, I seeee. Sooo, we have to find other way. We can observe. But we can't observe something that has already happened." Saren tapped her bottom lip with her index finger.

"Hey! We can look in sources of information that may have recorded events."

Saren was excited because now she knew that he would help her in her investigation by giving her ideas. She had often heard her mom say that it is often more important to know what *questions* to ask. Plus, she was going to learn to think like a business owner too.

"So, how *would* we know what kind of flowers we would need if Uncle Jonathan were not here? That would be a problem. How could I figure that out? I know: the POS computer."

Saren went over to the cash register and point-of-sale system. She logged in with her mother's ID. Seeing Saren log into the POS like a pro, the two teen boys came over to watch what was going on.

She pulled up a report showing the dates of prom for the last five years. As she typed, she started in on questions of her own for Uncle Jonathan. "So, who lives in that old cottage? How old is it anyway? It looks really old."

Uncle Jonathan was repotting plants that had outgrown their current homes. "I guess that's another thing that you'll have to figure out on your own."

She clicked a few more buttons and typed a few things out on the keyboard. The two teen boys stood on either side of her, watching her work.

"Wait—are you talking about the old mansion with the tower that's deep in the forest?" Logan asked. He looked at her as though she did not know anything.

"Yeah. Do you know it? Who lives there?" Saren stopped working and looked up at him in anticipation.

"Yeah, a creepy old witch lives there," Oliver said.

Logan bent over to get close to her ear and whispered, "The only thing we know for sure is that every kid that ever went snooping around there never came back alive."

Both of them made wicked laughing sounds like a couple of mad scientists.

Saran's eyes got big, and her mouth sagged open. Frost gave out a little whine.

"Don't you two Sprouts have somethings to do out in the barn?" Jonathan tried to hide his amusement. He was blessed with a lot of patience for kids.

Saren decided that if a creepy old witch really did live in the cottage, she would make friends with her and get to the bottom of the disappearances, if there ever were any. She was not going to be a scaredy-cat. She heard the printer go off back in the Crow's Nest. She retrieved the printout and returned to Uncle Jonathan.

"So, we sold on average twenty-three hundred corsages each prom over the last five years and twenty-one hundred boutonnieres, but the report doesn't show what kind of flowers were used. I added new buttons for rose, carnation, and orchid. So now as they're sold, we'll know what kind of flowers were used, and we or anyone in the future can run a report to find out. This year, I'll still have to get the answers from Uncle Jonathan's brain computer, but next year, we'll have recorded data."

"Very clever. That's one way to do it," Jonathan said. "Mystery solved for today. I think you're ready for your own computer login."

"Really?" Saren jumped up and down.

Jonathan chuckled. "I'll set it up while you're gone. Right now, I have a surprise for you." Jonathan took a watch out of the drawer. "It is a spy watch. It has a tracker and alarm on it. But what is the most important thing it does?"

"Tell time?" Saren raised one eyebrow and gave a wry smile.

"Exactly." Jonathan buckled the watch on Saren's wrist. "Now, it is time for Frost's walk—and remember your business hours."

"Got it!" She grabbed her satchel and Frost's leash. Then they headed through the expansive grounds of Emma's Nursery and to the hidden path behind the barn. Saren was proud of herself for solving that flower mystery so quickly. She had only been at the shop for about fifteen minutes.

The walk to the area of the cottage was much farther than she remembered. All that running the day before must have made it seem closer. Saren scanned the field and finally found the trail that she and Frost had made the previous day.

"Yep, there's that clump of sage that got you, Frost."

He gave a small bark in acknowledgement, and Saren paused to take in the scene's stunning beauty. The yellow and orange poppies decorated the meadow of tall light-green and yellow grass. She strained her eyes to find the hole in the forest wall. If she hadn't been there yesterday for the felling of that tree, she still would never have noticed the hidden cottage.

The meadow had a calmer air about it than the previous day—no chainsaws or workmen cutting down old trees and trampling young saplings. She retraced her steps back to the sage bushes. This time, they stayed put like normal bushes.

"Did we imagine that yesterday, Frost?"

He looked at the sage bushes with suspicion and stayed clear of them.

She took a big deep breath and looked around to get her bearings. It seemed like the cottage was right on the other side of the meadow, but all she could see was dense, dark forest. Exactly at that moment, a beam of sunlight broke through the forest and shone right on the house, illuminating one of its stained-glass windows, as if Saren were meant to find it. This sign from the heavens intrigued her further.

Exhilarated by her sense of adventure, she and Frost bounded through the field of poppies. The townspeople didn't go into the woods. It was considered dangerous, rough, and not worth the effort. Gnarly manzanita trees twisted and waltzed with thick oak chaparral. Maybe the witch rumor made the forest less appealing. The path was nearly impossible for an adult of regular height, but the going was significantly easier for a child and a small dog.

Frost snooped out the best route through the brush at the edge of the thick patch of oak chaparral. Saren felt invincible wearing hiking boots and leggings under her tunic top. Birds chirped gleefully, and a woodpecker laughed in the distance. The forest was so much more cheerful than the day before.

She and Frost made such quick progress through the brush that they were in the midst of the forest in no time at all. She could see the house more clearly now, even with so many trees still in the way. She walked from behind one tree to another, hiding from anyone who might be looking out the window to spy her. She wanted to be the spyer, not the spyee. When Saren reached the edge of the yard, she stopped cold.

Her eyes widened. The cottage and garden must have been built by angels. The roof-high wall of thorny vines was now only a few feet from the ground, about half the height of the rock-wall fence that outlined the house and inner gardens. The wall consisted of large, rough rocks like the ones her great-uncle had used to build structures during the Depression while working for the Civilian Conservation Core, which he called the CCC. Each rock had its own unique color and shape, fitting together like a beautiful three-dimensional puzzle.

Saren's first reaction to the miraculous garden was to take in a huge gasp of air. Her senses were greeted by a bouquet of fragrances full of honeysuckle and gardenia, with roses dominating the sweet aroma. Many varieties of rosebushes in full bloom lined the inside of the fence.

"How could that be? The irises haven't even bloomed, and it isn't time for roses yet." But there they were, like magic. The roses wore every imaginable color, gnarled and tangled into a massively wide but low barrier between the fence and the forest. The house was barely visible behind all the lush ivy climbing its walls. Saren had only seen ivy like that in the movies because the climate in the southern California mountains was far too dry for ivy.

Even though the sage had been peaceful, she decided to do some observing before making another attempt to get close to that thorn wall. Maybe the place had to sniff a person first, like a dog meeting a stranger. Still a good fifteen feet from the outer briars, Saren mounted a boulder and stood on top to peer over the rose briars and rock wall to get a full view of the yard. A colorful array of flowers danced around the entire circumference of the house. Saren couldn't believe her eyes. The flowerbeds were full of every kind of flower, as if the yard were Noah's ark for flowers. And they were blooming all at the same time. Daffodils of early spring conversed with marigolds of late summer. Tulips and irises of every color thrived with zinnias and chrysanthemums, while bluebonnets of Texas covered the ground below bright hibiscus blossoms of Hawaii. Saren spotted an assortment of daylilies.

But how could they all bloom simultaneously without withered blossoms? How did they get bluebonnets to grow here? she thought. Saren had only seen them in pictures, but her paternal grandmother, Dina Jo, had often told her of the fields upon fields of the delicate blue flower in her native Texas. Saren was glad she had been raised around Emma's Nursery and Flower Shop. Not every twelve-year-old would know how special this garden was.

"What kind of place is this, Frost? It's a miracle cottage."

If the yard was miraculous, the house was artwork. A winding pathway led through the lush lawn past a small grove of young pines and manzanitas to the covered porch that extended all the way around the house, supported by delicately carved spindles. The style was old Victorian in its finest hour, complete with a circular tower. The round tower stretched high above the second floor with paned windows around the entire circumference of the tower.

"Frost, that must be where the princess is held captive."

Beautiful and intricate trim hung from the eaves around the house. The paint was surprisingly fresh, a cheerful light blue-gray, more blue than gray. A warm yellow-white glow came from deep within the house, matching the trim of the gables. The windows above the covered porch were elaborate stained glass. The one on the left depicted two young women running in a meadow. In the one on the right, a lady was walking through a gate leading to a forest trail. The one in the center made Saren pause to examine it more closely because the details were too realistic, like it had been magically painted with glass.

It portrayed a handsome man with a beautiful lady with brunette hair, wearing a flowing dress covered in beautiful yellow roses, daisies, and small blue flowers. The dress flowed as though the couple were in a warm summer breeze that swept away all their cares and concerns, leaving only the love reflected in each other's eyes. Saren marveled at the way the two looked at each other with such knowing and love—the kind of love that endured through time. She hadn't really thought much about romantic love before, other than thinking certain boys were cute. But the picture made her hope that one day she would find *that* kind of love. She felt that whoever lived in this house was and would be truly loved.

The man in the picture was handsome in an average kind of way, but how he looked at the lady made him seem princely, wise, and powerful. He seemed to have not only a love for her physical beauty, but also a respect for her intelligence, her spirit, her naturally innocent heart, her talents, and her faults. He knew all about her and loved it all. Even though the woman was exquisitely feminine, Saren got the distinct impression that she was intelligent, maybe a professional of some kind, decisive and in control, yet not arrogant. She had chosen this man to love, and love him she did with all her heart. The man in the scene was vaguely familiar to Saren, but she couldn't imagine why.

Saren sat down on the boulder to let Frost take a breather. She retrieved her notebook from her satchel and wrote "Investigation Log" on the front of the notebook. She took down the time and her observations. So far, no sign of movement: people, animals or vegetation.

Turning her attention back to the garden, she noticed that the lawn was perfect and lush, without a single dandelion or tuft of crabgrass. Through the center of the lawn wound a stone pathway leading from the front porch and coming to an end at the rock wall. At its end, a round trellis covered in ruby-red roses grew so thick that it created a round wall where there should have been an arc. At one time, a grand round gate had likely stood there, like something a hobbit would have built. The middle area near the pathway was a mini forest of live oak saplings, pines, and manzanita trees with their beautiful dark reddish bark and twisted branches. The blanket of ivy below the trees was trimmed perfectly around the little grove, as if someone had taken a ruler and measured the distance between each leaf. Whoever lived there obviously took tremendous care of the place. Saren was determined to find out who or what was responsible.

Saren had moved on to admiring the fine lace curtains that hung in the first-floor windows. She figured it must be the parlor. They were bowed out in a curve so perfect that the glass itself must have been curved. Imagining how beautiful the inside must be, she examined each window. Suddenly, a shadowy figure appeared in the center window. Almost as quickly as Saren's eyes had focused on the person, she had vanished, seemingly into thin air. Still, Saren has seen clearly a woman with very long hair, wearing an old-fashioned dress. Even though she only saw her for a second or two, Saren was astonished that the lady in the window seemed to be entirely gray. Her clothing was various shades from light gray to charcoal, and her silver hair seemed to shimmer like tinsel on a Christmas tree.

"Frost, did you see her? Could that have been real? It had to have been an optical illusion. It must have been shadows making her *appear* gray."

Saren searched the other windows in the house for the gray lady. The tower had staggered windows around and along what Saren assumed was a staircase up to a room at the top. A shadow passed the first window covered in sheer curtains. In the next window up, the curtains were open. There she was. Yes, Saren trusted what she saw. The woman's skin was ashen, her hair silver gray, and her clothes shades of slate.

"The lady *was* gray."

Saren's mystery was now more mysterious. Resolved to discover the truth behind the fantastic garden and its strange patron, she watched a little longer before noting the time and everything she saw.

She glanced at the sky. "That's odd. It's still early, but it is getting dark. Come on, Frost. Business hours are over." They took off quickly toward home, excited to tell Uncle Jonathan about the gray lady and the miracle garden.

As they passed through the forest, it grew darker and darker. Frost put his ears back and his tail up and picked up his pace. Saren kept up with him at a trot. The darkness followed them out of the forest and into the meadow to engulf her. Saren could barely see in front of her.

"Frost, go!" she yelled. Stumbling over a bush, she fell flat on her stomach. Frost's retractable leash pulled out farther and farther. She scrambled to her feet and ran blindly in the direction the leash was pulling her. She couldn't see anything at all now, but she knew Frost's canine eyes could see even in the darkest night. Eventually, she could feel the soft earth under her feet, and they turned right down the path and toward Emma's Nursery, Uncle Jonathan, and safety.

"Please, Lord, help us get back safely."

After a short distance and couple of more falls, the darkness started to dissipate like a quickly clearing morning fog. As soon as she could see again, she scooped up Frost.

"You saved me again!" She hugged and kissed him. "My little hero!" After she'd put him down, they both ran along the path toward Emma's.

Chapter Six

Jonathan pulled up the trailer ramp, and Luke slid in the pins locking it in place. "You know, Luke, loading this stuff up together reminds me of the first day I ever stepped foot in Emma's. Amazing how one traffic accident—"

"Two. Ol' Blue would never have been born without the second one," Luke said.

"*Two* traffic accidents could change the course of our lives."

"That's for sure. My dad never waited until the day of to pick up supplies ever again, and neither have I. But, you know, you never did tell me what was up with you that day. You were acting so weird. I mean, I had never seen you act like that before or since. What's the story?"

"Dude, you were there. You know what happened," Jonathan said. He had to keep all those feelings of regret and loss at bay so he could do what he needed to do every day.

Jonathan stood on the running board of the pickup while Luke pulled the trailer to the front parking lot.

Luke chuckled. "Hey, I'm going to hang out until Saren and Frost make it back. I'm not sure Frost is one hundred percent just yet after his pincushion experience yesterday."

As Luke passed the front of the shop, Jonathan hopped down while the pickup was still moving. "I'll grab the root beers."

After parking the truck, Luke settled in the one of the old rocking chairs on the front porch of the shop. Jonathan handed him an ice-cold bottle of root beer.

"No really, why did you freeze up like that? Were you concerned about your dad or what?"

Jonathan felt an elusive—and probably temporary—sense of calm about the past. "Sitting here on this porch like Grampa used to does take me back..."

Twenty Years Earlier

WITH CEMENT ENCRUSTED on his shirt and his tattered San Diego Padres cap on backward, Jonathan bounced the basketball low and ducked under Luke's arm to shoot the basket. "Score!"

"You win! Being taller gives me no advantage when you're that fast." Luke retrieved the ball and continued bouncing it on the driveway of his family home.

"I'm stronger than you too."

"I don't know about that. Let's go best out of three."

Dina Jo, Luke's mom, came out of the open garage with the portable house phone in her hand. "Luke, it's your dad."

While Luke was on the phone, Dina Jo looked over at Jonathan. He was wiping the sweat off his forehead with the bottom of his shirt.

"How did you get cement on your shirt?"

"I was pouring cement before basketball practice this morning."

"Oh, wow. We could use someone who knows cement at Tasker Trails Landscape Architecture."

"Oh, yeah?"

"Why don't you come to work for us?" Dina Jo asked.

"Well, Luke already offered that, but I heard it's not good to work with your friends."

"That's who you should work with, especially if you trust one another."

"I never thought about it like that."

"I can get you one of Luke's shirts if you want to change."

"What for?" Luke had passed him the ball, and he began practicing his lay-up.

Dina Jo, paying no attention to the bouncing ball, continued. "Well, for one thing, you never know when you're going to meet your dream girl." She smiled slyly.

"Yeah, right." Jonathan did a couple of dribbles between his legs to show off.

Luke clicked the phone off and held it out to his mom. "Hey, Jonathan, one of my dad's employees crashed the company truck and can't pick up a load. He needs me to get it from Emma's Nursery. He said to bring a friend to help and that there would be pay involved."

"Wow, are they okay?" Jonathan asked.

"Yeah, no serious injuries. They were hit by a drunk driver, but they're fine. They got lucky because the truck was totaled."

"That's horrible. I'll be happy to help, but you don't have to pay me. I have already been paid in Dina Jo's fine dinners." He smiled at Dina Jo as he hopped in the passenger seat of Luke's old work pickup that was a hand-me-down from the business.

On the way, they hit a traffic jam caused by an accident. The rubberneckers were each passing slowly to get a good look in case there was carnage. At least five police cars flashed their blue lights.

"Look, Jonathan. That's them."

Two cops stood in back of an ambulance. One held a small clipboard and was taking down information from the two guys sitting on the bumper of the ambulance.

"That's Joel and Jesus. Joel plays the piano for our church, and he can really play some fun old bluesy gospel. He always says he was cousin to Ray Charles. Nobody can tell if he made that part up. I'm so glad they weren't hurt. Look at that crash."

The company pickup was completely smashed and mangled with an old 1970s mint-green Nova.

"Wait a minute—that's my old green Nova." Jonathan examined it to be sure and remembered Luke had said the accident was caused by a drunk driver. He looked around with dread. "Oh no!"

Just as they passed the crash site, a group of five officers were placing a handcuffed man into the back of a police car.

"That's my dad." Jonathan pointed at the man in handcuffs.

"What? You're kidding."

"I wish I were, believe me. Look, there's my Nova. Man, I worked for two years to get it running. As soon as I got it fixed, he took it over. He didn't have it for a month before he crashed it." Jonathan looked down, shaking his head.

"Oh, gosh, Jonathan. Do you want to stop?"

"No, your dad needs his stuff. Let's get your job done. Besides, I'll have to deal with him soon enough. Why do you think I'm always working? He wastes money on booze and bail so that my brothers and sisters have no food."

One officer directed traffic, encouraging cars to hurry along. Luke picked up the pace and left the accident scene in the rearview mirror. Jonathan wished he could.

Jonathan could see that Luke's demeanor had changed. He was no longer joking and light-hearted.

"Luke, don't sweat this, okay? This is just as normal in my family as sitting around the dinner table is in yours. I just wish it didn't affect good people like your dad and his employees." Jonathan gave Luke a reassuring smile.

Finally, the boys arrived at Emma's Nursery and Flower Shop.

Luke pulled the work pickup around back near the hay barn, where the load was waiting. A muscular older man wearing a big straw hat, dark-blue work pants, and a light-blue work shirt moved a large flat of flowers from his utility cart to the order staging area table. A yellow rosebud was embroidered over his left shirt pocket like it was stuck in his buttonhole.

Walking up next to him was a girl about their age. Her long chestnut-brown hair, which gleamed with natural ginger highlights, looked soft like silk. She wore a pale-yellow ball cap with a single yellow rose embroidered on the front, and her ponytail curled over her left shoulder and down to her waist. She was wearing long cutoff jeans and a tank top that said Emma's Nursery across the front, decorated with yellow roses that were similar in style to the one on the hat.

Jonathan had closed the pickup door, but he stood frozen with his hand still on the handle of the pickup door. Luke was already picking up his first bag of fertilizer.

"Howdy, Grampa!" Luke said.

"Howdy, Luke," the man replied in a gravelly, very grandpa-ish voice.

"Hey, Allison," Luke said.

"How's it goin'?" the girl replied.

Luke tossed the fifty-pound bag of fertilizer with practiced skill all the way to the front of the truck bed precisely where he wanted it to land. On the way back, he took the other way around the truck to see what was wrong with his friend.

Suddenly, a little sprite bounced out of nowhere and knocked Luke's hat off from the back. He had been waiting for it and reached out to gently grab one of the long French braids still lagging in the air after her leap. "Gotcha, Maddie. One of these days, I'm gonna tickle you to death."

She gracefully twirled out of his grasp with a ballerina toe turn on a kiddy's flat-toe sneaker.

"How'd you do that?" he asked.

The little girl moved like some kind of wild, graceful antelope. She was destined to be a great beauty one day, even though she put on the tomboy act with ball caps and overalls.

Now that his hands were free from braids, Luke smacked his friend roughly on the back of the head. "Dude, are you helpin' or what?"

While Luke was preoccupied with the twelve-year-old, Jonathan hadn't taken his eyes off Allison. Jonathan snapped out of his frozen gawking at Allison and walked over to the staged supplies. Luke patted Jonathan on the back.

"Grampa, this is my buddy Jonathan. Jonathan, this is Grampa and Allison and..."

Before he could say it, Madeleine blurted out, "Maddie!" jumping up with her arms out like she was saying, "Tada!"

"Nice to meet y'all," Jonathan said. He had his head down, acting bashful even though he wasn't at all shy.

"Nice to meet you too." Allison looked at him squarely with eyes so blue, they were almost turquoise.

He was not surprised that he had never seen Allison before, because it was obvious with the sharp look in her aqua eyes that she was in the college-prep classes at school.

He had a photographic memory but spent all his time working instead of studying, so his grades were barely passing. That was okay with him, because he was basically in school for two meals a day anyway. He hadn't figured out what history had to do with making a living. But if he'd known babes like this were in those classes, he might have tried harder.

Jonathan picked up two fifty-pound sacks of fertilizer and threw both of them with equal skill to the front of the truck bed.

"Show-off," Luke said under his breath.

Allison and Madeleine pitched in, helping to load the plants on top of the fertilizer bags. Then Maddie retrieved the invoice from the back pocket of her cutoff overalls and held it out to Luke. As soon as he had it within his grasp, she snatched it back and ran around the truck for him to chase her.

"Okay, Maddie, you can flirt with Luke later. His dad is waiting on this load." Grampa gave her an exasperated grin.

Grampa put his hand on the open window as Luke was putting the pickup in reverse. "Hmm, young man"—Grampa looked across Luke to address Jonathan—"you look like a strong, hard worker."

"Yes, sir."

"How many hours can you spare from school for working?"

Jonathan responded without hesitation. "Three before school and six after school, and all day on the weekends." He had been working odd jobs and hustling yardwork, but this looked stable, and if Luke's dad used this guy, he was a good guy. He didn't see any other workers around except the girls and the old man. He'd seen at least four lawnmowers behind the last greenhouse that looked like they needed fixing. Plus, he would have the opportunity to get to know Allison.

"What time do I start?" Jonathon didn't care that he sounded overly eager.

"Today, one o'clock." Then, shifting his gaze to Luke, he said, "Feed him lunch and bring him back over here."

"You got it, Grampa!"

They took off at about eleven o'clock. They had exactly enough time to get the stuff over to Luke's dad, get it unloaded, stop at his house for a sandwich, and get back to the nursery, which was a good five miles past the edge of town.

"Who are those girls to the old man?" Jonathan asked, trying not to sound suspicious.

"Grampa's granddaughters. They're always out there with him, hanging out at the nursery. I've been around them since I can remember."

Jonathan watched the foothills give way to a desert valley as they headed down into the city.

"Where does Allison go to school?"

"Our school. She's the same age as us, but she's on the college track."

"She seemed like she knew what she was doing."

"Yeah, Allison loves the plants and flowers. She tends them and makes sure they're in the right spot for light and water. She knows the name of every plant, flower, tree, or shrub. She's into it too, and not just because she grew up there. You'll never see a happier person than Allison digging in dirt or finding a new blossom on a distressed plant she brought back to life."

"Wow, that's cool." Jonathan's excitement grew. They would have a lot in common because they both enjoyed working outdoors. "What about the little one? She seems to really like you."

The temperature was cooling. Jonathan enjoyed the passing row of palms as they neared the harbor area.

"Maddie and I have always had a special understanding that if she needs anything, Luke fixes it for her. She's my girl." He smiled in a proud protective manner. "Little Maddie isn't as much into the outdoor side of the business; she helps her grandma with the books. She counts the money and makes out the invoices. She's only twelve, but she's smart and meticulous."

"So, Allison and you are not..."

"Dude, even though we only really see each other when we have to do something for our companies, Allison feels like a sister to me. She's fair game, but if *anyone* hurts her, they'll get a busted noggin."

"Cool, times two," Jonathan said, subscribing into the Allison-and-Madeleine protection service. The two boys looked at each other and somehow knew they would be lifelong allies.

Then, out of nowhere, a Prius slammed on its brakes and veered into their lane right in front of them. Luke tried all he could, but the right front bumper scraped down the side of the Prius as it spun out of control. As the Prius slid sideways away from the pickup, they glimpsed a dog in the roadway, trying to dodge traffic. As it spun, the back of the Prius hit the dog and sent him flying. He landed right in front of Luke's vehicle as it came to a stop. They were lucky no one had hit them from behind.

As soon as everyone stopped, Jonathan jumped out and ran to check on the lady in the Prius.

"Did I hit it?" she yelled at Jonathan through panicky tears. "The dog, the Australian shepherd?"

Luke had jogged around the pickup to assess the damage and heard the lady. He and Jonathan ran over to the dog. As they approached, the dog popped up from the ground, shook its furry coat, and ran over to greet Jonathan. The dog licked his face and hands like he had always known him. Luke patted him on the head, but he only had eyes for Jonathan.

A police car drove up on the median and asked if they were okay. After the officer wrote his report, they took their leave. As soon as Jonathan opened the door of the pickup, the dog jumped in. Luke laughed. "Well, it looks like we have a new member of the crew."

Jonathan petted the dog's neck. He had blue-speckled eyes and no collar or identifying tags. Jonathan released the dog, and he hopped into the back seat of the crew cab. "He doesn't seem to be giving us a choice." Jonathan stepped up into the pickup.

Somehow, they still arrived right on time, five minutes before one o'clock, for Jonathan's first day of work at Emma's Nursery and Flower Shop. The dog followed Jonathan out of the pickup and sat down behind him.

"I see you brought your four-legged friend." Grampa sized up the canine.

Luke relayed the events leading up to the dog following Jonathan on his first day of work.

Allison and Maddie were already petting and hugging the dog.

"What's his name?" Allison asked.

Without hesitation, Jonathan said, "Al." He was his first dog, his alpha dog, and he liked the sound of it because it started off like Allison.

Grampa had kind eyes and a jolly disposition, but he was a stickler for details. "The dog can stay as long as it doesn't affect your work, and you'll give him a job to do too. He can shepherd the birds away from the plants and learn to guard the perimeter."

"Yes, sir." Jonathan gave Grampa a serious nod.

"Okay, today you'll start weeding over there with the girls."

"I'm on it." He tried to keep a straight face, but inside he was giddy at the prospect of working closely with Allison.

He watched the girls at work for half a second and then jumped right in. He waved goodbye to Luke then pulled round sprouts out of a container, careful not to disturb the flowers.

"These weeds are clover sprouts. Once they get around the plant, they'll strangle it to death." Allison put her hands to her neck to pretend to be choking.

Jonathan laughed.

"Also, while you're on each plant, pluck off the brown leaves and dead petals," explained Allison.

"Do we use weed killer or fertilizer?"

"We're an organic nursery, so we don't use chemicals. We make our fertilizer ourselves with composting." Allison went on and on about composting and when to use it.

Maddie was pulling weeds and rolling her eyes toward Jonathan behind Allison's back, like a typical little sister. Allison was interested and serious about plants. Maddie was bored.

"Can I go?" Maddie whined. "You have help now."

"Fine. We'll finish up, but make sure you get the deposit ready for Grandma and have the floor swept. Okay?"

"Deal!" Maddie bounced and hopped back inside the shop.

"I'm really glad you're here," Allison said. "Grampa needs some-one strong around. I worry about him lifting all those fifty-pound bags at his age."

"I'll take care of that. Before you know it, Grampa won't have to do a thing except rock in his chair." Jonathan made a mental note to find out what would need to be lifted while he was in school and po-sition things as much as he could to save the old man's back.

Jonathan could hear a ruckus going on out in the front of the shop. Some lady was yelling at Grampa. Jonathan wondered who would want to yell at an old man like that. But being from the wrong side of the tracks, he knew the best thing to do was to not get in-volved in other people's business. So he put his head down and kept working.

Allison stopped and turned around. "What is Busy Bea doing here?"

Jonathan kept working. He could hear the loud woman getting closer. He heard two sets of steps approaching from behind him and figured the other set was Grampa.

"Dad, I want him out of here. I don't think it is appropriate to have him working with my daughter," the lady said.

"Now, Bea. Since when are you interested in the operations of Emma's? You haven't been out here for over a year. This is my busi-ness, and I'll hire who I want to hire. He's a good worker, and you have nothing to say about it," Grampa declared.

"Mom, what going on?" Allison asked.

"Where's Maddie? She has a dentist appointment."

"She's in the shop."

"I want you to stay away from him." Busy Bea pointed at Jonathan and stormed off.

A few minutes later, Maddie skipped back out to Allison and Jonathan. One of her braids was flopping loosely, coming undone.

"Allison, do you have an extra ponytail holder?"

"Sure." Allison dug in her pocket and retrieved one for her little sister.

"Don't mind Busy Bea, Jonathan. She's a crazy religious fanatic." Maddie made a circle around her right ear with her index finger.

"Madeleine! You shouldn't talk about Mom like that," Allison hollered in shock.

"Well, might as well let him in on the truth on his first day."

Maddie gave Jonathan a thumbs-up before trotting to her mom's car and hopping in.

"Busy Bea means well," Allison said.

"You don't have to make excuses for her. It seems like she can stick up for herself," Jonathan said with a little chuckle. He never stopped working but stole a glance at Allison every chance he got. He knew right then that all he wanted was to be near her and protect her.

"SO, IT WAS ALL ALLISON from the very start." Luke took the last swig of root beer from the glass bottle.

"Luke, could you ever have believed how impossible it would be to protect the ladies?"

"Nope, and Saren is due."

Luke got up from the rocking chair and tossed his bottle into the recycling bin just in time to see Saren and Frost trotting around from the back of the shop. She was covered in dust, but Frost looked fine.

"Did the forest kick *your* butt this time?" Luke asked.

"Something like that," Saren said. "Maybe I need to stash a change of clothes here so Mom doesn't get suspicious."

"Are you hurt?" Jonathan asked. He ran over to her and looked for injuries.

"No, but you had root beer without me!" she said, eyeing the empty bottle sitting on the porch next to the rocking chairs.

Jonathan chuckled, realizing that she was still only twelve years old. Maybe they had put too much of a burden on her by letting her do this, but he and Luke felt at peace about it underneath their desperation.

"I think the forest will calm down once it realizes you won't give up," Jonathan said. "It wants to discourage you, but if you can't be thrown off track, it will eventually start helping you."

Luke gave Jonathan one of his looks. Jonathan knew Luke didn't like talking about the supernatural, but he didn't deny its existence around that cottage.

Luke sat Saren down in one of the rocking chairs and squatted down to her level. "Saren, are you sure you want to keep going with your investigation?"

Saren looked exasperated but still showed no fear. She was intrigued. "Dad, are you kidding? After what I've experienced? No way. I'm more determined than ever to find out what is going on out there."

Luke looked up at Jonathan, who shrugged. "Well, okay. But if you get scared or think you could really be hurt, we have to stop letting you go out there. Got it?"

"Got it, Dad."

"Good."

"But, Dad, Uncle Jonathan, you're not going to believe what I saw! I saw the lady! She's gray, gray all over."

Chapter Seven

Standing inside the curved bay window, the Gray Lady eyed the lace curtain. "This is really pretty," she said—or maybe she'd just thought it. The beautiful lace curtain was the only thing she could see. A dark fog seemed to cover her eyes.

She listened and heard the old cottage settling. A tree limb scraped the side of the house in the gentle breeze. Was the sound really that slow, or were her ears in a fog too?

She wondered where she was. She didn't recognize the place. She wondered what day it was. She couldn't remember how she'd gotten to this lacy curtain. She had no idea what had happened a moment ago, yesterday, or the day before.

She rubbed her eyes, hoping that would help her vision. As she gazed at the intricate pattern of the lace curtain, her mind strained to put meaning to the shapes in the delicate fabric.

"*What is that?*" she thought. It seemed so familiar, yet she couldn't come up with words. She traced the design with her finger, and the curtain opened up a little, allowing in a stream of bright light.

Her eyes were on something farther away—a shape just like the one on the curtain. This same shape and similar shapes were scattered on the ground. She could make out the outlines of the forms. She studied the items, trying to find words for them.

Then she saw movement past the perimeter of the garden. At first, she jerked back in fright. But she couldn't remember what she was trying to avoid, so she peered out.

A child and a dog stood just outside the garden. The Gray Lady couldn't remember ever seeing another person before, yet the girl seemed somehow familiar. The fluffy little dog was strangely wonderful. He made her feel something that she didn't recognize, but she liked it.

The girl was peering into the yard at all the shapes the lady could not name. The girl wore a long tunic top covered with a print of the same unknown but familiar shape. The girl and the dog, like everything else she saw, were in varying shades of gray. The garden and the forest beyond blended with non-colors of gray like the morning fog. Distinguishing trees from grass was difficult because she could see only shape and outline in grayscale but no color.

The Gray Lady closed her eyes tightly, hoping the fog over them would clear. Searching the gray for the girl and the little dog, she found the girl standing on a boulder. She blinked a few more times, and as she watched, the girl's top emerged bright with rose, pink, vermilion, and red. The child's long brown hair flowed from her large yellowish hat. The dog was white and fluffy like clouds.

Color! They were in color! The child had rosy cheeks, and a brilliant-blue ribbon was tied around the dog's neck. Once the lady realized there were colors, something in her sparked. She rubbed her eyes again, and when she opened them, she looked for the child and the dog. They were no longer where they had been a second ago. They were closer to the garden fence. Once her gaze fell on the girl and the dog, the color began to spread outward from them like unrolling a painting of the forest and garden. The whole outside became colorful. The familiar shapes on the ground became recognizable as long-stemmed red roses cut and left on the lush green lawn. She looked back at the curtain.

"Rose..." Her voice was harsh and cracked as though she hadn't spoken in years. For an instant, she felt hopeful, even daring to feel calm.

Bang, bang, bang came a gavel from upstairs.

Jumping back from the curtain, she stumbled into the desk and sat down in the twirling leather executive chair. She looked around the room as if for the first time, noticing and appreciating the beautiful aqua color of the velvet chairs, the Persian rug, and the books on the expansive bookcase.

Finally, she looked down and saw her calico-print skirt in shades of gray. Her hands were sallow ash. The end of her long hair was oddly silver gray, as were her boots.

"Color, everything is colorful but not me. I'm gray—" Her voice cracked.

Bang, bang, bang. She heard a gavel from upstairs then a harsh man's voice. "Calling this trial to order."

As she focused on her ashen hands, they began to tremble. That familiar dread, shame, and condemnation washed over her. As she looked up, the fog rolled back over her eyes and covered everything again in its colorless gray mist.

Her small reprieve was over, and her autopilot continued. She rose and headed up the stairs, past the giant mirror, up the tower stairs, and toward the *clunk, clunk, clunk* of the gavel.

Chapter Eight

Jonathan, with Ol' Blue riding shotgun, sped his utility vehicle down the path around the curve through the forest and parked near the back gate of the cottage. Ol' Blue hopped out and made her rounds, checking the property perimeter.

Jonathan grabbed the bags of groceries from the storage bed. When he picked up the bags, one of them caught on the machete tangled with the loppers that he still kept in the back of his cart. After freeing the bag, he made his way toward the thorny hedge.

He smiled and shook his head, recalling the first few nights that he had been guardian over this place and its unusual resident. The hedge of thorns around the garden and house hadn't allowed him in. He'd had to fight the briars. He'd hacked and lopped for hours before finally breaking through—or maybe it had simply let him in. He'd come night after night. Each night, the task had been easier, until the hedge finally let him enter freely. He chose to believe that the hedge—or whatever or whoever was controlling it—realized he was not going to give up, ever. After the briar or the miraculous force realized he had only come to help, it calmed down and didn't even bother with him anymore.

He paused at the break of the briar that allowed access to the backyard.

"Saren and Frost are trying to help too. Just like me. They won't give up either. Maybe you could cut them a break." He spoke to the forest, the briar, and the angel—or angels—that had taken up watch over Allison. Jonathan had never been sure what it was, but he was definitely convinced that it must be an angel there for good and not evil. He didn't know why. He just believed with all his heart that something wonderful would eventually come out of all these odd miracles.

Whenever he was near the cottage, he felt peace beyond comprehension considering the circumstances. He was thankful for this peace. He knew it came from God or His angels. He prayed often that his trials would be cut short. He felt that they were coming to an end and with it a new set of challenges and a new life. He looked forward to whatever the future would bring.

He felt strange about relying on a twelve-year-old for the solution, but he knew instinctively that she was the only one who would be able to navigate the unknown territory. He believed that something here didn't want interference, but it would not harm Saren or Frost.

He passed through the thorny opening without incident then strolled slowly along the backyard path lined with singing flowers. He wanted to stop and listen to them, but the hour was late. On the porch, the old wooden planks creaked with his every step. Vining sweet peas in full blooms of purple and blue covered the porch ceiling. A thousand tiny voices came from the sweet pea blossoms, saying, "Good evening, Jonathan."

"Hello. What a beautiful night it is." Jonathan looked up at the blossoms, and they all clapped their petals with glee.

The bright moonlight lit up the scene, giving the garden an even more enchanted atmosphere. Jonathan found the old skeleton key on his chain. The door itself was a white-washed Dutch door. Grandma Emma had cut the antique door in half so she could enjoy the fresh air. The paned window in the top part could be opened while leaving the bottom door closed. Jonathan turned the key, and the latch clicked, giving him free entry into an expansive indoor courtyard with a huge fountain. The courtyard was lined with rooms.

He closed the door, leaving the top part open, then proceeded into the glistening white kitchen. He put on the chicken and potatoes to cook before doing his usual maintenance and safety check around the house.

Although the house mysteriously never needed any maintenance, Jonathan was meticulous about knowing exactly where everything was. As soon as he entered the dining room, he could see something out of place. The center lace curtain was open, and the desk chair was swiveled to the left.

He walked over and looked out the window. Roses littered the lawn—one more weird thing for Saren to solve. His brain hurt from trying to figure this stuff out. He started to close the curtain then hesitated. *If she's looking outside, maybe she's finally making progress.* He decided to open all the lace curtains. Maybe she was starting to enjoy the view.

The night was stunning. The bright full moon lit up the clear night. He took a deep breath and enjoyed the moment, looking around at the unusual garden. He should be used to it by now, but it still amazed and delighted him. In this garden, he felt only peace and love. That was how he knew that it was from the forces of good, not evil. He didn't doubt that the dark side attempted to spoil what was meant for good, but he believed with all his heart that good always prevailed in the end.

When he turned around, the parlor, which seemed more like a study, felt like a totally different place with the moon streaming in. He remembered how wonderful this room had been on that first Christmas he'd been invited to spend with Grampa John and Grandma Emma. Allison had been so beautiful when she'd answered the door still in her reindeer flannel pajamas.

She and Maddie had always spent the night here on Christmas Eve because when Allison was small, she worried Santa Claus wouldn't find her since her own home lacked a fireplace and chimney. So staying at their grandparents' cottage had become a tradition.

That was the first time Jonathan had ever received a Christmas present. He got four that year. Allison had given him a CD Walkman. He wasn't a packrat, but he'd kept that old Walkman. He felt his smile fade as he came back to the present.

He headed across the foyer and up the stairs. At the top of the stairs, he turned right, and at the corner of the balcony hallway, he quietly opened a bedroom door. Her silver hair gleamed in the dim moonlight penetrating the fanlight window above the heavily draped windows. The room contained two full-size beds. He opened the drapes and sat down on the unoccupied bed.

As usual, she was still awake, if her state could be called that. She usually fell asleep somewhere around midnight, and it was only eight thirty. She lay quietly, staring at the ceiling.

"I have some good news," Jonathan said. "Saren, you know the one I always tell you about? Anyway, Saren found the cottage yesterday. The forest attacked the Frostie Dog, poor little guy. That didn't stop her, though. She came back, and today, she saw you. Did you see her? Did you look out the front window and see her and Frost?"

Jonathan let the questions hang in the air. As usual, they went unanswered. He refused to show discouragement in her presence. He saved that for when he was alone in the wee hours of the morning. He looked at her ashen complexion and cloud-gray eyes.

"I miss you. Please see Saren and Frost. You would love them. Whatever this is, you can solve it. You're the smartest person I know. Now is the time. I feel it in my bones." He spoke with little emotion. He knew from experience that too much emotional expression was draining. He needed all his energy. His stomach growled. "That's my cue."

He stood up and smiled down at her. He adjusted her covers and left her to her silent staring. His chicken would need to be turned over, so he headed back downstairs. Once dinner was ready, he put one helping in a plastic container and the other on a paper plate. He poured out some dog food, filled up Ol' Blue's water bowl, and headed into his room off the courtyard to eat.

The room was stuffy and smelled like paints and potting soil. Maybe the potting soil was permanently in his nasal cavities. Regardless, he opened the window for fresh air. It was the first night the weather had been warm enough. The air smelled fresh and full of gardenia mixed with roses. He turned on the TV to catch the local news. He was nearing the end of his meal when a mockingbird flew in with a whoosh and sat on the windowsill. It cycled through several beautiful songs so loudly that Jonathan could barely hear the weather report. The bird continued its medley with a song that sounded like a frog croaking.

This got Jonathan's attention. He muted the TV and looked at the bird. It watched Jonathan while doing a perfect rendition of *ribit, ribit, ribit.*

"So, are you Kermit now?" Jonathan asked after taking his last bite.

"No, I'm not Kermit. He speaks English, you know, not frog. I'm Mackey."

"Mackey the Mockingbird. Okay. Well, that frog thing is impressive. I once heard a mockingbird do a ten-speed bike," Jonathan said.

"Not too many of those around here in the forest. But I can do a water sprinkler." The bird did a perfect impression of a sprinkler.

"Cool." Jonathan clicked the mute button to unmute the weather report.

"You don't need to bother with that. It is always seventy-five degrees and sunny in Southern California."

Jonathan took a deep breath. "Look, I don't really like talking to birds that much, so why don't you go impress some lady bird with your frog impression?"

"Why don't you want to talk with me? It is not every day you run into a talking bird."

"Yeah, well, I've had plenty of talks with birds around here, and they're always bad. So beat it."

"Ohhh, you met Jay. The blue jay."

"Come to think of it. It was a blue jay that usually comes and talks *at* me."

"Yeah, that's him. He's a half-empty kind of guy. But not me. I'm not just half full. I'm full, baby. No empty around here."

"At first, I thought it was pretty cool, but it turned out to be a trick. He would just tell me all the things I did to drive her to do what she did. And he was right. If I had been there for her when she needed me, none of this would have ever happened. So here I sit, trying for redemption."

"Dude, you're redeemed."

"Man, bird, whatever, I know Jesus died for my sins, but..."

"No *but* to it. You're doing what you're here to do. It won't last forever. Okay."

A blue jay landed on the windowsill and shrieked loudly.

"Is that necessary?" Mackey flapped a few times and settled a little to the left of Jay.

"You're going to be in this mess until you die," Jay said. "You asked for it. You got it. You don't even have to die to go to purgatory. You're already there." Then he shrieked again.

"Guys, could we not have a bird-brain conversation tonight? Please?"

"Well, you don't have to be insulting," Jay said. "I was just trying to help."

"You're never trying to help," Mackey said. "I really think sometimes that you're trying to take the half full from people and fill up your half empty, but empty can't ever be filled."

"Good point, Mackey," Jonathan said.

The remote crashed loudly onto the floor, and Jonathan woke up. He looked around for Jay and Mackey, but they were gone. He took a deep breath. "Geez, I never know if they're real or just a dream." He turned off the TV and crawled into the bed. He fell into a dreamless, birdless sleep.

Chapter Nine

Saren and Frost arrived at nine o'clock in the morning, much earlier than her appointed time for working at Emma's. The fog produced by the Pacific Ocean's marine layer gave the nursery a spooky Halloween feel, even though it was spring. The shop and flower display area were already packed with customers. Several Sprouts were working today.

She looked around and spotted Uncle Jonathan in the vegetable-and-herb section behind the colorful perennials. He was talking with a police officer. She took off Frost's leash to let him greet Ol' Blue and stuck it in her satchel.

She decided to eavesdrop on their conversation. Maybe they were talking about her case. She stealthily made her way around the other side of the shop, out of the view of Uncle Jonathan. She weeded the tomatoes then the basil here and there to seem inconspicuous while getting closer and closer. From her position, she took a deep breath, enjoying the Italian-herbed air. She decided this was a good spot.

"Carly was just here yesterday, buying tons of tomato plants. Did she forget something?" Jonathan asked.

"Yeah, peppers. We can't make the salsa without the peppers. Right?" The officer held a jalapeño pepper plant in his hand.

"She must not like peppers."

"You know what? She does hate bell peppers. Maybe she 'forgot' them accidentally on purpose." The officer chuckled. "By the way, how is your investigation going?"

"You know, I haven't done anything with it in such a long time. I got frustrated and put everything up. I never got very far with it anyway. Everyone was so closed-lipped. Besides, would it fix her? I just don't know."

"Well, I don't know if it would. But it might give her some justice. Now that I made detective, I would be happy to help if I can. We're busy, but if you need me to look somebody up, just give me a call."

"Man, I really do appreciate it. I might take you up on that." Jonathan took the officer's card and shook his hand.

"Also, consider calling some of the old numbers again. Sometimes people will talk after time has passed. What has it been now? Thirteen years? People change; they have regrets. There's a real possibility of finding someone who'll be willing to help now."

"Thanks, Frank, good idea. Now for those peppers. You have a jalapeño. Let's get you some chilies." Jonathan turned around to find Saren weeding and eavesdropping.

"Well, well. This is Saren. She's an aspiring detective herself."

"Saren, this is Detective Brennen."

"Hi." Saren smiled proudly.

"Really? What case are you working on?" Detective Brennen asked.

"The case of the mysterious prom flowers," she said, trying to sound mysterious, then she smiled mischievously at Jonathan. She'd seen enough TV shows to know that a cop was not likely to take her seriously if she started spouting about gray ladies and enchanted forests.

"Oh, that sounds challenging." He smiled and glanced at Jonathan then back at Saren. "If you ever want a tour of the detective office, give me a call. We'll show you the ropes." He handed her a card of her very own.

"Cool!" She jumped up and down and looked at Uncle Jonathan. "When can we?"

"We'll talk to your dad about it. How's that?"

"Yeah!" She adjusted her satchel that she still wore across her body. It had almost fallen off in her excited jumping.

They heard a loud group chatting and looked toward the front of the shop to see what was going on. A group of white-haired women were stepping off a shuttle bus with "Cherish Independent Living" painted on the side.

"Saren, it's too busy here right now to train, so you're free to walk Frost. Take your time. I'll see you when you get back."

As soon as his name was mentioned, Frost bounced over and watched with excitement. Saren reattached his leash, and they trotted out toward the back of the nursery and into the woods.

Even as their voices faded into the background, she could hear Officer Brennen and Uncle Jonathan talking more about a long-ago investigation. She had a feeling that it had something to do with the Gray Lady. Perhaps she was a missing person and no one knew who she was. She made a mental note to herself to find out who had been missing thirteen years ago or if someone had been found.

She had only been to the cottage after school so far, so she was excited to see what happened in the morning. And since she had more time, she would go deeper into the forest and closer to the wall for a better look.

She approached the rock wall cautiously, but all the vegetation acted like vegetation. She spotted a thick manzanita very close to the briar that lined the garden wall. One of its branches extended out parallel to the ground about three feet up. Right next to it sat a large boulder almost as high as the branch.

"Excellent," she whispered to Frost. She climbed up and sat on the branch with her feet dangling. Frost looked up and gave her a soft whine. She reached over to the top of the boulder and patted it twice. "Up, up."

Effortlessly, Frost jumped the three-foot boulder and sat. He busied himself pawing at a black beetle that had taken up residence on the gray granite with black dots, hoping to use it as camouflage. This would be a great spot. It was high enough to get a complete view of the garden, but because of the tree foliage, they were hidden from sight.

Saren took out her investigation log and noted her position and the time. She looked at the previous page, which listed questions to be solved.

1. Who lives in the mysterious cottage?
2. Why and how was the forest enchanted?
3. How long has the forest been enchanted?
4. How do all those flowers bloom together simultaneously?
5. How and why is the lady gray?

Saren contemplated her next action as she waited for the gray lady to appear. Maybe she should just knock on the door and ask the lady who she was. *There has to be a reason that wouldn't work, or Dad and Uncle Jonathan would have suggested it.* She added question number six.

1. Why do Dad and Uncle Jonathan consider this an investigation?

Plus, the Sprouts at the flower shop had made this place sound scary. *"No one ever came back alive."* She wondered if that was true, but she suspected they were pulling her leg. However, the forest had tried to get *them* twice. Maybe that was why someone was missing.

1. Find out if there was a missing person case in this area

within the past thirteen years.

Turning back to her daily log, Saren focused on observing. She examined each window starting with the bay windows. Through the now-open lace curtains, she saw a gray figure get up from deeper in the room then go into the foyer, take a big hat off the hat rack, and head for the front door.

The front door had a shiny cherry finish and a stained-glass window picturing a single burgundy rose. It reminded Saren of the one in the Disney movie *Beauty and the Beast*. Saren wondered if the beauty or the beast lived there—or both. But this was an entirely different kind of story.

At that moment, the door swung open slowly and steadily. Like fog rolling in off the ocean at night, the shadowy gray figure emerged. She was the most remarkably contradictory thing Saren had ever seen. Long silvery-gray hair flowed, curling down under the giant gray hat. She wore a smoke-colored smock over a charcoal-and-drab-gray calico prairie-style dress with a light-gray lace petticoat peeking from under the plentiful skirt. Her feet wore dark charcoal-gray combat boots.

"What is up with this lady?" Saren whispered to Frost.

At first glance, her long silver hair made her seem very old, but upon closer study, she seemed to be merely twenty-six or twenty-seven. She was beautiful in a tragic way and a little creepy. She moved so slowly and smoothly, almost ghostly. She carried pruning shears in her ungloved hands.

What is she doing with that? Because the yard and everything in it was perfect, Saren couldn't wait to see what the woman would choose to prune. The garden was so still that Saren barely breathed for fear of being heard. She hoped that Frost would behave quietly too. He seemed to have the same thoughts as they both watched the odd woman glide slowly across the luxurious garden. Then his ears perked up, and he looked to the left.

Saren pulled her gaze from the lady to see what Frost had spotted. It was the black snake in a tall rosebush in the center of the lawn. The bush was unusual in that the roses and thorny foliage stood on a thick trunk, and it was groomed to a perfect sphere of roses. Saren was surprised she hadn't noticed that rosebush before, because it was clearly the centerpiece of that area of the yard. It was almost as if the bush had been cloaked with an invisibility cape this whole time.

"*Weird*," Saren thought then turned her attention back to the long black snake which Frost had spotted. It had yellow eyes and a deep-purple forked tongue. It was coiled around the thorns of the rosebush. Saren was astonished, because it was clearly the same snake that had landed on them. Her first reaction was to warn the Gray Lady. Instead, she waited and observed.

The snake was also watching the Gray Lady approach.

Frost let out a soft, low warning growl. Right then, the snake turned abruptly toward Saren and Frost, and it seemed to look Saren right in the eyes.

Frost stood up and stuck his tail between his legs as if in imminent danger. Saren startled, upsetting her balance on the tree trunk. She flipped backward off the branch. In her attempt to stop her fall, she took a couple of limbs down with her. She managed to tighten her hold with her legs, preventing a hard fall on her head. She ended up hanging upside down on the branch from bended knees.

Frost jumped down from the boulder to consider Saren's predicament. He decided to help her by licking her upside-down nose.

"Frost, you're not helping," Saren whispered. She put her hands down on the soft ground covered with clover beneath her. With a grunt, she athletically and quietly kicked her feet off the tree to the ground, forming a downward-facing dog pose. "We're not here to do yoga either," she whispered.

She found her hat inside a shrub and returned it to her head. She quickly collected her satchel, along with her journal, pen, and her Nancy Drew book that had scattered in the process. Saren had been so creeped out by the stare of the snake that she'd momentarily forgotten the Gray Lady.

"Let's go," she whispered. She didn't have to tell Frost twice. He bolted out ahead of her, taking the retractable leash to its limit. When they'd made it out to the path, Saren put her hands on her knees to catch her breath. Frost doubled back to her to see why she'd stopped.

She stood up straight and looked around. Her willies had vanished. She had a renewed determination to stick around today and observe the Gray Lady. "We're not going to let that ol' snake scare us off so easily."

Frost looked up at her with surprise as she headed back across the clearing and toward the cottage. He stood on the path, looking toward Emma's, as Saren headed closer to the forest. Once the leash was at the end, Saren stopped and gave two gentle tugs. Frost looked one more time toward Emma's, as if to convince her to abandon her cause. Unsuccessful, he slowly followed Saren into the forest.

When they arrived back at the manzanita tree and the boulder, Frost gave a soft whine like he was ready to leave. Saren put her right index finger to her lips. She looked around the forest floor and picked up one of the branches that she'd knocked off in her fall. The leafy branch was just the right size to block her from being seen. Doing her best bush impression, she slowly rose to peer over the briar, the fence, and the inner rose wall. Hoping the Gray Lady hadn't heard her commotion, Saren checked to see if she had been discovered. Not spotting the gray lady or the snake, Saren scooted back-

ward up on top of the boulder, holding up the branch for camouflage. The boulder was surprisingly flat on top and comfortable.

Blooming clover covered the ground below the stone. Frost had
settled down and already started to chew on one of the tiny yellow
blossoms. "Perfect," she whispered to Frost, "we can sit here all day,
undetected."

The snake had made no spooky return. Still, just in case, she decided not to examine that particular rosebush too carefully. She figured if she didn't look for it, the dark serpent wouldn't exist.

Even though it was midmorning, the mountain cast a deep shadow over the house and garden. The air was still heavy with gray
morning mist. With a start, Saren blinked to make sure she was
seeing correctly. The mist seemed to be moving. Then there she
was—the Gray Lady, in flesh and blood, gliding slowly like a cloud
across the lush green grass.

She didn't look like a witch at all. She didn't look like a princess
either. She looked, well, sad. The woman's odd old-fashioned style
paired with boots completed her gothic grayscale fashion. The boots
were not unlike the ones Grampa had worn in combat. Saren wondered what battle the woman was fighting. Saren was relieved to see
the boots were, in fact, on the ground.

On the lady's head was the biggest hat Saren had ever seen. Made
of a tightly woven gray straw, it was plain. It was neat and clean, just
like the rest of her appearance. The huge hat shielded her entire body
from the sky—as if she were hiding from God.

As she walked, she only looked down, never straight ahead or up.
Because of this, Saren couldn't get a look at her face. She could see
the woman's hair coming out from underneath the hat and flowing
like silk down her back. Her hair was shiny silver. However, the texture of the long locks was of a young girl's hair rather than an old
woman's. Somehow it didn't jibe. Saren wondered if she was one of
those Goth chicks who had dyed her hair silver. Saren marveled at

how beautiful it was. Then the sunlight broke over the mountain, dispersing the shadows, and it streamed bright rays right onto the woman's face.

She must be a princess or something. Saren had never seen a face so beautiful. Except for the ashen hue and gray around her eyes instead of apple-colored cheeks, her skin was fair like Snow White's. Her eyes, squinting from the unaccustomed sunshine, were smoky gray and sad to the depth of her soul. Not only sad, but tormented.

Saren was amazed that someone so beautiful, with such wonders around her, could be so distraught. Her eyes look glazed over with smoke, almost like that blind old dog from the headstone maker's yard. Saren wondered if the woman could even see through those eyes. Because of her youth, Saren had never seen someone transcend life into such a dark abyss.

The Gray Lady stopped when she reached the center perfectly round rosebush. This was the very same rosebush where Saren and Frost had seen that creepy snake. Saren made sure she looked carefully at the Gray Lady. She didn't want to look at the bush to avoid the snake. She hoped that the snake was gone now and would not harm the Gray Lady. She wondered if she should warn her. Ultimately, Saren decided that she would warn her if it looked like the Gray Lady was in danger. Saren hadn't seen any sign of the snake since she fell off the tree branch. Maybe she had scared it away.

The Gray Lady began cutting the beautiful crimson roses off the most perfect rosebush in the yard. The roses fell randomly on the lush green grass, and there they stayed. The Gray Lady seemed to be the Morticia of gardening.

Suddenly, a red spot appeared on her hand. She was pruning the rosebush without gloves, and the thorns pricked her fingers. She didn't notice or care but simply kept clipping, letting the drops of her blood fertilize the ground.

As the Gray Lady cut off the blossoms, Saren made notations in her journal like a real detective would. At first, though, her details resembled notes from a horticulture class rather than a detective's case. Flipping back a page, she added to her list of questions that needed answering in order to solve the mystery of the Gray Lady and the miracle garden.

1. Does the blood in the soil account for the different seasons of flowers blooming all at the same time?

The Gray Lady had been pruning or rather relieving the bush of blossom after blossom. She worked her way around methodically. Saren figured the woman would gather the roses up at the end and take them into the house to make a bouquet. While the Gray Lady trimmed, she seemed to be speaking to the rosebush. At first, Saren thought she was talking to the plants to make them grow. The conversation was not a very encouraging one, though. Saren strained to hear what the Gray Lady said.

"No, I didn't want to. He forced me."

"You stayed with him for months after," said a deep, low voice. "Why did you continue?"

Saren looked around for who could be speaking. She didn't think roses could talk, and if they did, they wouldn't have such a deep voice. She didn't see anyone. She looked down at Frost, and he was taking a nap. *Some guard dog.*

She looked in the direction the Gray Lady was looking. Blended in with the remaining crimson roses sat three bright-red cardinals. The middle one opened its beak, and a higher-pitched male voice came out.

"What did you hope to gain by ruining a man's career?" the middle cardinal asked.

"You cannot trust your prayers," said the cardinal on the right, with the deepest voice. "God will not hear you now."

The cardinal on the left shook his head in disapproval. "Tsk, tsk, tsk."

All three cardinals frowned with their harsh black-masked eyes and shook their heads in condemnation.

"I did everything you asked." Her voice hoarse, the Gray Lady sounded hopelessly defensive.

Suddenly, there it was again, the snake. Saren sat straight up in case the Gray Lady needed her. But the black snake showed no signs of coiling to strike. It twisted and curled deep in the bush, revealing only its head to get close enough to hiss the words right in the Gray Lady's ear.

"You cut that one too ssshort again. Where are your ssscruplesss? You are usssselessss." The snake spoke with a snooty-sounding French accent.

"Sorry." The Gray Lady looked even sadder.

Saren decided that this kind of snake could be far more dangerous than the kind that strikes. He might have poisoned the Gray Lady's spirit in order to collect her soul.

"You asked for it," the cardinal on the left said.

"No, I didn't want to," the Gray Lady said. "He forced me."

"You stayed with him for months after. Why did you continue?" the deep-voiced cardinal asked.

"What did you hope to gain by ruining a man's career?" asked the middle cardinal.

"You cannot trust your prayers. God will not hear you now," said the deep-voiced cardinal.

The cardinal on the left again shook his head in disapproval. "Tsk, tsk, tsk."

All three shook their heads again in disapproval.

The exact sequence repeated like a loop until every last rose was clipped and dropped onto the garden floor.

Forty-two minutes after she began clipping the roses and bleeding from the thorns, the Gray Lady had succeeded in ridding the most perfect bush in the garden of every single blossom. She neatly wiped the blood off the gardening shears with an old-fashioned lace handkerchief and placed them in her smock pocket. The roses lay haphazardly in the lush yard wherever they had fallen. The Gray Lady pivoted slowly on her heels and made her way to the porch. Her movements were almost dreamlike in their sluggish, liquid motion. Her head hung even lower as she went in. She looked like she was completely defeated and demoralized. *No wonder the woman is so depressed.* Saren marveled that the woman hadn't shooed away the birds and killed the snake. After all, they were just birds.

Wait, but birds don't talk. Saren burned to run to the Gray Lady and say something encouraging. But she just watched as the woman disappeared behind the cherry door.

Stunned, Saren sat on the boulder. She examined the wasted roses longingly, shocked the Gray Lady had done all that work just to leave them there. She was tempted to gather them up and make a bouquet. But she didn't want to have a run-in with that snake again. So she flipped her page back and added a question.

1. What is the purpose of cutting the roses and leaving them there?

2. How and why are birds and snakes talking to the Gray Lady? Why are they so mean to her? Why does she accept it?

This is day three of my investigation, and all I have is more unsolved mysteries. I hope I start to get some answers soon instead of more questions. She realized that she was being very twelve. Surely a thirteen-year-old would have more patience. *More questions will lead to more answers. Remember, the key is asking the right questions. Yeah, I'll look for even more questions. Eventually the answers will come.*

Through the stained-glass window on the door, she watched the Gray Lady hang up her hat and smock in the foyer and head up the stairs to the tower again. Saren wanted to know what she was doing up in that tower.

Chapter Ten

The Gray Lady sat on the antique divan in her usual blank, colorless state. Something felt different. She could feel warmth, light, on her face. Unusually intrigued, she looked up straight ahead. The morning sun filtered through the fog and the trees and into the windows, shining gray and bright in her eyes. She blinked a few times and looked again. *Yes, light. Is it a... yes, a garden? Oh, it is beautiful.*

A small grove of gray trees rose out of a perfect but gray lawn. She panned the yard to the right. Her eyes widened. Red, she could see red. The most beautiful crimson roses she had ever seen stood out in a sea of gray forest. The blossoms were the only color she saw.

"*Oh, Maddie would love these roses.*" She clapped her hands together in delight. "*They're the perfect flowers for her bridal bouquet. I'll have just enough time to gather them and make her bouquet before the wedding. I'm the maid of honor. I have to get dressed too. I had better hurry,*" she said, though her mouth never moved.

Even though her mind was excited, she felt as though her body were walking through molasses. She slowly and smoothly got up, put on her gardening smock hanging by the front door, and donned her wide-brimmed hat. She walked across the porch and down the steps.

Why is this taking so long? I should be there already. I'm going to be late. She was halfway across the spongy lawn when she saw movement outside the garden on her left. Out of the corner of her eye, she saw a girl sitting on a tree branch, hiding behind some leaves, and a dog sitting on a big rock. *Oh, maybe they have come to visit me. I haven't had a visitor in so long. Have I had a visitor? I don't remem-*

ber ever having one. I hope they come to talk with me. Then suddenly something happened, and they both disappeared. Her heart sank.
*"No, I was just imagining a new friend. I'm stupid to think anyone
would come visit me."* Then she saw the girl and the dog running away
through the forest. *"I must have scared them away. I don't deserve a
visit anyway. Besides, look at the time. I'll be late for the wedding."* She
plodded along as slowly as ever, gliding toward the rosebush.

The black snake coiled around the thorns, but his head and a
good portion of his upper body were outside the bush, turned in the
direction where the girl and the dog had been. He turned his yellow
eyes at her.

"Well, it'sss about time you ssshowed up," the snake said with
his slithery purple tongue in an arrogant-sounding French accent.
"You're ssso late. *Where* have you been?"

"I don't know, where are we?"

She looked around her. The rosebush and garden were gone. She
was in an expansive cafeteria. Plates and silverware clanged in the
background. A tall dark-haired man had a painful grip on her arm.
He was escorting her around the endless sea of tables and young people with backpacks and books and hamburgers on the tables.

"What are you doing flirting with those guys?" he asked in a
thick French accent.

"Who? Nothing. I don't know what you're talking about."

She didn't know who the man was, but he did seem familiar.
Whoever he was, she was afraid of him. She wanted to get away, but
he had a firm hold on her arm. She felt like even if he let her go, she
still couldn't escape him, as if he had a grip on her very soul.

It was coming back to her now. Her friends would not be arriving
to help. He had been perfectly polite to the boys she was talking
to. They had been fellow classmates, and they were talking about an
upcoming assignment. He cracked jokes with them and came across
as completely charming. When he was no longer within earshot of

them, he changed. They would have no idea anything was wrong. She couldn't tell anyone, because who would believe her over a professor?

"That's what he wants you to believe," said a familiar gravelly voice that sounded as though it belonged to an old man.

"Who said that?" Suddenly, she was back in the garden again, looking at the rosebush through smoke-glazed eyes.

A mockingbird fluttered his wings then sat back down on a branch.

"Don't pay attention to that ol' snake. He's as old as the earth itself. He tells nothing but lies," the mockingbird said in a very Grampa-ish voice.

"Ssss... You have nothing original to sssay," the snake said.

"Where are your ssscruplesss? You are ussselesss," the mockingbird said to the snake, imitating the snake's voice perfectly.

"I don't have time for all this. I have a bouquet to make." Unconcerned with the presence of the snake, she put her hands deep into the bush to clip the rose with as much stem as she could. She examined the beauty of the single long-stemmed rose blossom.

"What a pity. You have cut it too ssshort. You are ussselesss."

Just then, three bright-red cardinals flew around, pushing the mockingbird off his perch, and landed on the bush.

"You asked for it," said the cardinal on the left.

She stared at their red feathers then closed her eyes. When she opened them, she saw only red dots at first. Blinking then looking around, she found herself in a small room with a bare bulb over a table. The brightness of the bulb made the gray room seem dark in spite of its brightness. Three men stood around her. They wore dark suits and white shirts. One wore a white tie with red spots. The one with the deep voice wore a tie decorated with red feathers, and the third man, whose tie was adorned with cardinals arranged in diagonal rows, was losing his hair and had combed what was remaining over.

All three were nondescript vanilla-type American white men. They each asked her questions at the same time. They all had an accusing tone. They thought she had done something wrong. What had she done? She didn't know. They were accusing her of ruining a man's career. They cycled through the same questions over and over again. They were never satisfied with the answers.

"You asked for it," one said.

"No, I didn't want to. He forced me," she said.

"You stayed with him for months after. Why did you continue?" another asked.

"What did you hope to gain by ruining a man's career?" the third asked.

"You cannot trust your prayers. God will not hear you now," the first said.

All three shook their heads again in disapproval.

"You cut it too ssshort again. You are ussselessss," the snake said.

She flashed back to the garden. Disappointed she hadn't pleased the snake, she let the perfect rose fall haphazardly to the green grass, as it was now considered to be trash.

She tried again, reaching her whole arm into the bush. Eventually, she had to get it right. Then the cardinals began their questions, and the cycle repeated itself. Each time, she became more and more distraught and depressed. She could no longer remember why she was cutting the flowers. She continued until the bush held no more blooms.

She then put her head down in sorrow and utter defeat. Feeling like nothing more than a wisp of smoke being sucked under the door in search of fresh air, she streamed back into the cottage to hide.

Chapter Eleven

Saren and Frost jogged all the way back to the shop. She couldn't wait to tell Uncle Jonathan about seeing the Gray Lady and how she'd talked with birds and that creepy snake. Saren considered not telling him about the snake. Her father and Uncle Jonathan might stop her investigation if they thought it was too dangerous. Anyway, she was still twelve. Maybe a thirteen-year-old would be able to not talk about the snake.

The forest had behaved itself today. Uncle Jonathan was right—it must have realized she meant business. Despite her excitement, she was troubled by how sad the Gray Lady had been. The lady had believed that stupid snake. She seemed ashamed of something that she had done. Saren wondered if she actually *had* done something bad. Either way, the woman must not know about forgiveness. Maybe that was why she was so gray. *I would be gray, too, if I thought God would never forgive me.*

Still deep in thought, she slowed her pace as she came to the back door of the shop building. She figured Uncle Jonathan was getting lunch ready for his crew in the break area. He always fed everyone. Most of the Sprouts were from low-income families, and usually, the other employees didn't think far enough ahead to bring their lunch. So he made his famous sandwiches every day. He could have been a chef as easily as a horticulturist.

Saren decided to practice her spy skills. She gave Frost the "shush" sign. He slowed down to a crawl so that his dog tags would not jingle. She stealthily and quickly went through the back door and snuck behind a storage shelf at the same moment Uncle Jonathan said loudly, "What are you doing?"

She jumped then realized he hadn't been talking to her. She tiptoed to see over the big bags of wild-bird feed to see Donny, one of the Sprouts, pressing Megan, one of the teen employees, into a corner.

Megan hollered, "No, stop. Let me go!"

Chapter Twelve

"Okay, Frank, you're all set to grow salsa," Jonathan said. He watched Frank close the tailgate of the pickup.

"It sure gets busy here, doesn't it? No wonder it was hard for you to spend time investigating what happened to Allison."

"Yeah, it is, but that's not the reason. I just couldn't get anywhere." It had been like a brick wall, almost like trying to investigate in the Eastern Block during the Cold War.

"Like I said, no one would talk." Jonathan put his head down. He really didn't want to talk about this. It brought up such horrible memories. He tried to put it behind him and focus on the present and future, but the past haunted him, ate at him. He hid his bitterness well, but he felt like if he had just been someone else, someone from an important family, he could have found the answers that could have helped Allison. Maybe he could have at least gotten justice for her.

"Jonathan, are you okay?" Frank ducked down to capture Jonathan's gaze as he looked at the ground.

Jonathan had been lost in thought, thinking of when he'd been searching for Allison. The color of his skin had put ridiculous limitations on him that he did not accept. He only knew Frank as a customer and didn't want to mix business and personal. The situation couldn't get worse, though. At least now he was on his home turf. "Yeah, I just have these flashbacks sometimes. You know? About when Allison went missing."

"Jonathan, really. What happened back then?"

"Well, she didn't call me or her sister back for two days..."

Thirteen Years Earlier

THE POLICE STATION smelled like old mildew under Lysol, microwave popcorn, and scorched dust from the furnace. It was too hot in the building. The thermostat must have been set for eighty-five degrees. It was late February, and it had just snowed two feet.

"Where do we report a missing person?" Jonathan asked the receptionist, who was eating a taco, his tie and the shelf of his protruding belly littered with grated cheese.

He slurped the bottom of a soda loudly then said, "Sit down over there."

Jonathan and Maddie sat down in the waiting area. "You think Luke will be okay running Emma's while we're here?"

"Don't worry, Maddie. You should know by now Luke can handle himself," Jonathan said.

"Where in the world could Allison be?" Maddie was hiding both her thumbs in her closed fists.

Knowing that was Maddie's nervous tell, he gently picked up her right hand and freed her thumb. "Don't let them see that you're nervous. We have to go in one hundred percent confident that we know what we're talking about."

"Really?"

"Yeah, I know that from dealing with the cops with my dad. Use direct, short statements."

"Got it."

"So, Maddie, when you saw Allison last, did she act normal to you?"

"No, Jonathan, you know she didn't."

"Right, so that's what you're going to emphasize. We already know that Mort is lying to the cops. Why would he come to the wedding if he wasn't in a relationship with Allison? We need them to investigate him. He's at the bottom of this. I know it."

A tall and thick police officer walked toward them with an arrogant swagger. "Mrs. Madeleine Tasker, you can come back now." The police officer spoke through his overgrown mustache. The middle-aged man eyed Maddie and Jonathan with suspicion. His words were police professional, but his tone dripped with contempt. He had not introduced himself. His badge read Drexler.

Maddie and Jonathan got up to follow him, but Officer Drexler put his hand on Jonathan's chest. "Where do you think you're going?"

"I'm with Mrs. Tasker."

"We only need immediate family."

"He is. I mean he's like family, and he's our business partner. I want him to come too."

"Only immediate family can file a missing person report."

"That doesn't make any sense," Maddie said rather loudly. Her hands moved with her words for extra emphasis. Her eyes widened in panic. Fearing for Jonathan's safety, she moved the officer's hand away from Jonathan's chest and abruptly stepped between the officer and Jonathan.

"Fine. He can sit *outside* my office." He ushered Maddie into an office and pointed at a chair right outside the door. "Sit," he said to Jonathan in a commanding tone, as if he were speaking to a pet.

The office was stark and seemingly unused. No file cabinets or family photos. The desk supported a small stack of forms waiting to be filled out. Jonathan tried to have an open mind, but so far, this police officer seemed like he had joined the force for the power trip, not to help people. He focused on being grateful that the door had been left open so he could hear what was going on.

"So, what seems to be the problem?" Officer Drexler shuffled some papers and clicked his retractable ballpoint pen back and forth.

"My sister is missing. Her name is Allison Louise Scott. She has long brown hair, blue eyes. She's five feet... Officer, you're not writing this down."

He tapped the desk with the pen impatiently. "Let's start with why you think she's missing, then we'll get into the description."

Mattie took a deep breath. Her right heel tapped the floor quickly. Jonathan could tell that she had been offended that the officer did not seem to believe that Allison was missing. She controlled her emotions and spoke plainly and clearly without wavering. "After two days of trying to reach her by phone, Jonathan and I drove here from Southern California. Her roommates haven't seen her for two days. She hasn't attended any of her classes. *No one* has seen her or heard from her."

"When is the last time you saw your sister?" He leaned on the desk with both his elbows and laid his pen on the desk.

"At my wedding in San Diego, three months ago." Maddie sat up straighter and looked at the unused pen.

"Did she act unusual at the wedding?" He picked up his pen and clicked it twice. He still hadn't written anything down.

"Yes, she wasn't herself at all. She seemed nervous, but then at the reception, she opened up and was herself again as long as that guy wasn't around. She brought this professor she had been dating to the wedding."

"What was his name?"

"Professor Mort Hebert. He's French and a horticulture professor. He was snooty and wasn't friendly at all. Allison seemed afraid of him."

"What makes you say that?" He moved some papers around on the desk.

"Well, she was finally relaxing and acting normal at the reception. We were dancing and having fun. Mort was talking with other guests. My mother came over and told Allison she had been neglecting her date. As soon as she went over to him, her whole demeanor changed into this serious person none of us recognized."

Officer Drexler leaned too far back in his chair, causing its springs to scream in protest. Then he yawned.

"I saw them walk out of the reception and walk back to the greenhouses. She was gone for a long time. So we all went looking for her. My husband saw her running from the greenhouse to the barn. Jonathan went to look in the shop and offices. He found Mort looking through my grandfather's file cabinets."

"Why would he do that?" Officer Drexler retrieved a handkerchief from his back pocket and wiped his nose.

"He was looking through my grandfather's research notes. He was a well-known researcher in the field of horticulture, and that's Mort's field as well. We believe he was attempting to steal research results that hadn't been published since my grandfather passed away last year and planned to pass it off as his own."

The officer sat back up and impatiently slapped the desk with both hands. "So back to your sister. She ran to the barn."

"Yes, so, anyway, I found Allison in the bathroom of the barn apartment, crying and cleaning blood off of her maid of honor dress."

"What was the blood from? Was she wounded?" The officer finally sounded interested.

Maddie hesitated a second. "She said that she had unexpectedly got her period. But she had her period the week before."

The officer looked up at the corner of the ceiling. Bringing his gaze to Maddie, he tilted his head. "With all due respect, Mrs. Tasker, it sounds like your sister had sex and was embarrassed about it. It happens all the time with these girls that attend religious colleges. These places really just teach them how to lie."

"If she disappeared by her choice, she would have told me. We're very close."

"You may not be as close as you think."

Another officer came in. He was tall and broad and looked like he was habitually angry. "That him?" He pointed out the door toward Jonathan.

The officer behind the desk nodded and sucked his teeth loudly. The tall officer grabbed Jonathan suddenly and handcuffed him.

"What are you doing? Wait!" Maddie yelled.

Standing quickly, Officer Drexler seized Maddie, pinning her on the desk, and handcuffed her. "So, you want to go where he's going, huh?"

A female officer happened to be walking down the hall toward them. "Come on, Joe. I'll take it from here."

She motioned for him to uncuff Maddie then asked her to sit down. The tall officer still had a painful grip on Jonathan, even though he was in cuffs.

"I'm Detective Gonzo. After your phone calls the past two days, we contacted Dr. Mort Hebert. He tells quite a different story. He says that your sister was infatuated with him. She was a student with a crush on her professor and they never dated. But she was practically a stalker. He said he saw her two days ago and told her not to contact him anymore. Jonathan James had picked her up from his office, and that was the last time he saw her."

"That's impossible," Maddie said. "Jonathan was running Emma's Flower shop back in California two days ago. That whole story is a lie."

"We're going to hold him until we can verify his whereabouts."

They took Jonathan into a holding cell full of drug addicts, homeless guys, and a couple of shoplifters. He had seen this type of place plenty of times, but he'd never been on the inside. He was always wasting his hard-earned money bailing his dad out. He'd been glad to be in America, where the authorities couldn't condemn a kid for the crimes of his family. He hadn't lost hope in American justice.

Boyfriends were always the prime suspect. He wished he were her boyfriend. He would do whatever he could to protect her.

But right now, he was wasting time. Every minute counted, and it was supposed to snow again tonight. If her car broke down on the side of the road, she could freeze to death. He closed his eyes and prayed for her to be found and for his release so he could help.

They held him for six hours. Luke had faxed them numerous orders Jonathan had taken, proving he'd been there all day. Plus, Luke and Maddie provided substantial alibis, which the police didn't believe at first, but after several hours of questioning, they released Jonathan.

"What finally made them let me go?" Jonathan asked, opening the car door for Maddie.

"I asked them why you would drive me all the way here and do all you have for us if you wanted to hurt Allison. Mort's lies actually deprived them of motive."

Jonathan made a right turn onto the interstate on ramp toward the airport.

"Where are we going?" Maddie asked.

"I'm sending you home so you'll be safe from any more traumatic drama. Plus, I won't have to worry about Emma's with you there. It's obvious they have no interest in looking for her. I'll stay until I find her. Maddie, I promise I'll find her."

"SO, FRANK, YOU SEE why I haven't put much hope in law enforcement," Jonathan said.

"Yes, that's completely understandable. It's incomprehensible that you could be arrested while trying to report your friend as missing. What was going through your mind while you were sitting in that cell?"

To anchor himself in the present, Jonathan closed his eyes and breathed in the fragrance of the eucalyptus trees shading the parking lot.

"To be honest, all I could think about was Allison. She was somewhere, and she needed my help, but I was stuck in there with a bunch of potheads and petty thieves. All of us had failed her."

The parking lot was beginning to fill up again, but Jonathan tuned out all the buzz of activity around them.

"How old were you at the time?"

"Same as Allison, twenty-one."

"So, if you were twenty-one, then Maddie was—"

"She was eighteen."

"Wow, you guys were so young to be handling this on your own. Don't get me wrong. I'm not siding with those cops, but where were Allison's parents?"

Jonathan crushed a rock of gravel with his work boot. His demeanor remained professional.

"They were at home. Come to think of it, we asked them if they wanted to come with us to Utah, and they just started mumbling about something they had to do at school. They're both teachers."

"Didn't you think it was odd that her mom and dad didn't call the cops or go looking for her themselves?" Officer Frank asked.

"At the time, we didn't think much of it. They weren't involved with their kids much. But now that you mention it, that is weird. What do you make of it?"

Officer Brennen took off his hat and smoothed down his thick black hair.

"They know something, something they wanted to hide."

"How do we expose them so they have to tell us?" Jonathan asked. A bumblebee buzzed between them and hovered over the blossom on Officer Brennen's pepper plant.

"We need to find out one key element, and then the dominoes will fall. Did her parents know this Mort guy?"

"Yes, they met at an event. In fact, Allison's mom insisted she go out with him. Allison didn't want to at first."

Officer Brennen put his hat back on and took his notepad out of his back pocket.

"Okay, I think we have something there. Tomorrow, when I get back to the station, I'll run a search on our Professor Mort Hebert." He wrote the name down in his notebook and returned it to his pocket.

"Thank you, Frank, I really appreciate it."

"No problem, and we'll make sure you get some of this salsa when we make it."

"Jonathan," a customer hollered. "Jonathan!"

"Thanks, man." They shook hands, and Jonathan jogged back into the shop.

Chapter Thirteen

"Hi, Jonathan!" He heard the voice over the buzz of the crowd. He turned to see a familiar face. She had been a cheerleader when he and Luke were on the varsity basketball team in high school. She was now a school counselor and song leader in the church Maddie and Luke attended.

"Hey, Tamika, how have you been?" He gave her a friendly wave as he made his way toward her through the crowded display area.

She wore a bright smile and many long braids twisted into intricate patterns adorned with numerous beads. She gave him a strong hug and held on too long for Jonathan's comfort. She took a step back and looked at Jonathan. "Boy, you're looking good."

Jonathan chuckled shyly. "Thank you, so are you. How is Melvin?"

"Oh, him? I kicked him to the curb." She waved her hand away. Her tone changed to slightly spurned. "So, you're still working here after all these years. I grew out of cheerleading, but you never grew out of your high school job." She snickered and flicked her braids back from her neck.

"Well, I'm still happy." Jonathan offered her a satisfied smile.

"Don't you think they're taking advantage of you, making you work all these hours?"

"I'd be taken advantage of myself. I'm the managing owner."

"No way—you?" She shook her head. "Imagine that, you were that kid from the hood always covered in dirt."

"Yep, I like dirt. Now, how can I help you?"

"I need centerpieces for a party I'm throwing."

"Okay, just head into the shop, and one of the ladies in there will make that happen."

Before Tamika got a chance to say anything else, three other young ladies jockeyed for Jonathan's attention, so she headed on inside. Jonathan patiently worked his way through each customer's request, keeping it professional and deflecting their attempts to make the conversations personal in nature.

Jonathan carried an armload of plants toward the cash register for a customer. She was deep in excited conversation. "Do you know who you look like? Darius Rucker. Do you sing?"

"No, ma'am. I'm a plant guy." Jonathan smiled at the lady, wondering if it was the hundred or three-hundredth time he'd heard that. He wondered if every African American guy had looked like Charlie Pride back in 1970s.

As they stepped through the crowd, Jonathan instinctively took inventory of his employees around the shop. He had four boys from the Sprout Bible Study and Horticulture training group working outside, two teen girls who had been working with him for two years, and Iris, a semi-retired lady who loved flower arranging. He immediately noticed that Megan and one of the Sprouts were absent. Iris was at the design table, making centerpieces.

"Iris, have you seen Donny or Megan?"

"Oh, Megan went to the bathroom." She turned to look at Jonathan. "But you know... she has been gone for way too long now. That's not like her."

"And Donny?"

"I don't know. I assumed he was outside with the rest of the boys."

"Iris, can you please help them ring up this line of people."

Jonathan went into the display area, where Tamika was browsing while she waited for her arrangements to be made. "Tamika, I need your help with something."

"Sure."

With Tamika following, Jonathan walked quickly back through the design area and storage room. Donny had Megan pinned in the corner between the water fountain and the wall, holding her by each wrist.

"No, no, stop. Let me go." She looked exhausted, like she had been trying to get away for a while.

"What are you doing?" Apparently, Donny didn't hear him.

"Donny!" Jonathan said firmly with authority. His deep voice boomed.

Donny backed away and turned around. Tamika wasted no time and ran over to Megan.

"Come here, honey." She sat Megan down at the break table and sat next to her with her arm around her, comforting her. Megan broke down in sobs.

"What do you think you're doing, Donny?" Jonathan asked.

"Nothin'," he said with his head down.

Jonathan grabbed another chair. "Have a seat."

He sat down in the last chair in front of Megan. "Tell us what happened here."

"I came out of the bathroom, and he trapped me there." She pointed at the corner.

"Liar!" Donny jumped out of the chair.

"Sit down. You'll get your turn... maybe," Jonathan said.

Donny sat back down.

"So, anything else you want to tell us, Megan?" Jonathan asked.

Megan was still crying.

"Donny, what the heck?"

"She acted like she liked me," Donny said defensively.

"Okay, but when she said, 'No, let me go,' what were you think-ing?"

"I thought she was just playing hard to get."

"Why would you think that?" Jonathan asked. "Are you guys dating?"

"I thought we were. Then all of a sudden, she was like, 'No.'"

Megan had calmed down and blew her nose loudly.

"Boy," Tamika said, "you better know a girl means no when she says no." She looked back at Megan. "Honey, tell us your side now."

"Yeah, we went out last week. And I *thought* I liked him. He didn't tell me that he was going to be working here. I was nervous dating an employee would endanger my job. I need my job so I can save up to pay for college. So when I saw him, I asked him what he was doing here. He said he worked here and not to worry about it." Looking over at Donny, she asked, "Why didn't you tell me you were going to work here?"

He shrugged. "I thought it would be a fun surprise."

"Well, it's not. Is anything fun about this?"

"Kinda." He chuckled.

Jonathan gave him a look, and the serious look returned to his face.

"So, we just have a few more questions," Jonathan said. "Did he touch you inappropriately?"

She looked at Donny then Tamika.

"Donny, go out to the barn, load that fertilizer on the trailer. I'll talk with you later," Jonathan said.

Donny slouched off out the back door.

"Okay, honey, you can answer the question now," Tamika said.

"No, he didn't. But he was holding me by my wrists, and I couldn't get away to get back to work. I was afraid of messing up my job."

"Don't worry about your job. You're a good employee, and your job is safe, okay?" Jonathan spoke calmly.

Megan let out a huge breath in relief. "I'm so sorry for this mess I caused. I can do extra work to make up the time."

"Megan, you do not need to apologize. I want you to hear this and believe it. You did nothing wrong here. Donny didn't treat you like the lady that you are and that you deserve to be treated as. Okay?" Jonathan reassured her.

She gave a weak smile. "Okay."

"So, do you want to press charges?" Jonathan asked.

"No, I just want this to be over with."

Just then Frost shook out his fur, revealing that he and Saren had been hiding and listening the whole time.

Jonathan, with his back still to Saren, said, "Okay, young lady. That's enough snooping for one day. Come on out."

"I'm not snooping."

"Getting defensive doesn't a good spy make," Jonathan said.

"Okay."

"Okay, and...?"

"I apologize for eavesdropping, Megan. Hi, Sister Tamika."

They did a poor job of holding back their amusement at Saren's games.

"So, Sister Saren, I'm glad you're here," Tamika said. "When did you arrive on the scene?"

"Right when Uncle Jonathan came in and caught Donny pressing Megan into the corner."

"So you saw what happened?" Jonathan asked

"Yes."

"That makes you a witness," Jonathan said.

Megan started to cry again. Tamika put her arm around Megan to comfort her.

"Megan, why are you crying?" Saren asked.

"Saren, a young lady's reputation is very important," Tamika said. "If she feels like something has ruined it, that can be very devastating. Do you understand?"

"Yes, you mean if you did something bad or even if you didn't and it gets out, that could make a girl ashamed... and turn gray."

"Yes, gray," Tamika said. "That's an interesting way to put it. So we're both going to help Megan by keeping this to ourselves, aren't we?"

"Yes, ma'am." Then turning to Megan, Saren said, "Megan, don't worry. I can keep a secret. So please don't turn gray. Whatever you did do or didn't do or may do in the future, God can forgive all of us if we ask Him. He has a big unlimited lake of forgiveness." Saren put both her arms out to show how big it was.

"I couldn't have put that better myself," Tamika said.

"Okay. So we'll call both your parents and have a conference this afternoon. You can talk with them and make your final decision on pressing charges. Okay?"

"Okay."

"Tamika, do you mind sitting with Megan while I make these calls?"

"No, of course not."

"Saren, help your Uncle Jonathan out. Make the sandwiches today, okay?"

"I'm on it." Saren jumped up.

Jonathan went to assess the situation in the front of the shop. Most of the customers had been helped, and Iris was back to making centerpieces. He phoned both sets of parents, and they said they would be right over. Then Jonathan headed out to the barn.

"Dude, really?" Jonathan said.

"Jonathan, I'm so sorry," Donny said. "I'm not a creep, okay?"

"That's to be determined. Right now, you *are* a creep and other choice words you could be called. That behavior can land you in jail. Is that what you want?"

"No, really, I thought she was just cranky and messing around."

"Even if that were so, why are you doing it on the clock? Do you think it makes you more charming if you jeopardize a girl's job? Look, if you get between a girl and her money, you'll have problems every time. Are you going to pay for her college tuition, rent, books, car, gas, electricity?"

"No, I just started here this week. I haven't even got my first pay-check yet."

"So, you're broke, and you jeopardized your job too. What a way to woo a girl. Listen, women want security above all. If you're ever going to get a girl, keep her, and have a great life, you'll need to have and keep a steady job. You ever hear 'no money, no honey'?"

"Yeah. I heard that."

"That stuff is true."

"Okay, I messed up."

"And when a woman says no, she means no. Even if she's your girlfriend."

"Got it."

"Not the fifth no either. The first no."

"Okay, okay, I messed up. It won't happen again."

"I'm glad you realize it, because now you won't be trusted with women until you prove yourself. Work out here in the barn until the parents arrive and we find out what Megan wants to do. Are you good? I have to get back to work now."

"Yes, Jonathan. And again, I'm sorry. I know you've given me a huge opportunity. I really hope you give me another chance."

Jonathan took off his cap and rubbed the top of his head. He closed his eyes and put his hat back on. He opened his eyes back up, examined the teen for a moment, and turned to head back to the waiting customers.

Jonathan knew the risk he took every time he hired one of the Sprouts boys. They all came from rough backgrounds. There was a fine line between helping these kids and the potential destruction of the business that he worked so hard to protect and grow. He believed that God would continue to preserve Emma's and nurture the boys he took under his wing. The hardest part was deciding if helping one boy meant enabling him to hurt someone else.

Donny's mom and Megan's dad both arrived within the hour. Donny's mom was horrified by the situation. Her worst nightmare was having a son who would take advantage of a woman. As a single mom, she wanted to make sure Donny was punished but didn't end up with a criminal record.

Megan's dad, on the other hand, didn't see what the big deal was. "Boys will be boys. Megan better learn how to be tougher. That's why she'll pay for her own college if she wants to go," he said. He insisted that Jonathan keep the boy on staff. He believed that Donny had learned his lesson.

For Jonathan, dealing with parents of employees was the hardest part because they were often entirely self-serving. Donny's mom didn't want the situation to make her look bad, and Megan's dad didn't want it to cost him any money. Neither of them seemed to put much thought into what would be best for the kids. Once again, Jonathan had to make the tough decision.

Iris and one of the other Sprouts had just finished loading up Tamika's centerpieces.

"You're still here?" Jonathan asked. "I'm glad, because I wanted to thank you for helping me out with Megan."

"No problem. She really is a sweetheart. By the way, how did you know what was going on?"

"A teenage boy and a teenage girl are missing?" He shrugged.

"I see, but why did you come get me?"

"I knew the girl would be embarrassed, and I thought it would be easier for her if a woman was there too. I knew you would handle it just like you did. So, thank you."

"How did it go with the parents?"

"You wouldn't believe it, but Megan and her father both insisted that I keep Donny on. Then his mother suggested that he be punished by making him work the early shift. I told her that wasn't really a punishment since that's the easiest time of day around here. But I decided to go with it and teach him how to fix lawnmowers. We haven't had a dedicated mechanic since I took on management duties. Now I hardly have any time for it at all. He seemed genuinely excited about it. I guess for him, it will be punishment because he'll have to get up early and be off by the time the girls get here."

"Wow," Tamika said. "Jonathan, this is so like you. You always did put others before yourself, even to a fault. You know you should fire that boy. Your company could be liable."

"Doing what is in the best interest of others is always in the best interest of the company. Grampa used to call it 'God's economy.' He did things for people that didn't make business sense, like when he hired me. Then he built out that loft apartment in the barn for me. I've tried to follow in his footsteps. That's all."

"Wait, what? He built you an apartment?"

"Yeah, he called it my bachelor pad. I'd been working here for about three months and I had been staying in Luke's garage..."

Twenty Years Earlier

ONE PARTICULAR DAY, the sky opened up, and buckets of rain came down. It rained so hard, the dry creek that was rarely more than a series of puddles since the decade-long drought was about to burst its banks. Jonathan had been fixing a lawnmower in the barn and came up to the shop to order a part when the rain came down. When he finished his business, it was already an hour past quitting time.

Grampa sat on the front porch, talking to Grandma Emma on his portable shop phone.

Jonathan came out of the front door and leaned into the rain, examining the plants to make sure they weren't getting too pummeled to bounce back.

"Jonathan, they're so happy to have actual rain, so don't you worry about them plants. They'll be as happy for it as I am." Grampa smiled with a satisfying rock of the chair and without moving the phone away from his conversation with his beloved Emma. "Honey, I'm going to have a talk with Jonathan, and then I'll be home. How long before dinner's ready?" He listened intently to his wife then finally said, "You got it."

Turning to Jonathan, he said, "Have a seat. You worked enough today. Take a load off."

Jonathan felt odd about sitting around, but he loved the old man, and whatever he had to say, Jonathan knew he would benefit from it—if not now, then in twenty years.

"Yes, sir." Jonathan sat down obediently. Like most teenagers, he would be ready to hop right back up again.

"It is funny how young people don't know about resting. Resting is as important as eating and working and almost as important as sex." Grampa was not looking over at Jonathan but gazed out at the sheets of rain.

"Do you like working here?"

"Yes, sir, very much, sir."

"What don't you like about it?"

"Nothing. I love everything about it. I know I don't know much yet, but I want to learn everything about this business. Every plant and what makes it happy, to all the equipment and repairs. I love being outside. It is so nice here."

"So, what are your plans for your future? College? Military? Family?"

"College is a waste of time, and I'm not interested in killing people. I could learn all about plants and equipment and fertilizer from you and your friends. My future is here with Emma's Nursery. I could see myself working here forever."

"You might not ever make much money, Jonathan."

"I don't care about money. I like fixing things and watching plants grow. I've only been here a few months, and already, I walk through town and see plants that I know you grew from a seed, now thriving in someone's yard. I can see being happy doing that myself."

"What about when I'm too old and my kids take over? What then?"

It had never dawned on Jonathan that anyone would ever want to sell Emma's Nursery. But Grampa's children weren't interested in the business. His son was a lawyer who liked fancy suits, and Madeleine and Allison's mom and dad were school teachers, bookworms, not outdoor types.

"I could help Allison and Maddie run it. They'll need someone to do the heavy lifting and mechanical part of the business."

"So, at the ripe old age of sixteen, are you making a lifelong commitment to this company and this family?"

"Yes," Jonathan said.

"What about your family?"

"Every paycheck, I give money to my mom."

"Ahhh, that's why you're always broke."

Jonathan smiled with guilty pride. But he didn't see why he needed money.

"I'll tell you what we'll do." Grampa sounded like he was about to make a grand announcement. "You know how we've had all those men over giving us quotes about a perimeter alarm system?"

Jonathan nodded, wondering how the two pieces of the conversation went together. Even though Grampa was in his early seventies, he was still very sharp and always had a point.

"Would you be willing to stay here and watch the place at night? There will be extra pay in it for you."

"Absolutely!" Jonathan was not concerned about where he would sleep, eat, or bathe.

"So, here is what we'll do. We're going to build out the loft in the barn into a small bachelor pad for you. You can live there as long as you want, with no obligation to stay living there. You'll get additional pay for watching the place at night.

"Don't worry about your dog. Al is to be properly trained to guard the property while you're sleeping. You're still going to finish high school, and assuming you do not lose your mind, you'll have a job and a place to call your own for as long as you want it. If you can get that old flatbed truck behind the barn running, it's yours. I'll pay for any parts it needs, so charge them to the shop."

As Jonathan's life was laid neatly out for him, the phone rang twice and stopped.

"That would be our dinner bell. Emma insists you stay for dinner and that we drive you home."

Jonathan was so excited that he wanted to run a hundred miles. He couldn't believe his good fortune. This old man had taken him in and was teaching him everything, and now he'd promised him a job forever. The best part was that he would be working with Allison. It was more than he could ever have dreamed.

But a few days later, a shiny long black Cadillac pulled into the parking space sideways in front of where Grampa and Jonathan were working on the sprinkler system in the lawn outlining the parking lot.

"Oh no, Grampa, that's my aunt Patrice. She works in the mayor's office, and she's always up to no good."

"It's okay. Don't worry," Grampa said.

"Mr. Murray, you're going to be hearing from child protective services," Aunt Patrice said.

"Feel free to call me Grampa. Everyone does," Grampa said in his usual friendly yet gruff voice.

"Jon Jon"—Aunt Patrice ignored Grampa and pointed her long manicured index finger at Jonathan—"you should be ashamed of yourself. Now you know your mother needs help at home. You're out gallivanting all across town. Remember that time I had to bring you home from that party?"

Aunt Patrice lowered her shoulders and her voice and addressed Grampa. "Don't get me wrong. He's a good kid. Don't get in no trouble. He can thank me. Whatever he knows from the Bible, he learned from me." She put her hands on her hips and leaned back proudly.

"Aunt Patrice, you know no one has ever called me Jon Jon. You never found me at a party. I gave *you* a ride when you were drunk after that revival, remember?"

"Don't you sass me, boy." She came over and towered over him. She was a tall, hefty woman wearing three-inch-high heels that took her well over six feet. Jonathan knew that she often used her height to intimidate people.

Grampa cleared his throat loudly to get her attention. "Certainly, we'll welcome a visit from the social service folks."

"His mother is in bad shape. She needs an operation. She can't feed her children. She needs Jonathan at home."

Jonathan started to refute the lies, but Grampa raised his right hand to stop him. Jonathan closed his mouth.

Grampa smiled. "Ms. Aunt Patrice, we'll be happy to talk with Jonathan's parents should they choose. Meanwhile, is there anything else we can do for you?"

"Oh!" she said in a huff. She turned on her spiked heel, and Jonathan wondered how it was strong enough to hold up such a large woman. "You'll be hearing from our lawyers." She plopped into the Cadillac and sped off with a squeal of tires.

"Grampa, she works for the mayor's office. Will they make me go back home?"

"Don't you worry about it. I called social services before we started construction. They have a file on you. They know you have been living at Luke's. As long as you stay in school and don't have any run-ins with the law and your parents don't object, they won't bother with it."

"My parents never cared before. I don't know why they would now. Unless Aunt Patrice causes a stink."

"Maybe we could get her and Bea together."

"Yeah, on the Fourth of July. We wouldn't need fireworks." They both chuckled as they got back to work.

"SO, YOU SEE, TAMIKA, I'm just following in Grampa's footsteps."

"I can see how this was mutually beneficial. Grampa had a good long-term employee, and you had a job and a knighthood in Allison's kingdom."

"Yeah, that's right. Still Lancelot." He looked down and, with his boot, dug up a small weed coming through the asphalt.

"But you know she loved you too, right, Jonathan?"

"Yeah, I know she did."

"So why didn't you go for it?"

"I regret it every day of my life. But back then, she just seemed so out of my league. I mean, I was from the hood. I wanted more for her than..." He looked at the sky.

"What? Oh, I see. You didn't want her to have to deal with being *us*?"

"Yeah."

"You know she never cared about that. She wouldn't. She wasn't like that."

"Yeah, but she also didn't know what it was like either. I guess maybe it was my own insecurity. Her parents were adamantly against us dating. Then I started looking at it from their point of view. What would life really be like for her if we walked into a restaurant and they gave us the worst table. Ladies grab their purses when I walk by just because of the color of my skin. I didn't want that for her."

"But, Jonathan, she would have had you. She would have experienced so much more having you than she ever would have cared about a dining or shopping experience. Can't you see that? You took away *her* choice."

"*Now*, I do. I did give it a last-ditch effort at Maddie and Luke's wedding. I actually proposed. But she was so caught up in what her parents wanted. I wish I had tried harder and made a stand. I could have prevented this. If I had been bolder, stronger. My delay cost her... much more than dinner or shopping. It cost her everything. I could have saved her."

"Don't be so hard on yourself. You're doing all you can and more than anyone else would have ever done."

"Thank you, Tamika."

"By the way, whatever happened with your aunt Patrice?"

"Oh, nothing. Like the rest of my family. We didn't pay attention to it and never heard from her again. In fact, I haven't seen her since."

"Uncle Jon Jon!" Saren yelled, popping up from the other side of the bush.

"See you later, Nancy Drew." Tamika slid gracefully into her car with a smile.

"Oh, no you don't." Jonathan took off after a giggling Saren, chasing through the colorful display of flowers.

Chapter Fourteen

Saren and Frost headed out early to get some spying in before church. The Sunday morning sunshine glistened as she arrived at Emma's. James Earl Jones boomed the New Testament over the nursery-wide speaker system. Sunday was Uncle Jonathan's Sprout training class. The older Sprout boys were grafting branches into potted trees while the younger ones were learning the art of pruning topiary bushes. She waved at Uncle Jonathan, who was busy instructing his newest Sprout. When they saw their mentor wave, all twenty of the boys looked up from their projects. Some of them waved at her, and all of them hollered, "Hi, Frostie Dog!" The voices woke Ol' Blue, who was lounging on the front porch of the shop and came to greet them.

Not wanting to be delayed, Saren said, "Come on, Frost. Let's go." She took off at a jog. Even though she was in a dress for church, she still managed to run surprisingly fast in her ballet flats.

She arrived early at her big rock before the Gray Lady came outside. She was shocked to see the central rosebush lush with stunning sanguine roses. The roses on the ground the previous day were gone.

"Frost, look—the roses are back. How is that possible?" Although she couldn't be sure quite yet, it appeared to be exactly as it had been when she'd first seen it.

Suddenly, she spotted the evil-looking snake slithering around in the bush and let out a quiet gasp. This time, she sat perfectly still so as not to attract his attention. Frost sat at attention and glanced at Saren for direction. Saren slowly put her index finger to her mouth and quietly said, "Shusssh." He didn't make a sound, but his ears were back, and the hairs on his neck bristled.

Saren's only explanation for how the roses could have grown back to full blooming glory overnight was that it was one more miracle of the cottage. New questions formed in her mind. *Who is causing the magic? Is it evil from the snake? Some kind of spell put on the Gray Lady? Miracles carried out by angels under God's direction?* With the beauty juxtaposed with the sadness of the Gray Lady and the evilness of the snake, it looked like it was some kind of spiritual warfare going on in this small section of the natural world.

Soon, the Gray Lady followed the same slow procession to the rosebush that Saren had seen before. The Gray Lady approached the rosebush and the snake with a kind of dread, like walking into her own funeral, or worse. She stood there for a moment, and the snake slithered up to her face. The Gray Lady nodded, and with shame, she proceeded to cut the roses off the bush again. Saren watched as the seemingly identical scene from the previous morning played out. Then came the three cardinals who talked to her from the bush.

This was weird. Like déjà vu. Except it was actually happening over again. Saren quietly took out her notes and followed the scene. It was repeating over again word for word. The Gray Lady was stuck in some kind of loop like a ghost in a horror movie. Saren had an epiphany. She must be reliving some traumatic experience, like a ghost, except she was still alive.

Saren turned the page and made a new list of possible clues to the past trauma.

1. Interrogation by three "cardinals."
2. Obsession with roses.

She flipped back a page. According to her notes, this scene would go on for another thirty-five minutes, until all the roses were cut off.

Saren set her spy watch for thirty-three minutes. She looked around and slid silently off the rock. Before Frost moved, she took off his collar so the jingle of his tags would not give them away. Staying as low as she could, she made her way down the briar-lined wall toward the back of the cottage. Saren was cautious but relieved that the briar hedge acted exactly like a briar hedge. Finally, the hedge ended, giving her passage into the backyard. It was just as miraculous as the front yard. Hundreds of different flowers from different seasons bloomed hardily, all together in beds lining the flagstone pathway and porch. The summer flowers conversed with fall flowers while the spring flowers hummed songs softly.

Saren wanted to see if they really were real. She reached down to touch a daffodil petal and rubbed the soft yellow petal between her index finger and thumb. She gave it some more pressure, testing for moisture.

"Do you mind?" the daffodil asked in a sophisticated feminine voice.

Saren jumped back. "Oh, pardon me. I wanted to see if you were real."

"What is your conclusion, young lady?" the daffodil asked.

"You're real enough, all right. I hope I didn't hurt you."

"No, we're sturdier than we look."

All the daffodils nodded, chiming in with tough-sounding comments. Frost sniffed the talking flower suspiciously.

"Don't you even think about it, buddy," said a calla lily with a deep masculine voice.

"Oh, he would never dream of it." She picked up Frost and continued down the backyard pathway leading to the back door.

She hoped she would have time for a long conversation with the flowers later. She had so many questions for them, but right then, she had a burning desire to get into that tower. She had a strong unexplainable intuition that she would find something important up there.

She stepped cautiously onto the back porch and tried the door latch. Locked. She looked around for other ways in. All the windows on the back of the house were closed. She looked for something she had not yet seen. She looked at her watch—only twenty-eight minutes left before the Gray Lady would go back inside.

"How can we help you?" a hundred tiny voices said in unison.

Saren looked down toward the flowers lining the porch. All the flowers looked up to the porch ceiling. Saren looked up.

"Hi," said the sweet pea blossoms that vined across the ceiling of the porch, creating a beautiful purple-and-blue ceiling. All the tiny blossoms spoke at once in high-pitched voices. "How can we help you?"

"I'm trying to get in so I can find out why the Gray Lady destroys the rosebush in the front yard."

"Why didn't you just say so? We can help." The vines that trailed creating a green, purple, and blue wall on the end of the porch opened up like a curtain, revealing an arched passageway through a giant hedge.

"Cool! Thanks." She started into the hedge.

"Watch out for the jay," the sweet peas said. "He lies."

"Who?" She turned back to find the sweet peas hanging down beautifully, acting like regular mute flowers.

Saren shrugged and, with the Frostie Dog right on her heels, ran through the arch. The corridor turned right then left then right again. At first, she thought perhaps it was a labyrinth and wondered if she would meet a mighty Minotaur or goblins. But then the hedge opened up to the side of the cottage right at an open window. Saren quickly popped the screen off the window and crawled inside. Frost effortlessly and quietly jumped the three feet up to the windowsill.

Saren found herself on a twin bed in a well-lit room that smelled of paint and popcorn.

The room had an unusually high ceiling with three large windows high above providing good light. Paintings, some finished, some not, filled the room. The unfinished canvases were stacked in rows. The finished ones hung on every inch of wall. They all featured the same woman. The woman seemed familiar somehow, but Saren couldn't place her. The woman in the painting had the same hair as her mom, but her eyes were blue instead of green. One painting looked like it had been recently abandoned, and a new one sat on the easel. It depicted the same woman holding the hand of a girl about Saren's age. The child was leading the woman down a path.

A loud squawk startled Saren to the core. A blue jay landed on the windowsill. Frost jumped down onto the bed and perked up his ears.

"You're breaking the law. You call yourself helping, but all you are is a criminal."

Saren was not surprised the blue jay could talk. "Shut up you, blue jay."

"*Steller* jay. Don't you know anything? I'm much too beautiful to be confused with a common *blue* jay. You are a *dumb* thief. You'll find yourself in jail, where you belong."

Saren picked up a long-handled paint brush sitting in a jar of cleaning solution and poked at the bird. He squawked loudly and flew away. She closed the window.

Saren jumped off the bed and stepped out into a large indoor courtyard with rooms around it. She tiptoed across the courtyard to the back door. She unlatched it in case she needed to make a quick getaway. Turning back around, she headed into the archway leading into the kitchen. It was decorated with a monotone white, but she didn't take time to examine the details. She had to see what was in that tower.

She passed through the dark dining room and the parlor. Through the bay window, she could see the Gray Lady still at work. The house smelled old and stale like it had never been opened up to the fresh air. The cottage was silent and still. She was confident that no one else, at least that was human, was currently in the house. Whoever stayed in that art studio bedroom was gone for the time being. She didn't think that the Gray Lady was the artist. The paintings were too full of color and hope.

Saren quickly ducked across the foyer and bounded up the stairs. At the second-floor landing, she noted a balcony-style hallway that looked down over the foyer with a giant mirror leading to several bedrooms. The room in front of her had a different kind of door—it had to be the tower access. It was slimmer than the others and had a crystal knob. She tried the knob, but it didn't turn. It didn't have a keyhole, so how could it be locked? She tried again and pushed. The door popped open from a spring-loaded latch.

"Cool," she said and sprinted up the winding stairs. Every window, she checked to make sure her hypothesis was correct. The Gray Lady was still in the garden.

The spiraling stairs spilled up into a small round room that had been used as an office in an earlier era. Windows circled the entire room, except for the fireplace on one side and the French doors that led out to a balcony. Frost sniffed around the room while Saren looked through the sheers to see the Gray Lady far down below in the garden. Satisfied she would not be discovered, she looked around the tower office.

It had been an elegant space at one time, with an L-shaped desk, comfortable executive chair, and stylish paintings. But the walls were littered with thumbtacks and tabs of scotch tape with pieces of paper still on them, like someone had papers up all over the room in every spot, even on the paintings, then one day suddenly took them all down in frustration without bothering to take down the tacks or the tape.

Some burned papers were in the fireplace, but it looked like someone had changed their mind and put out the fire. One paper was charred on the edges and had been doused so that the ink ran, making the words unrecognizable. She looked through the desk and found nothing but empty file folders and the usual office supplies. She sat down in one of the guest chairs near the fireplace. She took a breath.

She believed she'd been led to this room. The hedge was confirmation. But why? There was nothing here. She looked at the ceiling. *There's something I'm missing. Something obvious.*

She looked at the floor. Another drowned and singed paper stuck out from the corner of the desk. She grabbed it and looked around the desk to the French doors. Outside the doors lay a spacious balcony, and on the other side of the balcony was a door. She fiddled with the latch on the French doors and realized that she had actually locked it. The door had been unlocked already.

Frost pawed her foot and whined.

"What is it?" She looked down at him then followed his gaze up to the ceiling of the balcony. "Oh!" She gasped and jumped back.

A dozen bats hung motionless from the ceiling, wrapped up in their wings.

Saren put her finger up to her lips and looked at Frost. He put his ears down like he wished they could just leave.

"Fine, you stay here," she said to Frost. He happily sat down and waited at the door.

Saren tiptoed under the sleeping bats to the door. The knob was rusty and didn't turn at first. Using both hands, she worked the knob, which made a soft creaking noise and released to allow Saren entry.

A puff of cold, damp air hit her in the face, causing bits of dust to cloud her vision momentarily. She grabbed her spy flashlight out of her satchel and lit up the dark expanse. At first, she saw only more darkness. The space was so big, the flashlight didn't hit anything. Moving from left to right then up to down, she came to a floor just left of center from the door. It was the attic. On the left was just rafters, heating ducts, and space, but on the right was a built-out floor littered with stored items. Whoever had built it had no fear of heights. No rail or warning existed before a fall would send a person crashing down three stories onto a wood-planked ceiling far below.

Suddenly, she realized no one knew where she was. If she did fall, they would never look inside the cottage. The lying jay was right—she was breaking so many rules. But she felt like it was about to give a big payoff. Right in front of all the storage were two old-fashioned steamer trunks, each with a monogrammed emblem on the top. One had a blue *A*, and the other a green *M*. Remembering the blue eyes in the painting, Saren opened up the blue lettered trunk first. Right on top was an accordion file with papers spilling out of it. The papers all had a little piece missing from them. Some of them had been wet but were readable. At least they would be readable in enough light. She shoved all the papers into the file and put the whole accordion file into her satchel. Glancing at her watch, she saw she had only two minutes. She couldn't believe that the time had gone by so fast. Even so, she couldn't resist peeking into the other chest.

She flipped it open, finding a wedding dress carefully packed and wedding album with pictures sticking out haphazardly. She thought it was odd that the album was not put together. Something must have made this bride not want to see these pictures. She flipped open the cover. The top photo was a group shot of the wedding party. It was her mom and dad with Uncle Jonathan as best man, and most of the other people, she recognized but not all. She didn't have room for the whole album, so she snatched up the group photo and put it in her satchel.

Her watch said she had three seconds. She began tiptoeing across the balcony, and just as she was under the bats, her watch alarm went off. In the doorway, Frost jumped with a start. All the bats woke up at once. Saren froze and looked up. They all glared at her with angry eyes. As if one of them had said, "Get her," they swarmed Saren.

They knocked off her hat and pulled at her hair. They flew past her, scratching her arms. In attack mode, they flapped in circles around her. She started to feel the trickle of blood running down her arms. She grabbed up her hat from the deck. She returned it to her head and pulled it down over her face, running back across the large balcony. The bats bit at her feet and tried to trip her, but she made it back into the office. She was able to shut the French doors before most of them made it into the house. Two of them, however, circled overhead inside the tower office. Saren and Frost ran down the spiral staircase, Frost's nails slipping on the hardwood. He was running down so fast, his feet got ahead of his head. He tumbled down the last five steps head over paws like a bowling ball, right into the back of Saren's calves, making Saren skip the last two steps. She put her hands out to the wall and landed hard but upright on the landing.

She burst through the door next to the giant mirror just as Frost rolled down the steps and out the door. She snapped the spring latch shut behind her, trapping the two remaining bats in the tower stairwell. Luckily, Frost rolled into the banister of the balcony hallway. He returned his feet firmly on the floor and gave his fur a fierce shaking.

Just then, Saren heard the front door downstairs open and close. She looked around then ran to the other side of the balcony hallway, where she hid in the corner. Frost hid behind her. The Gray Lady had removed her hat and gardening smock. Her fog-like motion poured slowly and fluidly up the stairs, with her silver locks becoming visible before the rest of her grayness.

Boom, boom, boom. The distinct sound of a judge's gavel echoed down from the tower. "Court is now in session. Where is our witness?" The mysterious gavel boomed again.

The Gray Lady disappeared behind the tower door, leaving it ajar. The bats must have followed her up, because they were nowhere to be seen.

Frost and Saren quietly made their way around to the stairs before they lost all restraint. They ran with all their might back through the house and out the back door, leaving it wide open. They didn't stop running until they reached the path back to Emma's.

Saren took off her hat to smooth her hair. She examined her arms, which had been clawed by the bats. Her arms had no scratches or evidence of her run-in with a dozen bats. Her hat was also just like it had been when she'd put it on that morning. It was like none of it happened, except it had.

She began to feel a strong compassion for the Gray Lady. She thought about the snake, the bats, and the jay. Her mission was no longer just a mystery to solve, but a tormented soul to free.

Chapter Fifteen

The Gray Lady felt like she had to drag herself into the house. Even if she could never feel glad, she was at least relieved to be inside, away from that snake and those dreadful birds. The moment that the relief came, though, she heard the gavel. *Boom, boom, boom.* "The court is now in session. Where is my witness?"

She dreaded every step up the curved stairway. Her heavy feet felt like cement blocks. She was so tired. She was so sorry. Why did she still breathe? Her eyes wanted to close, but they did not. Against her own will, she trod up the stairs. She thought at first that she'd heard something. She paused but didn't look around. *No, no one is ever here. I'm in some kind of alone purgatory with no other faces. That's my punishment. I deserve my punishment.*

She opened the tower door. Two bats ushered her upstairs.

"You're late. You have kept the judge waiting. Why won't you tell the truth? You know it is a bunch of lies. You think you can destroy men. We'll make sure that you'll never succeed," the first bat said.

"Go on," the two bats said in unison as they prodded her into the tower office.

She opened the French doors and stepped out on to the patio.

The bats were flying around. "Why did you leave the door open? Can't you do anything right?" the first bat said.

She closed the door to the attic. "I'm sorry. I don't remember leaving it open. I'll try to do better."

Boom, boom, boom went a gavel. "The court is now in session," said a loud bat.

Chapter Sixteen

Jonathan sat at the outdoor worktable, finishing up the last of the scheduling for the working Sprouts. He had twenty in his class, and eight were working after school and on Saturdays. That was far more than he needed. He still had the two youngest ones, ages twelve and thirteen, in front of him, jabbering about when could they begin working.

"When you're old enough. You know the law." Jonathan shook his head.

"*Law smaw*," the thirteen-year-old said.

"Exactly, that proves that the law is correct at setting an age of *maturity* for earning money. With earning money comes responsibility. Part of responsibility is *respecting* and following the law. Otherwise, we're just a bunch of wild animals. Are you guys wild animals?"

The younger boy began howling like a wolf. The older boy laughed and punched him in the arm. The three of them strolled over to the parking area, where the moms were picking up their boys.

"Hi, Jonathan."

"How are you, Ms. Johns?"

"I'm good. Hey, do you ever need any help with the Sprouts class? I mean, I'm free on Sunday morning."

"Wow, that's so nice of you. But I'm good." Jonathan gave the woman a shy smile. He could see that she wanted to get to know him better and was using the offer as an excuse to spend time with him. Jonathan was skillful at not hurting feelings and keeping conversations professional.

They both looked up to screeching tires turning into the parking lot. An old rusty 1980s Chevette pulled up in front of Jonathan and Ms. Johns. A woman with a cigarette in her hand, sporting a colorful sleeve tattoo, exited the car, yelling at a teen boy in the passenger seat.

"I heard you take boys." The woman took a drag from her cigarette and opened the passenger door. Before Jonathan could say anything, she yelled to the boy, "Get out!"

A tall teenage boy got out of the car with his head down. He had neatly trimmed hair and wore a plaid shirt buttoned all the way to the top button. The woman got back in the car and drove off.

"Excuse me, Ms. Johns," Jonathan said, turning away from her. He walked over to the new arrival. "So, young man, what is your name?"

Just as he was about to speak, Saren bounced up to them. "Hi, Ethan!"

"Hi, Saren." He sounded dejected.

"Ethan, this is my Uncle Jonathan."

"Hi," Ethan said.

"So how do you know Ethan, Saren?" Jonathan asked.

"Oh, he goes to our church sometimes."

By now, all the other Sprouts had been picked up and were gone.

"Okay. So, Ethan, what's going on?" Jonathan asked.

"Well, my mom and I got in a fight this morning. She didn't come home last night. Then she showed up drunk and smoking. I have asthma, and I asked her not to smoke in the house. She told me that it was her house, and then she drove me here."

"How old are you?"

"Sixteen."

"So, what do you want to do?"

"Breathe." He attempted to take a deep breath but wheezed instead.

"Do you have medicine?"

"Yeah." He pulled an inhaler out of his back pocket and breathed in sharply.

"So, are you good, or do you need to go to the doctor?"

"No, I'll be better in a minute."

Jonathan considered Ethan's situation. He seemed to be in charge of his physical well-being. That was good news. He knew from experience in dealing with teen boys that they needed to feel in charge of their own lives. The sooner they became responsible and autonomous, the better off everyone would be. He felt that Ethan needed some time to process what had just happened. "Okay, so I have some errands to run, and I'm going to run Saren to the church. Would you like to go to church today?"

"Yeah, I would like that."

Jonathan knew that Luke and Maddie would keep an eye on Ethan's health and emotional wellbeing. "You can go home with Saren's family. I'll pick you up at Saren's house later, okay?"

"Sure. Thank you."

"Saren, we'll put Frost in the barn with Ol' Blue, and I'll bring him when I come to pick up Ethan."

"Got it," Saren said.

Jonathan got the dogs situated then the kids dropped off and headed to the hardware store for sprinkler parts then to the grocery store. He enjoyed Sunday mornings because some people were at church or running on the beach, and the rest were sleeping off the party from the night before. The few Sunday morning shoppers were laid back and minded their own business.

He thought about the new boy, Ethan. He wondered how it would work out. All he knew for sure was that he would do what he could to guide the boy in his time of need. Maybe the church social services would offer help. But usually, they called Jonathan anyway when there was a situation that had to do with teen boys. No one wanted them. They were considered dangerous lost causes. But Jonathan didn't believe in lost causes; he refused to think that way.

The grocery store was cool and bright. The mister hissed, sending small particles of water over the green leafy vegetables. Watered-down 1960s tunes played in the background. The apples smelled good, and he gathered a bunch of them into a plastic bag. The smell of freshly baked bread wafted past him. He imagined Allison there with him. She'd loved the aroma of baking bread. She would have taken a huge breath in through her nose to savor the aroma. He smiled to himself, enjoying his make-believe moment.

"Hi, Uncle Jonathan." He turned around to see who was addressing him so familiarly. The only person who ever called him that was Saren. His siblings and their children only contacted him when they wanted something, and they hadn't allowed their children to get to know him. He would barely have recognized them, and they would *not* recognize him. So, when he turned around, he wasn't sure who he would find. He found no one at first, then he looked down.

"Oh, hi there."

"Remember me? I'm Lauren, Saren's friend."

"Honey, you should call him Mr. Jonathan. He's not *your* uncle," the girl's mother said.

"Yes, I do remember. How are you?"

Two boys ran up, tossing bags of chips into the grocery cart like it was a basketball hoop.

"You guys are going to crush those chips before we get them out the door." Their mom adjusted the groceries. "This is Tristen, Lauren's twin, and their older brother, Kaleb. I'm Lila."

"Nice to meet you all."

"You're the one that teaches that Sprouts class out at Emma's nursery, right?" Lila asked.

"Yes, that's right." Jonathan shifted his footing, wondering where this conversation was going. He really didn't have the heart to dodge another single mom today. They always looked so sad after he didn't take their bait.

"Do you have room for a couple more Sprouts? These two need a male influence in their life. I would really appreciate it."

She was all about the kids. He could see it in her eyes.

"Sure, but it is early. We start at seven a.m. sharp." He looked at the boys. "It's a commitment for the boys and the parents to get up that early on a Sunday morning." He wasn't surprised to see that they were paying attention to him. He didn't know why, but he saw eye-to-eye with most boys he met.

Before the boys could speak, they all jumped from a sudden commotion happening at the front of the store.

"Go to the back storeroom and stay low," Jonathan ordered the family.

He ushered all the shoppers in the vegetable and fruits to go to the back of the store.

Running to the front, he found two teens fighting outside in front of the store. One was a large boy around six feet tall, and the other was small and skinny. The small one repeatedly attacked the larger boy, who pushed him down.

"What's your problem, *boss*?" the bigger boy asked. After every sentence, he called the smaller boy "boss." And at every utterance of the word, the smaller boy got angrier.

Jonathan came out of the store to see the larger boy pushing the other boy so hard that he flew into the parking lot, narrowly being missed by a car. This didn't deter him. He got up and charged the other boy again.

Jonathan yelled, "Oliver!"

Oliver ignored Jonathan and continued his charge. The larger boy looked at Jonathan, who shook his head. The larger boy took a step back just as Oliver would have made impact, causing him to crash into the store's brick siding.

Jonathan had just made it to them when two police cars pulled up with the sirens blaring. The first set of officers jumped out with their guns pulled, pointed at Jonathan.

Jonathan put up his hands. The two kids started to run away. The other police car pulled in front of them. The officers got out without guns and asked them to return to the front of the store.

"Fellas, he's on our side. Put those away," Officer Brennen said. "Hi, Jonathan."

"Hi, Frank. I'm glad *you* showed up." He gave the other two officers an annoyed look.

"Jonathan, this is Officer Mike and Officer Bill. This is Jonathan, who owns Emma's Nursery and runs the Sprouts program."

"Oh, sorry, we got a call about an active shooter. Anyone have weapons?"

"Not that I've seen. These two were fighting. It was personal, not random."

Frank's partner, Randy, brought over the two teens.

"Oliver, you've been doing good ever since you started Sprouts. This is the first call we've gotten about you lately. Are we going to have to go another route with you?"

"No, sir," Oliver said, looking sideways toward Jonathan, hoping he would vouch for him.

"What's your name?" Frank asked the other boy.

"Kyle Connor."

"Well, Mr. Kyle Connor, when you mess with people, you don't always know what you're unleashing. It could be dangerous for you, them, and the public," Frank said. "What do you have to say for yourself?"

"I apologize for picking at him."

"Okay, I could write you both a ticket and give you a ride home in a police car. Is that what you want?"

They both shook their heads.

"Jonathan, you mind taking another Sprout?"

"Sure, I'll make them partners." He chuckled. "I'll take them both home. But, Frank, can I talk to you for a minute?"

They walked a few paces away from the others.

"A boy got dropped off at Emma's this morning. The mom acted like she was giving me the boy. He's at church with Saren right now. What should I do?"

"Give me his name, and I'll call social services for you and set up a visit. Do you have a place for him to sleep?"

"Yes, he can stay at the barn loft."

"You'll be hearing from someone this afternoon."

"Thank you, Frank. I really appreciate it."

"No problem. Just doing my job, but *you're* not. These are not your problems." Without turning his head, he rolled his eyes in the direction of the boys. "Why do you do this, Jonathan? Why work with all these problem boys?"

"Well, I don't really look at them like problems. I see them as potential problems that haven't popped yet. If no one pays attention to these boys, they'll go out there and hurt girls and women. We as men have to teach them how to be men. If they don't have a father, how would they ever learn it? This is my way of protecting women—by teaching men how to control their testosterone and channel it in a productive, constructive direction. I believe that what happened to Allison was caused by a man, maybe a whole system of men. I can't stand by and watch boys turn into monsters when it could be prevented with a little bit of kindness and attention."

"*All* this is for Allison? Wow. Well, you should get paid or something."

"Yeah, well, treasures in Heaven, man."

Frank smiled and nodded.

"Oh and, by the way, can you spread the word to your buddies to stopping pulling guns on me? I can't do any of this if I get shot."

"Absolutely, I will. Those two are idiots, and I'll have a talk with them and the rest of the department too."

After dropping off the two boys at their houses, Jonathan drove home with the groceries. He wondered if he would be doing any of this if he had married Allison and never let anything happen to her. He was sure that he would have been like everyone else, happy and involved in his own life. As it was, though, he had no life, only grocery store make-believe and the life he saw in others.

Chapter Seventeen

Usually, Saren enjoyed church, but this Sunday, it seemed to take forever. The only thing she wanted to do all day was go through the documents in her satchel and look at that wedding picture. The suspense was killing her. Even a thirteen-year-old would not be able to wait *this* long. She wished she could just ask her mom about it, but she had been sworn to secrecy about her investigation. Saren hated keeping secrets from her.

Saren wondered how she was going to tell her dad and Uncle Jonathan that she'd broken into the cottage. She'd wanted to tell Uncle Jonathan as soon as she got back to the nursery and ask him about the photo. But with all the chaos at the nursery with Ethan, she hadn't gotten a chance. It would have been easier before she had all day to build up guilt over breaking and entering and stealing.

But she didn't feel like it was *really* bad, because after all, something was terribly wrong with the Gray Lady. Saren believed she could help her. Plus, her dad and Uncle Jonathan wouldn't let her investigate the mystery if it weren't important.

At home, they all piled out of the car. Her dad had insisted she put her satchel in the trunk to make room for Ethan in the back seat. She decided to leave it in the trunk until later, hoping that her dad would not get it out for her. He would definitely notice something unusual was inside it.

"Ethan, make yourself at home," Madeleine said. "Saren, why don't you show Ethan around? Maybe he would like to play ping-pong."

"Sure, Mom." Seeing Ethan's mom dumping him had made her want to make Ethan feel welcome, but she was still anxious to get to look at those papers. "Mom, let's have tacos for dinner."

"No, we have a guest, and tacos do not a Sunday dinner make. We're having fried chicken and all the fixings. Why are you so impatient today? Are you starving or something?"

"No, just... never mind." Saren's hands were clammy, and her stomach had a distinct twinge of excitement. She could not have cared less about food, but she quickly adjusted her disappointed expression to a friendly one and turned to Ethan. "Want to see the back yard? That's where the ping-pong table is."

After what seemed like forever but was only just over an hour, Uncle Jonathan arrived with Frost and Ol' Blue. They had dinner and conversation. After doing the dishes, Saren took Frost on a short walk. The sun was quickly sinking behind the mountains. From about a block down the street, Saren could hear voices coming from her front yard. Uncle Jonathan, Ol' Blue, and Ethan were getting ready to leave. Uncle Jonathan and Ethan waved goodbye, and Saren waved back.

Just as soon as Uncle Jonathan's pickup was out of sight and her family were back inside the house, Saren tugged at Frost's leash and hurried back home. She snuck into the garage to retrieve her satchel from the trunk of the car. She was pleased to see it was undisturbed. She looped her satchel over her head and onto her shoulder crosswise then called to Frost, who had been sniffing the unopened bag of dog food in the corner of the garage.

Frost sounded like a herd of paws as they ran up the stairs with all of their might and blazed down the hallway. With a swoosh of the door, they were safely in her room with the smuggled documents, at last. She opened her closet door so that if anyone tried to come in the door, it would get hung up on the closet doorknob. They would still be able to get in, but it would buy her time to hide the stolen papers.

She put a trashcan filled with empty soda cans next to the door so that if someone did open the door, they would knock it over, giving a loud warning and buying her even more time.

Once she was satisfied with her booby trap, she dumped the contents of the accordion file onto her bed. The papers were different colors, and she wondered if the colors corresponded to anything. They all seemed to be in the same handwriting. It was clearly a man's handwriting. It was definitely names, phone numbers, and notes from an investigation. Some of them had a series of acronyms after them, like *lmom* for "left message on machine" or *na* for "no answer."

A few of them had dozens of these and other acronyms. Some had just a few. He really wanted to talk to these certain people, but they were dodging him for some reason. Some of the names had titles such as Bishop, Professor, or Doctor.

She began sorting the files into stacks. She decided the people with titles might have been some kind of consultants or experts of some kind. The other names must be friends, relatives, or colleagues.

The paper that had by far the most unreturned calls was titled simply "Lisa." This person must have been a close personal friend. Saren glanced at her spy watch. It was 8:17. The phone number had a Utah area code. It would be 9:17 there—just early enough not to be completely rude and late enough that they might just answer the phone. She hoped Lisa still had the same phone number.

Saren opened her door just far enough to grab the portable phone off the hallway table next to her door.

Her mom came out of the bathroom at that exact moment. "Saren, who are you calling at this hour?"

"Lauren," Saren lied.

"You two can talk at school tomorrow. It's time to get ready for bed."

"Yeah, but, Mom, this is an emergency. I left my assignment for first period in her backpack."

Her mom eyed her suspiciously. "Fine, but make it quick."

"Thanks, Mom." Saren quickly reset her door trap and climbed back into the middle of her bed, surrounded by stacks of multicolored papers, and dialed Lisa's number.

The phone rang four times. Just as Saren was about to give up, she heard an elderly woman say, "Hello."

Saren tried to sound as grown-up as possible. "Hello. May I speak with Lisa, please?"

"No. I'm sorry, but Lisa has not lived here for many years. What is this all about?"

Saren could hear a sitcom playing loudly on a TV in the background.

"I'm investigating a disappearance of a young woman that happened thirteen years ago. I believe that Lisa may have some important information."

"Oh, I see. Well, I'm her mother."

She was getting somewhere. "Oh, Mrs.... What should I call you?"

"Mrs. Lovelace, dear. I'm sorry, but I haven't talked to Lisa in twelve years."

"Oh no. What happened?" In her excitement, she slipped back into her regular voice.

"You sound a bit too young for this conversation. How did you get this number?"

She decided to level with Mrs. Lovelace. "I am young, ma'am, but I am investigating a mystery. Do you know anything about a disappearance of one of Lisa's friends thirteen years ago?"

"Well, yes, I do remember her telling me about a roommate that disappeared."

To contain her excitement, Saren looked out her bedroom window and focused on the fog drifting over the moon.

"What did Lisa tell you?"

"You see, my Lisa didn't really like the girl because she didn't think it was right for her to marry someone she didn't really love. You see, my Lisa was secretly in love with her roommate's fiancé. They had been seeing each other just before the girl's disappearance. Lisa was afraid to tell anyone because she thought they would blame it on her. But she had nothing to do with it."

Saren wondered if this fiancé had done something bad to the missing girl. Somehow, she didn't think Lisa did. She sounded like a victim herself.

"Wow, that must have been so scary for her. You say that your communication with her stopped the next year. What happed to Lisa?"

"Hold on a minute, dear." The TV in the background lowered to a whisper. "So, after her roommate's disappearance, she kept secretly dating the man. I was the only one that knew about it. She gradually called me less and less over that year, and then I lost her." Mrs. Lovelace sounded sad and on the verge of sobbing.

"Lost her?"

Mrs. Lovelace blew her nose with a loud honk. "Yes, she disappeared without a trace."

"Was there an investigation?" asked Saren.

"No, her car was gone but nothing else. They thought she just left. No one would search for her."

"What do you think? Do you think she ran away with the man?"

"I believe that she's dead at the bottom of Utah Lake or somewhere like that."

"Oh, I hope not. What was the man's name that she had been dating?"

"I wish that I knew. She would never tell me anything about him because the relationship was supposed to be secret."

Saren heard her mother's footsteps in the hallway. She lowered her voice as much as she could. "Do you think that her disappearance is linked to her roommate's?"

"I wouldn't think so because they found the roommate alive in the mountains, and my Lisa didn't disappear for several months after that."

"What was her name?"

"I never knew. Lisa just called her 'my roommate.'"

Saren's door opened, knocking over the trashcan with a loud crashing sounds of soda cans rolling out of it, and then, with a "wham," the door caught on the closet doorknob. "Saren, how many times have I..."

"Sorry, Lauren, I gotta go."

"Oh, no dear, my name is Betty. Please call again. I get so lonely."

"I sure will. Thank you so much. I really appreciate it." She clicked the end button.

Saren scooped up and hid the contraband just as her mom untangled the door and entered.

"...asked you to close your closet door? You're going to give someone a bloody nose one of these days."

"Sorry, Mom." But Saren was not at all sorry. She had succeeded in shoving the accordion file under her bed and hiding the wedding picture behind her pillow before her mom entered.

"You dropped something in the hallway." Madeleine held out a water-stained yet readable lime-green Post-it note that read "Lisa 801-555-6810 pcd."

Saren panicked on the inside but stayed frozen on the outside.

"Saren, it's a big responsibility working at Emma's. I know you're young, but you need to make sure you don't accidentally bring messages home with you. I'm sure Uncle Jonathan needs this phone number. What if it's an order?"

"Uncle Jonathan's?" Saren put her hand to her forehead. She decided that a thirteen-year-old would have definitely caught on that this was Uncle Jonathan's handwriting. Saren recovered quickly. "Oh, sorry, Mom. I'll make sure I give it back to him first thing when I see him tomorrow." She couldn't wait to interrogate Uncle Jonathan about why a file full of *his* handwriting was in that cottage attic along with her parents' wedding pictures.

Madeleine crossed the room to hand the sticky note to her daughter, then she looked at it again. "What does 'pcd' mean? Did you develop a new code for orders?"

Saren was quick on her feet. "Pansies, crocus, and daffodils. It's a new spring flower gift basket we're putting together. You get blooming pansies with daffodil and crocus bulbs to plant in your garden. This must be our first order of it." She took the paper from her mother.

"Saren, that's a brilliant idea. That way the recipient has something to enjoy while they're waiting on the bulbs to bloom. Did you think of that?"

"Actually, I did." She had *just* thought of it. She would have to tell Uncle Jonathan about her new idea. Considering the other notes about Lisa, she figured that "pcd" stood for "professional call dodger."

"That's very useful. Excellent." Madeleine kissed her daughter on the forehead. "Okay, time for bed."

"Hey, Mom, how come you don't have any wedding pictures on the walls or anything?"

"Your father and I don't need pictures to remind us of how much we love each other." With that, her mom was out of the room.

Definitely fishy. Her mom had pictures of them all over the house, including pictures of Uncle Jonathan. Plus, she never gave one-line answers and left it at that. Something must have happened at the wedding, something of which she didn't want to be reminded.

Saren snatched the photo from under the pillow. The large group wedding picture also included some extended family and friends. Her parents looked so young and happy. Her mom's dress was flowy satin and lace with a tulle veil. Her dad and Uncle Jonathan had on tuxedos with green-and-gold plaid bow ties. Maddie's bouquet was an elaborate arrangement of long-stemmed red roses with ferns and Queen Anne's lace. Her dad's boutonnière had three red roses. The bridesmaids carried smaller versions of the bridal bouquet. The lady right next to her mom was dressed in an emerald-green taffeta-and-lace bridesmaid dress. She had the same hair as Madeleine—the same chestnut brown as Saren's. The bridesmaid looked so much like Maddie, just a tad taller and with blue eyes instead of green. Saren recognized her grandparents, a few other relatives, and family friends. She recognized everyone except one person—the bridesmaid. *Who is she?*

"Saren!" her mother hollered from down the hall.

"Okay, Mom." She carefully put the picture back into her satchel and went to brush her teeth. As she crawled into bed, she burned with anticipation to question Uncle Jonathan. It was going to be a long day at school tomorrow, waiting to talk to him.

"Knock, knock."

"Come in, Dad."

Luke sat on the edge of her bed. "Saren, how are you feeling?"

"Good."

"Let me check you over. Hop out of bed and come here." He checked her neck and her back then her arms and legs. "Did you get bit by anything today, Saren?" he asked in almost a whisper.

"Yes and no," she whispered back.

"Is it a yes or no?" he whispered somewhat impatiently.

"No."

"You look all right to me. Goodnight, Saren."

"Goodnight, Dad."

She wondered how some men ever learned anything when they insisted on such short answers. She would have told him about the bat bites that had disappeared, but he didn't ask that, so technically, the correct answer was no. She would mention it to Uncle Jonathan, though. He was never in a hurry like her dad—probably because he was already at work when she was talking to him. Dad was always coming from or going to or dealing with some kind of crisis.

Uncle Jonathan had a ton more crises dealing with all those boys, but he didn't get impatient with them. Sometimes he was strict and unbending but never impatient. Saren thought maybe it was in the genes. She wasn't very patient either, like her dad.

Oh, school tomorrow will take forever! Her class would be going to the city library. *Oh yeah. Perfect, the librarians will have ways to look up the cottage and what happened thirteen years ago and missing persons and the wedding.* Now she only had to get through tonight!

Chapter Eighteen

Jonathan patted his belly as he led Ethan, Maddie, Luke, and JD out to his pickup. The night was dark and clear. Having a nice normal dinner with Maddie and Luke's family made him feel refreshed and renewed enough to help Ethan. Although he had never been dumped on a doorstep like Ethan had been that morning, he knew what it felt like to be unwanted by your family. Although Jonathan gave to his family generously, they had never shown him anything but harshness. Jonathan hoped to show Ethan the source of all love through Christ if he hadn't found Him already.

Jonathan unlocked the passenger side with his key and opened the door for Ethan.

"Where did Saren and Frost go?" Ethan asked.

"Oh, she went to walk Frost." Luke pointed down the street, where Saren was waiting on Frost to finish sniffing a bush.

Ethan waved goodbye to Saren as he got into Jonathan's pickup. "Thank you again for the delicious meal, Ms. Madeleine."

"My pleasure. You're welcome anytime, Ethan," Maddie said.

Luke tapped the hood twice.

Jonathan drove slowly down the dark lane toward Emma's and his barn loft. He led Ethan through the barn and up the stairs into his loft apartment. It was tidy, organized, and sparse. Jonathan owned the minimum for his comfort, which was not a lot. Since he was usually covered in potting soil by evening, he kept his clothes and personal items at the barn loft so that he could clean up before heading to the cottage. Since he had been sleeping in the cottage studio, his loft bed had often been used by others in need, like Ethan.

The decor had not changed since he'd first moved in many years ago. Allison had found all the decorations and furnishings for him long ago. He had loved them then because she'd chosen them. He loved them now for the same reason.

He decided to hang out with Ethan for a while before heading out to the cottage. He knew teen boys were always hungry, and even though Maddie had cooked a huge meal, Ethan would still be happy with a snack. He showed Ethan around then got him some fresh towels, pajamas, and a change of clothes for the next day. The boy was a little taller than Jonathan, but otherwise his clothes would fit Ethan.

He snatched a bag of chips from the top of the fridge and some salsa from inside it and poured the salsa into a bowl. He tossed Ethan a cold bottle of water and grabbed one for himself. He clicked the TV remote to the sports channel and bit a chip.

"Thank you so much for doing all of this for me. I really do appreciate it," Ethan said.

"No problem. It's how we roll."

"This place is really nice. I mean, am I taking your spot, or is this like an extra place you have for random people who get dumped on your doorstep?"

"Maybe... something like that. What do you think this place is?" Jonathan asked.

"It feels like a special place for someone who is well loved by a girl who likes to decorate."

Ethan pointed his chip at the wall full of shelves that held a few books along with figurines and dried flowers made into elaborate and artistic designs. The flower containers were creative things that a teen boy would relate to like an old Converse high top, an old beat-up baseball glove, and a tin with a label that said "pork and beans" on it.

"What? You can tell I didn't decorate this place?" Jonathan asked and smiled.

"Well, yeah, you have a more hardcore but soulful vibe, and this place is kind of very high-end teen suburban." Ethan shoved a handful of chips into his mouth.

"Wow, that's very perceptive of you, and you're right on track. Maybe you're a gifted decoration reader, or you heard something."

"Nope, neither, but I'm interested now. Who did decorate this place for you? Ms. Madeleine?"

"No it wasn't her, but you're warm," Jonathan said.

Twenty Years Earlier

THE SUN SPARKLED, AND the air was fresh from the major rainstorm the day before. Jonathan felt new, as well. The day before, Grampa had announced that he wanted Jonathan to live on property. That was more generosity than he could ever have imagined existed. Plus, he was going to get to bring Al, whom he had nursed back to health after that accident.

He would make the old man proud. He had already started fixing up the old lawnmowers in the barn, and they had already sold two of them. He'd picked up a few jobs fixing other people's mowers as well. Now he could take on more work because he would be there all the time. He could fiddle with engines before and after the shop closed, so he wouldn't take time out from the nursery work to fix mowers.

The barn at the back of the Emma's property was a weathered gray work barn full of old equipment and gardening tools. The upper loft was accessed by a ladder where they used to keep the hay back when the property was used as a ranch. On one side, the loft had wide sliding barn doors leading to a landing where the hay could be tossed up from the ground for storage or back down to ground level for selling or feeding. Small stacks of old hay littered the loft, which hadn't been used in decades. The setup was ideal. Jonathan could get up and tinker on engines and lawnmowers in the middle of the night when he got enough sleep. No more commute.

Grampa John had a few friends over to help with ideas for the loft apartment, including Luke and his dad, Bobby.

The early morning had been chilly because of the lingering storm from the night before, but the day had turned warm and unusually humid for Southern California. When Allison and Maddie arrived that day, the men were already out at the barn. Wearing sweatshirts, Allison and Maddie jogged all the way out to the barn.

"What's going on?" Allison asked.

"We're going to build out a bachelor pad for Jonathan in the barn," Grampa said.

"Now when someone says, 'Do you live in a barn?' you can say yes!" Maddie said.

Luke flicked her cap off from the back, and she returned the favor with a punch in the arm.

"Cool. So you're going to *live* here?" Allison asked Jonathan.

He nodded and beamed his toothy smile at her. He could see Allison's mind working quickly and decisively.

"So, Grampa, can I help design it?" She jumped up and down. "Please?"

"Ask Jonathan. It's his bachelor pad."

"Please."

Jonathan beamed from ear to ear and waved his hand toward the door of the barn.

Maddie, standing nearby, rolled her eyes at him. Looking over at Luke with her own puppy-dog eyes, she promptly punched Luke in the arm and ran.

"Dude." Luke made fun of Jonathan and ran to chase Maddie for punching him.

Allison didn't wait around to see the shenanigans her sister was getting into. "I'll be right back."

Jonathan watched her run all the way to the office. She took off her sweatshirt on the way. She meant business. She was getting ready to work. He smiled to himself.

Jonathan saw that Allison respected and adored him, but she hadn't caught on to his romantic affection for her. She acted like they were best friends. Jonathan loved their easy, relaxed relationship. He felt closer to her than he did with anyone, even Luke. He hoped living there would open up the relationship to something more.

Still traumatized a bit by Busy Bea's cruel outburst on his first day of work, forbidding him to work with her daughter, Jonathan was reluctant to openly pursue Allison. He didn't want to put Allison through dealing with her mother. He knew how important her mother's approval was to her.

Jonathan had long since given up seeking approval from his family. He had come to realize that living for the approval of others only caused them to ask more and more of you until you had nothing left at all. Besides, he knew that if he was to be happy, he had to take responsibility for his own happiness. No one else could do it for him.

He thought Allison would soon outgrow her blind obedience to her mother. He hoped that her mother's meddling would not cause Allison pain, but he suspected that Busy Bea's own selfish ambitions would override what was truly best for Allison. He wished Allison could see that for herself. If Allison could only see herself through his eyes, she would know how wonderful she was. She was so full of joy, delight, strength, compassion, and caring. She fearlessly included everyone. She'd never even seemed to notice that his skin was so much darker than hers. She'd told Jonathan on numerous occasions that she didn't know why her mother didn't want him around. It made zero sense to her.

Jonathan watched Allison reemerge from the back door of the shop, armed with a notepad, clipboard, and pen. Without even slowing down, she bounded into the barn and bounced up the ladder.

Jonathan looked at Grampa, Bobby, and Luke. Their amused expressions said, "Go ahead, you put her in charge, so you better see how she wants it."

Jonathan, scrambled up the ladder, unaccustomed to being led by a girl, but he strangely liked it.

The grown men chuckled.

"Allison," Grampa hollered up, "give Bobby the plans when you're done, and we'll get started tomorrow."

"Okay, Grampa," she said without stopping her task. Clipboard in hand, Allison drew the shape of the loft. For someone so young and untrained, she skillfully began outlining the space. "We'll make this your balcony," she said, opening the double barn doors that led out to the hay-receiving landing.

"So this will be your living room." She took two steps into the room from the "balcony." "Over here, we'll put your kitchen and give you a window over your double sink." She motioned to the left with her whole arm.

She paused to record her decisions on the "blueprint." She laid the kitchen along one wall with the fridge at an L on the wall they would add for the bathroom. She paced out three feet square. That should be enough room for a shower.

"Do you need a tub?" Jonathan raised his eyebrows with indecision.

"No, with a tub, you won't have room for a closet. Okay, so here is your shower, sink and toilet, and we'll put a long closet here with folding doors, next your bedroom." She erased the closet. "Instead, we'll put your closet on this side so you'll have privacy from the rest of the barn, and we'll have your bathroom door open into the bedroom. Put your bedroom door here."

She walked out of the "bedroom" pretending to shut the door, and through the "kitchen" into the "living room."

"Yep, your TV can go there, couch, coffee table and kitchen table right here." She pointed, indicating the spots for the various furnishings.

"There, you have everything you need. Can you think of anything else?" she asked Jonathan, but before he had a chance to answer, she said, "Oh, wait. What about Al?"

Jonathan smiled and gave her a thumbs-up.

"Cool. Okay, so you'll need stairs, unless Al is a talented ladder-climbing dog." She giggled.

Jonathan was beside himself with excitement, but all he could do was smile at Allison. He hoped his mouth would grow into his feelings.

"Cool?" she asked, and Jonathan nodded quickly. He loved the plans, especially since Allison had made them.

The next day, they started construction. Once all the other work was done at the nursery, Jonathan would run back to help with construction between customers.

The girls took on extra responsibilities, as well, so Jonathan didn't have as much to do. He would arrive at a plant to find it had already been doted over by someone equally skilled. He also enjoyed working construction.

Allison talked nonstop about couches, tables, and fabric for the curtains. If he had a cot, he would be happy. He was slightly nervous that she would make it too fancy and he would mess it up. After all, he had a dirty job, always dealing with dirt, plants, fertilizer, motor oil, grease, and the like.

But her ideas were rustic, complementary to a loft apartment in a barn. They had a lot of old wood from taken-down fences, and they enclosed the walls with that rather than drywall.

Allison found a used black leather couch in great condition. They made a coffee table and matching end table out of old railroad ties and fence planks. Grandma had some old ratty chairs out in her art studio, so Grandma, Allison, and Maddie painted them with lots of cheerful colors.

After about a month, Jonathan was ready to move out of Luke's parents' garage and into his very own loft apartment. He could hardly believe his blessings. The best part about it was that Allison was so excited to be involved with it. Some would have thought she was taking over, but he loved to see her spirit uninhibited, and he would let it flourish.

"YOU SEE, ETHAN, I WAS blessed with this place and an amazing decorator." Jonathan downed the last of his water.

"So, what happened with Allison? Did she ever figure out you liked her?" Ethan grabbed another handful of chips.

"To be continued. How are *you* feeling?"

Ethan sat up with his mouth full. He chewed quickly to respond. "Me? Are you kidding? This was the best day ever."

"Yeah, but you have to think about your mom eventually." Jonathan looked at Ethan with compassion.

"I have, I don't want to go back. It's chaos over there all the time. You're not going to get into any trouble for letting me stay here, are you?"

"No, I notified the authorities about your situation. They said you can stay here if you're comfortable with it until everyone decides what to do.

"I'm starting a training session on repairing lawnmowers tomorrow morning at seven if you're interested. It will be over in plenty of time for school."

"Yeah, that would be great. I want to help out around here too. You know, to earn my keep." Ethan picked up the empty chip bag to put it in the trash.

"Okay, we'll see what your talents are. So, are you good? I mean to be here by yourself?"

Ethan returned the salsa to the fridge. "Yeah, no problem, I'm used to it." He brushed the crumbs off the coffee table into his hand and put them in the trash.

"Okay then, I'm heading out. There's cereal. Make sure you eat breakfast and be ready to go at seven tomorrow morning. Around here, we're on time and honor our commitments."

"Got it. Thanks again, Jonathan."

Jonathan stopped at the bottom of the stairs to listen for the click of the lock on the loft door. As soon as he heard it, he hopped into his utility cart, where Ol' Blue was already waiting in the passenger seat.

As Jonathan and Ol' Blue drove the utility cart through the forested landscape, the night was foggy with a chill in the air. The utility cart didn't have headlights, but Jonathan could see well in the dark. An unexpected patch of fog added a challenge, though. As he came around to the cottage, something seemed amiss, but he couldn't put his finger on it. When he pulled up to the backyard entrance, he was shocked to see the back door wide open. He flew inside, and Ol' Blue bounded up the stairs ahead of him. He rushed into the upstairs bedroom and put his hands on his knees, bending over in relief.

She was there and okay. Her silver strands of hair glimmered in the faint moonlight. Everything in the room was as it always was. He adjusted her covers and moved a strand of silver off her ashen sleeping face.

Going back down the balcony hall, he realized the tower door was open. He slowly opened the door all the way, entered the stairwell, and closed the door behind him. Climbing the tower spiral staircase, he could hear the bats flapping around. Two bats circled the loft office, screeching in distress, unable to get out. He opened the balcony door, and they flew out into the night. No other bats were there at the time.

He had repeatedly tried to get rid of the bat infestation without success. He didn't want to hurt the bats, but he didn't want them pooping all over the balcony floor. He had built a wonderful bat house and put food in there, but they were obsessed with the tower balcony. He flicked on the porch light to assess the damage. He didn't really need the light to know there was a mound of guano in the usual spot, but he hoped to find evidence of who had opened the door to the tower in the first place.

His mouth dropped. The attic door was ajar. His heart leapt almost out of his throat. *The drop-off... If Allison had...* He refused to finish the thought. He would put a lock on this door tonight.

He stepped inside the massive, damp expanse. The light from the balcony illuminated the gloomy, stale air. Thick dust wafted through the beam of light, tussled by the night breeze. The dust was so thick that at first, he suspected that the fog had permeated the attic by way of the open door.

He looked around and listened to determine if any bats had gotten inside. Nothing moved. Everything seemed unchanged. He turned to go back out, and the beam of light illuminated the left side of the trunk adorned with the blue letter *A*. He was shocked and amazed by what he saw. A thick layer of dust blanketed the trunk, except four very small spots outlining four very small fingers. Saren was bolder and more resourceful than they'd thought.

He opened the trunk and found exactly what he expected to find: no accordion file. She'd been thorough. She had gathered up and taken every single scrap. He knew that he shouldn't condone breaking and entering, but his heart swelled with pride. If she didn't leave a stone unturned in this trunk, he knew she would have looked in the other one.

The other trunk was not closed all the way. Popping it open, he found Luke and Maddie's wedding pictures all spilled out. He couldn't tell for sure, but he figured she hadn't been able carry them all so she'd taken one or two of them.

He was glad to step back into the fresh night air. As Jonathan closed the attic door, his back pocket vibrated.

It was text message from Luke. *AM.*

He texted Luke: *Check for bites.*

He figured the bats had been asleep when Saren passed under them, but he wanted Luke to look her over.

Finished with the security check around the cottage, Jonathan went back into Allison's room. He sat on the extra bed and watched her. He'd heard that coma victims could hear even though they couldn't wake up. He often came in to talk to Allison while she was asleep, hoping she would hear him. He tried while she was awake too, but he found it more frustrating. He feared that his negative vibes would leak out into his tone of his voice and exacerbate her condition. So, he spoke to her in her sleep. Maybe she could feel the companionship they had once had and might have again when she was better.

"Hi, Allison, you probably didn't see her, but you had a visitor today. Saren, your niece. She's so curious. She's determined to find out about you since she discovered the cottage. I think she'll find your cure or at least show you the way. You can trust her. She won't stop or give up on you either. She doesn't know about giving up.

"Just like you, Allison, you went to that stream to find answers to something. You didn't give up. Keep working it out. You are free. You just have to realize it.

"Alli, I was thinking about that day when we drove up to Julien after I got that old truck running. On the way up there, we hiked to the top of Stone Wall peak. You were leading, and you went down the wrong path and got off the trail. You were so upset that you'd made a mistake and got us lost. We had to jump a ravine and work together and trust each other to find the trail again. But along the way back to the trail, we found that amazing babbling brook. We sat beside it in the warm afternoon breeze. We didn't know where we were, but we didn't care. After we talked on the banks of that creek, you finally accepted that if you hadn't taken the 'wrong' path, we would never have found that beautiful, peaceful place. It was our own special place.

"That day, you were so beautiful. You looked happy and free with the wind in your hair and the sun on your face. You overcame your self judgement and laughed about it. Freedom and joy radiated from you. I know that joy is still in there. It's a part of you.

"I'm so glad you're safe. I miss you. Find a path, Allison, even if you think it's the 'wrong' path. Find your way back to us."

His words seemed to echo back to himself unheard. He watched her silver hair glimmer in the dim moonlight as he closed the bedroom door.

Chapter Nineteen

Saren sat at her desk, writing in her spy notebook while waiting for the teacher to announce the arrival of the bus that would take them to the city library. The students joked loudly and jeered each other like it was the last day of school. Saren, however, didn't participate in the sixth-grade revelry.

She was checking over her notes in her spy notebook so she would be fresh and have her mind ready so that no time would be wasted. She might not get another opportunity to do this kind of research again for a while. She started a new page titled "Library." She wrote:

1. Find out who went missing thirteen years ago.
2. Wedding announcement to see if it lists the wedding party.

Saren just realized that she didn't know her parents' wedding date. They had never celebrated their wedding anniversary as far as she knew. That *was* strange. Most people did, she assumed. She tried to imagine why her parents never mentioned their wedding or anniversary. Saren had the feeling the reason they were hiding their wedding pictures had something to do with the mysterious woman in the photo. *And why was Uncle Jonathan's handwriting in that trunk?*

A sudden loud hand clap nearly startled Saren out of her chair. She sent her notebook, pen, and books flying in all directions. All the kids around her cracked up.

"Gosh, Saren. What were you doing? Reading a horror book or something?" Lauren asked.

Saren laughed with everyone at her own fright. "Something like that." She gathered up all her belongings from her classmates who had helped her pick them up.

The teacher clapped his hands again and announced that it was time to board the bus. The students created a ruckus as they filed into the hallway.

"Quiet down!" hollered the teacher.

"Saren, where have you been anyway?" Lauren asked. "I called your house three times over the weekend, and you were never there. What's up?"

"I've been busy," Saren answered.

"Come on, what? Have you got a boyfriend you didn't tell me about or something?"

It was their turn to get on the bus. Saren was happy to have some distance from her friend's questions, but she knew Lauren would not just let it go. She boarded the bus first and chose a seat near the back of the bus. Lauren held onto the seat in front of Saren and spun on her heel, landing gracefully in the seat next to her.

"Lauren, how did your dance audition go?" Saren asked.

Saren chatted with Lauren about the audition all the way to the library to keep her questions at bay. She would have to figure out how to ditch Lauren when she got to the library. She didn't want Lauren to ask questions about things that she couldn't explain. Plus, this was a secret investigation. She couldn't risk her mom finding out. She'd made a promise.

At the library, Saren and Lauren stood in a long line for the computers.

"Hey, Lauren, I'm going to the bathroom. I'll find you." Saren jogged around the corner and straight to the librarian behind the big circular desk.

"Hi, Ms. Rainer." She had noticed the woman's name tag.

Hearing her name made her look up and smile. "How can I help you?"

"I want to find out information about a missing person, a woman. It would have been about thirteen years ago."

"Yes, yes, I remember that so well, myself. Her name was Allison. I remember it because my sister has the same name, and the whole thing gave me the chills. Come upstairs. We'll have the newspaper article in microfilm. Have you ever used microfilm before?"

"No, ma'am."

"Well, you're in for a real treat. We have every newspaper ever printed in San Diego County right here." Spoken proudly like a true librarian.

They crossed the main lobby to the grand spiraling staircase. Saren crossed behind Ms. Rainer to the other side so that her classmates wouldn't see her. She didn't want any tagalongs.

"So, Ms. Rainer, what do you remember about this *Allison*?"

"Yes, I was just out of college, and it made my blood run cold. She was going to college in Utah, and she went missing during a snowstorm. I remember some family members going on the news, pleading for help to find her. But the police named her a runaway. But who runs away at twenty in the middle of a snowstorm? It just didn't add up. Poor girl. I never heard any news after that if they found her or not. But I don't think the authorities put much effort into searching for her."

Ms. Rainer pulled out the microfilm for the year in question. "Here we are. Try March or April first. It seems it happened around spring break, so maybe March."

Ms. Rainer showed her how to load the microfilm reading machine. A newspaper image popped up on the computer screen next to the machine. Ms. Rainer pointed out how to print a copy.

"Good luck." And with that, Ms. Rainer was gone.

Saren searched the *San Diego Tribune*, going through each day, each page. She feared she would run out of time before she found anything. She could hear the teachers down the hall gathering up the students to leave. She searched faster. Finally, she found a missing girl on the second to last page of March 31. The headline read:

Missing
College Student: Allison Louis Scott, a student attending a Christian university in Utah, is missing, according to family members. Ms. Scott is twenty years old, five feet five inches tall, with blue eyes and brown hair. She was last seen leaving her campus apartment. She grew up in East San Diego County. No foul play is suspected.

The last five words of the article stuck in her heart like a dagger. She wondered what kind of person would print that when they didn't know where the girl was, but that concern was for a different time. Right now, she needed to know if this was the missing girl Uncle Jonathan and Officer Brennen had been talking about. Those last five words made her confident it was. Her burning question now was *"Is this missing girl the Gray Lady?"*

The article included a small, fuzzy picture. Saren squinted at the photo to see if it could be the Gray Lady. The shadowy picture featured a teenaged girl with an outdated shoulder-length hairstyle and a huge joyful smile. It was almost impossible to translate the joyful face into the tormented expression of the Gray Lady. Plus, the big hat the Gray Lady wore made it even more difficult to tell.

Saren stared at the photo. With her imagination, she added a big hat and gave the girl long silver hair while simultaneously trying to picture what the Gray Lady would look like smiling. Her concentration paid off. It was her. She was sure of it. In triumph, Saren slapped the desk with both hands. "That's her. The Gray Lady is the missing girl, Allison Louise Scott!"

She had no time to relish her discovery; Saren heard Lauren call-ing her name from down the hall. She quickly printed the page and gathered up her stuff from the table.

"Come on. Everyone is waiting for you!" Lauren snatched up the paper out of the printer and sprinted down the hall, with Saren right behind her.

"Well, it's about time, Saren," the teacher said when they arrived at the bus. "We almost left you."

Lauren and Saren boarded the bus without comment. Once seat-ed, Lauren looked at the fuzzy image of the missing girl. "She kind of looks familiar in the same way a random stranger resembles a movie star."

She handed the printout to Saren. "What's this for anyway?"

"Oh, I'm doing a paper on crimes against college girls." Saren didn't feel *too* bad lying because she was doing more than writing a paper—she was trying to solve a missing person case and help a tor-mented soul in the process.

"Oh, that sounds depressing." Lauren leaned over Saren to look at the article. "She was pretty. Did anyone ever find out what hap-pened to her?"

"I don't know yet. Hopefully, I will. What makes her look famil-iar to you?" Saren asked.

Lauren took another look. "Well, she kind of looks like your mom. Like a younger version of your mom. Don't you think?"

"Yeah, you're right." Saren's heart dropped for a moment.

"Your mom didn't go missing, did she?" Lauren ducked as a ball of wadded-up paper flew past, narrowly missing her head.

Saren caught the ball and tossed it back over her head without looking.

"Oh, not that I know of. Besides, this girl has blue eyes. My mom has green ones like me." Saren's mind flashed back to the blue *A* and green *M* on the trunks in the Gray Lady's attic: *A* for Allison and *M* for Madeleine. Her mother's maiden name was the same as the girl's last name, and the resemblance was spooky. Suddenly, Saren realized that the missing girl had to be a close relative of her mother's. Surely a thirteen-year-old would have figured that out already.

Lauren continued, "How did you... Oh, they put the eye color in the article. I was wondering how you knew her eye color since the picture was in grayscale."

"Grayscale!" Saren said a bit too loudly, struggling to contain her emotions. Saren shuffled through her backpack and located her parents' wedding picture. While the photo was still inside the backpack, she folded it so that Lauren would only see the mysterious maid of honor and pulled it out of the satchel.

"Seriously, Saren, that missing girl looks so much like your mom, it's creepy," Lauren said.

"Creepy?" Saren showed Lauren the picture.

"Wait, that's the same girl," Lauren said.

She was right. *Allison Louise Scott was my mom's maid of honor!*

She dug her silver pencil from her colored pencil pouch. The mysterious maid of honor wore a lovely green satin-and-tulle gown and a fancy updo. Her forced smile spread flat with sad eyes. Saren drew shoulder-length silver hair on the maid of honor then added a broad-brimmed hat.

The bus turned sharply, nearly making Saren draw a line across the maid's cheek. With a shading pencil, she skillfully turned the colorful maid to grayscale in spite of all the turns and bumps of the bus. She finished just as the bus came to a stop in front of the school.

"Someone is not going to like you drawing on their picture, Saren."

"Nope, if I solve this mystery, they will love it."

Saren held the maid of honor away from her to get a distance view. It *was* her. The maid of honor was the Gray Lady. Saren immediately grabbed the missing girl's picture and placed it next to the wedding photo.

Lauren had been glued to Saren's activity at every turn. "See? I told you that is her. But where did you get the bridesmaid picture?" Lauren asked.

Saren smiled at her proudly. "That's a long story."

Everyone else had already stood up and began filing off the bus.

"Saren, you are definitely going to get extra credit on that paper." Lauren got up to exit the bus.

With the pictures still in her hand, Saren followed, glad that her next class was the last of the day. She couldn't wait to tell Uncle Jonathan what she had found. She quickly hurried through her assignment then pulled out her investigation log and the photos.

On a blank page, she wrote:

Two mysteries solved.

1. *The Gray Lady is Allison Louis Scott.*
2. *Mom's maid of honor was the missing girl, the Gray Lady.*

- *How they are related is unknown. Why the Gray Lady has been kept secret is still a mystery.*

Saren finally had some answers. She couldn't wait to interrogate Uncle Jonathan and her dad. They knew a lot more than they had let on. She was burning to find out.

Chapter Twenty

Having just finished preparing his corporate orders for pickup, Jonathan stepped into the frigid air of the walk-in refrigerator, where the cut flowers were preserved while waiting to grace someone's custom floral arrangement. For many years, Jonathan refused to think about Allison while at work, but now, he allowed himself to hope that Saren would make a difference. His mind wandered to Allison as a teen. She had never liked going into the refrigerated room. She'd complained that her chill bumps lasted for an hour after. Every time she'd needed something in there, she would find him and ask him to go in for her. He'd never minded it. Her blue eyes peeked in from the display window as she pointed at the exact flower she wanted.

"No, not that one. That one," she would say, her voice muffled by the thick glass. She had been so particular about finding just the right individual flower for each arrangement. No wonder she got so cold—it took her forever to decide. To him, most roses looked pretty much the same, but to Allison, an individual flower could make or break an arrangement. She could take as long as she wanted as far as he was concerned. It was time he got to spend with her. Maybe she took so long because she got to spend time with him too. He chose to believe that was true. He wished he were picking out the perfect flower for her right now.

The bells dangling from the front door of Emma's jingled, bringing Jonathan out of his daydream. It was still early for customers. The shop didn't officially open for another two hours. It was Iris arriving for her shift right on time.

"Good morning, Iris. Here is an order for you to work on. It needs to be ready for pickup at nine. I already got the flowers out for you."

"Oh, thank you, Jonathan. That walk-in chills the arthritis in these old bones." She sat up on the work stool Jonathan had gotten her to preserve her energy.

As Jonathan walked out to the barn, he enjoyed the morning air. The clouds hung low over the Southern California mountains, creating a cozy fall feeling even though it was nearly May. Due to the expectation of rain, no gardeners were to be found on this early weekday morning. The only corporate client who would be expected was Luke. Tasker Trails Landscape Architecture was on a time schedule, and unless rain actually arrived, their foremen would keep their jobs moving. But Jonathan knew business was the secondary reason for Luke's visit. Saren had learned something.

Jonathan walked in to the barn to check on Ethan and Donny's progress in their first day of mower repair training. Ethan squatted in front of a lawnmower, squirting starting fluid, while Donny pulled the cable to start it.

"Why do I have to pull?" Donny asked. "It's your turn."

"Because you were squirting the wrong place and making it worse," Ethan replied.

Donny stopped to take a breather.

"Donny, you have to pull faster than that. No mower would ever start at that speed." Jonathan held out his hand to Ethan for the starter fluid.

Donny crossed his arms. "Fine, show me. This piece of junk is ready for recycling."

"This is recycling. Saving it from the landfill."

"I got it." Ethan stood up to grab the pull cable.

Jonathan held the starter fluid in his hand, ready. "Okay, go."

Ethan gave the cable one quick jerk, and the mower came to life.

"Good, now give it some gas. Not too much," Jonathan said.

Donny, acting out his frustration, kicked a bottle of motor oil, splattering it all over Ethan. Luke drove up to the barn loading area just in time to see Ethan covered in motor oil.

"Dude, what happened to you?" Luke asked as he opened the back door of his shiny navy crew cab pickup.

"Luke, can you please show Ethan where the degreaser soap is?" Jonathan bounded up the stairs to the loft to get Ethan another change of clothes.

"Sure!" Luke retrieved an extra-large pizza from the backseat. He set the pizza down on the worktable and led Ethan into one of the stalls that had been used for horses in an earlier century. Now it had a large sink, a washer and dryer, and shelves holding random supplies for fixing mowers.

Jonathan arrived with the fresh clothes. "Hurry and change. You don't want to be late for school."

"Or pizza!" Luke said.

Jonathan came back out of the laundry room to find Donny angrily pacing the length of the barn.

"Donny, sit down a minute and talk to me. What was that all about?"

"I can't do anything right. I'm such a loser."

"Why would you say something like that?"

"You know why. I messed up the job I liked. Now I'm on punishment work, and I can't even get that right."

"That's why you're a Sprout. You're learning and growing. How do you feel about fixing lawnmowers?"

"Like I'm being punished. Like a failure. I wish I could take it back."

"Okay, first of all. Getting up early is punishment. But this job is something the company needs. I used to do it, but I'm too busy on management tasks to tinker anymore. This was my favorite job and my favorite part of the day when I was your age. So this isn't a 'punishment job.' Do you think Ethan should be punished?"

"No, he didn't do anything wrong."

"So, who is really punishing *you* right now?"

"I don't know."

"You're punishing yourself. You're judging yourself. You're shaming yourself."

"So?"

"So the best way to handle criticism is to take responsibility for it, accept it, and learn from it so you can move on with your new and improved self."

"I'm taking responsibility. I know what I did was wrong."

"What you're doing is blaming yourself. If you blame yourself, you give yourself an excuse that you're just flawed in some way. Like saying you're a failure. That keeps you locked in shame, which stops everything. If you stop, do you think you can grow?"

"No." Donny shook his head and seemed to be considering what Jonathan was saying.

"So taking responsibility means that you accept one hundred percent of what you did and you're willing to learn from your mistakes and move on into the future. Can you learn if you're moving?"

"Yes, and Sprouts are moving even though you can't see it. But over a few days and weeks, you can see it."

"Yes, teens are growing even when you can't see it. You just look up one day and they're men running businesses themselves." Jonathan pointed both his thumbs at his chest. "You get it," Jonathan said.

Ethan came out of the laundry stall, looking fresh.

"I hope he gets it, because the pizza is getting cold," Luke said.

"Pizza!" Saren yelled, sliding down the railing from the loft.

Jonathan shook his head.

"Saren, you better be careful who you eavesdrop on. Some people won't like it," Luke said.

"Noted." She gave her dad a salute. "Uncle Jonathan, I have a million questions for you."

"Saren, Ethan, and Donny, let's load up my trailer. You'll have to grab your pizza and eat it on the way. Hurry, or you'll all be late for school."

"But, Dad, I have to talk to Uncle Jonathan!"

"So did I, but too much drama this morning. We'll try this again after school."

"Ohhh-kaaaay." She sounded very disappointed.

With all of them working together, they had the trailer loaded up in just a few minutes. With nearly cold pizza in hand, they piled into the crew cab.

"Bye, Uncle Jonathan. I'll see you after school."

"Okay, Saren. Ethan, are you coming back here after school?"

"Yes, if you don't mind."

"Not at all. I'll see you right after school then. Donny, take tomorrow off and think about what we talked about, okay?"

"But... yeah. Okay."

"Dude, you look like a soccer mom!" Jonathan said to Luke.

"Yep, you're just jealous!" Luke gave Jonathan a Cheshire cat grin.

Jonathan wasn't an envious type, but he did aspire to have a wife and children. Maybe that was why he seemed to be collecting teens to mentor. He wished Allison were there as his wife. They would have had a bunch of kids by now. He hated that she had missed so much life. He hoped with all his cells that she wouldn't miss any more. But that would take a miracle. He had very good reasons for believing in miracles, though, especially when it came to Allison.

Chapter Twenty-one

Cold pizza was a lame consolation for not getting to talk to Uncle Jonathan. Saren missed talking to her mom. She had practically avoided her presence completely since starting this adventure. She hoped she would be able to tell her soon. Now that she had experienced it herself, Saren could understand why her mom was so upset about her going to the cottage. But somehow, she knew that it was not all evil. Maybe she *should* have been afraid, but she just wasn't. More and more, she was coming to the realization that she was there to somehow help the Gray Lady. What a twelve-year-old could do to help a magically gray gardener of the Morticia variety, she had no clue.

Frost sat waiting for her at the door. Luckily, her mom was upstairs in her office when Saren got home. "I'm heading out, Mom!" She grabbed Frost's leash and said, "Walky walk walk!"

Frost jumped up and down in excitement as they stepped outside. As they arrived at the nursery, Saren's heart sank. It was completely packed. She had forgotten that it was prom week. The shop was crowded with moms ordering corsages, boutonnieres, and centerpieces for afterparties. The nursery plus the research projects funded by universities were the busiest parts of the business. The flower shop was mainly for display, but during prom and wedding season and around Valentine's Day, it got extremely busy.

Saren released Frost and stepped inside the shop.

"Hi, Saren. We need your help before you head out. You're just the person for the job." Jonathan handed her the order slip that read,

"One-of-a-kind centerpiece for a small table." He passed her a bowl with water-soaked green foam inside it.

Even though she was excited for her investigation, she enjoyed flower arranging. She made an asymmetrical masterpiece with tropical flowers, her specialty.

"All done, Uncle Jonathan," she said.

"Really? You're just going to leave it there like everyone will know who it's for until it wilts?"

"Oh, yeah." She picked out a flower-shaped cardholder and carefully placed it in the arrangement before attaching the order ticket to it. She put the entire arrangement into the walk-in refrigerator.

The second the door closed, Uncle Jonathan said, "You're free!"

She dodged and ducked all the customers to head for the nearest exit. With the front door bells still jingling, she took off at a run toward the forest trail. She figured Frost could catch up to her.

"Walky walk walk," she hollered, and Frost immediately appeared at her side. She reattached his leash, and they darted past the greenhouses and barn into the forest. Nearing her usual spot, she could see that the roses were already lying on the lush green grass.

Clunk, clunk, clunk came from the side of the house up high. Recognizing the noise, Saren went around carefully to the side of the house. A big forested mound sloped up from the garden on that side of the house. When on top of it, she was nearly eye level with the second story. She found a large log on the hilltop under a large jacaranda. She marveled at the beauty of the dark-lavender blossoms thick on its branches. It was outside of the boundaries of the miracle garden and was indeed blooming in its own natural time of spring. One of the boughs had become large and heavy, and like billowing ruffles, it extended nearly to the ground in front of the log.

"Excellent," she whispered. She sat down on the log concealed by the jacaranda branch.

She was high enough to get a good view of the tower balcony and close enough to hear what was being said.

A bat with a white tuft on its head banged a gavel with its wingy hand. "This trial is come to order! Where is our witness!" The bat sounded very cross and ill-tempered.

Just then, the Gray Lady stepped out on the balcony. The rest of the bats, over a dozen of them, swirled around her. Their wings sounded like rustling papers.

Saren stood up to get a better view and slipped her head through the purple veil of flowers. Then one of the bats spotted her. The majority of them left their posts on the tower balcony courtroom and surged toward Saren. Before she could react, they swarmed her, knocking her to the ground. She stumbled back over the log and fell, landing hard on her back.

When her body hit the ground, her mind transported into the mind of the Gray Lady. Her ears heard bat wings flapping all around her, but the sound morphed into papers being rustled by a dozen men. Her view of the cottage tower became a dark room with an endlessly long table of scowling men. It was a vision... No, it was a memory, a recurring memory.

Chapter Twenty-two

C *lunk, clunk, clunk.* Allison jumped with each blow of the gavel. "The trial is now in session," said a stern-looking man with white hair.

"We call our witness, Allison Scott."

A roar of papers rustled as Allison stepped from the bright fluorescent-lit waiting room into the dark conference room. Three lamps hung from the high black ceiling illuminated the long mahogany conference table. Allison didn't know why it was impossible to see how big the room was. She didn't know if it was darkness that surrounded the table or her own tendency toward tunnel vision in times of extreme stress. Her eyes didn't adjust. She looked to the left, and the long table seemed to go on for a mile. Around the table sat men. All the men looked similar, each wearing a short haircut, dark suit, white shirt, and expensive silk tie. She imagined they all wore wing-tipped shoes, perfectly polished, hiding under the table. The room smelled like a strong collage of expensive cologne. It made her nose twitch into the beginning of a sneeze. She held her finger under her nose to prevent the further embarrassment of a sneeze.

All the eyes of the men were upon her. They were a humorless, harsh-looking lot. She didn't recognize a single man in the group.

She looked for her bishop. He was not present. The door attendant bid her to sit down at the first chair on the side of the table next to the head position, where the white-haired man with the gavel sat. She hadn't gained the courage to look up and saw them only out of the corner of her eye. She felt hot, as if each man's gaze were burning her with coals. The man directly across from her gave off the most intensely hostile look. As she gained the courage to raise her chin, she discovered that Professor Mort Hebert sat directly across from her. He looked exactly like he had the first day she'd ever seen him. He was wearing that same suit he'd worn when blessing the sacrament.

"What is *he* doing here?" she protested.

"Young lady, you will not speak out of turn."

Now she was not only scared and humiliated but angry. After breaking off her engagement, she'd told the bishop what had happened. He'd insisted that she appear before this tribunal as a witness against Mort. The bishop told her it was her duty to prevent the same from happening to other girls. "I was assured he would not be here while I testified."

"He has to be here. It's *his* trial." The man sitting next to her spoke with sarcasm.

Mort smirked and peered at her with cruel eyes.

"When did you first begin dating Professor Mortimer Hebert?" asked one of the men down the long table.

"After the University Gala about eight months ago."

"When did you first have intimate relations?"

Allison took a deep breath. "At my sister's wedding, he for—"

"Just the answer, please," the white-haired man said, cutting her off. "How long did you have relations with Professor Hebert?"

"He for—"

"Please answer the question only."

"Two months," she said and put her head down. "But he forced me," she blurted out, interrupting the next question.

"We always have a choice, young lady. Where you alone?"

"Yes."

"You know that you should not be alone until after you're married."

"You say he forced you. Why did you stay with him for two months?"

"I was ashamed."

"As well you should be. That will be all."

Her stomach churned. She didn't fear throwing up, because she hadn't eaten since breakfast the previous day. She couldn't feel her body, but somehow, she stood and stepped into the bright lights of the waiting area. Tears didn't bother to well up. They jumped out of her eyes even though her expression remained blank. She dreaded that someone she knew would see her before she could wipe her tears.

She ducked into a back stairwell, sat down on a step, and put her head in her hands. That hadn't gone at all like she'd thought it would. She had hoped that she would finally get to tell her side of the story and be vindicated. But they didn't care about what really happened as long as they had someone to look down on. They offered no help or support, only cold indifference and judgement. She considered going to the police, but after this many men had dismissed her, why would they be any different?

The bishop had listened to her testimony in much the same way. He had offered no counsel but required her to meet with him each week for more confession. The following week, while she was at work at the horticulture center nursery, her supervisor sent her a note saying that she was to report to the Standards Office.

At the Standards Office, the receptionist, who had mostly likely typed the letter inside, handed her an envelope without looking at her. Allison opened the letter as she walked back into the corridor.

February 29, 1987

Miss Scott,

Due to your unworthy behavior, you have been excommunicated. This in turn is an automatic expulsion from any church-run university. This also results in termination from any church-run employment and residence in any church-approved student housing. You may apply for reinstatement in one year's time upon approval of your presiding bishop.

Sincerely,

University Standards Office

Her need to be heard and understood, to be told it wasn't her fault, was intense. They all said it *was* her fault. After all, she had broken the rules. She'd been alone with him. She'd trusted him. He was an elder in the church and a professor. She'd never dreamed he would violate her like that—then give her the ultimate insult after.

She no longer loved him. She couldn't see why she'd ever thought she loved him, especially after seeing Jonathan.

Oh, why didn't I just stay at the reception? Why! Why! She broke down in uncontrollable sobs.

Eventually, she wandered home late, hoping her roommates would all be asleep. She took the phone into the closet and called her mother.

Her mother listened to every word without interruption. She believed that her *mom* at least would take her side. She explained that she would have to tell her father.

The next morning, she called her mother back to see how it had gone with her father. "Mom, what did he say?"

"I told him that Professor Herbert forced you. He knows it isn't your fault. So it's okay."

That was it. Her parents were okay with her being forced. Neither of them offered any disapproval against Mort. From their point of view, as long as she had been raped, it wasn't her fault, so she was clean.

Allison was devastated that her parents thought it was okay for her to be raped. Her virtue and well-being didn't matter to her parents. Her worth was apparently equal to her good standing in the church. She had lost both. Her grandparents were dead. Her sister had her own life now, and Jonathan needed to move on. She was not worthy to be Jonathan's after all this. She was nothing. She was blank. In her own mind, she'd become void.

Chapter Twenty-three

Jonathan glanced at his watch as he strolled through the greenhouse, checking the moisture and temperature of various specialty areas. Saren was staying past her office hours, and he began to feel concerned. Hearing a faint jingle but distinctive tinkle of Frost's dog license and his ID tag, he relaxed and looked up toward the greenhouse door. At first, he thought that Saren was running toward him, but he couldn't hear her footsteps or the rattle of the clasp on her satchel. He began to quickly walk toward the jingling. He could hear Frost's paws pounding the dirt path at a full-on run. Frost had evidently used his canine superpowers to find Jonathan. He burst through the hanging plastic strips of the doorway into the greenhouse with his leash trailing behind him, his tail down.

Frost whined and quickly moved his feet like an Irish folk dancer. Frost's anxiety dance and Saren's absence threw Jonathan into a panic.

He unlatched the dangling leash. "Show me where she is, boy."

Frost immediately took off through the plastic strips. He ran past the barn just as Luke was driving up with his trailer. Without bothering to finish parking, he threw it into park, killed the engine, and bolted after Jonathan. They both sprinted to keep up with Frost. The dog ducked under some brush, and Jonathan and Luke lost him for a moment. Frost must have realized they were no longer behind him, so he barked three times and waited for them to catch up. When they had eyes on him, Luke gave him his emergency whistle, and Frost returned to Luke. Jonathan handed the leash to Luke, who quickly applied the clasp.

"Okay, boy, let's go!" Luke said.

Frost took off like a bullet, pulling Luke through shrubs and low-hanging trees, with Jonathan close behind. Frost jumped over a boulder and landed right next to Saren's head. Luke dropped the leash and bent down to Saren. Frost jumped on her belly and sniffed her motionless mouth.

"Frost, down," Jonathan said.

"Frostie Dog!" Saren whispered and slowly opened her eyes.

"Let's get you up," Luke said.

Her feet were still on top of the log she'd fallen over. With Jonathan on one side and Luke on the other, they picked her up and sat her down on the log. As they were moving her, she became more coherent.

"I was inside her. I blacked out, and then I was her." Saren put her right hand up to her head as if steadying herself from dizziness.

"Dad, it's Allison. We have to check on Allison. She ran down the tower stairs, and she... She was so upset." Saren tried to get up, but her dizziness returned. She sat back down. "We have to see if she's okay."

Jonathan looked at Luke in shock. They hadn't told Saren her name.

"Go ahead," Luke said. "I got Saren. I'm going to take her home. I'll call you when I get her settled."

With a nod, Jonathan took off toward the back door of the cottage. He raced through the house, finding no sign of Allison in her usual spots. He bounded up the stairs. At the tower door, he stopped. He took a deep breath and opened the door. Allison sat on the second-to-last step. Her ashen face was expressionless, yet tears flowed down the tear-stained streaks like rainwater through a dry creek bed.

Jonathan was stunned. This was the first time he had found her anywhere but her usual haunts, which were limited to only four locations: her bed, the couch in the parlor, the kitchen table, and that rosebush. This was also the first time she'd cried or showed any emotion at all. Maybe she had cried when he was at work, but he'd never seen any evidence of it. He was convinced that this was new behavior. He allowed himself to become hopeful that she was starting to feel. Maybe she was starting to come back.

He wondered how long she had been going into the tower stairwell. He popped in at random times, so the tower thing had to be new.

"Allison?" He got behind her and lifted her by her elbows and stood her up. Coming around to face her, he said, "Allison, Allison."

He took her in his arms and hugged her. She didn't respond to his embrace. Her arms just hung nearly lifeless from her shoulders.

"Allison, please come back. Please, I miss you. Maddie misses you—Luke too. You could get to know J.D. and Saren. Saren is quite a character." He pulled back from her and smiled.

She looked toward him without seeing him. The flow of tears had stopped. He guided her down the hall to the bathroom. He wet a washcloth and cleaned up her face. He led her downstairs to the kitchen and sat her down at the table. He put a glass of water in front of her. She drank the whole glass without stopping. He watched her with wonder. He pulled her pre-prepared dinner out of the fridge and slid it into the microwave.

He set her now-warm plate in front of her, and she ate slowly, methodically. Jonathan sat down across from her.

"Allison, how can you not *be* here when you *are* here?" Jonathan hadn't spoken to Allison while she was awake in several years. He had worn himself out day after day, trying to reason with a mannequin. Maddie had made herself physically ill trying to reach Allison.

Jonathan had finally begun trying to communicate with her in other ways. He'd started painting in hopes that the paintings would make her think again, feel again. But they had not. After that, he had all but given up.

She still ate, dressed herself, bathed, and slept, yet she didn't communicate. His hope swelled inside his chest now. He found himself talking to her like he did before. Except this time, he didn't plead with anger or desperation. He spoke to her like she could really hear him.

"Allison, remember on the dance floor at prom? Do you remember what you said?"

Twenty-three Years Earlier

THE INLAND SAN DIEGO sky was so blue, it was almost purple in the late-spring air. Jonathan knocked on the front door of the cottage. Grandma Emma answered the door.

"Oh, Jonathan, you look so handsome. Come on in."

Jonathan checked his royal-blue bow tie in the foyer mirror. His hair was newly cut and smooth. His face was freshly shaven. He looked down at his shiny rented shoes and rubbed one toe on the back of his pants leg to get it even shinier.

"Don't worry, Jonathan. You look amazing. Allison really admires you. You know that, right?"

"She does?"

"Yes, she loves how you're always so confident and you always know what the truth is. That's a rare gift."

"Grandma Emma, does she know how I feel about her?"

"Jonathan, listen to me carefully. She does know, but women need to be told. We start to doubt ourselves after a while. Make sure you tell her. We women need the words."

They both heard a click, and Grampa John came down the stairs backward, carrying his camcorder.

"Be careful, Grampa," Grandma Emma said.

"Woman," he said gruffly, and Grandma Emma smiled. "Okay, action."

Allison appeared at the top of the stairs. The royal-blue gown with a hoop skirt floated down the stairs with Allison's matching blue eyes gleaming.

"Alli, you are so beautiful," Jonathan said.

Grandpa panned to Jonathan's expression of pure love and joy.

Grandma Emma handed him a corsage, which she had made herself. Jonathan slipped the elastic band over Allison's lace-gloved hand, securing the white roses garnished with forget-me-nots. The forget-me-nots had been Jonathan's idea. He knew they were her favorite.

"Oh, no one is going to have one like this. Thank you!" She kissed him on the cheek and hugged her grandma and grampa. Then Allison pinned a matching boutonniere to Jonathan's tuxedo. After pictures, Jonathan led her by the hand down the cobblestone walkway through the front garden and out of the gate with a round arbor of pink roses.

Jonathan opened the door of his pickup and helped Allison in. Grampa had offered to loan him Grandma's Cadillac, but Jonathan was so proud that he had fixed the old truck, he declined the offer. Besides, they need the Caddie to pick up Busy Bea and Spencer to take them to dinner. Grandma and Grampa had promised to keep Allison's parents busy during the prom so they wouldn't discover Jonathan had taken Allison at least until after the prom. Since they taught at the high school, that was a tricky undertaking.

The gym had been decorated with sparkly streamers and glittery everything. It was magical. Foreigner played loudly over the speakers as Jonathan took Allison's hand and led her to the dance floor. He felt free. The music swelled.

He looked in Allison's eyes. He couldn't believe how blue and clear they were. They looked at him with complete trust—and love.

"Alli, I love you."

"I love you too," she said as a single tear flowed from her left eye.

"I don't just love you because of the sparkly lights and the romantic music. I love you with dirt on your face. I love you when you're upset because Busy Bea won't give you a break. I've loved you from the first moment I saw you. I'll always love you."

The music faded, and the beats of a fast pop tune came on. All the other couples separated and jumped around, dancing to the beat. But Allison and Jonathan didn't separate. They had no interest in separating. They gazed into each other's eyes in the middle of the dance floor, lost in each other. They wished this moment could last forever, but suddenly, Luke and Maddie ran up. They were dressed in jeans.

"What are you guys doing here?" Luke had opted to take Maddie to the movies because she was not yet a junior and wasn't allowed to go to prom. He'd refused to go without her. The music changed, and a song about a man-eater blared.

"This song is appropriate!" Luke said over the music.

"Wait, what!" Jonathan said.

Jonathan looked around. Allison's parents were talking to the DJ.

The music changed. The DJ announced, "This is for your parents."

A 1960s psychedelic song came on. The haunting voice said something about Alice getting ten feet tall. Busy Bea grabbed her husband and dragged him onto the dance floor, waving her arms in the air. Jonathan grabbed Allison's hand and ducked behind a group of basketball players dancing with their much-shorter dates.

"Ladies, your parents are hippies. Look!" Luke said, ducking with Maddie hiding behind him.

Allison peered between the basketball players and saw her parents dancing.

"I don't believe it. Shocking. Maybe they did have fun and hid it from us," she said to Maddie.

The music switched a current 1980s tune. The parents kept dancing, but they were moving closer and closer to them.

"Come on, Allison. Let's go," Jonathan urged as he pulled her hand toward the door.

"No, I don't want to go. We're having so much fun. They weren't supposed to be here!" She was on the verge of tears. "I want to tell them about us. I'm tired of not being open about how I feel about you, Jonathan. It's so unfair."

"I know it is. This world is not fair." If Jonathan thought that Allison could have handled her mom and dad's disapproval, he would have gone over there to plead his case. He believed that her father would not be happy, but he would be reasonable. Busy Bea, however, had made her opinion known from the second she'd even heard he would be working with Allison. She would flip out if she saw them dating. He couldn't bear to see Allison hurt.

"Look, we have to go."

"Jonathan, okay, but we'll work this out somehow. Right? We have to. Promise me that we'll work this out. We'll be together openly."

"I promise."

"Here they come," Maddie said. "They just saw me. Go, I'll take the heat."

Jonathan could hear Busy Bea scolding Luke and Maddie as they made their way through the crowd.

"Maddie, you know better than this. Luke, you'll be in detention for two weeks."

Outside, the cool evening air hit Jonathan. Allison looked fresh and beautiful. Jonathan didn't know how he was going to keep his promise, but Allison looked so much happier now. He would think of something.

Jonathan drove toward the beach. The grandparents weren't expecting them home until midnight. They walked and talked on the beach in their formal clothes. Allison hiked up her hoop skirt to walk in the water in her bare feet.

"Do you have any ideas?" Jonathan asked.

"You mean about Busy Bea? No. Maybe we can hypnotize her."

"Maybe I could just join your church."

"You would do that?"

"I would. If that's what I have to do. I would."

"Honestly, I wish it were that easy."

"Yeah, I have a three-strikes-you're-out problem. Broke, black, *and* unsaved, according to them."

"Well, you solved two of them, and being black is not a strike. That's their problem, not yours. Hey, I have a plan. I'll go to college. Come home and see you as often as I can. When I graduate, we'll announce that we're together. I'll be an adult. You'll be an adult, and that will be that."

"That's four years from now, Allison."

"I know, but I'll be busy studying. You'll be busy running Emma's. Then we'll work it out.

THE ANTIQUE PHONE RANG, bringing Jonathan back from prom night. He left Allison still eating slowly at the kitchen table and briskly walked to the foyer to answer it.

"How is she?" Jonathan asked without waiting to find out who it was.

"Full of questions. And yours?"

"Still nothing. But something has changed. I just don't know what."

"Let's do a beach walk with Saren tomorrow at six a.m."

"I'll meet you guys there." He hung up and returned to the kitchen table.

She'd gotten up from the table and was walking with her dishes. She put them in the sink and, in her slow plodding walk, headed to bed. Jonathan followed her through the dining room and parlor. When they got to the foyer, he came around to face her, stopping her.

"Allison, I love you. I just want you back to your old self. Please find a way to come back. We'll start fresh. We'll forget about what other people want. You'll only do what you want. You can do this, Allison. I know you can. You're strong. You're stronger than you think you are. God has preserved you for a purpose, and only you can find out what it is. But together, we can work it out. Remember?"

Her ashen complexion and stony expression remained, but one tear from her left eye came down her cheek. She was *trying*.

Chapter Twenty-four

Allison said with unmoving lips, "Jonathan, Jonathan." In her mind's eye, she saw a vision of a new journal she had begun a lifetime ago with "Jonathan + Allison" written across the front page.

Jonathan, Jonathan. The name echoed through time. Through her mind. The word itself brought warmth and safety. She felt love and joy at the sound of the name. She felt her cheek wet on one side. She felt. She wanted to be Jonathan, to be warmth, safety, honor and loyalty. To be love.

No, she wasn't Jonathan. She was betrayal. She was cold, betrayal, destruction, hate, and dishonor. She had abandoned all she loved, especially herself. She deserved isolation. She was not worthy of a Jonathan. That name. She couldn't see a face. Only a name. Jonathan.

She was not worthy. She would punish herself more. She would, at last, allow herself to long for Jonathan.

Chapter Twenty-five

S aren focused on the first rays of day that shone like an outline of a spiderweb over the eastern mountains. The deep, dark ocean still blended with the pre-morning sky, making the western horizon impossible to decipher. The cold, wet sand felt good on Saren's bare feet. This was her favorite spot. She knew her dad had chosen it because it was secluded, and its isolation worked as a kind of truth serum. Words spoken on that beach could be left there unhindered or taken back to begin a new venture or embark on another leg of an old struggle.

"So, Dad, who is Allison the Gray, and why did you guys never tell me about her?"

Luke looked at Jonathan suspiciously.

"What?" Saren asked.

Jonathan chuckled and rubbed his nose. "That's what your dad calls her, Allison the Gray. How did you learn her name?"

"No, seriously. Why is there apparently a relative of Mom's that is living so close to us, and I don't know her? Why is this all such a big secret?"

"Saren," Luke said, "we're here this morning to tell what little truth we know. We'll start with what *you* have found out, and then we'll answer some of your questions. Deal?"

Saren felt a little disappointed but recovered quickly. "Deal."

She took a deep breath. She wanted to sound professional and not let bitterness enter her tone. "Okay. First, I found Uncle

Jonathan's handwriting on a bunch of notes and my own parents' wedding picture in the Gray Lady's attic."

"Saren?"

"I know, Dad. It *was* dangerous. Whose idea was it to build out an attic with a drop-off like that? Plus, I got attacked by bats. Anyway, I survived it."

"Okay, we'll talk about that later. Go on."

"Then I found an article at the library about a missing college student, Allison Louise Scott. After studying the picture, I realized that she's the Gray Lady. Then I compared her to the wedding picture and determined that Allison the Gray was your maid of honor, Dad. Who is she in the family?"

"Unfortunately, Saren, we can't give you those answers yet," Luke said.

"We wish we could," Uncle Jonathan said, "but we made a promise not to."

"Okay, but if you don't tell me, I'll just figure it out myself."

"We have no doubt about that," Luke said.

"So, you know her name. What else have you found out?" Jonathan asked.

"I've told you everything so far up until last night, when you guys found me passed out. When I blacked out, it was like I became her. I could see what she saw and hear what she heard."

"You know that's impossible, Saren," Luke said, showing impatience.

Saren was looking at her dad. Jonathan was on the other side of her. Her dad looked at Jonathan.

"Go on, Saren," Jonathan said. "*I* want to hear more about it."

"Well, Allison the Gray is seeing a trial. I think it's on some kind of daily loop, because I saw her go up there that first day that I discovered the cottage. Then I heard the gavel that day I broke into the tower. So it must have been some kind of traumatic experience for her. Maybe the cause of her... condition. But the weird thing is that she was called as a witness. It was not *her* trial."

"Whose trial was it?" Luke asked. He seemed to finally be putting his skepticism aside.

"Someone named Professor Mortimer A-Bear. But I don't know who that is."

Luke looked at Jonathan.

"Luke, I burned everything with his name on it." Jonathan turned to Saren. "Did you hear that name from your mom or Busy Bea?"

"No, just the vision," Saren said.

"The only way she would have known that name is from that vision," Jonathan said.

"Okay, I agree," Luke said. "Saren, I want you to describe the trial. You mentioned a gavel. What did the courtroom look like?"

"It didn't look like any of the courtrooms I've seen on TV." Saren thought for a second. "I know—it looked like that fancy room with that long, long table in that skyscraper downtown... except it didn't have any windows."

"A conference room," Luke said.

"A church trial," Jonathan said.

"To excommunicate a man, they need, I think, a dozen men for a hearing. It would have seemed like a trial to Allison," Luke said.

"Were there twelve men at the table?" Jonathan asked.

"I didn't count them, but around that many for sure."

"If they excommunicated him, that explains why he just vanished from the university," Luke said.

"Yes, but it doesn't explain how he's nowhere to be found," Jonathan said.

"What is that? Excommunicated?" Saren asked.

Luke responded, "It's when a church decides that a person has done something bad, like committed a sin, and they kick them out of the church. In this particular church, they believe that they won't go to Heaven if they're excommunicated."

"Gosh, can a bunch of old guys keep someone out of Heaven? I thought only God could do that."

"We don't believe they can, but some people do," Luke said.

Jonathan followed up, "We believe that we're saved by grace. Which means—"

Saren interrupted. "That when Jesus was crucified, He was the sacrificial lamb for all of our sins. To be saved, we need only to believe in Jesus and that He died and rose again. So, all of us who believe in Him will live forever with Jesus."

"Exactly," Jonathan said.

"Wait, I don't get it. They believe in Jesus, too, but why do they think they can control the destination of souls?"

"Well, some religions get doing good confused with judgement. When we're true believers in Jesus, we want to do good. Right?" Luke said.

"Right. So?" Saren asked.

"Some religions get it backward. They think doing good gets us into Heaven. They forget that we're saved by grace."

"Why? It seems like it's a lot easier," Saren said.

"Yes, and that is how Jesus intended it, but grace is the opposite of what humans are used to."

Saren looked at the horizon and listened to her stomach growl. "Oh, I get it. The world is used to buying a dozen donuts and getting an extra one for free. But with Jesus, we don't have to buy the dozen. He just gives us one."

Luke chuckled. "Yeah, you're catching on."

"So wait, Jesus gives us this free gift of forgiving all our sins and gives us eternal life. Then there are these guys who step in between Jesus and people and tell them that they have the power to forgive or not forgive. And these people believe that if those guys kick them out of their church, they're kicked out of Heaven?" Saren said.

"Yes, that's right," Luke said.

Saren walked in silence for a while, taking it all in. She looked at the ocean, which was still dark, but a streak of light had found its way to a distant cloud over the Pacific. She felt very grown-up now. Her childhood beliefs that all was good on the Earth were over. She thought about the dark sky and ocean. "So, the world must be very dark for someone who thinks they have been kicked out of Heaven. They may only be able to see a small sliver of light like that wispy cloud way out there over the black ocean."

"Yes, Saren, that's why we're here—to show them that there's light for them. They need only to ask Jesus to forgive them, and he will," Luke said.

"Is that what you're doing with the Sprout boys, Uncle Jonathan?"

"I try. All I can do is show them the path, but they have to walk it. We all have free choice."

"Dad, does Allison the Gray believe that those men can kick her out of Heaven?"

"She did. Yes. We don't know what she believes now. Or if she can think at all."

"So why is she reliving someone else's trial? Who was that guy?"

"She was engaged to him. Whatever he got in trouble for, she must have been involved," Luke said.

"So, you mean... ohhh." Saren felt her face become hot, and her ears felt like they would catch on fire. She clamped her chilled hands over her ears to cool them off. Saren could see her dad and Uncle Jonathan chuckling in their bellies but with serious faces, trying not to show their amusement.

"Remember, the other day? What happened with Megan? It must have been something like that," Jonathan said.

"Oh, so why would she get kicked out if it wasn't her fault? And why wouldn't she be replaying her own trial?"

"Saren, unfortunately, in some cultures, it doesn't matter if she was forced. The woman gets the same amount of blame. As for the trial—only men have trials. She would not have had one. It would have happened without her being present, and she would have simply been sent a letter."

"Busy Bea," Jonathan said. "She would have gotten one." He sounded angrier than Saren had ever heard him. "She had to have known this *whole* time."

"Wait... Why would Grandmother Bea be involved? Who is Allison anyway?"

Now Jonathan uncharacteristically seemed even more agitated.

"It's okay, Jonathan. That information most likely would not have helped Allison. But now it may help Saren help Allison. Clearly, having Saren snoop around the cottage is making changes to her and her surroundings." Then he looked down at Saren. "We can't tell you everything until we can tell your mother, okay? So for now, this is still just between the three of us."

"Okay, maybe I should just knock on the door and talk to her."

"Let's just be patient. We've tried the direct route for years, unsuccessfully. I have a feeling that you *will* meet her very soon. It will have to be her doing, or it won't work. Okay?" Luke said.

Saren's expectation was rising because her dad was rarely wrong when he had one of his "feelings".

"Okay, but Dad, you guys gotta give me something."

"Have *you* told us all you know yet?" Luke asked.

"That's all I know so far. I didn't have enough time at the library to search to see how she was found. What happened after that? At least tell me that part."

"Luke?" Jonathan asked.

"Go ahead. Tell her how you found her," Luke said.

Saren jumped. "What? You found her!"

Thirteen Years Earlier

JONATHAN RAKED HIS fingers through the nearly two months' worth of unshaven beard while his other hand gripped the steering wheel. He would find Allison no matter how long he had to search.

Jonathan turned into the police station parking lot. He picked up several fast-food bags from the passenger seat and carefully stepped out of the car and onto the icy sidewalk. His boots turned into skates as he slipped on the ice and slid into the glass double doors. Once inside, the melting snow on his boots caused him to squeak across the marble floor to the reception desk, where he deposited the bags.

"Jonathan, you have to stop bringing us food. It's against the rules. You know that." The young male officer sat at the reception desk without looking up from the computer.

"Anything?"

The officer picked up the phone, dialed, listened for a few seconds, and hung up. Without looking up, he said, "No."

"Did you really call the detectives, or are you just faking me out every day?"

Finally, the officer looked up at Jonathan. "Twice a day. You come in here twice a day. They *said* they'll call you if they have anything." The officer had the air of a sarcastic uncaring robot.

Jonathan turned quickly on his heel and squeaked back across the lobby and out the door. After two months, they hadn't given him the time of day. But he couldn't give up. He also couldn't rely on them—not after they'd arrested him when he and Maddie reported Allison missing.

He continued his daily morning routine. He drove straight to the university security office. Even though he'd spoken to her every day for the past two months, the young lady behind the reception desk smiled a blank, polite smile like she had never seen him before.

"How can I help you?"

"I'm looking for Allison Louise Scott."

"We cannot give out information about students or faculty," she said, sounding like a recording. He had spoken to many people in the university and the church offices. They all gave the exact same canned response. But he kept trying, thinking that eventually, they would have to show they were human. Today was not the day.

He proceeded to the bishop's office.

"The bishop is unavailable. We cannot give out information about students or faculty."

His next stop was the donut shop, then the Horticulture Department, in hopes of finding information about the mysterious Professor Mortimer Hebert. He entered the back way through the greenhouses like a student or worker to avoid the gatekeeper that sat at the front desk of the department, who believed her job was to stop everyone.

"Good morning, Professor Bluff," Jonathan said to his old friend and long-time client.

The horticulture specialist with white hair turned from his plants and smiled. "Good morning, dear boy. You must stop bringing me donuts." He patted his protruding belly. "My wife is starting to notice. I got a lecture this morning."

Jonathan chuckled. "Maybe I'll bring you some yogurt tomorrow."

"Oh, no you don't. You can't turn me into some health food nut." He gave Jonathan a compassionate smile. "I'm so sorry, Jonathan. I haven't learned a thing. I have calls in to almost every horticulture department in the world, and no one has seen him at all."

"When was the last time Mort was here?"

"It was two days before you showed up here with Madeleine, looking for Allison."

"Tell me again what happened that day? It seems like they both disappeared at the same time."

"It does appear that way. The day after you arrived looking for Allison, we received that letter from the office of the President of the University, stating that Professor Hebert would be taking an indefinite leave of absence. His office and apartment had already been cleaned out, and he was gone."

"Allison couldn't have gone with him, because she hadn't moved out of her apartment. The only thing missing was her backpack, which she always had with her. She didn't even take her toothbrush."

"You don't have to convince me. It's baffling that the police won't search for her. It doesn't seem logical that a young woman would leave with a man and not take her toothbrush and other toiletries. Also, why would a tenured professor clear out and disappear like that? The police based their entire case on the fact that her car was missing. They assumed that she drove it somewhere intentionally."

"Yes, all these things we know. But we don't know where she is and if she's okay." Jonathan sat down on the stool and put his head in his hands. "I don't know what to do now. I'm out of ideas, Professor Bluff."

Professor Bluff pulled up another stool and sat down beside Jonathan. "Jonathan." He put his hand on Jonathan's shoulder. "Jonathan."

Jonathan finally looked up.

"I want to try something. What have we to lose?"

Jonathan nodded.

"Look around, what do you see?"

"I see a lot of tables with a variety of tropical plants. Vines hanging from the rafters draped heavy with exotic fruit that I don't recognize."

"Good. Now take a deep breath and focus. You want to be fully in the present for this to work. Okay?"

"Yes, got it."

"Picture Allison in a place in this area. Where would that be? Maybe a place you both went at one time. Close your eyes and see her. Do you have it?"

Eyes still closed, Jonathan nodded.

"Now tell me where you are."

"We're in that café on the outskirts of Spanish Fork, right at the foot of the mountain. Do you know the one?" Jonathan looked up at the professor.

"Yes, yes. Close your eyes. Go on. Tell me about the last time you were both there together."

"It was a sunny August day when Grampa John and I had driven Allison to college for the first time. After we got her moved into her dorm, we took a drive down through the Spanish Fork canyon. We stopped for a late breakfast at the most isolated restaurant we had ever seen. It was at the foot of the mountain, across the street from a large creek. It was hot and dry that day, but the birds were singing.

"Allison said, 'Look, the water trickles like it has no fear of being evaporated.' She stood there looking out downstream like she wondered where something with no fear went. Like she wanted to follow it. Like it would give her the answers to her personal riddle." Jonathan opened his eyes.

"If something had gone terribly wrong for her, she would have wanted to start again. It was the beginning of her time here.... That's it, Professor Bluff. That's where she is. I haven't thought to look there. We haven't been back to Spanish Fork since that day. I had forgotten about the place. But now I'm sure... She followed the stream. Oh no, the cold. I got to go."

"Godspeed," Professor Bluff said as Jonathan rushed out of the greenhouse.

After forty-five minutes of driving at dangerous speeds on icy roads, he pulled up in front of the restaurant. He got out and looked around. The place was barely recognizable because at least two feet of snow blanketed everything.

A man with a white beard was shoveling snow on the walkway to the café door.

"Excuse me, sir, have you seen this young woman?" He flashed Allison's picture.

"No, I haven't. I just shovel snow. Hardly ever look up. Go on in and ask for Becky. She's the owner. She's always here."

"Thank you."

A puff of warm air hit Jonathan as he entered the café. The front of the restaurant served as a gift shop, with various displays of locally made crafts like crocheted blankets, pottery, and handmade jewelry. A middle-aged woman with a puffy bun on the top of her head greeted him.

"One?" She had an air of authority and experience.

"You're Becky," Jonathan said.

"Yes, how did you know?"

"It's obvious you own this place." Jonathan gave her a warm smile. "I love the food here, but today, I'm looking for someone. Have you seen this girl?" He held up Allison's picture.

She studied the picture, taking her time. "Yeah, I remember her. She came in—what? Must have been two months ago. She sat in the corner booth all afternoon. For at least three hours. I remember her because she wrote in a fancy notebook the whole time."

"Did she say where she was going when she left?"

"No, but she seemed off somehow. Like she had gone off the deep end. I asked her if she was okay. She just nodded and left."

"Did you see which way she went?"

"She went toward the canyon." Becky pointed out the window toward the mountain with a menu.

"Thank you, so much."

Jonathan jogged down the newly cleared walkway to his truck. Finally, he had a shred of information. He was excited, hopeful, and full of worry and anxiety at the same time. She was close—he could feel it.

The café had been the last structure for many miles. He rolled the pickup slowly down the country highway that ran along the creek. His search concentrated on the area near the creek. The roadway up ahead turned south, away from the creek, which ran east to west. He looked north and saw a glimmer, a reflection, something shiny. He pulled the truck around on the narrow highway, nearly entering the creek during the U-turn. He drove as far off the road in front of the glimmer as he could without getting stuck in the snow.

A mound of snow over four feet high stood between him and the glimmer. He realized the glimmer was the radio antenna of a car. The snow plows had buried it. He took a deep breath to control the anger welling up in his stomach. It was as if someone had deliberately tried to hide the car.

He scampered and slipped his way over the long-frozen mound. It was late April, but the snow hadn't yet melted. The car was buried beneath nearly three feet of snow. He dug his way to the window to peer in. He immediately recognized the custom steering wheel cover he'd given Allison so her hands wouldn't get too hot in summer. The irony stuck in him like a knife in his side as he examined the car. He could see her journal in the back seat of the car, but there was no sign of Allison.

He quickly dug out the back door and crawled inside. Flinging off his gloves, he flipped to the last page of the journal. It was stained with tears. He skipped to the last two lines:

This stream was not afraid of evaporating and now it is not afraid of freezing. It flows even in the coldest day. If I can find the source, I can ask it. Maybe I can join it.

A new kind of panic struck Jonathan. *Join it... Join the stream?*

He ripped out the last two pages and stuck them in his pocket as though they were a map to finding her. Then he took off at a trot down the edge of the creek. The snow was still frozen and about a foot thick, so treading on top of it was easy, although occasionally slippery. He ran and ran down that creek.

"Please, God, please let me find her. Let me find her alive." He shouted to the sky and white field of snow on his right and the mountain on the left. He had been crying in desperation and frustration for almost five miles. The sun was quickly dropping behind the mountain.

Then he spotted a tree root on the edge of the mountain that created a small cave with a large overhang of rock. He stopped running and crossed the creek, getting his pants wet up to his thighs, but he didn't care. The temperatures had hovered around freezing for the past several months. If she was there, she would be frozen to death. Jonathan couldn't see anything yet, but his hope sprang up when he saw the snow was melted inside the small cavity.

Deep in the earth, there she was, wrapped in a sleeping bag. Allison was unconscious, but her cheeks were red, not blue. The cavity was so small, Jonathan couldn't fit his broad shoulders into it.

Right then, a strange dog flew past him and into the cave and nuzzled Allison's cheek. Jonathan coaxed the dog out of the cave, but she was reluctant to leave Allison. He could barely reach the feet end of the sleeping bag. The dog began pawing at the end of the sleeping bag as though trying to help pull Allison out. The dog then grabbed the sleeping bag with her teeth, and together, they pulled Allison out of the hole.

Weakly, Allison opened her eyes.

"Allison, Allison!" He hugged her, but she was silent.

He picked her up, still inside her sleeping bag. She drifted in and out of consciousness as he jogged while carrying her in his arms nearly five miles back to the truck.

The dog trotted at Jonathan's heels the entire way back there.

Busting in the door at the restaurant, he yelled, "Call 911!"

Becky ran out from the kitchen. "Oh my God! You found her!" She hurried behind the hostess desk and called 911.

After laying her on the floor in the gift area just inside the door, he grabbed several crocheted blankets off the display shelf and wrapped Allison in them. Rubbing her arms, he held her tightly, hoping his body heat would stave off further hypothermia.

The dog lay next to Allison as if she had been in the habit of keeping her warm all this time. All the employees came from the kitchen and dining area to bring Ziploc bags full of warm water to help warm her up. It was between mealtimes, and the two customers occupying tables offered coats to add to the warmth.

The ambulance was there within five minutes, the EMTs prepared to rush her to the hospital. One of the officers asked if Jonathan wanted one of them to drive his truck to the hospital so he could stay with her. So they did and took care of the dog for them too. The policemen nicknamed the dog Blue Angel. The dog was a blue heeler with bright-blue eyes, and it was obvious that she had been keeping Allison alive, maybe even bringing her food.

The doctors at the hospital said that she was a miracle. No one knew how she had survived out there for so long. Her sleeping bag was a special cold-weather bag, but that still didn't explain how she was only slightly malnourished with no sign of frostbite. A person could have frozen to death after only one night out there. She had survived two cold months.

"ALLISON WAS IN THE hospital for a long time. She didn't speak or seem to recognize anyone. She was what they called 'walking catatonic.' She's been that way ever since. For thirteen long years."

Saren had been riveted by the story. As soon as Jonathan finished, she asked, "So, is that why she's gray? Did the cold and frostbite do that to her?"

"No, she was pale but colorful then. The gray came later."

"So that was the same Blue Angel that had Ol' Blue with Al?"

"Yep, she was a very special dog."

They were back at their pickups.

"I have to get you fed and to school on time. So the rest will have to wait for another day," Luke said as he opened the door for her.

"Another beach walk?" Saren asked while doing a pirouette in the air. She momentarily felt very twelve. She hoped that thirteen-year-olds still jumped for joy.

The men chuckled.

She gave Jonathan a hug. "Uncle Jonathan, Allison the Gray would have died out there if you had given up! I always knew you were awesome, but I didn't know you were a *hero*." She pulled on his sweatshirt to get him to lower down. She gave him a kiss on his cheek and hopped into the truck.

He smiled sweetly at her. Jonathan gently put his hand on Saren's hand that lingered on the rolled-down window. "Remember, Saren, the only real hero is God. He had to show me where she was. I believe He showed *you* where she is. It's no accident you happened upon her cottage. You'll have a role to play in her recovery."

"I hope it happens soon. It would be wonderful to have a new friend. Especially a friend that's already friends with..." She examined Uncle Jonathan's face then turned to her dad. She couldn't read their expressions. "Or a relative to... or something with you and Dad and Mom... and apparently Grandma Busy Bea."

She got nothing from them. She wondered how they could keep a secret so well. However, Allison the Gray's involvement with her family was secondary. Saren wanted her to come back into reality from whatever kind of torment she was experiencing. Hearing the story about how no one wanted to help find her gave Saren a new wave of compassion that further cemented her determination and resolve to help Allison the Gray.

Chapter Twenty-six

Saren and the Frostie Dog bounced into Emma's. "Hi, Iris. How's it going?"

"Very well... and why are you not in school today?" Iris asked, sounding suspicious.

"No school... Teacher's training. I actually forgot about it. Dad took me to school, and no one was there." Saren chuckled. "It was like the Twilight Zone. All the people had vanished."

"I see. Well, lucky you."

"Yep!" She did her signature leap and spin. "Where is Uncle Jonathan?"

"He's out all morning visiting clients."

"Oh, yeah. Well, if he comes back before I do, can you please tell him that I'm here and working on the assignment he gave me this morning?"

"No problem. What is the assignment?"

"Sorry, Iris. Top secret," Saren said, trying to sound like a real spy.

The bells on the front door jingled, announcing a customer.

"Okay, we both better get to our tasks." Iris made her way toward the front of the shop and the waiting customer.

"Thanks, Iris."

Saren and Frost quickly exited the shop through the back storage room door. It opened up to the path between the rows of greenhouses. Saren jogged and Frost trotted through the grove of greenhouses. She was so excited. If she hurried, she could get to her boulder before Allison the Gray emerged from the cottage.

It had become easy for her to navigate the forest and find her favorite rock and spy perch. The forest was behaving itself, as were the animals, today. She no longer feared the forest since the day it had helped her break into the cottage. She now believed that the cottage, garden, and surrounding forest were actually protecting Allison the Gray. It seemed to have accepted that Saren was there to help her too.

When Saren made it to her boulder, there was no sign of Allison the Gray just yet, but she was due any minute. But something seemed different. The boulder was flatter and larger on top. As Saren sat down, she looked around to see if it really was the same rock. She was positive it was. But now it had more room on top, and it was more comfortable. The forest had adjusted the rock for her.

"Thank you," she whispered, looking up at the canopy of boughs. She once again marveled at the miraculous beauty of the cottage and garden.

She quietly pulled out her notebook, took a deep breath, and relaxed. Frost found a cushy spot on a bed of clover and lazily chewed on the clover blossoms. Saren was confident Frost was not interested in exploring, so she unclipped his leash to make him more comfortable. He looked up at her as if to say, "Thank you," and he put his front paws on the rock. The rock had made room for him, so she made a pillow out of her satchel right next to her.

Saren patted the satchel and whispered to Frost, "Up, up."

He obediently complied and, in a single leap, landed squarely on the satchel. He circled a few times and lay down, resting his head on his front paws. Although he looked like he was about to nap, his eyes were fully open and seemed to be cautiously focused on the rosebush.

She was no longer shocked but still astonished to see the central rosebush lush once again with stunning sanguine roses. The roses on the ground from the previous day were gone. This time, she decided to draw the rosebush. She wanted to see if it magically reappeared exactly as it did before or simply grew back overnight in a new arrangement. Although she couldn't be sure quite yet, it appeared to be exactly as it had been the first time she'd seen it and every time after that.

She was surprised to realize she was no longer afraid of seeing the snake. She wondered if she had gotten braver or wiser or if she had just gotten used to the fear—she didn't have time to think about it now, though. She wanted to finish her sketch before Allison the Gray started cutting off the blossoms.

While studying it, she suddenly spotted the snake slithering around in the bush; she let out a quiet gasp. This time, she sat perfectly quiet so as not to attract his attention. Frost, sensing her tension, sat up at attention and glanced at Saren for direction. She slowly put her index finger to her mouth and as quietly as she could said, "Shusssh."

He didn't make a sound, but his ears were back, and the hairs on his neck bristled.

The snake didn't seem to notice them, so Saren continued her sketching, moving the pencil softly so the snake wouldn't hear. While drawing, Saren contemplated how the roses could have grown back to full blooming glory overnight. She could come up with no explanation other than it was one more miracle of the cottage. New questions formed in her mind. *Who is causing the magic? Is it evil from the snake? Some kind of spell put on the Gray Lady? Miracles carried out by angels under God's direction?* With the beauty juxtaposed with the sadness of Allison the Gray and the evilness of the snake, some kind of spiritual warfare seemed to be going on in this small section of the natural world.

The door opened, and Allison the Gray followed the same slow fog-rolling procession to the rosebush as before. She approached the bush and the snake with a kind of dread, as if walking into her own funeral. She stood there for a moment, then the snake slithered up to her face and began talking to her.

"You ssstrive oncccce more to sssucccceed. I don't sssee why you perssssissst."

Allison the Gray nodded, and with shame, she proceeded to cut the roses off the bush again. Then the three cardinals arrived. Saren watched as the identical scene played out once again. Allison the Gray pricked her fingers with the thorns and bled all over the roses one more time.

Saren looked around the garden, examining each area closely. The briar lining the inside of the stone fence was now much smaller and thinner. It bloomed with a variety of roses. The walkway wound across the lawn over near the small grove of manzanitas and young pines then ended at the rock wall.

Suddenly, she became excited and sat up tall. Frost pricked up his ears and watched Saren. On previous observations, the rock fence along the walkway had been thick with briars on both sizes, but now, at the pathway's end, the thorny briars were gone, exposing the rock wall on both sides. The area over the rock wall under the rounded trellis was clear as well. Bloodred roses bloomed over the archway, leaving the area under it open.

"Frost, look! The wall is now *passable*," she whispered. With too much enthusiasm, she pointed at the archway, with her whole arm outstretched.

Quickly, as if taking it as an invitation or a command, Frost unexpectedly bolted off the boulder. He bounded through the forest around to the walkway. He jumped right over the cleared rock wall and through the round trellis like a dog show champion.

It was such a shocking surprise that the cardinals scattered in three different directions. The snake slithered so deep into the bush, he was no longer visible. Allison turned so quickly toward the approaching canine that her full skirt flared out. She put her pruning shears into her gardening smock pocket and squatted to the approaching fluffy canine.

He trotted right up to Allison the Gray with a full wag-wag greeting. Without thinking, Saren ran after him, her books and pens flying in all directions, but it was too late. They had been found out.

The Gray Lady held her hand out for him to sniff. Then she petted his fluffy head, leaving dots of her blood on his white fur, giving him a pink-polka-dotted coiffure. For a split second Saren thought she saw a smile form in the woman's eyes, then it faded quickly. But as she petted Frost, her demeanor seemed to soften. She looked a little less sad, but still very distraught. The Gray Lady rose slowly and peered over the fence at Saren.

"I'm so sorry to bother you, ma'am."

"Where did *you* come from?" the Gray Lady asked, walking slowly toward the rock wall. She didn't appear afraid or nervous.

Saren detected only curiosity and wonder—two traits she hadn't observed in Allison the Gray so far until now. Saren took a deep breath. She realized this was the first time Allison had spoken to a human since her disappearance. "I was sitting over there, watching you. I was so curious when I came across your house and your unusual garden that I had to discover the mystery behind it."

"I'm not accustomed to visitors, but would you like to stay for tea?" the Gray Lady offered. She swooshed her blood-dripping hand to the ground and back toward the front door in a macabre gesture of hospitality.

"Absolutely, we would love to." Saren was so excited.

"Oh." The Gray Lady cleared her throat as though she hadn't spoken in decades. She slowly waved her blood-wet hand back up toward her chest. "Allow me to introduce myself. My name is Allison," she said with a slow, old-fashioned way of speaking that reminded Saren of an old vampire minus the Romanian accent.

"I'm so pleased to finally meet you, Miss Allison," Saren said politely. She was compelled to call her Miss because her manners made it seem like she was an old lady, but her face showed that she couldn't have been more than mid-twenties, in spite of her oddly silver-gray silken locks. "My name is Saren, and you have already met Frost aka the Frostie Dog."

Allison the Gray looked down at Frost, who was looking up at her and seemed to be waiting for instructions. She slowly waved her hand from the dog to the front porch steps leading to a covered porch that wrapped around two entire sides of the house. She didn't have to invite the dog twice—he bounced over the grass and flowers then up the steps, where he turned and looked for Saren.

She quickly collected her scattered belongings into her satchel.

Allison turned and headed for the house in her usual slow, creepy pace.

Fearing that Allison would get too far ahead and she would lose her opportunity, Saren sat on the rock wall, threw her legs over, and passed under the round trellis. The lace trim of her tunic top caught on one of the fence rocks. She freed herself and bounded cheerfully toward Allison.

If Allison had noticed Saren's delay, she didn't let on. Her pace was her usual steady plodding rhythm.

Being so close to Allison, Saren could hear the rustling of her floral-print taffeta skirt and the lace petticoat underneath. The print was stunning. Saren had never seen a taffeta skirt with a floral print before. How odd to wear this with the *Little House in the Prairie*-type work smock.

Allison's long hair glistened silvery even when shaded under the huge sun hat.

Saren was finally on that perfect front yard. The lawn was spongy and lush under her feet. Now that she could get a better look, tiny flowers covered the ground of the flowerbed like a quilt. She breathed in the sweet air filled with living potpourri of gardenia, jasmine, lilac, roses, and other flowers.

This was better than she'd ever dreamed. Allison the Gray was not just speaking but inviting her in. Saren could barely contain her excitement at the promise of conversation with Allison the Gray. Plus, she would get a chance to check out the inside of the cottage. When she had broken into the tower, she had scarcely gotten a glimpse.

Saren couldn't wait to find out why she had such a beautiful home and a miraculous garden—and was still so gloomy and always wore the same drab varying shades of gray. In fact, Allison's whole being reminded Saren of the nearly blank gray of the mist on the mountains in the west right before dawn. She seemed constantly and permanently in shadow. Saren made up her mind at that moment to see to it that Allison's sun rose. Saren's determination was established, her purpose was fixed, and she knew this woman's life depended on her.

As Saren reached the front steps, Frost's tail was wagging so fast that it lifted him a little off the freshly painted bluish porch planks. He was whining with anticipation and looked like he could explode with excitement. Frost personified how Saren felt under her composed and poised stride. Saren reached down, trying to grab Frost's collar to put on his leash. She wanted to have her full attention on Miss Allison, and she knew that Frost would want to explore everything.

Saren blinked to adjust her eyes from the brightness outside to the darkness of the interior. She was finally inside. Saren had been dreaming about the details of the inside. She had no thoughts of danger when entering the strange house. She felt as though she had known Allison all her life.

Saren burned with so many questions, she would have to concentrate on not bombarding Allison with too many at once. She would take her time. If she were in the mystery, she would only be on chapter one.

Chapter Twenty-seven

Saren's eyes and ears were wide open as she entered the cottage, alert for swarms of bats. She was proud of herself for not jumping up and down like she really wanted to. Instead, she remained calm and focused. No time for childish behavior—she had a mystery to solve and a troubled woman to help.

Allison's Dr. Martens squeaked on the entryway floor. It was ancient oak with wide planks and a dark finish. The floor was well worn underneath the shiniest finish Saren had ever seen. It was a stunningly beautiful contrast. Frost tentatively skated across it on his toenails.

Saren's eyes went up and up through the spacious and high-ceilinged foyer. In front of her was a huge wall covered with paintings. A wooden staircase leading up to the second floor swept off majestically to the right side of the grand entry. An elaborate black cast-iron railing of leaves and vines curled up the staircase. Certain leaves had been painted gold for accent.

Looking around, Saren felt like she had walked into a museum or a getaway cottage of a princess—and maybe she had. Maybe *that* was Dad and Uncle Jonathan's big secret.

Allison slowly removed her giant hat and hung it on the antique hat tree next to the door. She began methodically untying her smock from the back. Her fingers had formed scabs and no longer bled.

While Allison was occupied, Saren examined the artwork. A large painting about five by four feet wide took the left-of-center position. It was a larger-than-life painting of someone who looked identical to Allison but had chestnut brown hair and seemed joyful, hopeful, and content. It was hard to believe that it could be Allison. She looked just like the maid of honor in Maddie and Luke's wedding picture. She wore a soft, timeless flowing dress with yellow roses on white with emerald swirls of foliage filling in the blanks, sprinkled with wild blue flowers. The blue flowers brought out the nearly-violet blue color of her joyful sparkling gaze. The sun was streaming through branches of trees, and the girl in the picture was surrounded by all types of flowers. She had a little bichon frise dog in her arms. It wore a blue-and-yellow plaid satin bow tied around his fluffy neck, reminiscent of the bichons in paintings of European princesses. The fact that Frost was also a bichon couldn't be a coincidence. In fact, the dog in the painting could have *been* Frost. She wondered who the painter was. Clearly, it was someone who knew Allison the Gray *and* Frost well.

Allison removed her gardening smock. Blood soiled the light-gray fabric. Saren wondered why the smock had no stains on it. It seemed to her that it should have many years of bloodstains, but it was completely clean except for today's red spots and smears. Saren wondered if the smock became clean miraculously and simultaneously with the restoration of the rosebush.

With sloth-like motion, Allison hung the gardening smock on another hook of the hat tree. The gardening shears still in the pocket clanged against the trunk of the brass tree until they came to rest. The many dings and worn-off finish of the brass trunk showed where the shears had hit—this exact process had been going on for many years.

Saren appreciated the syrup slowness of Allison's actions since it gave her a chance to look at everything. But Saren had been so captivated by the painting that Allison had already turned left into the parlor and was nearly out of sight. Frost, like he was on a treadmill, repeatedly slipped on the floor at the end of his taut leash in his desire to keep up with Allison and urge Saren onward.

Saren wanted to study the painting and make more comparisons to Allison, but she forced her eyes to just scan the surrounding paintings. They all included the same young woman in different daily life scenes involving others, such as one in a loving embrace with a young man. The center painting featured a garden scene of a woman's feet wearing Dr. Marten boots starting down a path that was lit by rays shining down from a Bible passage. Oddly, the words were not in English.

That's weird, Saren thought.

Allison had already disappeared into the next room to the left, and Frost was starting to whine. Saren followed Frost toward a double-door-sized archway that led into a formal parlor. In the parlor, the elaborately carved fireplace held the center of attention. The painting above it was the same woman, a technicolor Allison, walking arm in arm with a younger girl as though sisters. The other girl reminded Saren of her own mother but much younger. She couldn't be sure. Come to think of it, she didn't remember seeing *any* pictures of her mother as a young girl. She wondered if the same trauma that had caused Allison the Gray to lose her color had also affected her mother. Maybe that was the reason she had no old pictures of herself in the house and always had sadness behind her eyes.

An antique cherrywood desk sat nestled in the lace-adorned bay window overlooking the front garden. The inward-facing desk surprised Saren, considering the splendor of the supernatural garden. The aqua velvet chairs and Victorian sofa framed a glossy cherrywood coffee table displaying an antique family Bible.

Mahogany bookcases guarded a large collection of folklore, fairy tales, romances, and inspirational fiction. Whoever had collected these books was a connoisseur of happy endings. Saren didn't think it was Allison's collection. If she read these books, she couldn't have been so distraught all the time.

Allison passed through another wide archway with shiny dark wood molding and came into a small formal dining room. On the left was another bay window covered with lace curtains and heavy roman shades. Beautiful curio cabinets filled the corners of the dining room. As Saren blinked, adjusting her eyes to the darkness, she glimpsed glistening figurines of Biblical scenes that seemed to glow all on their own. An empty crystal vase in the center of the oak table seemed to cry out to have roses in it to show off.

The dining room was so dark that Saren bumped into a baker's rack on the right side of the room. A matching china cabinet on the back wall was filled with gorgeous china decorated with delicate blue flowers and pink roses that sparkled even in the dim lighting. Although the contents of the room were cheerful, the gloom gave Saren a feeling of foreboding.

Something definitely seemed off about the place, and she hesitated—but Frost didn't. He was still pulling her forward with a full wag-wag motion.

He must really like Allison, thought Saren. Most people he ignored, a very few he despised, and some he adored. As Saren made her way through the dark room, she heard the water faucet running. When she entered the narrow threshold of the kitchen, the bright sunlight streamed through the lace curtains on the back window at the far end of the kitchen.

She heard the kettle hitting the burner and a pilot light's *click, click*. With a loud whoosh, the gas burner came to life to heat the water for tea.

As Saren waited for her eyes to adjust to the brightness of the kitchen, she paused to listen to the tinkling of teacups meeting the grooves of their saucers. Straight ahead, a farm-style oval wooden table painted white with weathered edges and shaker-style chairs were nestled into a pleasant breakfast nook in the back bay window.

Allison arranged the tea cups. They had delicate yellow flowers, and the matching teapot sat on a round handmade crocheted doily. It must have been *the* teapot that inspired the children's song, she decided. Saren was still smiling about the thought when Allison looked up and gave her choices of tea: ginger, chamomile, or Sleepy Time. Saren chose ginger, the least relaxing of the teas, as she didn't want to fall asleep anytime soon.

"Please have a seat at the table. It will be a moment until the water boils," Allison said softly, sounding sort of humdrum, as though bored with life. She moved like she was walking underwater. Saren wondered if she took some kind of psych meds that made her act like that.

Saren tugged on Frost's leash to get him to abandon the fascinating scent under the fridge and beckoned him to lie down on the light-cream braided rug under the white farm table. The kitchen, unlike the rest of the house, was monotone in varying shades of white. The countertop was whitewashed birch with an inlaid mosaic in different shades of white tile, creating a stunning image of angels watching over a young woman in a white field. At first glance, Saren thought the white field was full of white flowers, but on closer inspection, she determined it was snow. The snow's texture differed from the rest of the scene and appeared to be glistening. The entire mosaic scene was all white, as though the angels were viewing her from Heaven and could only see through the purity of Heaven, therefore the Earth appeared in hues of white. Saren had never seen such a piece of artwork. She thought how odd it was to have a snow scene in Southern California, where it never snowed. She had seen snow only on the rare occasion that her parents took her up to Julian in the mountains.

Allison moved the teapot from its sideboard position and placed it directly on top of the young woman who demanded so much attention from the angels.

Did Allison do that on purpose? Even though Saren was young, she knew sad people didn't like to see happiness. It somehow made their sadness worse—unless they wanted to be happy. Whoever had decorated this place loved happiness and loved the girl in the mosaic. Saren wondered if it could be Allison being protected by the angels. She wondered what or who they were protecting her from.

Saren pulled out the white shaker chair at the left end of the table and sat down. Frost sat down, too, looking around with a waning wag on his back end. The counter created a horseshoe-shaped island that extended from the left wall of the kitchen, holding up a double white porcelain sink. To the left of the sink was an old water pump left over from the days before running water. On the opposite side of the kitchen, next to the set of built-in glass cabinets where the tea set had come from, was a stately white refrigerator that looked to be one of the first of its kind. Silver chrome letters spelled out *Westinghouse* across the front.

"Milk or honey?" Allison asked in her crystal-cold tone.

"Yes, please," Saren responded with the best manners she could muster. After all, this was a real tea party.

Allison pulled the long lever that opened the refrigerator and retrieved a quart of milk in a plastic container. Saren was surprised to see a normal milk jug; she half expected to see an old glass milk bottle emerge from the antique fridge. That confirmed she hadn't stepped back into time.

What is this place? Saren hoped it was good and not evil. As that thought floated across her mind, the tea kettle whistled, breaking the deep quiet of the old Victorian cottage like a shattered plate-glass window, and she hoped Allison didn't see the noise had startled her.

Allison poured the hot water into the teapot. Picking up the tray, she brought the tea set fully loaded over to the table, complete with a small matching serving plate of gingersnaps. Allison poured the tea into the cups and passed one of the cups and saucers to Saren.

"Thank you, Miss Allison." She wondered how many questions she could ask and how quickly and still be considered polite. She didn't worry about it too much, but she did hope Allison started the inquiry first.

Instead, she looked down into her cup as though she were trying to read tea leaves. By the looks of it, she was going to sit there and be sad. Saren didn't have time for sad—she had a mystery to solve.

She cleared her throat and mustered her courage. "So, Miss Allison, do you live here alone?"

Allison looked perplexed. "I think so. Did you see someone else?"

Not wanting to give away that she was practically a bona fide stalker and hadn't seen anyone come or go on her watch, she said, "No, actually. You must not get many visitors since you don't have a real road up to the cottage."

"No, Saren, I can't remember having a visitor before. I can't really remember *anything* before today," Allison responded quietly, seeming a little embarrassed. She looked back down at her tea with an expression of intense dread and seemed to be bracing herself for criticism of some kind. "Where did *you* come from?"

"We live in the neighborhood on the edge of town. One day, walking my dog, we found your cottage after some men cut a tree down that had blocked the view of your house. Since then, we've been coming here every day because the garden was so beautiful, and we hoped we would meet you and see what you were like." She paused, watching for a reaction, but Allison kept looking into her cup.

"Frost and I were hoping to make friends with you and visit you all the time. Is that okay with you? Would you be my friend?" Saren asked hopefully, sitting on the edge of her chair, her teacup between both hands.

"I don't know if I can. I mean, I don't think I'm very good at being a friend."

"Why would you say that?"

"Since I don't have any friends, I must not be good at it."

"Well, you said you didn't remember anything. Maybe you just don't remember your friends. Do you think that's possible? After all, you were friendly with Frost and me." Saren's friendliness was undaunted.

"Well, that is true. Hm, I had not thought of that. I don't *remember* having a friend before." Allison kept looking at her teacup as though she were drowning in it.

Saren searched Allison's empty gaze, saying with compassion, "You really don't remember having a friend, do you?"

Allison shook her head. She didn't seem to feel sorry for herself, but rather at a loss for how to escape a cleverly devised trap.

"So, Miss Allison, you mentioned that you didn't remember having a friend or really anything? What is the last thing you do remember?"

"The last thing I remember was being cold in a room with a bare light and three men in suits asking me questions."

"Ohhhh, is that what you're seeing when those three cardinals come to talk to you in the garden?"

Allison sat up in surprise. She looked up from her tea for the first time and looked straight at Saren.

Oops! Saren had given herself away already.

But Allison didn't seem to notice what her question implied. "How do you know about that?" Her shoulders slumped, and her head dropped into her hands. She seemed like she was trying to shrink or disappear completely.

Oh no, that's what she does. She makes herself disappear. It was like she wanted to disappear from herself. "Oh, it's okay, Miss Allison. I could hear the cardinals too. As odd as it seems, they *were* talking to you."

"Was I not supposed to talk to them?" she asked without moving her hands from her face.

"You're a grown-up, so you can talk to anyone you feel like talking to, but I don't like them. They're not very nice."

"No, you are right. They are not nice."

"So those three men that show up as cardinals, what do they want?"

"I don't know, I don't know." She shook her head and lowered it toward the table so quickly that her forehead smacked the table.

"Oh!" Saren got up to see if she was okay. Her face was still planted into the table. Saren put her small soft hand on the back of Allison's silver head. She stroked her hair. "It's okay, Miss Allison. Really, I'm just here to help you. Tell me what is so upsetting about this. How do you feel right now?"

Allison slowly picked up her head, still looking down into her hands. Being closer to her now, Saren could see her eyes were swirls of gray clouds. No tears fell from them. Instead, cloudy gray mist floated out of them like a fog over the grass at dawn. "How I feel? Coerced."

Suddenly, Saren felt very twelve. She cleared her throat. She stooped over a little to be at eye level with Allison. "Coerced? What do you mean?"

"They wanted me to lie."

"Lie? What for?"

"They want me to take back what I said that got someone in trouble."

"Did the person do something bad?"

"Yes, yes, he did. The first person I told made me tell more men. He said that if I did, I would save other girls from getting hurt by him."

Saren remembered what Uncle Jonathan had said about maybe what happened to her was kind of like what happened to Megan. "You did the right thing. You saved some other girls."

"But it doesn't matter if I did the right thing."

"Why doesn't it matter?"

"I don't know, but doing the right thing gets the same punishment as doing the wrong thing." Allison looked a little more under control, so Saren took her seat back at the table.

"Well, that doesn't make much sense to me," Saren said.

"I don't think we're supposed to understand it," Allison said.

Saren had heard her grandmother Bea say that. She realized it must be something her church told its members to keep them from finding out the truth. Allison must have been involved in something the church wanted to cover up. "Hm, okay. Well, what do you remember after that?"

"The next thing I remember I was here in this perpetual garden, day after day in the perfect world with this perfect weather, except I wonder why I'm being punished by being put in such a perfect place to remind me of all my transgressions, failures, lies, sins, and faults." Allison sounded bitter and hopeless.

"Miss Allison, have you considered that you may be here as a reward for something or because someone loves you very much and wanted to protect you?"

Allison looked at Saren with complete astonishment, finally looked at Saren through her murky gray eyes. "No, I didn't think of that."

Saren decided to change the subject to lighten the mood. "So, Miss Allison, what's your gardening secret? How did you get all those flowers from different seasons to bloom all at the same time?"

"Well, I don't know. They're just there."

"What do you mean 'They're just there'?"

"They're there. I don't remember before now."

"What about the rosebush? How does it grow roses back so fast?"

"The roses grow back?" She looking at Saren with disturbed confusion. "Yes..." She looked oddly contemplative. "I had déjà vu when I went out there today. Are you saying that I did it before?"

"Yes, I've been watching for a few days, and you go out there every day."

"And every day, they grow back?"

"Yes, I'm not sure, but it looks like they grow back exactly as they were before."

Allison took a sip of her tea.

"What are you trying to do with the roses? I mean, why do you leave them on the ground?"

"I don't know. I have a feeling that I have a goal when I go out there, but then he tells me I'm doing it wrong. That I can never get it right, so I cut another one, but it never is the way it should be until they're all gone. Then I have done nothing but destroy the beauty that it once was and wasted the flowers."

"When you say 'he,' do you mean that talking snake?"

"Yes, do you know him too?"

"Unfortunately, we've... met. What makes you feel so bad when he talks to you?"

"I see that I've ruined the beautiful rosebush and the garden. I realize that I'm a hopeless failure."

"I don't know what you're talking about. Your garden couldn't be more perfect. It's as if God sent his angels down from Heaven to make it very perfect. It's the most beautiful and miraculous garden I've ever seen. And I've seen a lot of gardens because my family owns a gardening shop and nursery." Saren lost herself for a moment in her enthusiasm for the garden. She knew she sounded a bit like a know-it-all, but she wanted to make sure that Allison knew how magnificent her garden actually was.

Saren realized that it didn't matter what *she* thought. She was here to find out what *Allison* thought. "Wait—what do you mean? What should it be?" Saren tried to sound patient even though she wasn't.

Allison looked perplexed. "Um, I'm not sure what it should be, only what it's not supposed to be."

"How does that make you feel?" Saren was trying to understand, but to her, it was illogical to proceed based on how something was not supposed to be.

"Bad, very bad." Allison put her head down.

"So these cardinals and the snake that make you feel bad, do they have names?"

Allison looked up at Saren again, seemingly excited that she could recall something. "The cardinals, I don't know... but the snake is called Dr. Death."

Suddenly, Saren's spy watch alarm went off. They both jumped, waking the Frostie Dog, who had been enjoying a nap on the rug.

"My office hours are up," Saren said. "I have to go now."

Oddly, the whole day had gone by, and it had only seemed like an hour. Saren wondered if it was part of the spell of the cottage or if it was because it was such an exciting day.

"Yes," Allison said with the most confident voice she had heard so far.

"Yes, I need to go."

"No, *yes* we can be friends. I would like very much to be friends with you and aka the Frostie Dog."

Her formality of speaking made a giggle swell up in Saren's stomach. But she was a big girl and stifled it. "Oh, good. I would like that very much too. Is it okay if I come see you tomorrow?"

"Yes, please do." She sounded like an American vampire again.

"It was so much fun meeting you, and thank you for the tea and cookies."

"I'm sad to see you go."

Allison showed Saren and Frost back through the white kitchen, the dining room, the parlor, the grand foyer, and to the front door. The rose-stained glass window in the front door was even more beautiful from the inside looking out. The sun was low in the horizon and shining directly through the rose, creating amazing lens flares without a lens. Stunned by the beauty, Saren froze in her steps when she stepped into the light.

Not hearing her steps any longer on the shiny oak floor, Allison looked back slowly to see what Saren was doing. Allison gazed at Saren with an uncharacteristic sense of wonder.

"Saren?" Allison said softly and let the rising tone of the single word rest with the implication of a paragraph-long question.

"Look at how the sun comes through the window, lighting up the stained-glass rose. Beautiful!"

Allison's smoky eyes looked like full moons behind clouds in fall, like they wanted to glisten but were covered with a thick fog. Allison followed Saren's gaze and returned her blank stare.

"Don't you see it? Look!" Saren said softly and looked up, pointing at the stained-glass window sparkling with light. She turned her attention to the little rainbows all over the walls created by the sun through the window.

Allison continued looking at Saren, who pointed around. "Oh, you must be so used to seeing this that it's boring to you now, right?"

Allison looked truly puzzled and disturbed. "Saren, where?"

"Everywhere, rainbows, here, here, here..." Saren continued pointing at all the rainbows. When she was finished cataloging them, she finally snapped out of her excitement to realize that Allison didn't see what she saw. Allison the Gray stared at Saren blankly, then her eyebrows furrowed, her eyes narrowed, and her bottom lip protruded nearly to her chin. Her head sank even though her bitter eyes remained fixed on the wall of unseen rainbows. The intensity of her expression could have rubbed off on a weaker soul or a less joyous kid, but Saren marveled at why someone could look so miserable among such visual wonders.

"Do you have something wrong with your eyes?" She had made up her mind to give Allison an eye test on her next visit. She could make up her own eye chart like the one they used at school but use colors too.

"The only bright thing I see is *your* eyes." Allison broke the sunlit spell by opening the door.

"Thank you for your hospitality and for the tea. Come on, Frost. Let's go." She tugged at Frost's leash to tear him away from sniffing Allison's boots. She could tell that he liked her by the way he wagged his tail. He seemed to be hurt that Allison hadn't acknowledged him again after their initial greeting. But she looked so sad the whole time, like something was really wrong, and had been for as long as she could remember... if she could remember.

Saren decided that after the eye test she would find out what made Allison sad. With her objective set, she stepped over the threshold and onto the front porch of the cottage.

"We'll see you tomorrow, Miss Allison!" She looked back from the spongy grass at the bottom of the freshly painted blue-gray porch steps and flashed her biggest smile. She trotted past the little grove and the rosebush, intentionally ignoring its sinister inhabitant, and went back over the rock wall under the arc of garnet roses.

Chapter Twenty-eight

Jonathan leaned back in the executive chair across the desk from Madeleine, who occupied the guest chair in the crow's nest. He could see the customer area and the work areas through the big plate glass window of the office.

"Saren has been coming here every day for over a week," Madeleine said. "She's been so excited to get here that I hardly get to see her anymore. How is she doing?"

"Oh, she's a hard worker, dedicated and focused. Just like her mom. Oh, and thank you for bringing by these pants. But I really don't need them." Jonathan glanced out through the crow's nest window then at the clock on the wall above the window behind Madeleine. Saren was due back any minute.

"Jonathan, at some point you have to realize that you're the face of the company. You can't run around with holes in your pants all the time. And when are you going to trade in that ratty old cap for a new one?"

"Hey. This hat has character. Besides, it knows as much as I do."

"It can probably walk by itself too." She chuckled. "Where is Saren anyway?"

"Oh, I have her working on a special project out back. She's due back at the shop any minute."

At that moment, Saren and Frost came flying past the back work-table and dodged customers through the display area. Once she saw him through the crow's nest window, she stopped abruptly. Frost stopped so fast with his front paws that his hind end seemed to back up, causing his tail end to pop up. She could see the back of her mom's head through the window. Jonathan could see an unusual amount of excitement all over both of them.

He calmly twisted his head to the right while simultaneously listening attentively to Madeleine. Saren took that as a cue. She ran closer to the window, jumping up and down, mouthing, "I met her. She talked to me. She talked to me!"

Frost, caught up in the excitement, jumped up and down too. But since he had moved so close to the window, Jonathan could only see flops of ears, fur, and tail at the top of the bounce.

Jonathan nodded slowly, giving Saren acknowledgement, but allowing Madeleine to think he was nodding to her.

"Oh, here they are now. Maddie, thanks for bringing the pants by. Here's the mail."

"I wish you wouldn't put them in a trash bag."

"Have they ever gotten thrown away yet?"

"No, but..."

Jonathan put his hand on the desk, getting ready to stand. "Saren needs to give me a progress report, and then she can ride home with you. Do you have fifteen?"

"Sure, I'll go see if Iris needs anything while I'm here."

They both got up. Jonathan opened the crow's nest door for Madeleine.

"Hi, honey."

Saren ran over and gave her mom a hug. "Mom, I have important business with Uncle Jonathan," she said, trying to sound like the executives that her dad had meetings with.

"Of course. I'll be hanging out with Iris."

"Thanks, Mom." She grabbed Jonathan's hand, and they both ran through the shop and out the back door. They passed through half of the greenhouses before they were sure they were far enough away so no one would hear.

"Uncle Jonathan, I talked with her. With Miss Allison." Saren was breathing so heavily with excitement and running that it was almost hard for her to talk.

"What are you saying? Did she talk *to* you?"

"Yes, yes, she did. She invited me in for tea. She made tea and gingersnaps, and we talked."

"She can see you?"

"Yes, she does have this weird fog that comes out of her eyes, but she can see me. I don't think she sees colors, but she communicated with me *and* Frost."

"What did she say?"

"She doesn't remember much. She seemed very distraught. Those cardinals represent three men that once interrogated her about her getting someone into some kind of trouble."

"Really? What else?" Jonathan was bending down to Saren's level and had his hands gently on her arms.

"That snake, she calls it Dr. Death. Do you know who that would be?"

"Oh, my gosh." Jonathan stood up and paced in a circle. "I knew it." He came back to face Saren. "Remember when you had that vision with the bats and that trial. You came up with a name."

"Yes, Professor Mortimer Hebert."

"That's right. Well, he was Allison's fiancé when she disappeared. Me and your dad couldn't stand the guy. He was French and snooty, and we didn't like how he treated her. Anyway, since he went by Mort, your dad and I used to call him Dr. Death. He hated that name."

"Wait, why did you call him Dr. Death?"

"Mort means *death* in French."

"That snake has a French accent! So, he's an anthropo-something of Mortimer Hebert?"

"Anthropomorphism. Yes, it must be." Jonathan grabbed his phone out of his back pocket and texted Luke "611." That was their code for an emergency meeting but not to send him into a panic like 911 would. This was a *good* emergency.

He immediately turned back to Saren. "You run along home with your mom. Remember, not a word to her. I already called a meeting with your dad. We'll most likely tell her what we've been up to tonight, *if* your dad agrees. I'm going to see Allison right away. Good job, kiddo."

He gave her a peck on the check and sprinted toward the cottage. From where he was, it would be quicker just to run than to go back to get his cart. He didn't want to spare one second.

He ran through the cottage's back door and into the courtyard. He stopped to listen for her. The house was deathly silent. He ran through the kitchen, dining room, and parlor. He looked out past the desk to the garden, where roses still littered the lawn, and stopped cold at the archway that led to the foyer.

She stood with her hand still on the doorknob, as though she had just closed it after Saren's visit. At least thirty minutes must have passed, and she was still frozen there. He had never found her anywhere in the house except at the table, on the sofa, in her bed, next to that rosebush, and most recently, the tower stairs. This was new. After thirteen years of exactly the same, *new* had to be good.

"Allison, Allison..." Jonathan said calmly and softly, so as to not startle her.

She didn't move. She seemed to be looking for something on the wall. She reached out her hand to touch the wall. She seemed tormented. Her eyes swirled with haze, and the steady stream of fog floating out of them dissipated in the fading sunlight streaming in through the rose stained-glass window of the front door.

Jonathan gently took her by the arms and guided her into the parlor. He turned her around like a life-sized doll. He backed her feet up to the sofa and sat her down. He sat next to her. Picking up her hand, he said, "Allison, I heard you had a visitor today."

She looked straight ahead, just like she had for the last thirteen years. He had no doubt she had spoken to Saren. She was not the kind of kid who ever lied. But Allison was not going to talk to him... or she couldn't.

Profoundly disappointed, he couldn't even stand to be there at that moment. He left Allison where she was. He ran back out of the house into the backyard. He fell on his knees and cried. He had cried only twice in all this time. But this time, he had been filled with so much hope and his disappointment was so intense, he actually cried for himself. He loved her so much, and he mourned that love that couldn't be received.

After a few fleeting moments of anger and anguish, he calmed himself. He regained control over his emotions and headed back into the cottage.

He returned to the couch and sat next to Allison. Even though she couldn't communicate with him, she might still hear him. So, he decided to tell her about a beautiful day, the most amazing day he could remember.

"Allison, my favorite day of my life was with you. Remember the day that you discovered I had been raising forget-me-nots for you all on my own?"

Seventeen Years Earlier

JONATHAN FINISHED TAPING up the insulation that Allison held around a Hawaiian plant. A rare wintery day was falling on Southern California. They had worked all day insulating all the tropical plants. Many of their corporate customers had called them for advice on how to handle the unusual and imminent frost that had been forecast. Allison had decided to stay at Grandma Emma's cottage for the weekend to help out. This was her usual routine so that she and Jonathan could hang out more without Busy Bea knowing.

That frosty Saturday night, Grampa decided that they would make a big bonfire in the middle of the tree section of the nursery. They brought all the other vulnerable plants near the fire that were too big for the shop or greenhouses. Maddie, Luke, Luke's parents, and Grandma Emma were there. It was cold, but the fire was friendly. Grandma brought out hot chocolate for everyone. They roasted marshmallows and had s'mores. It was the first time Jonathan had experienced a campfire setting. He loved it.

The glow on the faces, the laughter, and the banter warmed his soul. They were having a wonderful time. It was just like Grampa to take an unexpected weather event that should have been stressful or even devastating and turn it into a memorable family-and-friends gathering.

As they sat around the fire with sticky fingers and full bellies, the lights flickered.

"Here it comes," Grampa said.

"What?" Maddie hollered.

"The rolling blackout. I was hoping it wouldn't make it out to us. But it looks like it—" A static-electric sound interrupted Grampa. The lights flickered two more times and went out.

If not for the large campfire, it would have been pitch black. Nothing beyond the firelight was visible in the unusually deep cold of the winter night.

"Wait for it," Grampa said in his deep gravelly voice.

They sat in silence and darkness for ten seconds, just enough time for Allison to grab Jonathan's hand. They could hear engines coming to life one after another. Then a few seconds later, the lights came back on in succession. They had only the essential lights, heating lamps, and heaters on already, so they didn't need to make any adjustments.

They looked around and could see that the last greenhouse was not receiving any power. Grampa started to get up.

"I got it, Grampa." Jonathan jumped up.

"Okay, the toolbox is already out there."

"Thanks, Grampa. You always think of everything."

"I want to help." Allison followed after Jonathan.

"Allison, take this flashlight too. You should always have your own light. Never depend on someone else's."

"Thanks, Grampa."

Jonathan waited for her to catch up. He preferred for her to be in the front so he could see her. He felt like he could protect her better in case anything unforeseen were to happen.

Just then, a raccoon jumped down from the roof of the shop and ran across their path. Allison jumped back. She put her hand over her heart and waited. A split second later, a tomcat burst out of a bush, chasing the raccoon. Allison startled so badly, she spun around right into Jonathan's arms.

"It's okay. It was just ol' Sylvester chasing off a raccoon. Doing his job. You really didn't have to come, Alli. It's cold out here. Plus, this generator stuff is dirty and grimy."

"Are you kidding? I love the smell of motor oil almost as much as roses." She chuckled.

He loosened his hold on her, and they continued down the path.

"Well, I'm glad you came. But let me know if you get too cold. I have blankets and jackets right there in my barn loft."

"Okay, or you could keep me warm." She smiled at him mischievously.

"That sounds like fun, but this is kind of an emergency." He put his right arm around her and rubbed her arm briskly to warm her up.

"I know. I'll stay focused."

They found the toolbox quickly, and Jonathan checked for corrosion around the battery.

"Jonathan, what do you really want out of life?" Allison asked.

"This. Fixing a generator in the middle of the night while the most beautiful girl I've ever seen holds the flashlight."

"That's sweet, but what about after this?"

"After this, I have a surprise for you."

"Really? What kind of surprise?"

"If I told you, it wouldn't be a surprise."

"Fair enough. But seriously, what's in the future for you, Jonathan? What do you want?"

"I want what every man wants."

"Such as?"

"What Grampa has. Beautiful wife who loves him, successful business doing what he enjoys. And God to worship."

"It sounds simple."

"It does, but somehow, I don't think it is."

"Okay, Alli, you do the honors. Toggle it three times to the top first, then down to start." He took her flashlight from her to free her hand so she wouldn't have to take her other hand out of her pocket.

"Grampa says I should have my own light."

"You are light."

She smiled at him. "Okay, here goes. Toggle up, up, up... start."

The engine roared to life.

"Okay, now hit that switch."

With a flick of a switch, she sent power from the generator to the warming lamps and heaters. All at once, the greenhouse lit up.

"See? You are light."

"*I* didn't do it. What did you do to fix it?"

"You were here. I didn't do much. It just needed *you*. Enough of working. Your surprise. Close your eyes."

He led her by the hand through the greenhouse. Jonathan could already feel the warmth of the heating lamps penetrating the cold night. He hugged her from the back and whispered in her ear, "Here we are. We're no longer in the coldest day in the history of SoCal. It's springtime in Alaska. Open your eyes."

In front of her lay a six-foot-by-three-foot table filled with blooming blue flowers with yellow centers.

"Forget-me-nots! Jonathan, how in the world?" She jumped up and down, clapping her hands. "I can't believe it." She turned around and gave him a bear hug. She pulled away to look him in the eye. "Did you grow these?"

"Yes, Grampa gave me my own section and told me to do something new that would be popular and profitable."

"So you picked *my* favorite flower."

"He didn't tell me I couldn't be sentimental. Why do anything unless *you* love it?"

"Jonathan, that's absolutely the most romantic thing I've ever heard of." She gave him the first kiss that he had dreamt of for a lifetime.

"ALLI, YOU WOULD BE so proud. Those forget-me-nots have become a best seller for Emma's. We're the primary producer of them for the entire country. We've won awards and honors because of them. But still, I really grow them just for you.

"Please come back to us. We all love you, Maddie and Luke and Saren and little J.D., who you haven't met yet. He's all personality. We miss you. I believe you can hear me." He spoke calmly with kindness and compassion.

"Remember what Grampa told you that night? 'Allison, you need to have your own light.' You have your light. You are light. You can find your way out of this darkness. If you can't follow *my* voice, follow Saren. She'll guide you out. She's so much like you. She's smart, and she never gives up. I know you're in there. I know you haven't given up."

Allison's gaze remained straight ahead. She didn't respond to Jonathan's reminiscing. He stopped talking and just looked at her. She was still so beautiful, even though her skin was ashen. Her breathing became deeper and deeper, as though she were having an emotion but couldn't let it out.

Steam flowed from her eyes, and a fine mist rose from her arms like sweat. Her clothes were becoming heavy with moisture. Her hair became wet around her temples. He ran into the bathroom and put cold water on a washcloth and brought a dry hand towel.

He washed her face. She felt hot to the touch. He swabbed her arms then dried them. After a few minutes, she began to breath normally again. He let her sit on the sofa while he made dinner.

When he came back to get her, she was gone. He ran upstairs. She had changed into her nightgown and was in the bed, sound asleep.

Her skin was now dry, but a fog hovered over her forehead. He believed it was going away. He considered calling a doctor, but what would he tell them? "A woman in an enchanted cottage is sweating fog?"

Doctors would not be able to help, but this was new. New had to be good. It had to be this grayness trying to leave her. It *had* to be.

He sat down on the other bed in the room and watched her. "Allison, you know what I want. But I never asked you what you wanted. We all just assumed that you wanted to work at Emma's. Your parents assumed you wanted to marry that Mort character. I believed you really wanted to marry me. But did anyone ever ask you what *you* wanted? Did you ever ask yourself what you wanted? What do you want, Allison? Was it this cottage? The way it is, so perfect? Is that what you wanted?

"You have to believe now that you're the most blessed of all God's children. You have come through so much and lived in a miracle for so long. I hope you know how much you're loved not just by us but by God Himself. Whatever you want, God will give it to you. He promised. God cannot break promises. So don't be afraid to come back. Find your light and connect it with God's light, and together you'll find your path back to whatever you want your life to be."

Chapter Twenty-nine

Allison the Gray closed the door behind Saren and Frost. She could see them bouncing across the lawn and over the rock wall then disappearing into the forest. She was excited to have a visitor. She could feel for the first time. She didn't want them to go. She was afraid she would lose herself in shame again once they were out of sight.

She had momentarily forgotten to hide while Saren was there. The girl was so young and cheerful. What had Saren seen on the wall? She didn't think the child had delusions, but what was it? She tried to see it. She touched the wall on one of the spots where Saren had pointed. The wall was rough with texture, but it didn't look different than any other piece of wall.

She stood there, puzzled, frozen in her quandary. She closed her eyes, trying to remember what the girl had called it. *Rainbow...* She tried to remember what a rainbow was. She closed her eyes and saw color—an arch like the one over the garden wall where the dog had jumped over. Yes, it was beautiful. It was full of color. She stood mesmerized by the vision in her mind's eye.

She watched the rainbow get bigger and bigger until it arched over the forest in front of a dark-blue sky. Allison looked down from the rainbow to a rolling sea of blue flowers. The sea of blue flowers like waves unfolded across the expanse and came to rest under Allison's feet. She bent down and picked a tiny blue flower with a yellow center. *A forget-me-not.* She didn't want the vision to stop, so she went to bed and tried to continue it into her dreams.

In the middle of the sea of blue flowers, a light flickered. It was a small, dim light, but it was there. It was her light. Her very own. It wasn't just a flame like from a candle. It didn't need any fuel. It was *alive*. It danced in the blue field, leaping for joy. Sometimes it twirled up into the air so high that it reached the rainbow.

The sun came streaming into the bedroom window. She opened her eyes, expecting to see a dancing flame in a field of blue under a rainbow, but she saw gray, just different variations of gray. The wonder of the long beautiful dream was broken. She was broken. For a while, she had believed she had her light, but it was just a dream. She didn't have a light at all. Colors were just fantasy and imagination.

She sat on the edge of her bed. She had a strange sensation, one she believed she'd never had before. She concentrated on it. For a change, it didn't feel bad. This felt different. It was a question. She waited, wondering if the question would form. It was a question she hadn't thought of before. She wondered what it was going to be. She knew it would come. She waited.

"What do I want?"

Somehow, even though she couldn't remember anything before her dream, she had the distinct feeling she had never asked this question before. *What do I want?*

I want to see color. I want peace from this constant tormenting shame. I want freedom from this limiting world. I want joy. I want... forgiveness.

She looked around at the room. It remained in black and white. She got up and looked out the window. Outside was gray and black and white. She put her head down and slumped. Nothing had changed.

Chapter Thirty

Saren could barely stand it. Her dad had told her they would tell her mother after dinner. "You know she handles things better with food in her belly," he'd said.

So all through dinner, Saren tapped her right foot. She ate very fast, hoping the others would as well. But the adults had the usual pace of eating and conversation. After she finished her last bite, she sat there for thirty seconds of painful impatience. Then she jumped out of her chair.

"I'll do the dishes." She picked up her plate and grabbed up J.D.'s plate too.

"Hey, I was gonna have seconds."

"A diet won't kill any of us for one day," Luke said. "J.D., help your sister with the dishes."

"Do I have to?" He picked up the glasses and moped into the kitchen.

The adults followed suit, taking their dishes to the kitchen counter.

"Maddie, we have something we want to talk to you about," Luke said. He put his arm around her waist to make her feel more comfortable and avoid setting off her internal alarm.

"Really?"

Jonathan followed them back toward the dining room. As he passed through the swinging door dividing the kitchen from the dining room, he mouthed to Saren so J.D. wouldn't hear, "Stay in here until we call you."

"What!" she mouthed back with indignation.

Once the adults were out of the room, she whispered, "Hey, J.D., you want to earn some cookies?"

"Cookies!"

"Shhh, not so loud. This is a secret operation. Do you want to help?"

He bent over and whispered, "Can I be a spy too?"

"Well, you'll be my spy henchman."

"What's that?"

"That's the person who makes the distraction while the spy is spying. See, he's just as important as the spy. Because without him, the spy can't do any spying."

"I don't hear dishes," Madeleine hollered.

"See? You just need to make dish sounds so they won't know that I'm spying. Get it?"

"Yeah, but I don't know how to do dishes."

"That's okay. Just put them in the dishwasher and make dish noises. Got it?"

"Got it."

She sneaked over to the swinging door and cracked it slowly, just enough to hear them.

J.D. dropped a dish.

"Don't break anything," Saren whispered to him.

"Okay," he mouthed back.

"So, Maddie," Luke began, "this is about Allison."

"What about her?" She raised her voice. "What's wrong? Jonathan?"

"Well, about a week ago, as you know, Saren found the cottage," Jonathan said.

"Yes, and... She wasn't supposed to go back there!"

"I know, honey, but..."

"But, but nothing. You know as well as I do that place could be dangerous."

"Creepy, yes. Weird, yes. But nothing bad or dangerous has actually ever happened out there," Jonathan said.

"Honey, Jonathan and I put together a plan so that nothing could happen to Saren. Besides, you know how she is. Do you really think she would have just let it go?"

"No, you're right. So that's where she's been going every day."

"I did have her help out at the shop too. So that was not a *complete* lie. But it *was* a cover," Jonathan said.

"Okay, so what has she found out? Anything we didn't know?"

"Actually, yes. She's gotten farther than anyone else ever has," Luke said.

"And..."

"Today, she actually met Allison."

"What do you mean *met*?"

"Frost jumped over the fence and ran up to Allison. She saw him and then saw Saren. They met. Allison had them in for tea and conversation."

"What! She's back? I was just there day before yesterday; she was unchanged. Wait, why haven't we been over there already? Let's go!"

Saren heard her mom's chair scoot back and clunk.

"Honey, here. Sit back down a minute," Luke said. "She's made progress, but she isn't *back* yet. Jonathan went out there, and she still didn't respond to him. But she's different. We think that's definitely positive. That's why we're telling you now."

"Since she didn't respond to me, we didn't want you to go out there until we were sure she'll see you. It was just too hard on me. So I didn't want you to have to go through that. Okay?"

"Yeah, okay, I understand. So, what now?" She regained her composure.

"Since she's responding to Saren, Jonathan and I think it's time to tell Saren everything. If she's going to really help Allison, she needs to know the whole story. She deserves to know at least what we know."

"Yes, I certainly agree. Saren, can you—"

Saren burst into the dining room instantly and ran to embrace her mother. "Oh, Mom, I hated keeping everything from you. I missed you!"

"Oh, sweetie, I've missed you too, all week."

Saren released her mom and took her spot at the table.

Dishes crashed in the kitchen.

"J.D., you can stop pretending to do dishes now. Go get ready for bed," Luke said.

He ran out of the kitchen with a cookie in each hand and dashed for the stairs.

"Mom, I have so many questions."

"So do I," Maddie said. "It sounds like you've been putting a lot of work into this. So let's start with your questions."

Saren wasted no time. "Who is Allison to us? I found your wedding picture."

"Allison is my older sister. She's three years older than me. We were always very close until that last few months right before she disappeared. Something happened to her, and no one knows what it was."

"Cool, she's my auntie. So why is she at that cottage and not with us or Busy Bea?"

"That was Grandma Emma and Grampa John's cottage. We used to stay with them a lot as children and teens. It was our happy place. I thought it would bring her back to be there. But it didn't. It changed her to gray. When that happened and she was still in a state of walking catatonic, I couldn't take it anymore. I didn't know it at the time, but I was pregnant with you. It was stressing me out. We feared for your safety if I stayed so involved *every* day. We decided that it would be for a happier childhood for you and J.D. if you didn't have to deal with a catatonic auntie that you could never know. So I went to see her a couple of times a week when you were with your dad and then later at school. It was the hardest decision I ever had to make for you not to know her. But we thought it was for the best."

Maddie started to cry.

"Why did the cottage turn her gray? And what is all the magical stuff about around there?"

"Jonathan?" Maddie said through her sobs.

"Well, I told you how we found her. Then came the waiting," Jonathan began.

Thirteen Years Earlier

JONATHAN HAD BECOME increasingly frustrated with the treatment at the psychiatric hospital. All they did was give her drugs that made her sleep. She was already asleep, in a sleep she could not or would not wake up from. Madeleine and Luke went to see her as often as they could, but they were running Emma's Nursery and Tasker Trails Landscape Architecture. Jonathan had refused to leave Allison alone in the hands of strangers. He stayed for all of the visiting hours. The rest of the time, he tried to find out what had happened to her.

Around the time when she'd been in the psychiatric hospital in Utah for six months, Madeleine and Luke came for their routine bi-weekly visit. They sat around in Allison's hospital room, debating what to do next.

"I think we should get her out of here. I don't trust this place. The longer they keep her sick, the more money they make. Why should they cure her? It would be bad for business," Jonathan said.

"Yep, you're right about that one," Luke said.

"But where would she go?" Madeleine asked.

"That's what we have to decide. I don't think she'll ever get better in a hospital. I think she needs to be around people who love her," Jonathan said.

"The logical place is home at Busy Bea's and Father's. But I can't imagine *that* being a healing environment," Madeleine said.

"Plus, they've only come to see her one time since she's been in here," Luke said.

"Yeah, that's out. So, where?" Jonathan asked.

"She could stay with us, but our apartment is too small, and it's on the second floor," Madeleine said.

"Can she do stairs?" Luke asked.

Jonathan shrugged. "I think she could. She walks around okay. And goes to the bathroom on her own."

They all sat in silence and stared at Allison, who stared at nothing.

"It's so weird. Like she can do everything except communicate with other people or maybe even herself. Why won't you talk to us, Allison!"

"Don't go getting upset again, Maddie. That wouldn't be good for you or her," Luke said.

"I'm going to get some snacks," Jonathan announced.

He went down the hall to the lounge, where the vending machines stood like soldiers guarding the Twinkies. As he was looking for Barbecue Lays, Madeleine's favorite chips, one of Allison's nurses came over.

"How are you holding up?" she asked.

"I'm good. Thanks, Beth. Maddie and Luke are here today. It's nice to see them."

"I'll have to stop in and say hello before they leave."

"They would like that. Hey, we're thinking of taking Allison back to SoCal soon. Do you think she'll need twenty-four-hour nursing?"

"Well, I'm just the head RN here. I'm not a doctor. But she eats, goes to the bathroom, and even bathes on her own when we prompt her to. She doesn't have any self-destructive behavior like falling or seizures or anything. I would say that she would need someone to sit her down in front of food and prompted her to brush her teeth and that sort of thing. She would be able to stay on her own for maybe three or four hours at a time. I wouldn't leave her overnight or for long periods, because she would not be able to respond to emergencies, but if someone checked on her at lunchtime, it could be doable. You would just have to see how it goes and make adjustments. But she doesn't really need nursing, just someone to take care of her."

Jonathan retrieved the last of the snacks he needed from the vending machine. "Thank you so much, Beth. We really appreciate your advice."

"No problem. I wish I could do more."

Back in the room, Jonathan passed out the snacks and soda to Maddie and Luke. "Hey, I just talked with Beth. She said that Allison doesn't need nursing, just someone to take care of her. I figured that if we tag teamed it between the three of us, we could do it. We just need a place for her. Obviously, she can't stay at my barn loft. Your place is out. It needs to be somewhere we can be easily all the time, even during business hours." Jonathan walked in a circle, eating hot Cheetos. He ignored Madeleine, who had been trying to get a word in. Finally, he turned around with his mouth full and said, "What?"

"What Beth told you is fantastic news. With that in mind, Luke and I have a solution. I can't believe we didn't think of it before!"

Jonathan looked at her then at Luke. He ate another Cheeto and shrugged. "And?"

"It's so obvious. You don't see it? Come on. What is the most obvious place? It's close to where we all work. It's vacant. We own it. It's Allison's favorite place in the world."

"Grandma Emma's cottage. That's it. Yeah, it's the obvious choice. I can't believe we didn't think of it before."

"Yep, it was left to Allison and me, so no need to get Busy Bea and Father involved."

"Well, aren't they her legal guardians?" Jonathan asked.

Madeleine turned her lips down toward her chin.

"Actually, Mrs. and Mr. Scott signed over authority to Madeleine," Beth said as she entered the room with a clipboard.

"Really! That's shocking," Madeleine said. "Why would they do that?"

"I was the nurse on duty that day. They said that they would not have the time to come here often, but you would, so it was logical."

Allison began shaking her head roughly, and Madeleine ran over and touched her hand. Allison yanked it back as though her touch were hot coals. Then Jonathan tried and got the same reaction.

"Y'all, give her some room. It's obvious she can hear what we're talking about," Luke said.

"Allison?"

As soon as she heard Luke's voice, she calmed down.

"It's working," Beth said.

"Luke's the only one that she didn't have a conflict with right before she vanished," Madeleine whispered.

Luke continued, "We're going to take you home to Grandma Emma's. Maddie and me and Jonathan are going to take care of you. We'll cook the foods you like, and you can just take it easy as long as you need to. We don't have to let Busy Bea come and see you. Okay?"

Allison was calmer now and still. Her breathing was heavy. Beth took her blood pressure. It was slightly elevated. However, after a few minutes she returned to her "normal" catatonic state.

"Yep, we have a decision," Luke said.

"I think it will cure her to go there," Maddie said. "She needs to remember how much she is loved. And how much she was loved before... She'll be cured there. I just know it."

"I believe so too," Jonathan said.

No one could have imagined what would actually happen when Allison arrived at the old Victorian house.

Luke had driven the big four-wheel-drive crew cab from work to Utah. Jonathan sold the old truck he'd bought for getting around Utah. It took them only a few days to orchestrate Allison's release.

Madeleine had brought Allison's favorite colorful floral print dress for her to wear on the trip home. She'd also stopped at the mall and purchased a new pair of pink ballerina flats to go with it.

Luke drove Madeleine, Jonathan, and Allison from the hospital to Grandma Emma's cottage. In the eight-hour drive, not a word was said by anyone. They didn't want to set off an unfortunate event like what had happened at the hospital, but Jonathan knew they each had a hope and prayer the new location would make a difference. A feeling of faith hung in the air, along with the expectation of something magnificent.

The cottage had been uninhabited for more than two years, and had been all but forgotten. No one had the heart to sort through their beloved grandparents' belongings, so when they'd died, the family closed up the cottage as it was. Their grandparents had always used an old dirt road that led from Emma's Nursery to the back door. Madeleine, however, insisted on taking Allison in through the front door because that was how they'd entered as children. Grandma Emma always expected her granddaughters to enter through the front door like important guests.

"Maddie, it's going to be tough to clear that path. No one has used it for over a decade," Jonathan said.

"I know, but it's important. It was a big deal driving through the forest."

"It won't be that bad, Jonathan. We'll stop at the shop and get a couple of machetes."

"We're going to need a bulldozer."

"It'll be fine. Whatever my little lady wants, that's what we are going to do." Luke gave Madeleine a confident and satisfying smile.

"Okay, we'll at least bring an ax. If that will bring her back, I'll cut the whole forest down by hand."

After retrieving the equipment from Emma's nursery, they drove around the base of the hill to the front entrance to the cottage. The wilderness had taken over the entire property. Trees, bushes, and weeds completely crowded the private road to the house. Approaching a faded street sign that read For His Glory Lane, Luke slowed the pickup and signaled to turn. A rusty antique chain stood sentinel over the untamed path. As Jonathan opened his door to get out and move the chain, it fell to the ground of its own accord. That was the first sign of welcome from the cottage.

"That was *weirrrd*," Luke drawled.

"Saves me a trip," Jonathan said, closing the door.

Luke put the truck into four-wheel drive and slowly proceeded over the chain. Madeleine braced herself for a bumpy ride over all kinds of forest vegetation.

Jonathan looked up to Luke for honoring his wife's wishes. He hoped that it comforted her. But this path was full of briars, oak chaparral and waist-high weeds.

Just as the truck wheel neared the first patch of overgrowth, to their shock, the forest opened up in front of them. It was as if some angels were magically preparing the path, creating a soft grassy dirt road with forest folding aside like the parting of the Red Sea.

Jonathan looked over to see Allison's and Madeleine's responses. Madeleine was in awe, completely lost in the moment. Her eyes were wide, and her mouth gaped open. Jonathan began to believe this was all part of some great plan for Allison.

Allison, on the other hand, had no reaction at all. Jonathan came to the conclusion that *this* phenomenon was doing more for Maddie than it was for Allison. If this didn't get Allison's attention, he couldn't wait to see what kind of magnificence it would take to cure her. He had no doubt she would eventually be cured.

"Wow, how is this possible?" Jonathan looked at Luke, the pragmatist of the group.

"I don't know, but it saves us a lot of work." Luke drove on.

They proceeded through the forest miraculously unencumbered.

"Dude, you're going to act like this is normal?" Jonathan asked.

"I didn't read the manual of how to act while driving through an enchanted forest."

"Jonathan, you know he can't take anything seriously." She patted Jonathan on the shoulder from the back seat as he pulled up near where the front gate had once been.

Luke and Jonathan simultaneously exited the vehicle, each with their own task to accomplish. Even though the forest had been mysteriously cleared, they still fully expected to have to chop through six feet of thorns to enter the cottage garden.

Jonathan and Luke had brought giant pruning loppers, an ax, and a machete to hack through the thick roses and bougainvillea that had lined the outside of the rock wall. Now they grew on both sides of the fence and into the break in the wall where the gate and the dilapidated round archway had been. The crimson roses were wild and had mingled with the border bougainvillea. They now closed the entire opening with a mass of thorns, thick vines, and withered, faded roses. The weight of the untamed rose vines had collapsed part of the arch over the gate.

Jonathan could see that coming back there was an emotional affair for Madeleine, and seeing it in ruins added to her heartache. Jonathan had so many amazing memories around this house and garden. And that was just a fraction of the memories Allison and

Madeleine had from their childhood. However, he still felt the love of the grandparents who had taken him in to be part of their family and given him this wonderful opportunity to run their business. He hoped that same love he remembered would bring Allison out of her trance or whatever had separated her from the world.

"Maddie, y'all should just stay in the truck. This is going to take a while," Luke said.

"We should stretch our legs."

Jonathan helped the women out of the truck while Luke headed toward the gate area.

"Faith," Madeleine said. She held her sister by the elbow and looked into her seeing-but-unseeing eyes with a smile. "Allison, it's Grandma's. We've brought you home."

Jonathan could see Madeleine's frustration waning. For the past six months, she'd tried to force Allison to talk, but now she seemed to take a more relaxed approach. Jonathan felt himself relax as well. He knew that God was with her, and whatever was happening was His plan.

Madeleine guided her toward the perfectly round trellis archway and gate that they had been through so many years ago. It had collapsed due to age, rot, and the weight of unpruned roses, but with Allison's first step, the semi-circular archway began to rebuild itself.

Luke was already at the gated archway, about to begin clearing it, when the briars started to shift. He jumped back. Jonathan assumed it was an animal moving the vegetation. But the vines kept moving in the same direction away from the entrance. Maddie watched Luke in confused shock then became engrossed by the moving vegetation. Luke looked back at Maddie and Allison. Unable to speak, he just pointed at Allison.

Madeleine and Allison took another step, and the briars shifted again. Maddie still focused on the moving rosebushes. Jonathan, still a few paces behind the women, was also captivated by the vines. For the moment, he didn't heed Luke's gestured warning.

"Jonathan!" Luke finally said. He held out his whole arm to point at Allison, his hand trembling.

Jonathan looked at Allison from behind. She seemed to be fading. At first, Jonathan was afraid she would disappear. But he soon realized only her color was leaving, not her substance.

Jonathan glanced back and forth between the moving vines and Allison. With each step Allison took, the archway supernaturally reformed itself. The briar cleared a perfect half circle area over the gate. Each thorn vine that cleared drained more color from Allison.

Madeleine couldn't speak. She watched with big eyes as the scene unfolded before her. She still had her by the elbow but hadn't yet looked at Allison. She hadn't realized Allison's transformation into grayscale.

Roses budded and blossomed right before their eyes. By the time Allison reached the gate, the rose trellis and gate were beyond their original beauty that her grandmother would have enjoyed.

"Whoa, Maddie, is this how it looked when you were kids?" Jonathan asked, mesmerized.

"No, this is something else," Madeleine said. She spoke reverently, completely amazed by what was happening. "It's like the glory of God has come to the cottage." Madeleine's voice was full of hope.

"A miracle," Luke said. "But what's up with Allison *the Gray*?"

Madeleine finally looked up at her sister, who stood three inches taller. Allison's face was pale, and her hair had turned from a reddish brown to a faded brownish gray. Her floral print dress and shoes were no longer brightly colored but looked like they had been in the sun for a decade. Madeleine let go of her sister's arm and shrank away from her.

"Oh my... What the... Honey? Jonathan?" Maddie's hopeful expression suddenly changed to horror.

"I don't know. Let's just get her inside. The cottage does seem to want her here, so I'm not going to argue," Luke said.

Jonathan took several deep breaths and prayed that this was all for the good. It had to be. He took Allison's elbow. He didn't want Allison to feel like there was something wrong with her. Maddie had just acted like she had leprosy, and Allison had always been very sensitive to other people's opinions of her. Her reaction to the mention of Busy Bea had sent her into a weird hysteric. From now on, Jonathan was going to make sure nothing and no one upset her. She needed to feel safe and loved.

They slowly walked toward the gate. Even though Jonathan had Allison mainly on his mind, he couldn't help but appreciate the awesome nature of this welcome home for her. The gate itself was in the picket style cut to form a perfect circle with the arch above it. Luscious red roses covered the arch and down to the ground on both sides of the gate.

Hesitantly, Luke reached out to the wooden gate to open it, but before he could touch it, the gate swung open on its own.

Luke waved his hand toward the gate, beckoning them enter.

Jonathan let go of Allison so she could go in first. Allison walked in her dreamlike state through the gate. As she passed through the threshold, her color began to change even more. Her skin turned a sallow gray, and her hair became a shiny, silky silver. As she stepped on the cobblestone path leading to the front door, the garden flourished from wild and unkempt to lush and inspiring. The remnants of Grandma Emma's flower garden mixed with forest wildflowers transformed into a miraculous collection of flowers from different seasons blooming simultaneously. The cottage itself perked up with fresh paint, and yellow light sparked to a glow from deep within it. The whole house and yard looked beyond warm and inviting.

Madeleine, Jonathan, and Luke were awestruck at the marvels of the cottage and in the landscape around them. But they were in shock at a different kind of spectacle when they looked at Allison. Whatever color grew in the yard seemed to have been literally siphoned right out of *her*.

Jonathan could see a terrible panic welling up in Madeleine. Jonathan nodded to Luke toward Maddie.

Luke put his arm around his wife and took his protective stance. "Honey, it's okay. I'm sure this is just part of whatever God is trying to show her or us. If we're going to accept all this beauty, the royal treatment of the forest, house, and garden welcoming Allison, maybe we should not freak out at what adjustments are made *to* Allison. Her color makes it all the more obvious that this is for *her*. Maybe this is something she needs."

"Yeah, you're right. I'm just so scared." She took a deep breath. Involuntary tears streamed from her eyes.

Luke said softly, "Maybe the angels have decided that if she doesn't want to see all this beauty and accept that it's for her, then maybe she needs to be gray for a while."

"Seriously?" Madeleine said.

"Allison *the Gray*," Luke said. "It has a nice ring to it. Let's only hope that she'll become 'Allison the Normal' rather than progressing to 'Allison the White.'"

Madeleine nodded.

"Let's hope she becomes Allison *the Normal*." Jonathan didn't know if he could handle Allison following a shadow monster down an abyss like Gandalf in the *Lord of the Rings*.

Snapping out of Middle Earth, Jonathan followed Allison down the cobblestone pathway through the garden and up the front porch steps.

Jonathan jumped ahead of her to open the door. He pulled out an old-fashioned skeleton key and inserted it into the lock. Luke stepped up onto the porch and looked at him with a questioning look. Jonathan shrugged.

Madeleine expected to do a lot of dusting and washing of linens, but as they entered the house, like the garden, it freshened itself up to the high standards of Grandma Emma herself.

They got Allison settled into bed for the night. Jonathan got established in his new quarters out in Grandma's art studio beyond the kitchen as the evening watch. Then he walked Luke and his very tired bride out to the truck.

By now it was way past dark, but the full moon illuminated the garden, giving it full visibility and an enchanted atmosphere. Arm in arm, the couple reversed their path through the lush lawn and toward the archway of wine-colored roses toward the four-wheel drive. Midway down the path, something moved toward them.

"Maddie, Jonathan, look," Luke whispered intensely.

A pair of yellow eyes with long vertical pupils floated smoothly to the top of the large solitary rosebush in the center of the lawn. The eyes seemed to rise out of the shadows, and a shadowy shape formed. It was a black snake, and it hissed then slithered up to face them. It stuck out its tongue to taste the air, seeming to sense their fear. "Sssshe'sss lossst." It tilted its head, looking sinister and satisfied.

Madeleine screamed and jumped hysterically. Luke grabbed Maddie by the hand, and they ran out of the garden. Instinctively rather than from fear, Jonathan followed. They hadn't seen the body because of the darkness of the night, but by the motions it made, they could tell that it was a sizable snake—a big talking snake.

Once outside the gate, Luke asked, "Did that snake have a French accent? Or am I hearing and seeing things?"

"It did," Jonathan said.

"Creepy," Luke said.

Safely inside the truck, Madeleine was still shaking. She looked back at the round trellis and gate as her husband closed her door. The gate had disappeared, and the rock wall continued as if a gate had never existed. The roses closed up the archway, creating a new and impenetrable wall.

"Luke, oh, we've got to get her out of there."

"You stay in the truck. We got this."

Jonathan was already pulling two sets of loppers out of the truck bed. "I guess we'll need these, after all," Jonathan said. He tossed one of the loppers to Luke.

"Unfortunately." Luke skillfully caught the tool with one hand.

They retrieved the machete and the ax from the bed of the truck and made their way to the wall where the gate had stood only moments before. They hacked and slashed at the thorns at the front gate area to no avail. It was as if they were made of steel. After fifteen minutes of no progress, Luke's machete broke in half.

"Holy smokes!" Luke said.

"Wow, this isn't working."

"Let's try the back way. It was clear when we checked from the courtyard."

They ran to the truck to get the extra axe.

"Maddie, we're going to try the back entrance. Stay put, okay?" Luke gave her a kiss through the window, then he and Jonathan sprinted to the back of the cottage.

It was grown up back there, too, but the thorn vines weren't as thick. They snipped and hacked. The vines cut, but they grew back just as fast. They cut and cut and hacked and hacked. After about fifteen minutes of hacking, the vines eventually stopped growing back. They broke through to the other side with a narrow path only a foot wide. Jonathan, being smaller than Luke, squeezed fearlessly through the opening. He hoped it wouldn't close back up with him inside, but quite the opposite happened. Once Jonathan stepped foot on the grass beyond the thorns, the gatekeeping briars relaxed and cleared a wide path for him.

"Thank you," Luke said to the thorny shrubbery. He bowed to it as if it were a valiant opponent then stepped through the opening.

Inside the backyard, Johnathan and Luke both took a breather and wiped sweat from their faces. Once their breathing quieted, they began to hear what sounded like tiny voices saying "Hurray, hurray!" and tiny hands applauding. They shined their flashlights down at the ground.

Flowers of all varieties lined the walkway and filled the flowerbeds around the house. Their little leaves clapped, and their petals formed mouths chanting, "Hurray, hurray!"

Jonathan and Luke looked at each other with astonishment. Neither of them wanted to be the first to admit the flowers were cheering for them. Jonathan knew Luke was a skeptical and pragmatic kind of guy. This would be hard for him to accept. Jonathan, on the other hand, took things as they came. He always believed that good things were about to happen. Most of the time, they did.

"Well, well, I've been talking to plants for all these years, but this is the first time they ever talked to me." Jonathan smiled at the little flowers. Looking at the group of daffodils, he asked, "Who *are* you? What's happening here?"

A hundred little voices sang in unison, sounding like miniature chimes, "Don't be afraid. She's safe here. She's loved here."

"What about that evil-looking snake in the front garden?" Luke asked.

"No place on Earth is completely safe from evil," they said. "God is here for her as He is for all of us. She has free will, just like us."

"So what do *we* do?" Jonathan asked, hoping these miracle voices would end this nightmare.

"Just like always, Jonathan. We all must work out our own salvation."

"It definitely looks like God is doing His part," Jonathan said.

"Unfortunately, the enemy may be as well," Luke said.

Jonathan looked down at the flowers to ask another question. "So..."

But the flowers no longer appeared animated. They were now just silent, beautiful flowers.

"Allison..." Luke said.

Jonathan ran to the back door. He fiddled with the skeleton key and gained access. They barreled through the house and bounded up the stairs. On the second-story landing, they slowed down and crept down the balcony hallway and into the bedroom.

The moonlight streamed in through the lace curtains and shimmered on Allison's newly silvered locks. Everything in the cottage was quiet. The men both took a huge breath of relief and headed downstairs and back out the back door.

Luke shined his flashlight apprehensively at the flowerbed.

"It's okay," Jonathan said. "That really *did* happen. You're not imagining things."

"So, what do we do now?" Luke asked.

"We trust the flowers." Jonathan spoke with confidence.

Luke chuckled. "Yeah, it sounds crazy, but yeah. Maddie won't be happy. She only saw the negative side of this place."

"Luke, buddy, I'm glad you're the one that gets to explain it to her."

"Thanks a lot."

"Well, just look at it like this. The forest and garden welcomed her and protected her."

"Yeah, from us."

"Maybe it wanted to see how much we would be willing to do to protect her. It's fine now. See?"

They walked back and forth through the cleared briar hedge.

"Okay, well, you keep these. Just in case it changes its mind by morning." Luke handed Jonathan the loppers.

Jonathan took them and nodded. Then he headed back into the cottage while Luke returned to his wife waiting in the truck. Jonathan ran up to the tower office to watch Luke and Maddie leave the forest safely. The tower office had been Grandma Emma's office. It really should have been called the crow's nest, sitting high above the forest and cottage. The lights of Emma's nursery were visible from up there, along with much of the edge of the city and neighboring properties.

As Luke drove the truck back out of the forest to the main road, the forest grew wild again behind them. When they turned onto the paved road, the rusty gate replaced itself as the western guardian over Allison.

Chapter Thirty-one

S aren had been completely absorbed in Jonathan's narrative. "So, then what happened? Did the bushes grow back overnight?"

"Actually, they did grow back, but not as much. Each time, they grew back a little bit less over the course of a month."

"So that's how you knew that the vegetation would chill out after a while."

"Yes, but it only took a couple of days for you. And it had helped you too."

"Yes, it did. So, what happened after that? Mom, did you ever go back into the cottage?"

"Yes, I did after a few days. I had to make sure she bathed and brushed her teeth and things like that. But it really freaked me out. Those talking flowers. I didn't like it. It was always so unsettling. I never went anywhere near the *front* yard again."

"Is that why you didn't want me to go there?"

"Yes. I was afraid. So eventually, I went to the cottage less and less, and Jonathan did more and more, because it was just so upsetting. She didn't improve much past eating, bathing, and dressing herself. I missed my big sister. I didn't want to be a depressed kind of mom. So I checked on her a couple of times a week, and we all found a way to separate our daily life from her in our own way. I soon found out I was pregnant with you. So your father and I tried to focus on the joy that you have always brought us, and Jonathan focused on the Sprouts."

"That's basically everything that we know. Saren, you have found out more than anyone has before," Luke said.

"It's way past your bedtime. I'll fill your mom in about what you have found out so far. Okay?"

"Okay, Dad. I'm so glad I don't have to keep secrets from Mom anymore. Mom, you're not going to stop me from going there, are you?"

"Could I stop you short of locking you in your room?"

"No way."

"We don't want to teach you to hide or lie. So you'll continue the schedule as you have been. We'll talk more tomorrow."

Saren said goodnight to Uncle Jonathan. That night, she dreamed of going to the ice cream shop with her Auntie Allison.

Chapter Thirty-two

Saren woke up an hour before her normal time. Her dad had already left for work, her mom was in her home office, and J.D. was still asleep. She took Frost out for a short morning walk.

As Saren entered the house, Madeleine called down from her loft office. "Saren, come up here, honey."

Saren loved her mother's voice. It was like a fresh spring of cool water flowing over her in summer, like a big comforting relief.

Frost's tags jingled as he raced Saren up the stairs. It was funny how such a small dog sounded like a stampede of paws.

As long as Saren could remember, her mom had been keeping books for the nursery business. Even when Madeleine was a child, Emma had her counting the money and recording it in the account book at the end of the day, the way it was done before computers.

Saren had heard many stories about Grandma Emma being a real stickler for details. She literally reconciled everything and inventoried everything. Her mom always said that the inventory drove Grandpa John nuts. He'd always said to her, "Didn't God chastise David for taking a census? How do you know we're not going to get punished for all this counting?"

"Don't pay any attention to him, puddin'. We women know that without us, the men would give away all their money or let it blow away in the wind," Grandma Emma would always say.

Saren caught her mom smiling as she finished entering in the last bill.

She clicked "save backup" and grabbed the last envelope to stuff with a check. "Perfect timing. I just finished."

"Oh good. I wanted to talk to you about Auntie Allison."

Her mom's smile faded. "Okay, shoot." She leaned back in her chair.

Saren sat on the edge of the guest chair. "Mom, what do you know about that Professor Mort, Dr. Death?"

"Well, I don't know that much actually."

"Anything, even something small, may end up being the key."

"Well, okay. Let's see. The first time I remember hearing about him was from Busy Bea. She'd just gotten back from visiting Allison at school, and she and Father had attended a gala. She went on and on about Allison dating this professor. I was shocked because Allison had been in love with Jonathan for years. I expected that, eventually, they would get married. But Busy Bea never wanted her to be with Jonathan. So she insisted that Allison go out with this professor."

"So, that's why Uncle Jonathan is so involved with this?"

"Yes. He still loves her and believes that she loves him."

"So why did she go out with that professor if she was in love with Uncle Jonathan?"

"Well, you have to understand Allison. My mother always had this hold on her. Like she was going to make her this perfect, perfect child."

"Gosh, so how did that make Auntie Allison feel?"

"Miserable. She never seemed to have any peace. The second she did one thing to please Busy Bea, she would have her do something else. Then Allison would just try harder the next time."

"So did she do that to you too?" Saren was filled with compassion for her auntie and her mom.

"Well, she tried, but I had the benefit of watching her do it to my older sister, so I just refused. I would disappear and go hang out with Grandma Emma. Busy Bea couldn't push her mom around, so I was safe. But Allison, she'd already been programmed like that from birth. So when Busy Bea insisted, she eventually gave in."

"Even when it came to her own love life?"

"Yes, even then. You see, Busy Bea was relentless in her attack on Jonathan. She didn't want Allison to have anything to do with Jonathan from the first day he came to work at Emma's."

"But, Mom, that doesn't make any sense. Everyone loves Uncle Jonathan. Why doesn't she like him?"

"That, you would have to ask Busy Bea yourself. I would have asked her if I thought she would tell me the truth. At first, I thought she was prejudiced, but now I think it was more of a status thing for her to get in the good graces of Grandma Scott."

"Oh." Saren considered this information for a moment. "So, what else do you know about Dr. Death?"

"Well, the only time I ever saw him was at our wedding. During the months leading up to the wedding, I didn't see Allison much. She was at college. She even stopped calling me on a regular basis—and Jonathan too. It seemed like Dr. Death didn't want her to talk to us. I got mad at her because she didn't come home and help with the wedding. I took it personally. But during the reception, Allison starting acting like her old self again, and it felt like it used to, being with her. We were very close up until this Dr. Death."

"Something must have happened at the wedding. Why don't you have any wedding pictures around the house ever?"

Madeleine looked down and closed her eyes. Finally, she looked at Saren with sad eyes. "We got married at Emma's and had the reception in the tree section. We were all having such a great time. Then Busy Bea came over and told Allison she was neglecting her date. Next thing I knew, she was dancing with Dr. Death. But after only half of a song, we saw them walking into the darkness toward the greenhouses. After a while, when they didn't come back, Jonathan and Luke and I went to look for them. We split up. Luke headed to the barn and Jonathan to the office. I was looking in the parking lot to see if his car was gone, but it was still there. Suddenly, your dad came running to get me. He said that he saw Allison running from the back greenhouse and into the barn by herself. So we both ran back to the barn. Your dad stayed at the bottom of the stairs while I went up into Jonathan's loft to get her.

"I found her in the bathroom, cleaning blood off of her dress and crying hysterically. I asked her what was wrong. She wouldn't say. I think she didn't want to ruin my wedding. She said that she'd started her period and it got on her dress. I bought the excuse. Then we got into a fight about why she hadn't helped with the wedding like she said she would. I was horrible and selfish. It wasn't until the next day when we were on our honeymoon that I realized that she had her period when she arrived home the week before the wedding and was relieved that it was over in time to fit into her bridesmaid dress. So the blood had to be from something else."

"You mean you think she was... abused?"

"Yes, something that she didn't want to happen happened. Something that she'd been saving for marriage had been taken from her. Anyway, that's what I think. I have no proof other than what I saw. If I had handled the situation with more compassion, maybe none of this would have happened. I was too selfish and thought only of my own happiness at a time when she really needed me."

"Oh, Mom." Saren ran around the desk to hug her mom.

"Remember what Dad always tells us that other people's bad behavior should not affect *our* unity."

"Yes, that's why he always says that. We weren't united, and we know what it costs us."

"We are united now."

"We almost are. We need Allison back to be fully united."

"I can't wait to see her today!"

"You'll get there a little early this afternoon. You have a dentist appointment, so I'll pick you up right after lunch, okay?"

"Cool. This is the first time I'm glad for a dentist appointment."

They both chuckled and headed down to make breakfast.

Chapter Thirty-three

Jonathan had a wonderful optimistic feeling that something was just about to change. He wanted to run around and sing, but he had to go through his day like every other day. "Okay, Logan, you and Oliver go fertilize the palms. Remember, just the right amount. Too much does what?"

"Burns the roots and wastes resources," they said in a singsong unison.

"Yes. Off you go."

He watched the two lanky teenage boys plod off toward the tree section.

Saren and Madeleine strolled through the colorful display area to meet up with Jonathan.

"Well, well, what a pleasant surprise. You're here early," Jonathan said. He squatted to pet the Frostie Dog. "How are my favorites?"

"We're good." Saren gave her signature leap and twirl.

"Hi, Jonathan, I came to talk to you because I wanted to let you know that I told Busy Bea. So..." Madeleine said.

"So, I should keep an eye out for flying objects."

"What? Why?" Saren asked.

"To see if she's flying in on her broom." With a chuckle, Jonathan picked up Saren's floppy hat and put it back down again.

"Something like that," Madeleine said. "She and Father are supposed to come over for dinner."

"I'll stay clear." Jonathan turned his attention to Saren. "Hey, what are you doing here so early?"

"Dentist appointment." Saren smiled to show him all her teeth and gave a thumbs-up.

Jonathan gave her a smile and a nod.

"Well, if you don't mind, I'll leave her here early. I have to go pick up J.D."

Jonathan patted Saren on the shoulder. "She can be here *whenever* she wants."

"Okay, you be safe at the cottage. Watch for snakes."

"Got it, Mom."

Almost before Madeleine had taken a few steps, Saren began jumping up and down, and so did Frost.

"Okay, Tigger, what?"

Saren calmed down and gave Jonathan her serious detective expression. "Uncle Jonathan, Mom told me about the wedding and Dr. Death being there and that Alli... Auntie Allison was upset in your loft. But where did you go? Where was Dr. Death at that time?"

"Oh, yeah. Good question. I went to the shop to look for Allison, but instead, I found Dr. Death sneaking around in the crow's nest, looking through Grampa John's research files."

"Really, wow. Why? What was he looking for?"

"I don't know. We thought maybe he was trying to steal some research. I could never prove that he got away with any, though. He disappeared the same time Allison did."

"Did his family come looking for him?"

"Not that we ever knew of. It never hit the papers or anything. He was just gone. Dr. Bluff got a letter from the president of the university asking him to fill in for his classes because he was on an extended leave from the university. But he never came back."

Saren had looked away from him. He turned around to see Officer Frank Brennen approaching in full uniform.

"Hi, there. How is our miniature detective?" Officer Brennen said.

"Hi, Frank." Jonathan shook the officer's hand.

"Hi, Officer Brennen. I'm good," Saren said.

"You haven't been by the office yet. How is your investigation going?"

"We have some new developments." Saren sounded very professional. She didn't know she was small any more than Frost did.

"Is there anything I can help you with?" Officer Brennen asked her.

"Can you find people?"

"We have resources for that. So, maybe. Do you have a computer hooked to the internet? I could log in, and we can see what we can find together."

"Sure, in the crow's nest." Jonathan led him back to the shop and offices.

Once logged in, Officer Brennen asked, "Okay, what's the name?"

"Lisa Lovelace," Saren said. "She was Allison's roommate when she disappeared. Her mom, Betty, told me that she'd been seeing Allison's fiancé behind her back, and then she vanished and has never been found."

"Oh, no. That's why Lisa never called me back."

Officer Brennen clicked on the computer.

While Officer Brennen searched, Saren began poking through old research files.

"What are up to now, young one?"

"Clues." Saren closed a file drawer and paused with her hand on another one. "Uncle Jonathan, which files did you catch Dr. Death looking at?"

"Well, it would have been in this drawer over here. Let me see."

Saren stepped back and waited impatiently.

He looked for ones that were recently dated to just prior to Dr. Death's and Allison's disappearances.

Officer Brennen suddenly clapped his hands together, startling Saren and waking up the Frostie Dog. "Here we are—a file on Lisa Lovelace. Yes, her case is still open and unsolved. It doesn't have many notes here. I just requested that the Utah authorities send me the original file. I'll do some more digging when I get back to the precinct. Great job, Saren. You're a natural."

"Thank you, Officer Brennen."

"You're more than welcome. I would love to crack this case with you, Saren."

Saren beamed a proud smile. "It seems like Allison's and Lisa's cases could be related. Don't you think, Officer Brennen?"

"It certainly does. By combining the information that we have for each person, we may be able to put together what happened to them."

"Okay, here it is. These are the last research results before the disappearances." Jonathan pulled a file out of the file cabinet and handed it to Saren.

"Artificial photosynthesis," Saren said.

"Hmm." Officer Brennen began clicking on the keyboard again. He spoke while typing. "Well, since I saw you last, Jonathan, I did some research on Mortimer Hebert. He really did vanish. There are no records of him after he left the university. He must have changed his name or died mysteriously." He lifted his hands from the keyboard and looked up. "Bad guys usually don't die." He resumed typing and talking. "Now, we know he was looking for files about artificial photosynthesis."

"Yes," Saren said.

Officer Brennen continued to click for a few more seconds. "Found him."

"You're kidding," Jonathan said.

"A Professor Bert Mortamer of the University of Lisbon has published several journal articles on artificial photosynthesis. Is this him?" He showed Jonathan a fuzzy black-and-white photo on the screen.

"I can't believe it. Yes. That's definitely him."

"Great. Okay. We're getting somewhere."

"Yeah!" Saren jumped up and twirled.

"Wow." Jonathan sat down and relaxed his shoulders.

Officer Brennen wrote a few notes on his pad. He stood up and replaced his notepad into its pouch on his belt. "I am heading straight back to the precinct to get cracking on this case. We really have something to go on now."

"Yeah!" Saren jumped and twirled again.

"Oh yeah, did you find what you were looking for at the nursery?" Jonathan asked.

"I did actually. I came to see you and Saren. I was in the neighborhood and decided to stop in."

"Wow, well, thank you," Jonathan said.

"We have a good start. I hope I find out more."

"I know you will," Saren said.

Jonathan and Saren waved goodbye to Officer Brennen. Sensing that Saren was itching to return to Allison, he released her to go. "You're free now, Saren."

"Thanks, see you later, Uncle Jonathan."

He watched her long hair swing back and forth under her hat as she jogged past the greenhouses and out of sight with Frost charging ahead.

Chapter Thirty-four

All morning at school then at the dentist's office, Saren contemplated how to go about finding out what had made Allison sad. The only way she could think of was to ask her—but she wondered if that was polite.

Saren settled on not asking directly because she didn't want Allison to get that feeling that the church ladies gave people when they pretend to be concerned, like: "Oh, Sister Whoever, you look tired. Is everything all right?"

They tended to do that when someone was looking particularly pretty and happy, and not at all tired. Many of the women would walk away looking drawn and tired because they believed the troublesome church ladies.

Saren had her suspicions about what had made Allison sad, but what she thought really didn't matter. She needed to know what Allison thought. She would focus on this goal.

She decided that girl talk would be better. After finding a topic, she would ask Allison how she felt about things in their conversation. Then she could ask if it made her glum. It would be fun to use the word *glum*, because it seemed to go with the antique Victorian setting and the formal style of Allison's speech.

Saren was beginning to look forward to the conversation and was determined to find a way to make it fun. If she had fun, maybe Allison would have fun too. Saren didn't dwell on troubling things, and she couldn't imagine hanging out with someone who was melancholy all the time. Now she knew that Allison hadn't always been a forlorn or sorrowful person.

With her strategy settled, Saren arrived at the enchanted cottage as Allison was finishing up her rose pruning for the day and, as usual, dripping blood on the green grass. Saren tried to avoid looking at the rosebush because it gave her such a twinge of pain to see all the beautiful flowers littering the lush lawn. The roses would grow back by tomorrow, so all was not lost. She wondered if anyone could really answer the question of how that worked.

She also avoided looking because she didn't want to attract the attention of the snake. She had a theory that if she didn't pay attention to him or even think of him, he wouldn't exist for her—and so he did not. As she was approaching the rock wall, a thought suddenly came to her.

Wait! She was reminded of the scripture she'd learned from Sunday school in Philippians 4:8 "Whatever is true, whatever is noble, whatever is right, whatever is pure, whatever is lovely, whatever is admirable—if anything is excellent or praiseworthy—think about such things and the God of peace will be with you."

That's it! Saren thought as her eyes widened. *I don't need to know what happened to Allison or why she's sad, and she doesn't need to care either. She needs to think about what is true, noble, right, pure, lovely, and admirable.*

"Hi, Miss Allison," Saren hollered with enthusiasm. She and Frost trotted through the tall grass toward the rock wall. Sitting on the wall, she swung her legs over and bounced through the round trellis. Even though the wall was four times his height, Frost jumped on top of the wall, wagged a few wags, and bounced off. He ran right up to Allison, looking for his greeting, and wagging so intensely, his tail reminded Saren of hummingbird wings. She wondered if Frost would take to the air like a fluffy bird if he changed the direction of his wag.

Allison looked down curiously at Frost. When she squatted, her taffeta rustled like old newspapers blowing in the wind. She took his face in both her hands and scratched behind both his ears, seemingly captured by the dog's gaze. Saren thought for a moment that she saw a smile twinkle across Allison's eyes, but her face refused to concur.

Finally, Allison broke herself away and turned her attention to Saren, showing a tinge of surprise, "Why are you smiling?"

"Frost likes you. He usually doesn't let anyone hold onto him for that long without getting bored and trying to get away. But he would have let you as long as you wanted."

"Really?" Allison slowly stood and resumed her tortured countenance.

"Come in, Saren. It's time for tea." She turned slowly on her heel, and with a swish of her skirt and petticoat, she was headed toward the front porch.

Saren followed Allison and Frost into the grand foyer, through the parlor, dining room and into the sunlit white kitchen.

This time Allison didn't tell her to sit. She must have assumed that she would follow the previous day's protocol.

She watched Allison fill the white porcelain teakettle with water from the tap. "Do you have a well here, or are you on city water?" Everyone in Southern California used bottled water unless they were on a well or had their own filtering system. Because of the drought, the city water had to be shipped in from far away and tasted of rusty pipes and swimming pool water. But the tea had tasted delicious, so they must have a special filter for the water.

Allison looked perplexed. "I *really* don't know." Saren thought it odd that the woman of the house would not know from where the water came.

She decided on another subject to break the ice. "What is your favorite color?" This was a typical question that twelve-year-olds would ask each other.

"I don't know." Allison spoke in a serenely monotone manner.

"Is it gray?"

How was she going to find out anything if she could not even find out her favorite color?

"You like gray, right? All your clothes are gray. That outfit is so beautiful. When I first saw it, I thought it was gray calico cotton, but when I finally got to meet you, I discovered that it was a calico taffeta print with a lace petticoat. Wow!" Saren said with her best girl-talk chatty demeanor.

"Really, it's beautiful?" An empty teacup made a tinkle as it hit the saucer and another as Allison placed the set on the tray.

"Oh yes, I know I'm a kid and haven't seen everything but I've never seen anything like it. Where did you get it from?"

"I don't know?" Allison said, looking even more tormented.

This conversation was not going anywhere. Saren got the impression that she was throwing salt on an open wound. She wasn't sure if Allison wanted to talk at all. She would ask something Allison would have to answer—then not talk until she did. Yep. That should work, so she looked around for some topic of conversation.

Allison picked up the tray and carried the teapot and two cups and saucers over to the white kitchen table and gently set them down.

Motioning to Saren to sit, she poured the tea. After passing the full teacup to Saren, she took her own place, but this time she sat next to Saren rather than at the head of the oval table. She faced the bay window, looking at the closed winter-white roman shade. She looked at it but didn't see it. Her eyes were far off like she was searching a field for a lost puppy.

She leaned in toward Saren and said in almost a whisper, "I'm sorry. I sound very rude. The truth is that *I do not know*. I can't remember much before I saw you yesterday."

Allison put her head down in sorrow.

"Wow! What can you remember?" Saren asked. She tried her hardest to express kindness and patience.

"I know I've been in this place for a very long time. So long, in fact, that I was not sure if I was still alive or dead and in some kind of Hell, or maybe I was a ghost haunting this house. Saren, am I a ghost?" She'd lowered her voice for the last question to an almost inaudible level, like she feared the other ghosts would hear her.

"Of course you're not a ghost," Saren whispered, then realizing whispering was not necessary, she spoke in a normal voice. "Miss Allison, you're alive and well. You may have lost your memory, but you are most definitely alive."

"How can you be so sure?"

"If you can fog a mirror, will you believe that you're alive?"

"Yes. That would be a clever test."

"If you fog the mirror, will you tell me the last thing you remember? Maybe together we can figure out what is going on with you."

"Yes, yes, I would like that." Allison replied with a near-Victorian formality that suited the surroundings.

"Where's the closest mirror?"

"I don't know." This time, Allison sounded less ashamed and added the first hint of curiosity to her voice.

"Okay, well, there has to be one around here somewhere." Saren was excited to explore the rest of the house.

Saren grabbed Allison by the hand and towed her to the only door leading out of the kitchen other than the one she came in through. She figured it had to lead to a hallway and eventually a bathroom that contained a mirror.

Opening the door, Saren found an indoor courtyard full of statues, fountains, flowers, and flowering trees in beautiful porcelain pots. The soft flow of the water in the fountains ran together like a refreshing symphony. Even though she was tempted to catalog the contents of the courtyard, Saren stayed on task.

To the left was a passageway that led outside to the sweet-pea-covered back porch. Across through the fountain area, she could see rooms lining the far side of the courtyard, each with plate glass windows for walls on the courtyard side. She headed first for the one the farthest from the back of the house. It had to be one with a bathroom inside, and it was also the biggest.

Upon entering it, she was overwhelmed by the aroma of oil paint and saw that it was the art studio she had come through when she broke into the tower. She looked at the open window for the talking jay, but all she heard were regular bird tweets in the distance.

With Allison's hand still in hers, she pulled her into the next doorway at the back of the studio. It was a half bathroom with only a toilet and pedestal sink with a gorgeous antique mirror over it.

"Here you are, Miss Allison." When Saren pulled the string on the roman-style shade, a glorious stream of sunshine illuminated the small washroom. "Go for it."

Allison approached the mirror as if it were a ferocious tiger that hadn't been fed. She put her mouth as close as she could without touching the mirror and gave out a long huff. The fog on the mirror hung thick and moist.

Saren rushed over and drew a smiley face on the fog. "Yep, you're really here. Let's go finish our tea before it gets cold."

Allison nodded. They made their way back through the courtyard and found their seats at the kitchen table. Comfortably seated and sipping lukewarm tea, Allison began with what she did know.

"I remember my grandfather. He owned a nursery. As a child, I wanted to study horticulture to help Grampa with his business. I stayed with him at work all the time, talking to the plants. My grandfather had a helper, a boy that lived in the barn. I remember being very fond of him. Yes, there's something about a little girl about your age being there too... Maybe it was a sister. I remember love."

These sounded like impressions rather than memories. She had to literally bite her tongue to keep from telling Allison about Uncle Jonathan and her mom to turn them into real memories, but she knew Allison had to remember for herself. Saren reminded herself to be patient.

"The next thing I remember, I'm in a small, bare dark room with a single light above me. I'm sitting in the chair, and three faceless men in dark suits, white shirts, and dark ties are standing around me, accusing me of something I did but didn't want to do and had no choice in doing, but I'm not sure. I felt hopelessly ashamed and damned.

"Then I remember being here, every day being the same, wearing the same clothes. And everything being gray. Most of the time, there's nothing but a gray haze except trying to trim that rosebush correctly and failing." Allison put her head down.

"Miss Allison, why did you think you failed at trimming the rosebush?"

"Because he tells me it's not right."

"Who is he?" Saren asked.

"The snake in the garden. Have you seen him?"

"Yes, both Frost and I have. He looked at us one day, and we got so creeped out that we nearly ran all the way home." Saren wanted to keep her side of the story short. She was far more interested in what Allison had to say.

Allison tore her gaze from the window blind and looked at Saren. "Saren, be careful with him. You're so strong and confident—I don't want you to ever lose herself like I have."

"Did you talk to the snake?"

Saren's eyes widened. "No, we were too busy high-tailing it. That's no regular snake. Average snakes don't talk or give girls and fluffy dogs the evil eye. That snake is clearly a demon or the devil himself. The devil only has three things he wants to do: kill, steal, and destroy. He definitely doesn't want to make rosebushes prettier. He would rather destroy them." Saren took a sip of tea and continued. "But those roses come back every day. Someone upstairs is regrowing them to show that demon snake and us that destruction has not won and that the snake won't win. I think it's to show you, Miss Allison. Those roses are like Jesus. He rose from the dead and defeated the devil and death. Jesus has already conquered the devil. You don't remember because you forgot everything.

"He has not managed to kill you, Miss Allison. He stole your peace. I believe with all my heart that if you get away from that snake's influence and focus on good things that Jesus has done, your memory and mind will come back to you."

"You really believe that?" Allison expressed her first sign of hope.

"Yes, I know it."

"You sound so confident." Allison looked down like she was going to drown in her tea again.

"My mom always reminds me about what it says in Philippians: 'We put no confidence in human effort. Instead, we boast about what Jesus Christ has done for us.'"

"Jesus?" Allison asked, somewhat snapping out of her inward persecution.

"Yeah, Jesus. He'll show you a way to remember if you want to. Look at what Jesus has done for you already. You live in this miraculous cottage. All you need to do is look around, and you'll see what He's done for you. Besides, why do you care what a creepy snake thinks anyway? That snake is just an evil poopy head. It's only Jesus you need to please. Miss Allison, promise me you won't talk to that snake or listen to him anymore."

"Yes, but what if I forget? I can't even remember who Jesus is."

Saren, unshaken by the admission, took Allison by the hand and led her to the parlor, where the huge, ornately decorated family Bible sat on the antique coffee table. She opened it up to the first scripture that she'd learned when she was given her first Bible.

Saren remembered finding her white Bible in the bottom dresser drawer. It had kiddy scribble in pink marker all over some of the pages. She was in kindergarten, but could already read her favorite books. She'd grabbed the Bible and thumbed through it to find several childlike pictures of familiar stories. Now that she could read on her own, she wanted to read for herself, but the Bible was so big, she didn't know what to read first.

After some contemplation, she took the Bible to her mother, who was sewing a new dress for her.

"Mommy, what should I read in this?"

"John 3:16. Here, let me see it." Madeleine stopped her sewing machine and took the Bible from Saren. She thumbed through the Bible then held it out to Saren, pointing to a passage. "See, John chapter 3, verse 16. Read that first."

Saren had spent the next several days reading it over and over until she knew it by heart. If Allison didn't remember Jesus, she should start like a little child. Saren quickly flipped to John 3:16 and pointed to the spot. "Miss Allison, read this verse right here."

Allison began to read, "For God." She looked over at Saren with a small gleam, showing that she was relieved she remembered how to read. "For God so loved the world that He gave His only begotten Son, for whosoever shall believe in Him shall not perish but have everlasting life."

Allison looked at Saren with wonder, her cloudy eyes swirling quickly. "Is that true?"

"Yes, he loves us, and we get to live forever too."

"Wow, God loves us?" Allison spoke with astonishment.

"Yes, Miss Allison. He loves us so much. I think he even loves you more, because you have a miracle garden. Your roses regrow every morning, even though evil cuts them down every afternoon. I'm not sure you realize it, but that's not normal. That's a miracle."

Allison looked up from the Bible and gazed outside. The sunlight was beginning to fade.

"Miss Allison, can you promise me you won't go out to the rose-bush tomorrow to trim it, at least not until I get here after school? There's definitely something malevolent about that talking, evil-eye-giving snake. We better get going, but I would feel a lot better if I knew you weren't talking to that snake by yourself."

"I'm surprised you actually believe that snake talks to me."

"Why wouldn't I believe you? The snake talked to Eve in the Garden of Eden, so why not here? Plus, this place is like the Garden of Eden. Maybe all Gardens of Eden come with talking snakes. Also, please think all night long about how much God loves you until I see you in the tomorrow."

Chapter Thirty-five

Allison watched Saren and Frost trot down the path through the little grove, under the tunnel of crimson roses, and over the rock wall. All the other days, she would have continued on her day of mindlessness. But today, she was still astonished by the newfound information that God loved her. She'd avoided thinking about God for so long. But now, with this Good News, she wanted to know more about God's love.

She stood staring at the closed door and looked out the stained-glass window. Then she thought about the snake and turned around. She was still in a contemplative daze, but this was a vast improvement over her usual thoughtless trance.

As she lingered in the foyer with her back to the door, her gaze drifted upward, and she saw a painting high above the archway that led to the den and eventually to the courtyard beyond the kitchen. She'd seen the painting many times, but this time, she really studied it. The painting featured a thick book with a light shining down from it like sunrays on a path where a woman's feet were starting up the path lit from the book.

She decided to examine this book. She'd learned about God's love from a book. This one seemed familiar. The pages had shiny edges, and it was bound in light-gray leather. Unrecognizable words rose from the pages. Words shined rays down, illuminating the dark forest path right up to a girl's boots.

"Wait!" Allison said, even though no one else was there. She was not in the habit of talking to herself. She first peered left into the parlor at the Bible on the antique coffee table, then back at the painting.

"It can't be." The Bible in the painting was identical to the one on the coffee table. The painted Bible had visible rays coming up out of the Bible with a phrase or sentence lifted off the page in the painted Bible, but it was unreadable.

She noticed the feet wore Dr. Marten boots like the ones she wore, but with the tops covered by pale-yellow lace. It was a soft, pleasing light color. It was definitely color. She was excited for a moment. She could see the color yellow. She could see a color. She considered her own feet and saw that her boot tops were covered by light-gray lace. The difference was subtle yet clear. She considered her own lace.

Hmm, the only difference is I'm all gray. For the first time, she had a hope that she would see color again. Maybe even be colorful herself. She walked through the rest of her day looking forward rather than down.

"What else have I not seen around here?"

Out of habit, she knew it was time for dinner, so she headed to the kitchen and removed the plate of already-prepared food from the refrigerator and warmed it in the microwave.

She raised the shades to look out the window. Then she sat at the table and peered out at the woods, lost in thought about Saren, the Bible passage, and the painting. She hoped she would remember this day tomorrow when she woke up. She still didn't have enough wherewithal to write herself a note, but she now had an inkling of hope of returning to her old self again.

After dinner, she washed her dish, glass, teacups, and teapot and placed them in the drainer next to the sink. She headed up to bed. Her habit had been such for as long as she could remember. There was a television in the den and one in her room, but she'd never turned them on or acknowledged their existence. Every day, she only looked forward to going to sleep again so she could be a non-person.

This day, however, was different. She hoped that tomorrow, she would remember the things she learned today, especially the fact that God loved her. She hoped that she would one day feel that love.

On the way up to her room, she looked around. For the first time, she noticed a huge mirror spanning the upstairs landing. At first, she caught the glimmer of the shiny gilded European Gothic—style mirror. The gold from the fading evening light reflected softly across the shapes of the mirror frame.

Her eyes followed the frame up to a gnarly entwinement of thorns with roses interspersed among the briars. Allison had to tilt her head back, looking almost all the way to the ceiling to view gold doves resting on the top corners of the mirror. The details and beauty of the frame was phenomenal.

She was so amazed by the frame that she walked to the center and gazed up at the top of the mirror. The mirror peaked in the center, reminiscent of an ancient cathedral arch. In the center peak was an open scroll with a rose nestled on the right top corner of it. The open scroll meandered to and away from the thorns like ribbon.

For the first time, she thought about what this mirror was trying to say. She decided to breathe on the mirror to confirm she was indeed alive and was not a ghost. When she made a line through the fog on the mirror, her eyes refocused on her own gray reflection.

She considered smiling at the silliness of thinking she was a ghost. But the grayness of her reflection made her remember her depression. She cocked her head to one side, and her silver hair shifted heavily at her waist.

In her sadness, her eyes remained fixed on the space where her reflection had been in the mirror. She froze in that position, struggling to overcome her sadness over her grayness enough to move. She managed to get her eyes to focus on what the mirror was reflecting, the painting above the hall in the foyer. Her urgency and curiosity moved her body to the side so she could see the entire painting.

The open book in the painting was clear, visible, and perfectly centered in the mirror. She couldn't believe her eyes. The mysterious words that stood out from the pages of the book were now completely readable. They were painted backward, to be read looking in the mirror.

It said: "Your Word is a Lamp for my Feet and a Light for my Path." She stood there stunned. Considering the boots, lace, and proximity of the painting, she decided the message was meant specifically for her. But what was the Word and where was her path? The book the words came out of her reminded her of the one Saren had shown her down in the parlor. She snapped out of her contemplative daze.

Looking around her, all was dark. The sun had sunk beneath the forest walls, and she stood in the hall with only the moonlight streaming in from the great arched stained-glass window above the staircase. She was too intrigued to go about her normal dismal sleep. Plus, what if she didn't remember all this in the morning?

This could be her only chance to remember who she was, why she was here, and why she was gray. She lifted her long skirt and headed back down to the parlor. She fumbled to find a light switch. She couldn't remember ever being down here in the dark before. She located the switch on the hall side of the archway that led to the parlor. The grand chandelier in the foyer flashed to life. The chandelier seemed too modern for this house. Its flat rectangular crystals reflected rainbows over the entire foyer.

"Wow, rainbows!" She was momentarily captivated by the beauty. She could see them. She could see all the colors. She looked around, and the rest of the room was still uncolorful. She would take it. She was grateful for the rainbows. Suddenly, she noticed that the chandelier was familiar to her, not because it was here, but because it was from "before," like an intense déjà vu. She wanted to explore the colors but didn't want to get off track.

She tore herself away from the rainbows and scanned the parlor for a lamp near the Bible. On the side table was a blue blown-glass lamp with an oversized shade. She quickly found the switch on the lamp and turned off the chandelier. She didn't want to draw the snake's attention to the house with too much light.

She sat on the couch and picked up the heavy Bible. It was so big, it covered her lap, and each side lay on the cushion of the couch. She used the satin ribbon attached to bookmark her place in John. She found Psalms 119 and started to read. At verse 89 and 90, she decided to ask Saren about faithfulness. "Forever, O Lord, your word is settled in Heaven. Your faithfulness *endures* to all generations."

She continued to read, reaching verse 105: "Your Word is a lamp to guide my feet and a light for my path." She read and meditated on His Word until her eyes closed of their own accord. She was swept away into a blissful slumber of hope. She dreamed of wild gardens where kittens and puppies played peacefully. Finding herself walking on a lighted path with darkness fading out into the background, she changed from gray to colorful Technicolor.

Chapter Thirty-six

Jonathan thought the day would never end. He hoped with all his heart that Allison would see him tonight. He was invisible to her. Saying silent prayers, he quickly locked the front door and made his usual closing-up check around the nursery property. After finally locking the back door, he jumped into his ATV, with faithful Ol' Blue waiting in her usual spot to ride shotgun, and they sped through the forest.

Approaching Allison's cottage, he could see a flicker of light on in the parlor. He turned left instead of his usual right, because he wanted to get a glimpse of her through the kitchen bay window. He parked on the right side of the house and entered the courtyard near the art studio area where he now stayed at night.

In thirteen years, she had never turned on a light. She was always in bed before sunset and didn't wake until after dawn. Jonathan had a deep pang of hope in his stomach. He didn't dare let that pang turn into butterflies. Ol' Blue made her usual security check around the perimeter of the property as Jonathan entered the courtyard and rushed into the kitchen.

He paused at the dining room table to assess the situation before entering the parlor. She sat with her head back on the high part of the antique divan with the giant family Bible open across her lap. He prayed she would turn around, run to him, and embrace him as the love of her life. But she was not moving and didn't seem to hear him arrive.

So he put his caregiver hat back on and softly approached the sofa. She was sound asleep. Astonished, he said to himself, "Did she fall asleep reading the Bible?"

"Allison? Allison?" Speaking softly, he tried to wake her. When she didn't stir, he moved the Bible back to its home on the coffee table and saw that it was open to Psalms 119.

"Hmm." He smiled. "That message took years for her to see, but she got it as soon as anyone got through to her."

He knew in his heart that God was faithful and was fixing Allison's broken spirit.

Jonathan was hopeful, but at the same time, he was bitterly disappointed. But he knew he couldn't afford to let his bitterness grow. He didn't want it to spill out to the rest of his life. He valued the atmosphere of positive thinking, hard work, and love that Grampa John and Grandma Emma had fostered at Emma's. He wanted to be able to maintain that atmosphere no matter what. He refused to give in to whatever enemy they were fighting.

Taking a deep breath, he sat down in one of the velvet aqua chairs and fingered the soft fabric. He watched Allison sleep. She was so beautiful in a tragic way. He prayed like he had never prayed that she would continue to want God. He had encouraged her to seek God through his paintings, but he suddenly realized he hadn't prayed that before. He had always prayed that she would recover and come back to him. Now, he realized that was a selfish prayer. She needed to be healed for herself, not just to come back to be with him.

He knew better than anyone that Allison needed and deserved to be her own person, but Busy Bea had trained her to do only what she was told. Busy Bea herself had been eager to please her mother-in-law and husband. She'd felt the need to push Allison to be a certain way to satisfy them. Jonathan had always encouraged Allison to please only God and herself. He and Grampa had had many discussions with her about trying too hard to please other people, especially Busy Bea.

Jonathan opened his eyes to see Allison unchanged. He prayed that God would see him through this without a bitter heart. Jonathan decided that he now loved Allison even more. He had grown past his selfishness and longing. He could now accept her friendship if she came back and didn't return his romantic love. A strange peace came over Jonathan, one he hadn't felt since before her disappearance. He would be content with whatever Allison decided for herself as long as she decided it for *herself*.

He rose to get her to her bed. He figured he would have to carry her up the stairs, but as soon as he touched her hand, she stood. She didn't open her eyes and was sleepwalking. He guided her up the stairs, pulled the covers back on her bed, sat her down, and removed her boots.

He smiled to himself about those boots. He had bought her several pairs of flip-flops, ballerina-type slip-ons, and slip-on tennis shoes, but she always chose the Dr. Marten boots and her grandmother's clothes that somehow turned gray when she put them on. They were beautiful, and the juxtaposition of the 1950s with the boots was very gothic. He personally loved the look, but the magical grayscale gave him the creeps.

He left her dressed. He had never violated her personal privacy, and he wasn't going to start now. So he swung her legs, rustling with taffeta and lace petticoats, up onto the bed and softly laid her head on the pillow. He covered her up and left her to her dreams.

Coming back down the upstairs hallway, he paused at the painting and the reflection in the mirror. He smiled at himself, pleased with his artwork. He smiled up at the ceiling and thanked the Lord for giving him the idea and for showing it to Allison.

"You could have showed her six years ago when I painted it, but, hey, I guess you had to wait for Saren to grow up enough to broker this deal. Anyway, thank you." Jonathan prayed all the time, but his prayers were of the informal type. He spoke to God like he would a much-respected friend. He believed that Jesus was his friend, and it had never occurred to Jonathan to talk to Him any other way. Sometimes he struggled with the fact that bringing Allison back was taking so long. It was such a waste of time. He wished he understood, but somehow, he doubted it would make him feel any better if he did. Besides it was Allison's life; he was just here to help her. He reminded himself of his new realization, so he set aside his feelings that urgently wanted to well up in him, wanting her back for himself.

He headed back out to the kitchen. He made himself dinner and meals for himself and Allison for the next day; then he picked up his plate of food and headed out to the studio. He simultaneously kicked off his shoes, turned on the TV, and set his food down at the bistro table in the courtyard.

Ol' Blue had returned from her patrol around the cottage and studio and was eating food from her bowl. She wasn't a greedy dog. She'd taken after her parents, Blue Angel and Al, who always looked after others before themselves.

Jonathan watched a basketball game. He loved watching sports. This was his usual habit: to drive his gardening ATV from the nursery, check on the house and Allison, then make dinner and food for the next day. He tried to make simple but nutritious meals for Allison. She always ate the food three times a day and seemed to be healthy.

After eating, he would sit and paint. He'd never known he was an artist. It'd started when he put a bed in the art studio as a way of watching out for Allison. He'd tried to sleep that first month but kept checking on her. He realized his being so neurotic was not healthy for either of them, so he forced himself to stay in the studio. A person could take only so much late-night TV, though. Jonathan had never needed much sleep anyway, and with four hours, he was good to go.

The studio had belonged to Grandma Emma. She'd loved all things color, and painting was her hobby. She had an entire storeroom off the courtyard of blank canvases and every type of paint and brush imaginable.

One night when Jonathan couldn't take one more late-night episode of *Perry Mason*, he started tidying up the studio. He found some books on painting and drawing and started looking through them. As soon as he first put pencil to paper, things looked real on the paper. He found that he loved it, and it was therapeutic.

He began painting things he hoped would come true. He decided to keep with the theme of the stained glass. It was his way of thinking about things that were pure in order to keep negative thoughts and sadness from encroaching on him.

Today, he decided to work on his newest project, which was Allison and Saren walking hand in hand out of the front gate. Allison was always in full color in the paintings. As he painted, that peace that he had felt when praying in the parlor came back to him. It expanded from his heart out of his arms and up to his head, where it became joy. For the first time ever, he painted with joy. Maybe Allison was not the only one who was being healed right now.

His joy gave way to forgiveness. Until this moment, he hadn't realized he'd been so hurt when Allison chose Dr. Death over him. He believed it had been his own fault. He'd never really pursued her like she wanted. He had been too insecure as a teen. But now he was a man. He had made his own way. He had grown Emma's business and started the Sprouts program. He was ready now to be the man Allison needed him to be. He forgave her.

He needed to forgive himself as well, because he believed he was partially responsible for Allison's tragedy. If he had only tried harder, maybe she would never have dated Dr. Death in the first place.

Jonathan decided he was going to clear his slate once and for all. When Allison did come back, he would be ready to start fresh with her, if that was what she wanted.

I forgive myself for any part that I may have had in Allison's tragedy. Also, I forgive Busy Bea. I blanket forgive everyone I forgot. Oh, except Dr. Death. No forgiveness for him. For him, we'll seek justice.

Chapter Thirty-seven

Passing J.D. and his friends in the front yard, playing with trucks, Frost led the way up the front steps.

Saren let the screen door slam and hollered, "Mom! Mom!"

Madeleine called down from her bedroom upstairs, where she was folding clothes, "Up here, honey."

Saren and Frost skipped steps, bounding up to Madeleine's bedroom. Rushing into the bedroom, she found her mom and a neatly stacked pile of towels perched on the bed next to a mound of unfolded laundry. On the TV, a woman was explaining how to make a thirty-minute meal. Madeleine clicked the remote and muted the cook.

Saren plopped down on the other side of the bed. Madeleine gave Frost a greeting pet. He circled the small soft rug next to the bed and curled up for his nap.

Madeleine reached for a tiny boy T-shirt. She held the T-shirt up to fold it, but then her anxiety got the best of her. She pressed the T-shirt to her chest with both hands and leaned toward Saren. "So, how is she today?"

"Mom, I really think she has gotten better since yesterday, but..."

"But what?" Madeleine let her hands and the T-shirt drop to her knees in alarm.

"Well, at first, she thought she was a ghost haunting the cottage. But now she realizes she's real. She doesn't really remember *anything* that good. I think she kind of remembers you and Uncle Jonathan, and your Grampa, but it seems like it's vague impressions, like when you wake up from a dream, not solid memories. But *that* is more than she had yesterday. She seemed more talkative and curious. Mom, we even talked about Jesus."

"Oh, Saren, I am so relieved. It seems like she really is coming back to herself again."

Saren was glad to see her mom's hopes waking up. She riddled her mom with questions about her Auntie Allison and the cottage while they finished the laundry. After finishing, they went downstairs to check on dinner.

Saren peered into the oven. "What? Lasagna! Apple pie!"

"Remember, Busy Bea and Grandfather Spencer are coming over for dinner tonight."

"Oh, yeah!" Saren jumped up and twirled.

Madeleine gave her daughter a suspicious look. "Why are *you* suddenly so excited to see them?"

"I have a million questions for Busy Bea. If we can just get Busy Bea to talk, we might be able to crack the mystery."

"You have my permission to quiz her to pieces."

"Cool."

"Now go tell your brother's friends it's time to go home and get J.D. cleaned up and changed while I finish dinner."

"Got it."

While J.D. was changing, Saren was sitting at the top of the stairs, fluffing up the Frostie Dog for guests, when she heard the doorbell ring. At the sound, Frost sprang into action as the official door greeter of the house, and Saren followed close behind him.

She usually dreaded her grandparents' visits because Busy Bea was always trying to get Saren to do things that she didn't want to do. She didn't really mind her grandmother trying to recruit her into her religion so much as her criticism. Grandmother Busy Bea often told Saren many things that she needed to improve. Saren was not typically sensitive to evaluation because she loved learning and improving, but the things Busy Bea wanted Saren to change were the very characteristics she liked most about herself, like the way she dressed or that she read a lot, too much according to Busy Bea.

"You're going to ruin your eyes with all that reading," Busy Bea would say. Saren figured if she rarely read, Busy Bea would tell her she should read more. Plus, Saren had decided changing oneself to suit someone else was not what a girl ought to do. She responded to her grandmother respectfully but always made it clear she would be her own person.

Saren opened the door. "Hi, Grandmother Bea."

Her grandmother gave her a stiff hug. Her clothes smelled like starch. Her hair was short and salon styled. She wore a tailored cranberry pant suit with three-quarter sleeves.

"Hello, Saren. You have grown." She looked at Saren from head to toe. "Your pants are a bit too short now, are they not?"

"You look well, Grandmother." Saren never acknowledged her grandmother's slights. She stayed Saren.

"Hello, Grandfather Spencer."

He ignored her completely, as usual. He passed her and went straight to his place at the head of the table. Saren started to tell him he had taken her dad's chair, but Madeleine came around the corner and put her hand on Saren's shoulder, placing Saren behind her.

"Hello, Father." She bent down and kissed him on the cheek.

"How are you, Madeleine?"

"Well, Father."

"And Saren and John David?"

"Both are wonderful. Thank you for asking."

J.D. jumped the last four steps of the stairs with a loud thud. Everyone turned to witness his entrance. He skipped into the dining room.

"Young man, come here. Sit down and talk to your grandfather." Grandfather Spencer's voice was formal and commanding.

J.D. jumped all the way there and took his seat. "Hi, Grandfather."

"We'll leave the men to their chat. Ladies?" Madeleine turned back to the kitchen, followed by Saren and Busy Bea.

"Mother, dinner will be ready in about fifteen minutes. Please have a seat."

Instead, Bea busied herself alphabetizing Madeleine's spices.

Saren thought it was odd that no one mentioned her Auntie Allison.

"Grandmother Bu... Bea, when was the last time you saw Auntie Allison before she disappeared?"

"That would have been at your parents' wedding." She scrubbed the top of the cinnamon bottle with a dishrag aggressively.

"Did you talk to her after that? Like on the phone?"

"Oh, yes, dear, many times."

"What did you talk about the last time you talked to her?"

"It isn't polite to ask such personal questions."

Saren looked at her mother. Madeleine gave her a nod to continue.

"Grandmother, why won't you answer that question? Did you say something you regret?"

"Heavens no."

"Then tell us."

"We don't talk about *her*." An ice-cold wall formed around the subject of Allison. Busy Bea acted like she wanted to forget Allison had ever existed. *No wonder Allison thought she was a ghost.*

"We need to talk about her. She is *alive*. She needs us, all of us. What did you talk about?"

"You're too young for this topic. We can talk about it in a few years."

"Allison has already lost thirteen years. I'm not waiting. I'll find out one way or another. It would just be easier for you if you told me yourself." Saren spoke boldly but softly and with control. She'd heard these last two lines on a TV show. It had worked then; she hoped it would work on Busy Bea.

Busy Bea put down the cinnamon. She'd nearly scrubbed off the entire label. Now it only said *Cin on*. She walked around the breakfast bar. She picked up her stiff, expensive handbag and flipped up the magnetic latch to retrieve a letter. She handed it to Saren.

Saren took the letter. The envelope was addressed to Mr. and Mrs. Spencer Scott from the office of admissions of the university Allison had attended. Saren realized instantly what it was. She pulled out the letter and read aloud.

> *"Dear Mr. and Mrs. Spencer:*
>
> *We regret to inform you that your daughter, Allison Louis Scott, has violated the standards of our church and university. She has been excommunicated. Therefore, effective at the end of the semester, she will be indefinitely suspended from any campus classes or activities on university grounds. All her eligibility for university jobs will be terminated immediately. All eligibility for university housing will terminate at the end of the semester.*
>
> *Sincerely,*
>
> *Standards Enforcement*
>
> *The Office of the President"*

When Saren finished reading, she looked up for her mom's reaction. Madeleine stood like a chef statue, her salad-chopping knife in her right hand and her left on a head of butter lettuce. Her eyes were focused intensely on her mother.

Busy Bea had slumped uncharacteristically in a breakfast bar chair with her head resting on her hand, which was propped up with her elbow on the bar.

"Mother, why did you hide that letter all this time? What if this information could have helped bring Allison back?"

"Madeleine, you know this can't get out. And I hope to Heaven you do not tell your father."

"You mean, he doesn't know? You hid this even from him?"

"Madeleine, I know you have divorced yourself from the church as a child, so maybe you do not understand. When you left the church, your excuse to help your Grandmother Emma was legitimate. But what happened with Allison... Your father was the bishop at that time. This would have ruined us."

"That's ridiculous. You didn't even know *what* happened. You were afraid Father or Grandmother Spencer would blame you. Didn't you? This was your way of protecting *yourself*."

Bea sat looking down. Saren went over to her and looked up at her face as only a small person could do. She saw regret there.

"Grandmother Bea? You *do* know what happened, don't you? Allison told you. She chose *you*, the only person whose approval she needed more than anything. She believed *you* would help her. But you didn't help her, did you? What did she tell you? What did you tell her?"

"Saren, I did what I did to protect her and the family."

"What was it, Grandmother? You have to tell us."

"I didn't know what to do. I was under so much pressure." Bea lifted her head. She put one hand on the bar and the other on her knee covered with perfectly pressed slacks. "She called the morning that she disappeared. She told me that Mort had forced himself on her at your parents' wedding. He had coerced her to hide it and do his bidding for the months after the wedding until she decided that her *salvation* was more important than her reputation or her status." Bea's tone said she disapproved of Allison's actions.

"She asked me if I'd received a letter. I said I did. She asked me what her father had said about it. I told her I told him that she'd been forced so that none of this was really her fault. So, now it was okay."

Madeleine was livid. "What? Mother! Do you even understand what you did?"

"I protected her. I suggested she find another university and stay there until the whole thing blew over and she figured out how to be reinstated into the church. We could make excuses about the weather or something to explain her transfer."

"Mother!" Madeleine drove the point of the knife into the cutting board with a loud thud.

"What, Madeleine?" Busy Bea still didn't seem to think she'd caused any harm.

Saren saw a fury welling up in her mom that she'd never seen before, but she didn't have time for a fight right now. She had to help Allison. Busy Bea—and to some extent, Madeleine—had been selfish when it came to Allison. They had put their feelings before hers. Saren decided that she would not do that to Allison. She would keep this discussion on track.

"Mother, you—"

Saren jumped off the bar chair and hopped right in front of her mother. Saren knew that she would not get away with that kind of rude behavior as a thirteen-year-old, but as a twelve-year-old, she could act like it was just a kiddy maneuver. "Grandmother, do you have anything else that could help us? Uncle Jonathan said Allison's journal was missing from her car after it was brought home. Do *you* have it?"

Busy Bea dug into her handbag, pulled out a tattered book with a floral print cover, and handed it to Saren. Madeleine released the knife in the cutting board and ran around the breakfast bar to look over Saren's shoulder.

Saren flipped to the back page. "Look, Mom. Two pages are missing, just like Uncle Jonathan said. This is *the* journal." Saren turned back a few more pages to the beginning of that day's entry. It was dated March 29, the day Allison went missing. Saren began to read aloud.

"*I'm at the end of what I know. I was taught to go to the bishop to seek forgiveness, but he gave none. He only talked about what I must not do. But not how I can be forgiven. I'll be ostracized from everything I've held dear. I want to believe that God can still hear my prayers, but the bishop told me that He wouldn't. Frankly, I'm too ashamed to even try to pray. I know the first time with Mort was not my fault. I didn't want it to happen, and I was powerless to stop it. But I put myself in that situation when I walked to the back of the grounds with him. He even accused me of not being virgin with blood all over my maid of honor dress.*

I didn't want to ruin Maddie's wedding. Then I was too ashamed to tell the truth. But later, my guilt got the better of me, so I went to the bishop, hoping for some release. But he simply told me not to take the Lord's Supper on Sunday and to meet with him next week. I was so humiliated when I passed the bread plate and then the water plate. All my friends down the row leaned forward to look at me. It was truly horrifying.

I want so much to call Jonathan and tell him everything, but Mom would be furious. Plus, I'm ruined now anyway. Mort was right about one thing. He told me that no good Christian boy would ever love me now. How am I supposed to expect Jonathan to still want me? Plus, I rejected him for Mort. I need to let Jonathan find a nice girl and forget about me. That way, he can have a chance at being happy. I love him enough to set him free.

Maddie was so understandably upset with me for not helping with the wedding. I hate, hate that I missed that! We had so many plans to do together for her wedding ever since we were children, but Mort was furious and cruel with me if I even called Maddie. Every time I mentioned going to help her with the wedding, he made me look stupid for wanting to do it. I don't want to bother her with my problems. She's starting on a new marriage. She'll have enough challenges.

Mom wants me to be with Mort, but I can't do that. I would rather be alone forever. I want to at least have a chance of seeing God one day. Right now, all I can do is isolate myself to try to work out my own salvation. I don't know what to do. I need time to myself to figure it out.

I can't go home, because Mom told me to stay away until I was reinstated in the church and established in another college and we could blame the weather on why I changed schools. I'm not sure I want to be reinstated. Everything I ever believed is now in question. The first time I ever saw Mort, he was blessing the Lord's Supper as an elder of the church. They seemed to side with him in that horrible trial that I had to testify at. I love God, and I want to be saved, but I don't want to be part of a church like that.

If only Grandma Emma and Grampa John were alive. They would know what to tell me. I don't know what to do—only what I can't do. I wish I could go back to the beginning. That wonderful day with Grampa and Jonathan at this very restaurant. I guess that's why I came back here to this restaurant where I am now. I wanted to see if I could feel their presence again. I miss them both so much. I remember the stream. It flowed like it had no fear of being evaporated. I want to flow like that with no fear."

"That's all up to the torn-out pages." Saren watched her mother.

Her face was turning bright red, and she was sweating from her forehead. Madeleine sank down onto a kitchen table chair. With her head down, her voice was low. "Mother, you had the letter. You had the journal. Why did you wait until now? Oh, never mind, but why give it to us now?"

Busy Bea just sat there. She didn't look up.

"Forget it, Mother. You're done giving us reasons, solutions, and advice."

"I'm still your mother."

"No, you gave that up with your legal rights as a mother to Allison when she needed you most and you prevented others from potentially helping her."

"I did what was best for everyone."

"Mother, you told Allison that—number one, it was okay to get raped. Number two, that no one cared if she'd been raped and suffered a trauma as long as it wasn't her idea. Number three, that Father didn't care if she was raped as long as it wasn't her fault. Poor Father didn't even get a chance to be a heel. You made an ass out of him behind his back. Number four, you told her not to come home. Number five, you washed your hands of her by giving custody to *me*.

"On top of everything, you forced her to be alienated from Jonathan, who she loved. And he loves her. He has proven that over all these years by taking care of her. You forced her to date that horrible guy who abused her from the start. Did you know he only wanted to date her to steal Grampa John's research?"

"You could have been a better sister. I know you two had a big fight at your wedding."

Saren was done with all this blaming. That was what had started Allison on the wrong track in the first place. "Okay, okay, Mom, Grandmother. Let's stop blaming each other. It sounds like the only person's feelings here that should matter are Allison's. I haven't heard anyone talk about how *she* must have felt."

"She wanted to clean up her life and then come back to the fold with her composure," Busy Bea said.

"No, no, Mother, no! She had a horrible thing happen to her. She went to you for compassion and comfort. She didn't find it. She didn't feel like she could come to me or Jonathan. She tried her bishop, and all he did was ruin the rest of her life by ostracizing her. No wonder. Who did she have to go to?"

"God," Saren said.

"Yes, sweetie, but when someone of her religion gets excommunicated, they're told and they *believe* that they have been cut off from God. So she didn't think that she could go to Him either."

"Whoa." Saren sat down on one of the breakfast stools. Now she understood the whole thing. "No wonder Allison went into the wintery forest looking for answers from a stream. She had no one else but a stream that she'd imagined unafraid one day." Saren looked at Busy Bea. She studied her expression, trying to get insight into her motivation. The silence was thick and the moment intense.

Suddenly, the oven buzzer went off, startling all three. But no one moved to turn off the oven. The buzzer continued. Luke came hesitantly in through the side door. He had been waiting for the discussion to die down before making his presence known. He quietly turned off the timer and retrieved the lasagna and pie from the oven.

"Are we okay here?" he asked.

Madeleine took a deep breath and went to give her husband a kiss.

Saren jumped up. "Daddy, guess what?"

"What?"

"Busy Bea had the letter *and* the journal all the time. Now we have everything we need to really help Auntie Allison."

"Oh great! Can we talk about it over dinner?" Luke picked up the lasagna and proceeded through the swinging door into the dining room.

Busy Bea looked like she was about to pass out.

"Come on, Mother. Time to face the music."

Saren waited until everyone had left the kitchen to follow. She really thought her grandmother was going to run out the back door.

But she didn't. She not-so-bravely filed into the dining room to await her fate.

Chapter Thirty-eight

The next morning, Allison woke up with the first ray of sun streaming through the window. Since there were no neighbors, only lonely forest, the window curtains remained open.

Allison blinked mindlessly, got up, and dressed herself. She headed downstairs with her eyes on the floor as had been her habit for at least the past decade. When she got to the upstairs mirror in the hallway landing, she paused.

Looking at her boots, she had an odd feeling that she was forgetting something. Her negative malaise had returned, and she thought, "Yeah, I hope I forget everything. I couldn't have done anything worth remembering."

She plodded downstairs to the kitchen and saw cereal already in a bowl on the table. She poured milk and ate it. After she washed her bowl and spoon, she headed for the front door, where she stood and stared at the rose stained-glass window. She didn't know what she was about to do, as if she'd been on autopilot or sleepwalking and woke up halfway through.

Allison turned and wandered through the old Victorian, feeling like something was different. Her stomach quivered. A feeling of nausea brewed inside her but didn't satisfy itself with purging. Her head was hot. Her skin had the uncomfortable sensation of porcupine quills poking her all over the tops of her arms.

She slogged back into the parlor. Something was pulling her. She stopped at the archway and looked around. The Bible on the coffee table was open. It was never open. She hadn't even known that it opened.

Her mind raced. *Was someone here? Did someone break in? Should I look around? What should I do? Do I care?*

"Hello?" she said quietly. Only silence answered. She took one step. The rustle of her own taffeta startled her. She jumped back. She tried to think what to do, but her senses sent her mind opposing signals. She was awake but asleep. She thought she was moving fast, but she wasn't.

She sat down on the Victorian sofa and gazed mindlessly at the open Bible. Her mind seemed to be like an old lamp with a worn-out power cord. It was mostly off, and with a wiggle, it might connect. After a long spell of being dazed, something moved outside, making her break her gaze on the Bible. There was a fight over her attention, but the Bible was not going to insist. Instead, it was going to lie there until she read it. But the enemy, although small and not powerful at all, was a master of distraction.

She'd caught sight of something moving, but hadn't actually been able to focus on what it was. What she *did* see was the most amazing, miraculously beautiful rosebush imaginable. She marveled at its color. Allison looked around at the bland gray of the house and garden, and right in the middle was this magnificent display of crimson-red roses. Her nausea turned to butterflies. Amazed by seeing color, she went to the window to get a better look.

They grew on a tall stable trunk in the center of a circle covered in pine needles, bordered by smooth beach rocks of varying color. Each one looked hand-plucked from the beach for beauty of its very own. The rosebush was naturally a rounded shape with dark green leaves. So many roses covered the entire sphere that Allison was sure it would fall over, yet it didn't seem to have a support stick attached to the trunk like most roses required. The color of the roses, deep like the color of thick blood, mesmerized Allison.

They're so beautiful. Yet she had an intense feeling of foreboding. She wanted them, to be close to them, to love them. She wanted to bring them into the house, but she was afraid of the roses. *They're so perfect. Ideal for Maddie's wedding. I have to help with the wedding.*

Allison headed for her smock hanging on the hook beside the front door. She put it on, along with her big hat, then trudged out the door and down the cobblestone path to the rosebush. She hesitated as she took her first step off the cobblestones onto the perfect lawn. *I wonder if I should even walk here.* But she wanted the roses, so she stepped onto the lawn. She already had her right hand securely around the pruning shears in her apron pocket.

Allison reached deep into the bush to snip the first one low so she would have a long stem for her bouquet. As she pulled the cut rose out of the bush, one of the thorns on the stem pricked her finger. She dropped the flower onto the grassy floor of the garden. A couple of droplets of blood from her finger fell onto one of the roses still attached to the bush.

Her eyes followed the blood drops. At first, the drops seemed to disappear into the redness of the rose. She stared at the blood drop and watched it flash like lightning as it turned the spot white. Astonished, she stepped back, whispering, "How could that be? What could it mean? Is someone trying to tell me something?"

"Yesss, you're bleeding all over the flowersss again." A snake slithered around the white-and-red rose. "Aren't you ever going to get thisss right?"

With too much shame weighing down her head and her eyes, she failed to look at the snake. She fell back into the same repeating routine. Only this time, all the flowers littering the lawn were partially white. Every blood droplet washed a clean white spot or two on each rose.

Chapter Thirty-nine

Saren finished all her assignments in time for the last bell to ring at school. Ignoring all her friends who attempted to involve her in afterschool plans, she rushed home to find Frost happily chasing a lizard from one bush to another. She nearly jumped over J.D. and his little buddies engrossed in their fantasy demolition derby. Saren skillfully avoided being demolished as she hopped across the yard, calling Frost for their walky walk walk.

She busted into the front door. "We're heading out, Mom." In one swoop she'd grabbed the leash and was off to the cottage. She and Frost trotted through the neighborhood to Emma's. Without slowing her pace, she looked around for Uncle Jonathan. He was inside the shop, carrying a flower arrangement and opening the door for an elderly woman. Saren knew he would see her soon. As he stepped outside, he looked in her direction.

She waved to Uncle Jonathan as she passed through Emma's without slowing down. He gave her a nod.

She already had her plan formulated. She didn't want to put Allison back in the spot that sent her down this gray path in the first place, so she would not reveal all that she'd learned the previous evening. She would continue as she had been with positive steps forward.

Arriving at the cottage, Saren and Frost bounced happily over the rock wall and dashed up to Allison, circling her as she was nearing the front steps. Saren thought they would surprise her and make her jump or laugh or *anything*. But it only resulted in a slow, soft

"Hello." With her head down, Allison looked even more gloomy than usual.

With a renewed boldness, Saren started asking Allison rapid-fire questions. "How's it going? How are you feeling today? Did you read a book? Watch TV? Hm... Do you have a TV? What music do you like? Do you have music?"

"Oh, Saren, come in and have some tea. You must be very thirsty after asking so many questions." She still wore the same humorless expression. It was simply a fact.

Saren *was* thirsty after running all the way there and asking all those questions. And she was only getting started.

As she stepped across the porch, Saren realized something very important. *Why was Allison outside? Was she cutting roses?* Saren didn't feel like looking at the rosebush today. She wanted to focus all her energy on Allison and didn't want to deal with that snake. So she followed Allison into the foyer, where she deposited her smock and hat on the hat tree.

Saren examined the odd painting with the unreadable words. She had no new ideas on the painting, so she followed Allison into the kitchen. Saren decided to get more interactive with Allison today. She leaned over the kitchen counter with her chin resting on her knuckles. Allison was busy washing the bloodstains off her fingers in the kitchen sink. Saren smiled to herself because Allison hadn't spent so much time washing the blood off the day before. She'd rinsed them off as though it were a normal handwashing before making tea, but this time, she actually scrubbed her fingers and nails clean.

Apparently, Allison had forgotten the previous day's discussion about not going to the rosebush. Saren needed another strategy. She wondered what had prompted Allison to go to the rosebush every day. She slowed her excited pace to mirror Allison's slow tone.

"Allison, tell me about the rosebush."

"What about it?"

"Everything. Tell me how you feel when you see it in the morning. What makes you feel like gathering your gardening tools and going out there to cut those roses?"

Allison quietly set the kettle on the stove and turned her face to Saren as if she hadn't heard the question.

"Do you remember seeing the rosebush this morning?" Saren asked.

"Yes, I do remember that." Allison raised her eyebrows and looked up.

"Okay, what did it look like?"

"It was so beautiful." Allison turned around and leaned casually against the counter. "The roses were so *red* that the color popped right out of the gray forest. Everything else was still like an old movie, but the roses were bright and red. They looked softer than crimson velvet." Allison waved her hands around while she talked for emphasis.

"Wow, that sounds pretty." Saren was surprised and relieved that Allison could see color. She opened her mouth to ask if that was the first time Allison had seen color. But she closed it. She didn't want to get Allison off track. It was tortuous, but she waited for Allison to say more.

"I decided they were the perfect roses for a wedding. Someone is getting married. Someone I'm supposed to help. But now I can't remember who I was getting the roses for."

She forgot the tea and started walking around the room like she was pretending to walk out to the rosebush. Saren carried the teacups to the table then gently took Allison by the elbow and guided her to her place at the kitchen table like she was a sleepwalker.

Allison continued in her dreamlike monologue. "I walked out to the rosebush. Attempting to cut a long stem, I pricked my finger on the first rose, and it started to bleed. The blood dropped onto some of the other flowers. I thought maybe I should wear gloves to cut roses. Then I heard him. He said, 'You're always bleeding all over the flowersss. Can't you do anything right? Why did you let this rossse-bush become such a messss? You should trim this bush correctly before it diesss. Have you no ssskill?' I was so ashamed that I couldn't see clearly because my eyes were welling up, even though I didn't really cry. I cut all the blossoms off too short or too long and left them on the ground. I cut off all the roses, the bush was left only leaves, and I saw him staring at me with those yellow eyes. He sat there accusing me. I couldn't tear myself away from him." As Allison talked, she pulled at her blouse sleeves. She put her hands on her face too hard, like she was trying to mold her face into something she could accept.

"Who was it?" Saren asked.

"It was the black snake with yellow eyes."

Allison remembered Saren and Frost, but she had not remembered any of their conversation—or she wouldn't have gone out to the rosebush in the first place. Saren decided to play along like Allison was telling her about the snake for the first time. She didn't want to add to her angst about her memory by pointing out petty details. Besides, it had to be great progress that she remembered her, Frost, and now that snake.

"You mean like the talking snake in the Garden of Eden?" Saren asked, to show that she was following her story.

"Yes, that's right," Allison said. "He tells me that I'm not doing it right. I try harder and harder, but I always mess it up, and once they're cut, I can't fix it."

Saren sat quietly for a moment to make sure that she was being a good listener. In that moment, the air was heavy, and Allison sat slumped as if she wished the chair and floor would swallow her whole.

Saren studied her. Now she knew how Allison could come to feel so bad.

"Did you know that the rosebush regrows every evening and is renewed every morning?"

"Yes..." Allison said. "Yes, now that I think about it. It's the same the next day, like I didn't do anything at all, which is a good thing because I destroyed it. So I go out to get roses for a wedding—I can't remember whose—and the whole process starts over again. What is wrong with me? Am I some kind of wind-up toy or insane?"

"Allison, first of all, you can't mess up a rosebush that regrows itself every day." Saren smiled, hoping that she'd said it kindly so Allison would not feel embarrassed. Apparently, the cardinals hadn't appeared today. That was an improvement.

"Saren, yes, you're right. It's the same every day, and I think I'm supposed to help with this wedding, then I fail again and again."

"Miss Allison," Saren said with an unusually shy tone, "did anything different happen today, anything out of the ordinary?" Saren was fishing to see if their conversation from yesterday had made any impact at all. Asking Allison to wait until she got there to trim the roses hadn't worked. Allison had gone about her normal day, yet something seemed different somehow.

Allison finally took her first sip of tea. No doubt it was tepid by now, but she didn't seem to mind. Setting the teacup back onto the saucer, she tilted her head. "Yes, now that you mention it. Something odd did happen today, very odd indeed."

"Do tell," Saren said, hovering over her cup and saucer.

"This time, when I bled on the flowers, wherever the blood soaked into the red rose petals, that spot turned pure white."

"Wow, another miracle." A song her mother often sang, "Between Thorns and Glory," instantly came to Saren's mind. Her mother loved listening to gospel music, and Saren knew many of the songs by heart. Saren's eyes widened, and she felt like she knew what God wanted Allison to see. Forgetting her formality, Saren asked, "Allison, what did you do with the red-and-white flowers?"

"I left them on the grass where they fell."

"Come on. I want to see." Saren stood without bothering to push her chair back, making a clunk against the floor.

"Very well," Allison said, "but, what about that snake? I don't want him to torment you too."

"I ain't 'fraid of no snake." Saren smiled loosely after imitating the Ghostbusters theme song. "Besides I have two things you don't have against him. First, I refuse to have conversations with talking snakes, and second, the Frostie Dog!" she said, referring to Frost like he was a superhero in need of a cape. She took off Frost's leash and grabbed Allison by the hand. With a determined march, the three headed toward the front door.

Saren began singing:

"Between thorns and glory, He put death to the test
He died and rose again on that third day
Now our crimson sins are white like wool
Our scarlet white like snow
Fulfilling all he promised long ago..."

Allison looked at Saren and raised her eyebrows as though she recognized the tune. Saren noticed a glimmer of excitement for the first time.

Saren could see the red-and-white roses on the lush green grass, and she couldn't wait to see one up close. She sang the song's chorus:

"He made us white as snow
He loves us so
He loves you so
He made you white as snow..."

She came to the end of the chorus as they stood in front of the rosebush, observing the roses on the ground.

"White as snow..." Saren let the last note fade out as she picked up a rose. It was remarkably beautiful with the stark white contrasting with the sanguine color of the rose.

Allison was scanning the bush for the snake.

"Miss Allison, don't look for it, and it won't be there."

"How do you know? We see what we want to see. Right now, we want to see the truth."

Saren carefully gathered up all the flowers on the ground and laid them across her left arm like a beauty pageant contestant. Allison kept her eyes on Saren's activity. Frost stood guard between them and the bush, sniffing the air occasionally.

"All done. Last one in is a rotten egg!" Saren announced as she headed for the front porch without turning back to make sure Allison and Frost were following her.

Allison was, in fact, right on her heels, and Frost lagged back a bit to give himself a running start to jump up the steps that were each only an inch or two shorter than he was. Frost made it to the door first, then Saren and Allison followed. They closed and locked the door behind them.

"Does that make me a rotten egg?" Allison looked seriously concerned.

Without moving her neck, Saren looked up at Allison from the corners of her eyes to see if she was kidding. Apparently not, and now she was going to have a complex about being a rotten egg. She sincerely hoped that Allison had a sense of humor under all that grayness.

"Oh, no, Miss Allison. It's just a kiddy game. It isn't real." Saren smiled at her. She wanted to make sure that Allison didn't feel made fun of. She'd seen the effects on some of her friends when they were made fun of by bullies.

Saren quickly changed the subject and softened the mood by breaking into song again, starting at the second verse.

"Between thorns and glory, He has plans for you
For good not disaster, for a future and a hope
Jesus shares with us His glory,

His joy, His righteousness
We're made free and pure in His own likeness..."

With arms full of thorny roses, Saren stepped into the parlor. She noticed the Bible was open. She leaned over to see it was no longer on John 3:16 but on Psalms 119. Saren smiled with wonder at Allison.

The cloudy haze swirled with recognition in Allison's eyes, and she joined in with the song. Saren beamed at Allison as she sang along. Saren had never dreamed that Allison would sing. This was a wonderful sign that she was getting better. Sad people didn't sing, and no one could sing and still be depressed.

"He made us white as snow
He loves us so
He loves you so
He made you white as snow..."

Saren's hope and anticipation soared with each note. Allison sang strong and clear with a beautiful voice. Her demeanor softened from her tortured state.

They reached the kitchen just as they sang the last note. Saren admired its monotone whiteness and wondered if the kitchen decorator had intended to show them what "white as snow" looked like since they had lived in the perpetual summer of Southern California, where it never snowed.

Saren gently laid the flowers over the white mosaic of the angels and the girl. She turned to Allison and started the song again. Allison joined in with her, and they sang the entire song again hand-in-hand. By the end, each had tears streaming down her face. They could both feel the presence of God's love surrounding them.

"Miss Allison, you know the song."

"Yes, I remember singing it with you before."

She hated to burst Allison's bubble. "Miss Allison, you couldn't have sung it with *me* before."

Allison turned her head. "Hmm, are you sure? Do you have a twin?"

"No! Do you remember someone like me?"

Saren watched Allison trying to remember. It seemed like there was something there, but Allison couldn't quite break the surface of it. Saren wanted so much to blurt out that she must have sang the song with Madeleine. But she believed that Allison needed to remember these things on her own. Others telling her anything hadn't worked in the past. So she focused on what Allison wanted to tell her.

Saren retrieved a large crystal vase from the cabinet, placed it gently in the sink, and filled it with water.

Allison closed her eyes. "I see a girl smaller than myself who looks like me only instead of blue eyes, she has emerald-green eyes. Do I have a sister, Saren?"

"I think you just might. We'll find out together." Saren set the vase down in front of the pile of roses. She wanted so badly to tell Allison and call her mom to come over, but she believed that Allison had to come all the way out of this herself.

Allison stood on the opposite side of the counter. She sorted the roses by stem length and handed Saren the longest ones first. Saren was amazed that Allison knew to start with the longest ones first. That was the way Uncle Jonathan had taught her to build an arrangement. He had shown her that it was easier to control the bouquet with the longest ones in place first when working with only a clear vase and not a foam base.

Calmly and quietly, Saren made a modern-style asymmetrical arrangement. Together, they worked to create the masterpiece. Saren was having so much fun, she didn't think to say anything. She soaked up the beauty of the flowers and Allison's comfortably silent companionship. Frost decided flower arranging was not interesting and opted to nap on the rug under the table.

"Isn't this silence pleasant?" Allison spoke quietly as to not disturb the peace in the air. "I can't hear those cardinals' accusations now—or that snake."

Saren thought about asking Allison more about the cardinals and the church men but decided that it might remind her of something negative, so she kept quietly fiddling with the arrangement.

"I remember the words of that song and singing it with a girl like you, Saren. She looked very much like you, but it was not you. Wait, I remember our conversation last night, talking about Jesus, and the painting and reading Psalms 119."

"It is *all* going to come back to you, real soon, Miss Allison. I just know it."

Allison had a peaceful expression and stopped handing flowers to Saren when the vase looked complete. Only a fourth of the flowers remained on the counter.

"That is so perfect," Allison said, giving a small Mona Lisa smile, like she was holding something else back.

Saren smiled bigger, astonished by Allison's expression. She could see that it was complex and grown-up, beyond her understanding.

"Come on, I have an idea." Allison rustled around the kitchen counter, and Saren followed her.

Allison started singing again under her breath; then Saren joined in, and they sang together as they reached the parlor.

Allison retrieved a rose-colored glass bud vase and a green glass one from the bookcase. She handed them to Saren and headed into the foyer. There, she picked up a tiny crystal vase from the side table next to the front door, handed it to Saren, and trotted up the stairs.

Saren's hands were getting full, but she didn't dare interrupt Allison, who was on a roll. She didn't know yet what Allison was on a roll to, but she was not going to be *a stopper*.

Allison paused at the bottom of the steps like she'd never been up there before then sprinted up. When she reached the top and realized Saren was not behind her, she peered down over the ornate railing.

"Oh, you can set those down on the side table there, and we'll pick them up as we go back by." This was the first time Allison seemed normal. She was kind of bossy, but in a good way.

Saren looked to her left where Allison was pointing. Against the wall next to the bottom of the staircase was a Queen Anne-style table with simple rounded legs and claw feet. It had a beautiful lace runner on it with a Chinese-style aqua jar and lid in the center and antique black phone on the left. She set the three vases down carefully on the right side.

She was going upstairs. This time, she wouldn't be running from bats, so she would be able to look around. She was so excited, she bounced up the stairs.

By now, Frost had realized they were missing and ran around the corner, turning so quickly in the foyer that his toenails slipped, causing him to slide across the floor, stopping right before his nose met the first step.

Saren looked at Allison for permission for Frost to come up.

Allison called down sweetly, "Come on, Frost. Come!"

Frost responded with extreme enthusiasm, even for him. With ears alert and flopping, he bounded up the stairs to Allison. She greeted him with a scratch behind both ears.

While Allison was playing with Frost, Saren busied herself with looking around. She could see the painting of the book better from up here. She wished she had time to pull up a chair and look closely at it, but there was so much else to see. The wide hallway landing had a huge, elaborate mirror. At first, she was distracted by the frame, but then she realized that it perfectly reflected the painting, making the unreadable words readable. "Your Word is a lamp for my feet and a light for my path."

Ooh—the words were backward. Duh! All of a sudden, she felt very twelve, deciding a thirteen-year-old would have definitely caught on to that.

Allison stood up and went past the mirror to another side table to retrieve a tall vase from the collection of gold containers in the center. Next to the mirror was the door leading to the spiral staircase and the round tower. She hoped Allison didn't go up there. The tower door was slightly ajar, and she peered in cautiously. However, Allison passed the tower door. Saren reached in and closed it just in case the bats decided to interfere with Allison's progress.

While Saren had been preoccupied with the tower door, Allison had snatched two vases from the bedroom. She passed Saren and the big mirror then quickly and gracefully descended the stairs. She picked up the small vase on the table, leaving the other two for Saren.

Saren quickly followed, picked up the two vases, and trotted to the kitchen. This time Allison took charge, and Saren took her place on the other side of the counter, handing Allison flowers upon request. Allison put the shorter-cut flowers in the smallest vase, then asked for the longer-stemmed roses first.

Saren was shocked at what a masterful flower designer Allison was. The arrangements were similar in style to pictures of designs her great-grandmother had made. The style was traditional and symmetrical with a full and luxurious feel, not unlike Uncle Jonathan's style.

Saren didn't think that there would be enough flowers to fill up all the vases, but each arrangement was completely full of bloodred roses with snow-white spots. It was like the roses had been multiplied like the bread and fish with which Jesus had fed the five thousand. They had already used most of the roses on the first arrangement, yet Allison made six more, some almost as big as the first one.

Once Allison was finished, they dispersed the seven arrangements to various parts of the house: the bedroom, hall, foyer, and parlor. They left the first, asymmetrical design by Saren in the kitchen on the white table.

After Allison and Saren cleaned up all the debris on the sink and counter, they sat down at the kitchen table for a snack and to admire their work.

"Wow! Allison, you went all out. This whole house smells amazing now. And you... Somehow, you seem different."

"Yes, I feel. Well, hungry. I've skipped lunch. I must no longer be a wind-up toy."

Maybe she has a sense of humor after all.

Allison gave half of her lunch to Saren—a tuna sandwich and some apple slices had been in the fridge—with a glass of milk. They ate and smiled at the red-and-white spotted flowers.

Saren could see the cloud cover over Allison's eyes swirling like it was trying to go down the drain, but it was taking forever because there was still a lot of fog. But she could faintly see her blue eyes gleaming through the heavy mist.

"Saren, I'm remembering. Not everything. But now I can remember you coming yesterday. I remember reading John 3:16. I saw the verse in the mirror and somehow recalled that it was from Psalms 119. I read it over and over until I fell asleep. I don't remember going to bed last night. This morning, I woke up in my bed, already in my clothes. But I didn't notice, and I continued the day like every other day.

"But now I won't be able to forget because I'll wake up with those flowers in my room and all the way to the kitchen. I'll remember the blood dropping on the red roses, turning spots white as snow. I'll remember the song from Isaiah 1:18. 'Come now, and let us reason together, saith the Lord: though your sins be as scarlet, they shall be as *white as snow*; though they be red like crimson, they shall be as wool.' I remember that scripture. Wow, I can remember the whole passage. Saren, I can remember it, but I don't know what it means. Is it some kind of magic trick, turning red to white?"

"It's magic only Jesus can do. It means like what you saw your blood do to the flowers. Remember, John 3:16: 'For God so loved the world that He gave His only begotten son, that whosoever believeth in Him should not perish but have everlasting life.'"

"Yes, yes. Jesus. I remember." Allison leaned in toward Saren, trying not to miss a word.

"Oh good. When Eve listened to the snake in the Garden of Eden, and then she and Adam ate the fruit of the tree of knowledge of good and evil, they brought sin and evil into the world."

"That's too bad. It could have been so good if Eve had just done what she was supposed to do." Allison looked sad again.

"But don't worry. I'm coming to the good news. So, they were kicked out of the Garden of Eden because of that original sin, and people on Earth have been sinning ever since. But God loved us and didn't want to lose us forever."

"I'm starting to feel God's love. But why would he love me? I mess up everything."

"Everyone does, not just you. That is why God didn't send Jesus into the world to *condemn* the world but to save it through Him. See, at first, God set up a system of laws and sacrifice with Moses. He gave us the Ten Commandments, and we had to sacrifice animals when we broke them, which was *all* the time. Even the Apostle Paul wanted to live the law, but no matter how hard he tried, he couldn't do it. He always, always failed."

"I see. Like when I mess up the roses."

"Yeah, you got tricked by that snake. We all get deceived and do things we shouldn't do. Sometimes we do them just because we want to and then regret it later."

"Wow."

"Jesus was the only person that didn't fail at the law. He was hated by those who got their social status from law—and they killed him."

"Oh no!" Allison grimaced in fear.

"I know, but turns out it was a good thing, at least for us, because the devil thought he had won that day. I'm sure they had one big party planned in Hell. But something weird happened. The Earth got as dark as night for three days. The light of the Earth was taken away, and on the third day, Jesus defeated death and rose to life again. Then when Jesus went to Heaven to His Father—our Father in Heaven—He sent us the Holy Spirit to guide us and comfort us."

"How do I get this Holy Spirit to comfort me?"

"You only have to believe that Jesus died for your sins and ask Him to help you."

"Really? That's it?"

"I heard that a lot of grown-ups have made it complicated, but it really isn't. God is sending you a sign that whatever has happened in your past, no matter what it is, the blood of Jesus cleans it like bleach, like turning the red flowers to white."

"Yes, I see. I can't remember what happened, but I'm forgiven?"

"Yes, the Bible says that the Holy Spirit prays with us and for us because we don't even know what to pray for sometimes—like you now. You don't know what to be forgiven for, but ask anyway, and you'll be forgiven, no matter what it is."

"What if it's so bad, it can't be forgiven?"

"That's impossible because only a direct betrayal of the Holy Ghost cannot be forgiven, and not remembering releases you from that one. You get to start from right now. Remember, God is faithful. He brought you this far, gave you a miracle garden, showed me your cottage, and made you friends with Frost and me. Don't worry. He'll finish the job."

Allison looked intense, with a childlike wonder in her eyes. "How do you know God is faithful?"

"First of all, this is my mom's favorite subject. Every time something happens, good or bad or neutral, she says God is faithful."

"How does she know?"

"She knows it from reading the Bible as well as from the stuff that happened in her life that she loves to tell me about and everyone else too. She even named me after her two favorite people of faith, Sarah and Jonathan."

"They seem so familiar, but I can't recall who they are."

"Okay, uh. Sarah is... I'll tell you Mom's version, because it's kind of cool. For a long time, my mom kept seeing the number 11:11. It would be that time when she looked at the clock morning and night for nearly a year. Often an invoice would equal $1,111.00, or the change she was given would be $11.11. Anyway, that number 11:11 kept popping up all over the place for over a year. She felt like it was some kind of sign, but she didn't know what it meant."

"That had to be a special sign for her. Like me and my spotted roses."

"Exactly, Mom thought that too. Then she went to a Joyce Meyer's women's conference, and Christine Caine was there. She's a preacher and writes books and stuff. The meeting was supposed to start at eleven o'clock, but it hadn't. When Mom's friend asked her for the time, it was 11:11."

"Oh, my goodness!" Allison said.

"My mom's friend agreed that it had to mean something. Right then Christine Caine said, 'Please turn to Hebrews 11:11.'"

"Up to that point in her life, she'd been taught that *we* are supposed to have faith. That scripture says that Sarah deemed God faithful so he made it so she could have a baby even though she was, like, a hundred. So Mom wanted to name me after Sarah. My Uncle Jonathan is named after Jonathan in the Bible. Jonathan encouraged David to have faith. So they named me Saren after Sarah and Jonathan."

"They were going to spell it 'Saran,' but they thought kids would call me Saran Wrap. Anyway, they spelled it S-a-r-E-n. So anyway, we know God is faithful, because He is. Miss Allison, you'll know too when you read the Bible and know for yourself—like that painting on the wall in the foyer with the backward words. I had wondered about that since I first saw it, but today I saw it in the mirror."

Allison chimed in, "'Your Word is a lamp for my feet and a light for my path.' Yes, I discovered it for the first time myself just last night."

"Wow!" Saren said after giving her a whole second of silence as to not interrupt her. "When you saw what the painting said, what did you do then?"

"I went over to the Bible and opened it up to Psalms 119. I don't know how I knew where to go, but I spent the rest of the evening reading that chapter. Wait, I even made a mental note to ask you about God's faithfulness from verse 90: 'Your faithfulness endures to all generations.'"

"It's cool you knew that on your own. Wait, you wanted to ask me about God's faithfulness. I don't think this is all a coincidence." Saren sat back in her chair and looked down, lost in contemplation. She knew it was deep, and she was only twelve. But it was all so beautiful and perfectly orchestrated; angels had to be involved. While she was thinking about the angels, she was gazing mindlessly down at Allison's boots, with the tops of the shoelaces covered with light-gray lace. "Miss Allison, I want to show you something you may not have realized. I finally did this second."

For the second time that day, Saren took Allison by the hand and led her through the house. They stopped in the grand foyer. The walls were covered with rainbows, signaling that it was time for Saren to be heading home. They had both ignored the rainbows because the painting was the object of their interest at the moment.

"Look, Miss Allison, the feet. They are *your* feet."

Allison looked down at her boots then up to the painting. When she looked down at her own boots, the angle was the same as if she'd painted it from her own perspective.

"What is it trying to tell me, Saren?"

It was obvious to Saren... but she didn't have a memory problem, and she loved puzzles. "Well," she said, trying to draw it out a little so she wouldn't sound like a smarty-pants. "It looks like whoever painted this wanted you to know that the Word is the light to *your* path. They think that if you read the Word, you'll be cured of everything that's wrong with you—and so do I. Look at how much better you are already on your first day reading God's Word."

Saren pointed to the painting with one hand and the Bible in the parlor with the other. "Check it out. That Bible is the same as that Bible; your feet are the same as the feet in the picture except the color of the lace and skirt, but it's yours. The words radiate up from the Bible, and the Bible shines a light down on *your* path."

Saren always loved those games in kid magazines where the objective was to spot the differences between the two pictures. Now she was glad she'd practiced it a lot.

"But wait, one thing is different. In the painting the path looks like the one through the front garden and the little grove, but instead of a rock wall, a gate finishes the circle of the half-round arbor."

"Yes, the gate looks like it would be a circle. Except the gate is open," Allison said.

Saren stood focused on the gate while holding Allison's hand when the image of Jesus knocking came to her. Inside her own Bible was a lifelike illustration of Jesus standing outside a rock wall and knocking on a wooden door.

"Allison, that gate means you opened the door for Jesus, and he came in. So in the painting you see that the Bible, is the light of your path, then you're able to find the gate, open it, and let Jesus in."

"Wow!" Allison put her hands to her head with concern. "How do I let him in?"

Only Allison could answer that question, so Saren waited. After a minute or so, Allison turned to Saren.

"The Word, the Bible, the answers are in the Bible. If God is faithful, then he'll show me what to do."

"Yep! He will."

Allison stood up. "Well, we have a plan of action. I'll remember not to go to the rosebush tomorrow when I see the roses, and I'll read the Bible until God shows me how to open the gate." Her take-charge personality was already coming back.

Saren was pleasantly surprised that Allison gave her a warm hug and Frost a scratch behind the ear as they left for home. She'd stayed so long that she had to just wave again to Uncle Jonathan. She couldn't wait to tell him all about Allison's progress, but she had to get home on time.

Chapter Forty

Jonathan arrived at the cottage later than normal. He had an unusually large order that he needed to prepare for early-morning delivery. After parking the gardening utility cart by the back door to the courtyard, he stepped into the large moonlit patio.

Jonathan had a feeling something was different, but it made no sense. He looked around the courtyard and inspected his room. All looked untouched, but there was something about the moonlight or the air. The atmosphere seemed fresher or fragrant in some way that he hadn't noticed before.

Jonathan breezed into the kitchen and took some chicken out of the freezer. When he turned around to put the chicken in the sink to thaw, he saw the red-and-white flowers beautifully arranged in the vase.

Saren's style was modern, artistic, and asymmetrical. He had tried to explain to Saren on many occasions when she was helping him that some people like symmetrical, but she would always add some way to make it asymmetrical—different, modern, and off-beat artistic. This was definitely Saren's artistry. He wondered about the variety of white-and-red roses. He didn't dwell on that because, like everything around the cottage since Allison had come home, it had an enchanted air about it.

He was more hopeful than he had been in years. The reality that some kind of change had happened soaked in slowly. After about a minute of staring at Saren's arrangement of strange roses, he did an about-face and hurried into the dining room, where he found another arrangement on the dining room table.

This one was not Saren's style. It was organized and arranged the way Grandma had taught him and Allison. It was traditional, full, luxurious, and perfectly symmetrical.

He stood with his mouth open for a few seconds, overwhelmed by the fear he would be disappointed if he thought she was back and wasn't. If she was fully back, Saren would have told him. But Allison must have made enough progress to make floral arrangements. Finding his courage, he was ready to move forward to whatever the future held.

Quickening his pace, he found the vase on the coffee table, also in Allison's style. Next to the beautiful arrangement, the Bible was open to 1 John 1:9: "But if we confess our sins to him, he is faithful and just to forgive us and to cleanse us from every wrong."

"Lord, forgive me for not protecting Allison." He crossed the threshold into the foyer. The moonlight streamed in through the stained-glass window, creating a moon rainbow that lit up the arrangement of the red-and-white roses on the entryway table. The stunning beauty and fairytale wonder of the scene stopped Jonathan in his tracks. He knew that this would become a painting one day.

He tore his gaze away to make his way up the stairs to check on Allison. He smiled as he passed the arrangement on the hall table and proceeded to Allison's room. Her silver hair was gleaming in the dim light. Jonathan could see something red next to her exposed ear. He got a little closer to see what it was. Out of the corner of his eye, he saw arrangements in Maddie's green vase and Allison's blue vase on their respective dressers.

Allison was sleeping soundly with one of the red-and-white roses cradled in her arms with the fully opened blossom resting on her cheek. She was stunningly beautiful with her silver hair and fair grayish skin. She didn't look real. He found himself questioning whether he had imagined an Allison—a beautiful fantasy based on a girl he once knew. Maybe this Allison was just a life-sized figurine of a beauty sleeping in a magical cottage.

She breathed deeply and restored his hope that she was real and would return to herself again soon. He bent down and kissed her forehead. He had never done that before, but he wanted to show her she was loved. Maybe in her sleep, she could feel the love he longed to show her... love that she couldn't receive while she was awake.

Chapter Forty-one

For the first time since her disappearance, Allison dreamed. Glistening white snow stretched out beyond the creek across the vast flat valley at the bottom of the mountain that seemed to rise nearly straight up from the snowy expanse. She sat in the restaurant, sipping hot coffee. She'd always loved coffee because it smelled so good. Her grandfather used to let her have some from his cup when she was a small child.

She knew she shouldn't drink coffee on an empty stomach, but she couldn't eat. Besides, nothing mattered anymore anyway. She'd been expelled, excommunicated, disgraced, and fired from her job, alienated from her friends, asked by her mother not to come home.

They had agreed to let her finish the semester, and she still had two months to go. She didn't know how she was going to do it. She was completely devastated.

How could I have put myself in the position to sin like that? How did I let myself get talked into staying in that relationship for so long? I've ruined my life forever. That jerk of a professor was right; no good Christian boy will ever marry me now. It no longer matters what happens to me. These horrible thoughts and worse circulated in her mind as she sipped the coffee.

She'd never wanted this. He had forced himself on her. She should not have been alone with him late at night, but she'd trusted him as an elder of the church and as an assistant professor to keep the church rules and the school rules. It had never dawned on her that he would do such a thing.

Afterward, he had accused her of lying about being a virgin. Taking her virginity without even asking was one thing, but then to accuse the virgin of not being a virgin with blood still on her dress was quite another!

Later, she had stayed with Mort because she needed him to be an upstanding elder in the church, a successful professor because he was a favorite of her mother's. Although he had presented her with no ring, he had proposed marriage to her. She'd thought that if they got married, it would all be set right in the end and save her from disgrace. He'd continually found excuses to put off giving her a ring, though. Her mother had insisted on buying the wedding dress.

During this period, she'd seen Mort act one way with her and another in public—showing her another side of her religion, dark and deceptive. Her belief in that church had started to waver, exacerbating and magnifying her guilt. She'd still thought Mort was an exception, not the norm, so she'd confessed to her bishop.

Now she realized that she should have confided only in God. She could have learned to lie well like all the others. But no, she was not that person, nor would she ever be. She would rather go to Hell with honesty than to be in Heaven with a bunch of liars and pretenders. She wanted to come clean. She'd believed there was a way through the leadership of the church. When she did, they had convinced her to testify at Mort's tribunal.

She'd been told that now she must seek God only through men in the church, that she no longer had the capability to talk to God directly. Deep down, she knew this was an evil lie, but realizing that the church she believed in with all her heart could be evil had made Allison lose all faith that she could find God. She didn't think God would want to find her ever again after all of this. Her life was void, and without God, she no longer cared about anything at all.

Staring into her coffee, she knew there was no way out of this jam. She sank deeper into her depression and negative malaise. She lost herself, staring into the coffee, into life's bitterness.

Suddenly in that dreaming state, she was in the harsh hot coffee without a flotation device, and it was becoming thicker, threatening to pull her under like quicksand made from anguish. Someone began stirring the coffee, making it harder to keep her head out of the hot, dark liquid. The men in suits and the professor took turns stirring. She was burning and drowning to death.

The brown coffee flashed to red flames then darkness and cold. She no longer felt or thought. Only the cold existed. She believed that she was in outer darkness, where those who were disenfranchised from God were cast forever—her own Hell. She was cold, but she deserved to be cold. Without the warmth of God's love, she would be cold and alone forever.

She blinked and saw the glistening white country field again. She was still cold, but now there was also a bright-white sparkling light. In the distance, she thought she saw an angel flying in. The angel was beautiful. He was still far enough away that she couldn't see his face. He was strong and full of love. He wisped over the snowy landscape like a strand of cloud that had come to life. He was as bright and quick as lightning.

Then she was warm and heard the hum of an engine. She couldn't see anything, but she could hear someone calling her name. *No, I must hide. They'll find out. I don't want to lie to anyone, so I'll hide. No one will know.* Like a child hiding under the bed from a house fire, Allison hid in her mind.

She'd wandered out of the restaurant and down the creek as it started to get dark. She'd brought her sleeping bag because she didn't intend to come back. She would hide.

She could see only her damnation and shame. Her past twenty-one years had been consumed by being a good church member and a good daughter, and she'd been rejected and publicly humiliated. She realized she'd been deceived.

She was truly stripped of even herself. They told her that she would not be able to pray to God until they said she could. She couldn't trust herself or be trusted. Only they could guide her spiritually. She was done. She no longer had any of her selfness left. She was open and vulnerable.

As the angel grew closer, she worried he was coming to punish her. How did she get herself into such trouble? She couldn't reconcile it or make the pain in her stomach go away. She believed that she would be consumed by guilty pain by morning—and it would be better if she were never found. Her family would believe she'd left for another life, and that would be the end of it. Her mother and father would be relieved. Maddie would be devastated, but at least she had Luke. Jonathan deserved a woman far better than her. He needed to find a wife worthy of him, and with her around, he never would.

In the middle of these defeating thoughts, she felt a warm feeling of love sweep from her forehead over her entire body. She strained her eyes in the brightness, looking for the white-winged angel flying in the whiteness of the evening fog over the snowy field. Her fear had subsided. She wondered if she dared to hope. She still believed it was pointless... but she dared. She had a glimmer of joy that he was bringing her hope of forgiveness. Forgiveness—this was the first time she'd even thought of the concept of forgiveness.

The angel finally arrived, fluttering above her. He wore white cargo pants that went down past his feet and a white polo shirt. A white ball cap covered his head. His wings were massive, and instead of feathers, they were covered with white pompous grass plumes. He hovered above her, saying, "Fear not. He is so rich in kindness and grace that He purchased our freedom with the blood of His son and forgave our sins. Because of the Lord's great love, we're not consumed, for His compassions never fail. They're new every morning." The angel raised his hands to praise God. "Great is your faithfulness."

Allison understood. The angel gleamed like the sun, and he finally got close enough for her to see his face. Jonathan, the face was Jonathan's. The angel was Jonathan. He was the one who loved her enough to never give up on her.

The angel impressed her with words without moving his lips and said, *"Love, God is love. Not judgement, not rules, not unreasonableness, not exclusion, not separation, not anything else. Love, God is about love. God is love, and all the humans that make up all these religions are trying to control the truth about the most basic yet most elusive need of all souls—love."*

Allison let the angel envelop her with his wings and carry her over the frozen white plain and soothe her in God's love.

JONATHAN WATCHED ALLISON as he rose from kissing her forehead. He noticed a small smile on her lips and followed a single tear flowing down her cheek and onto the cuddled rose. Her teardrop bleached the rest of the red portion of the rose white.

Jonathan gasped quietly. He believed that God was visiting her in her dreams and manifesting miracles for him to see. Maybe this was for him too.

He gazed at her flawless sleeping beauty and wondered if she would wake up if he kissed her on the lips. He smiled at himself over the childish thought, but this was God's work, not a fairy tale. He would let God finish it.

He mouthed, "Thank you, Lord," as he looked up to the ceiling while taking long strides across the bedroom and down the hall.

Chapter Forty-two

Allison woke up as the morning sun streamed in through the window. For the first time, she remembered her dreams—the horrible church men judging her and her hopeless feeling. She remembered the angel carrying her away to safety. She felt love like she'd been bathed in it. The rose she'd slept with was still cradled softly in her hands. She was astonished to see that it was nearly completely white, like the field and the angel.

She wondered if the angel had come there and transformed the rose. Maybe she would be transformed today too. Laying the rose aside, she stretched her arms up to the ceiling and hopped hopefully out of bed. She couldn't wait to tell Saren about her dream. She ran to the dresser and pulled out an old journal that had never been used. She remembered her grandmother had given it to her, but she'd thought it was too pretty to use and saved it. This was the perfect day to begin writing in it. A blue gel pen lay neatly next to the beautiful royal-blue journal. She sat on the edge of the bed and recorded the dream. This way, it could not get forgotten.

Finished with her entry, she closed the journal and placed it on the nightstand under the clear blue lamp. "This is a new day." She smelled and admired the beauty of the unusual roses in the familiar vases. For the first time since she'd been brought back to the cottage, she wanted to look at everything as though she'd been blind and could now finally see.

After she examined all the blue things, she slowly sauntered toward the chest of drawers with the green figurines. Stopping in the gap between the two dressers, she noticed a tiny frame on the wall. It was small considering the high ceiling and huge wall. It was a drawing of a flower with the saying "A day begun with God is always blessed."

Smiling, she knelt and prayed the Lord's Prayer. She was glad she remembered it. She added, "Thank you, Lord, for my new friend, Saren, and that beautiful dream of the angel and love. Lord, please let me know what you want me to do. I'm yours and will do your will."

She felt as new and fresh as raindrops. She hurried to the closet to get dressed. These clothes had been there from before she went to college, mixed in with keepsake dresses from several generations back. She enjoyed looking at all the clothes. She vaguely recognized each item, but the full memory would not come. They were all in grayscale. One that seemed somehow special to her was a floral summer dress with big gray roses on it. She put it on then chose a gray denim blazer with a gathered waistline with a tulle ruffle sewn underneath that created an exaggerated hourglass silhouette.

All dressed, she went downstairs and found pancakes in the microwave, still warm with butter oozing down the sides—further confirmation that it was a special day. She poured herself a glass of milk and sat down at the table.

Watching closely, she drizzled warm syrup on the pancakes. While she ate, she looked out the window. She watched the squirrels gathering acorns. Suddenly, it dawned on her that someone had been gathering her acorns.

Who made these delicious pancakes? How was this syrup still warm? She looked around, realizing she was in her grandmother's cottage.

If the snake had been inside, he would have told her to miss her grandparents and feel sadness and remorse that she'd been a burden. However, she felt nothing but love. She knew she was loved and well taken care of. She believed for the first time that she would owe nothing but love in return—mainly to God, who set things in place for her to be so well loved.

She did her breakfast dishes and headed into the parlor, which was more of a library. She looked around, marveling at the beauty of the room and the view of all kinds of gray flowers outside the front bay window beyond the desk. She smiled at the arrangement of white-and-red roses on the coffee table, proud of herself for remembering not to go outside and trim that rosebush again for the ten thousandth time.

She sat down on the couch while still looking at the window. "I need a new routine now that I'm not trimming rosebushes in the morning." She let her shoulders relax and her hands fall into her lap. Her gaze lowered to the Bible on the coffee table. "I know. I'll read the Bible."

As she pulled it over, the Bible seemed to open on its own, and one of the rainbows from the chandelier lit up a certain passage from 1 Timothy 15:17. Although it was an old King James Version, it miraculously read like a New Living Translation so that she could easily understand it. "This is a trustworthy saying, and everyone should accept it: 'Christ Jesus came into the world to save sinners'—and I'm the worst of them all. But God had mercy on me so that Christ Jesus could use me as a prime example of his *great patience* with even the worst sinners. Then others will realize that they, too, can believe in him and receive eternal life. All honor and glory to God forever and ever! He is the eternal King, the unseen one who never dies; he alone is God. Amen.'"

Allison sat and stared at the words on the page as they washed over her like a baptism. He was talking to her. God had patience for Paul, who had killed and persecuted followers of Christ, and He forgave and made him into the most prolific of the apostles. It was only logical that He had patience for her.

Allison soaked up 1 Timothy then 2 Timothy. Her eyes and spirit understood what she saw. 2 Timothy 1:9: "It's God who saved us and chose us to live a holy life. He did this not because we deserved it, but because that was His plan long before the world began—to show his love and kindness to us through Christ Jesus." Then 2 Timothy 2:8: "Never forget that Jesus Christ was a man born into King David's family and that He was raised from the dead. This is the Good News I preach."

Allison spent the morning surrounded by miraculous beauty that she finally saw, and she was so engrossed in the Bible that she read and read, going from passage to passage. She saw and understood the plan of salvation. It was beautiful and simple. Because God loves us, He had to reconcile sin, so He sent Jesus.

She realized the guilt she felt was a new kind of sin, because it showed she didn't believe Jesus had saved her and cleansed her of everything. She still couldn't remember what sins she'd committed, only the pain of the guilt that had been with her for so long. She felt her tormenting guilt slowly giving way to love, though.

She sat basking in God's love until Saren and Frost arrived. She was so excited to share with Saren her new understanding.

Chapter Forty-three

It was Friday, and school got out at noon because of a special sporting event. Saren was far too involved with her mystery to watch the event. So she skipped out and headed for Emma's.

Saren had decided to take some flowers to Allison. It seemed a little silly because she had so many all over the house and literally every flower in her garden, but Saren wanted to do something fun for Allison that was out of the ordinary. She didn't want to go out into the yard. She wasn't sure if she was ready to confront the creepy snake with Allison just yet. So she planned to avoid the yard and talk about that studio. Had Allison painted all those paintings? If not her, then who? Saren still had so many mysteries to solve.

It was right after noon, so she knew Uncle Jonathan would be making lunch for the employees. In fact, he was always at Emma's, no matter how early or how late she was there. But she didn't have time to think about what Uncle Jonathan did *after* work. She had a mystery to solve.

She pulled hard on the front door, enough to ring the giant jingle bells dangling from it, and entered the fragrant front display area. Uncle Jonathan's big smile floated around the corner, and he swaggered toward the door. Ol' Blue bounced around him with an anxious wag to greet her cousin dog and pal Frost.

"Ho ho whoo, looky who's here! My little favorite!" Jonathan hollered cheerfully as he passed through the work area toward the door. He picked her up and swung her around. Saren untangled herself and unleashed Frost so the two old doggie buddies could greet each other properly with a do-si-do of tail sniffing.

"Whatcha doing here so early today, young one?" Jonathan asked.

"Some special track meet at school, but I'm visiting a *friend* and wanted to take her some flowers." Saren gave him a knowing smile so that the employees wouldn't catch on.

"Oohh." He winked at her. "Do you have anything in mind?" Jonathan asked, treating Saren as if she was a very important adult customer.

"I don't know. Do you have any suggestions for the girl that has *every* flower?"

"I have just the right thing. Follow me." He took her back to the last greenhouse and weaved all the way back to the farthest corner table. It was covered in a sea of blue. Each tiny flower had five vividly azure petals with a yellow dot in the center.

"Oh, Uncle Jonathan, they're perfect!" Saren was jumping up and down, clapping her hands.

Jonathan couldn't help but beam. He stopped just to watch her joy. "You remind me so much of *someone* I once knew. She had the same exact reaction to them as you did. Even though she was about three years older then, than you are now. When she first saw them, she jumped up and down, joyfully clapping her hands, too."

Saren knew he was talking about Auntie Allison. But she had trouble picturing the sullen gray lady being as joyful as she was. *That would be so fun for her to get back to her joyful self. We would be able to be excited together.*

Saren came back into the present and did another jump and twirl. "Was she a *special* friend, Uncle Jonathan?"

"She was. Yes, she was my *very* special friend. She loved all flowers, but from that day on, these flowers were her very favorite. Grandpa often saved some for her. He always gave her the ones that didn't make it into a bouquet or were going to fade before they could sell. You know, her eyes were the same exact color of blue as these flowers. Do you know what they're called?"

"They're so pretty. No, I don't know. What are they?" She rarely got to go into that greenhouse. She thought they were the only flower *not* growing in Allison's garden.

"They're called forget-me-nots. They grow wild all over Alaska, Canada, and the northern parts of America, They're rare in Southern California. We started cultivating them in this greenhouse. Now we're the primary grower of them in all of the Southwest." Jonathan gathered a large bouquet of the delicate blue flowers. "The last day before... my *special* friend left for college, I made her a bouquet exactly like this one I'm making now. I wanted to ask her to forget-me-not, but that's too corny, right?"

Saren chuckled, feeling very grown-up. Uncle Jonathan had never talked to her about anything like this before. "Maybe if you said it like that." Saren paused to control her giggles. She gave him a sly look. "Was Auntie Allison your girlfriend?"

Jonathan cleared his throat at the question. "No, she wasn't. I sure wish that I had tried harder back then to make her my girl. Do you think these flowers gave her the message?"

"I guess it depends on the girl. But why didn't you tell her? Didn't you think she liked you back?"

"Well, yeah, I did think she liked me back, but she was so set on going to college. If I had told her how *much* I loved her, I thought maybe she wouldn't go to college and then years later would regret not going and resent me for stopping her. Plus, she was so smart. I wanted her to get her education. She'd planned to come back after college and work here at Emma's with Grampa and me. I figured I had time to sort it out. She'd planned to get a degree in horticulture and do research to develop new varieties of plants and flowers. But..."

"New varieties. That's exciting, Uncle Jonathan."

"Well, Saren, you know that your great-grandfather had a PhD in horticulture. As a young man, he decided that academia was not for him. So he started Emma's. He still wrote papers and did research, even though he wasn't at a university. Still, his little shop had become world famous for new varieties, and Allison wanted to follow in Grandpa's footsteps. It's too bad he didn't live to see her fulfill her dream and his dream for her."

"But she met that professor and turned gray instead."

"Yes, and I'm still waiting for her to come back to Emma's."

"Oh, Uncle Jonathan, why didn't you just let the flowers fall and swoop her up in your arms and tell her you wanted her for your very own?" Saren made gestures with her arms and wrapped them around herself like she was embracing someone. She twirled around. Being only twelve, she understood something about romanticism but maybe not as much as a thirteen-year-old would.

Jonathan shook his head in regret. "Yes, but she was too ambitious to go from high school to being a wife. So I gave her blue flowers and hoped she would forget-me-not." Jonathan looked down at the flowers with longing.

Suddenly, Saren took a step back and looked up at Jonathan in awe. "Wow, forget-me-nots... Do you think they'll make her remember now?"

Jonathan sat down on a stool so he would be at eye level with Saren. "I truly hope she does. I really do." He spoke with such intensity that Saren felt like it was really a prayer or maybe even a plea to God.

Jonathan hopped up from the stool. Recovering in his best fake cheerful voice, he said, "All done!" Jonathan picked up the finished bouquet all wrapped in paper tied with a blue ribbon like the one around Frost's neck. Then he ushered Saren through the greenhouse, into the back vegetable plant display area.

"Hi, Jonathan!"

Jonathan and Saren turned to see Officer Brennen walking quickly toward them.

"Hi, Officer Brennen," Saren said.

"Frank." Jonathan shook his hand.

"The lady in the shop told me that I would find you out here. I wanted to tell you in person."

"Good news!" Saren yelled.

"Yes! Those are nice." Officer Brennen pointed to the forget-me-nots. "So I alerted the FBI after we discovered the current identity of your Dr. Mortimer Hebert. He was taken into custody in Madrid, Spain."

"Yeah!" Saren jumped up and down and twirled. Frost joined in the celebration.

Jonathan took off his hat and wiped the sweat from his balding head. "Wow, Frank. You really did it. You got him."

"Yes, we got him. Thanks to you and Saren."

Frost gave a little whine.

"Oh, and Frost too." Officer Brennen chuckled. "He's wanted on two other counts of plagiarism, three other rapes, and a suspect in two poisoning murders. Each under a different alias. You know, after we cracked Allison's case, it didn't take long before the FBI found the others. So, it looks like we *will* get justice for Allison after all through the other cases."

Jonathan's expression changed from relief to worry. "What do you mean?"

"See, the statute of limitations on rape in California has passed for Allison. We will be able to get him on the plagiarism charges because there is no time limit for that."

"Isn't there a special clause or something for cases where the person can't come forward during the allotted time?"

"Unfortunately not, but since the other rapes took place in Utah, we will be able to prosecute there."

"We found Allison in Utah. The abuse must have continued there."

"Jonathan, that is a very good argument. I will present it to the DA in Utah."

"What if Allison can't testify?"

"Do we have any other evidence besides your eyewitness and the plagiarism?"

"Maddie saw her with the blood on her dress."

"That's good. But circumstantial. The best witness is the victim. How is Allison doing?"

Jonathan looked at Saren.

"She's doing better. She talks to me now. But we have evidence even if she can't testify."

"What evidence, Detective Saren?"

"We have her journal."

"What?" Jonathan spoke a bit too forcefully.

"Grandmother Busy Bea gave it to us last night."

Jonathan shook his head. "So she had it this whole time."

"Why would she not give it to the authorities or you to help with the investigation?" Officer Brennen took his hat off and scratched his head.

"Busy Bea didn't want anyone to know about what happened, and Allison explained everything in the journal," Saren said.

Officer Brennen pinched his eyebrows together. "But why?"

"She said it would ruin them, her, and Grandfather. Mom was really mad. I thought her head was going to explode."

Jonathan put his hand on Saren's shoulder. "Does your dad know about this?"

"Yes, and he told Grandfather Spencer. He didn't know she had it either."

"Wow! Yes, that will be the evidence we need to put him away," Officer Brennen said.

"I can't wait to call Maddie. She'll be thrilled to hear that Dr. Death has been found and will be prosecuted."

"Oh good, but what is the deal with their mother?"

"She has always been tough to deal with. One time during our high school years, Allison was working here with me. We were repotting plants. Bea came and saw dirt on Allison's apron, and she had a fit and went crazy at Allison for being dirty. Allison went into the storeroom to get another one. But Grampa came out and told Bea that he ran Emma's and not to bother the kids when they were working. She was dealing with dirt, and that's just what happens. You get dirty. But Bea could never accept it. She tried to make Allison into this impossibly perfect person. So when Allison disappeared, she chose to hide what she knew rather than to help Allison."

"Wow, you could almost see why Allison lost it." Officer Brennen put his hand on the side of his head. "Saren, did your grandmother reveal any other evidence?"

"Yes. Grandmother Bea also had a letter from the university that kicked Allison out of school and her apartment and fired her from her job."

"Okay. Do you think I could get a look at that letter?"

"Yeah, my mom has it. Why?"

"We may have a negligence case against the university as well since they didn't come forward with this information during the search for Allison."

"Wow, wouldn't that be great! Anything we can do about the police department that didn't respond?"

"Unfortunately, there's not much we can do to law enforcement. But we can ask for an internal investigation. If they find that the leading officer is linked to the university coverup, there will be repercussions."

"Well, I guess we can't have everything."

"Yes. Oh, and we found the other girl, Lisa."

"You're kidding. Where?"

"She was in a Lisbon homeless shelter. Her mother is there now to bring her home. Saren, you have definitely saved that young woman's life."

Jonathan put his hand on Saren's shoulder. She was uncharacteristically quiet. She seemed to be really feeling the impact of finding Lisa. Saren seemed to grow two inches right then.

"Wow!" Jonathan looked up at the sky then back to Frank. "Well, thank you so much for helping us on this case, Frank. You're the first cop to care about Allison... and Lisa too. We really appreciate it."

"I'm just doing my job. I'm just glad we can hopefully prevent this from happening to any other girls."

"I'll walk you out to your car." Jonathan turned to Saren. "You're free, young one."

"Okay, Thank you so much, Officer Brennen. Please let me know how else I can help," Saren said.

"Will do."

"Thanks for the wonderful bouquet, Uncle Jonathan. It's just perfect. My *friend* is going to love these. I can't wait to see her face. Frost, let's go." The two headed off down the wooded trail to the cottage.

"Is she going to see Allison now?" Officer Brennen asked.

"Yes, she's starting to remember some things, for Saren."

"Only Saren?"

"Yes, just Saren, but I'm hopeful. Wouldn't it be amazing if she gets justice and her memory back on the same day?"

The two men nodded and made their way toward the parking lot.

Chapter Forty-four

Saren bounced up and sat on the rock wall. When she swung her legs over to enter the miracle garden, she heard a hissing sound that made her pause. She looked around for the snake but didn't see it. She decided to ignore it like she always did. Frost seemed to have the same idea. He sniffed the air briefly then headed straight toward Allison sitting on the front porch bench. Saren released him from his leash. "Go ahead. Go see Allison."

He bolted as fast as he could with all his fur flowing back in the wind of his swiftness. He was up all the steps in one jump. Allison leaned down to scratch Frost behind the ears.

"Better watch out, Frost. Your tail is going so fast you might launch like a helicopter," Saren said.

Allison looked up at Saren, who saw a glimmer of a smile on Allison's face. Her eyes looked different today. Rather than the usual gray, a swirl of azure peeked out like a crisp blue sky shining through black clouds at the end of a dark storm.

"Hi, Miss Allison, how are you today?" Saren was so captivated by Allison's eyes that she forgot all about the flowers she was cradling in her left arm.

"Whatcha got there?" Allison asked, sounding unusually casual and normal.

"Oh, my goodness, I forgot. I brought you some flowers."

"Oh, for me?" Allison got up to accept the flowers. As she held them up to look at them, her eyes morphed into the exact same color of blue as the forget-me-nots. "They're forget-me-nots. They're like my eyes."

"'Allison, these are forget-me-nots,'" Allison said in a low voice, imitating her grandpa. Then she imitated another male voice, one that was far more youthful. "'Before you go, I wanted to give you these.'"

"'You know I could never forget you,'" Allison said in her normal but youthful-sounding voice. Allison spoke as if she were saying both sides of a conversation, maybe several conversations.

Saren thought that Allison sounded like she was imitating Uncle Jonathan. "Who... Who are you talking to?"

"Who... Who? Yes, where did you get these?"

"Uncle Jonathan said they were just the thing. Do you like them?"

Allison turned around and, staring at the flowers, whispered, "Jonathan." She smiled then suddenly clutched her chest then her head. She writhed in pain. But she didn't let go of the flowers.

"What is it?" Saren ran to her side but was afraid to touch her. "Allison, Allison! What is it? What's wrong?"

"I remember... It's too much. I don't want to remember. But now I remember. I know what I did." Allison slumped back and forth, and with a bang, she slammed her forehead onto the porch railing.

Saren was surprisingly calm. She figured it was good that Allison remembered, and so she pulled her close and had Allison sit back down on the porch chair.

Allison pulled at her clothes then scratched her own arms. She doubled over, holding her stomach with one hand and her head with the other. Her body and mind twisted in tormenting pain.

Frost laid his head down on the top of Allison's foot, trying to comfort her—then suddenly, he sat straight up.

That yellow-eyed black snake had slithered to the top of the steps and was watching the scene play out. "Well, well, well. Playing the innocccent again, are we?"

Frost turned to give the snake a low and very serious warning growl.

"I sssee you momentarily have me at a disssadvantage."

Frost positioned himself at the halfway point between the snake and Allison. Frost stayed his course.

"Sssaren, ssso sssweet, sssure of yourssself, are you? Are you ssssure, Ssssaren?"

"Don't listen to him, Allison. He's the devil. All he can do is throw doubt. He can't hurt you. Let's get inside."

Saren took a sport bottle of water out of her satchel. She aimed and squirted the snake right in the eye. She pulled Allison up, but she was still bent over in agony. "Come on, Miss Allison, you can do it. Come on."

Saren pushed her toward the door, and Allison finally moved her feet and lifted her torso enough to make progress. Meanwhile the snake shook his head and blinked his beady yellow eyes. He made several attempts to get past Frostie, who refused to fail as sentinel, barking and growling at the snake.

Saren was finally able to get Allison into the front door. As soon as they were inside the threshold, Saren whispered, "Come on, Frost. Good boy."

As Frost turned to go inside, the snake made for the door. Frost quickly trotted in, and Saren shut the door behind him. The snake was slithering so fast, it couldn't stop in time and smashed into the door with a series of thuds as the back end of him caught up and piled on top of himself at the door in waves.

Saren locked the door and peered through the clear part of the stained-glass window to make sure that the snake didn't try to get in some other way, but he was still trying to untangle himself.

Allison was in worse shape. Saren took her all the way into the kitchen to be out of sight of that snake and sat her down at the white table. Frost resumed his spot with his head on Allison's foot. For a few seconds, Saren just watched Allison. She didn't appear to be having a physical problem. She did, however, seem to be in some strange state of intense torment. Saren took both Allison's hands in her own. She started to pray in earnest. Being only twelve, she knew that she might not know what to pray for, but she believed the Holy Spirit would help her and pray with her. So she exercised her faith and prayed.

Chapter Forty-five

Allison felt a flush of pain sweep over her body like she was burning from her skin straight into her core. A flash of memories flickered through her like vicious licks in a flaming forest fire.

The first memory was meeting a man that she'd been warned of in a dream, but she didn't recognize the man when she met him. He was dark like a shadow, and sophisticated while sitting in an outdoor café as if in France, sipping hot black liquid from a tiny cup.

The memory morphed into a flame from the café that flared like a silent explosion before a mushroom cloud. She watched herself drowning in a pool of thick black-brown liquid. The scene pulled away to show she was a tiny being inside the espresso cup; then the vision refocused, and she was drowning in the brown of the shadow man's eyes.

Terrified, she choked on the brown liquid that stuck to her like thin hot tar. She tried to stay above, but a circular current drew her under like a giant evil hand was stirring the liquid. She thought she was going to drown in those cruel brown eyes.

The eyes turned into flames that beamed her into a greenhouse. She was pinned against a table, trying to escape but could not. Moments later, the shadow man was laughing—and she was crying.

Now she was on fire, burning with shame, humiliation, and betrayal. Huge licks of fire transported her smoldering into a dark room with old men sitting around a conference table. The conference room door opened, then a roaring blaze blew her out into the standards office of a university building. She was reading a letter that told her she was excommunicated, expelled, evicted, and shunned.

A flame came at her like a ball from the heavens that threatened to consume her. The smoke cleared to reveal her shame at her home church. In front of her family and all her friends, she passed the sacrament tray without partaking. She wanted to disappear as all the eyes of the congregation stared at her accusingly. The burning anguish inside her grew hotter until she saw the yellow eyes of the snake in the rosebush, accusing her.

Forgotten... Forgotten... She heard herself say the words over and over again in spite of the fire in and all around her. She'd been given the gift of forgetting all that had gone on in the past—but she had remembered only her shame. She was nothing but a ghost of shame. She'd become shame.

In the midst of the fire and flames that threatened to devour her, she accepted her fate and what she believed would be the harsh judgement of God. She accepted her role in her past, whatever it had been, and asked God for forgiveness. She'd never asked for forgiveness before because she'd assumed it had to come through the church men. But now she boldly stood in the flames and said, "Please, God in Heaven, forgive me for all and everything that I am. I love you, and I only wanted to please you, Lord."

She'd become so overwhelmed by the vision that she expected those would be her last words. Then a wave of cool, fresh watery peace started at the tip of her head and rinsed over her arms and body, all the way to her feet. Then a soothing love embraced her.

She saw herself sitting at the foot of a tree stump. Jesus sat on the stump, looking at her with compassion. "Allison, you are forgiven. Trust in me and believe it."

She accepted the gift from Jesus to be forgiven. "When will you release the shame?"

"Shame didn't come from me. It's within your own power to be free from it. Believe in me, and you will be free."

"I believe in you. I give my life to you fully. I don't know what to do, but I'll follow my feet. I believe that you'll guide me in your path."

He smiled then disappeared into a flash of bright white light.

Allison felt energized. She found herself surrounded by light so bright that she thought it would burn her, but it did not. Instead, it flooded her soul with goodness and love. She suddenly understood that the fiery light that had burned and tortured her all these years was not what she'd thought. She'd felt like she was being punished by God. But those singeing feelings were the shame imposed upon her by the church men, her mother, and herself. Shame had not come from God but others who'd wanted to make themselves powerful like God. They wanted to control her and everyone. But God did not control His creations. He gave them free will. He loved them.

Allison wasted no more time. She spoke into the light. "I choose the present, life, forgiveness, joy, and love. I choose to pass that love on to others. I choose the real, colorful world and all colors of myself."

In her vision, she saw a dark room where the men sat at the table, judging her. Then the black blended with the white to become the gray life where she'd used that shame to turn on herself. She'd brought this shame on herself because she had judged *herself*.

Then the gray turned to red, the blood of Jesus cleansing her to white. Surrounded once again by cloudlike whiteness, she finally understood that all humans fail. That was why Jesus came and sacrificed Himself. No one could follow the Commandments. All that evil snake had to do was to remind her of her failings, and she'd stayed in that gray state of shame, where no sun ever shone.

Although her personal grayscale remained, the grayness all around her swirled and drained from her sight. Color more vivid than she could imagine surrounded her. She saw all the flowers from every season blooming together. She bathed in the colorful world God was showing her. She didn't know why, but she could do this now that Saren sat across from her, fresh and young. She'd grown to love Saren as if she were her own daughter. Loving this young girl and this fluffy dog broke her habit of self-absorbed shame. She was no longer afraid to accept and give love freely.

She realized she had allowed her shame to block her from receiving or giving love to Madeleine, Luke, Jonathan, and especially to herself. She had abandoned herself.

Her eyes opened to see Saren's mouth moving in the shape of her name. As she focused on Saren, her hearing took a few seconds. At first, she could only hear the rush of water passing over her past and into her present like a wave washing over a crystal sandy beach on a calm, clear day.

She finally heard Saren asking, "Allison, Allison... Are you okay?" Allison nodded.

"Do you remember something?" Saren asked.

"Yes, everything is completely restored. Now I *choose* to forget the past and look forward to what lies ahead like Paul wrote to the Philippians. We really only need to know one thing in life: that Jesus loves us so much and that frees us, the only thing we have to do is believe it. We will fail, but Jesus is there to forgive us if we believe and ask Him." Allison smiled.

With courage in her heart, Allison took Saren's hands in hers. She looked intensely at Saren through eyes welling. "Jesus is Lord, my God, and my Savior. He saved me from all sin. He saved the world from all sin. I never understood that. I thought there had to be punishment. I thought I had to keep from sinning, to be perfect. He freed us. He saved us. They have no power to judge us. It's all a lie."

"Who?" Saren bounced in her seat. This was Allison's big breakthrough.

"The church men, they do not have the power. They only tell us they have it. But now I see. I finally see. Jesus brought us only truth and freedom and joy. Those church men wanted to control the love of Jesus, teaching us to block it with shame. They told me I couldn't pray. God would not hear me. I must reach God only through them. But it doesn't work like that. Jesus wants us to talk to Him no matter what. Sometimes we'll mess up. But when we ask Him for forgiveness, He does and He shows us His love."

As she talked about the love of Jesus and his beautiful plan of salvation, her fingertips began to glow with light. The light grew from her fingertips and passed over both her and Saren's hands, up to the elbows. They radiated a Holy Light.

Allison looked at their fingertips lighting up. She felt so joyful and free. She finally knew she was forgiven. She felt it.

She had blamed *herself* for being a victim of a date rape; then she became a martyr of the churchmen passing judgment on her. Taking the scripture too seriously and too literally *"For if we would judge ourselves, we would not be judged,"* her own judgment was so extreme and drove her so far into herself that she lost touch with reality.

Her thoughts shifted to Jonathan, the man who had always loved her and taken care of her. What a cruel thirteen years for him. She hoped he would still love her and forgive her. Her mind wanted to feel regret and loss of time with him, but the joy of forgiveness and reality made her determined to press forward to return his love and kindness.

She'd loved Jonathan from the first time she'd met him when they were fifteen. He was so full of joy and was the only one who encouraged her to be herself. She missed him terribly. With all her heart she wished that she'd accepted that proposal on the dance floor and married him that night at Maddie and Luke's wedding. But now she saw that he had waited all those years for her to come back to herself. It was all like a nightmare. But instead of feeling the horror of waking to reality, she felt peace and was excited to be free and start living her life now.

This all happened in an instant: this flash of past sin and the epiphany of forgiveness. Saren watched with big eyes of wonder and amazement, following the Holy Light spreading like sparklers up their arms and across their chests and down to their feet.

Allison continued, "I forsake my sins and surrender my life and my soul to you, Lord Jesus Christ. I follow you. My life is a testimony of your love."

As Allison declared her surrender to the Holy One, the light reached her face, and she felt her sallow, gray face give way to rosy cheeks and a peach complexion. Her silver hair faded and turned white like snow. Her summer dress popped back to roses on a navy background with brilliantly embroidered forget-me-nots twirling and swirling around the roses. Her charcoal jacket changed to dark-washed denim with a yellow tulle ruffle.

The forget-me-nots in the pattern on her dress became clear as they turned their characteristic shade of blue. She hadn't recognized them in grayscale, but in full color, the blue forget-me-nots stood out, accentuating the blue in Allison's eyes. Saren, caught up in the transformation, glowed right along with Allison. Her eyes never straying from Allison, Saren's face emanated joy and exuberance.

The lightning sparked around Allison's face, feeling like the source of life itself rushing through her. But the illumination didn't stop there. The electrical discharge spread over the table then to the rest of the house, covering everything as though Allison were the epicenter of an atomic explosion of the Holy Spirit. Every cell of her body felt joy, love, and vivid color. The sparkles like lightning lit up the entire house and garden and swirled upward, consolidating and cascading into a heavenly cloud.

After a few seconds, their eyes focused. Allison and Saren both shed tears of release, happiness, and joy. Overwhelmed by the presence of the Holy Spirit, they basked in the eternal and infinite love they had experienced. Then Saren gave Allison a huge hug.

The room was unchanged, but Allison could see out past the dining room, parlor, and bay window that the yard was wild and mangled. The miracle blessing of the cottage was released, and the place had returned to its natural wild state.

Allison, focused on Saren, reached out and caught up a long white streak of hair in her hand. "Saren, look!"

Saren looked at the lock of her own hair in Allison's hand. Saren took the strand. Her mouth dropped open, and her eyes widened. "I guess I got it too, a little bit. But check yourself out."

Saren lifted a lock of Allison's long hair. "*All* your hair turned white! And look! Your clothes and your face. You're in color again! You're no longer Allison the Gray. You're Allison the White!" Saren spread her arms out over her head in a grand gesture. She jumped up and twirled around so fast, Allison thought she would launch to the ceiling.

Chuckling, Allison looked down and examined her own hands and hair, then she noticed her dress. "I remember this dress. It's the one I wore the day I left for college. Jonathan came to see me off. He gave me a bouquet of forget-me-nots. I wanted to stay, but I wanted to go. I wish Jonathan could have come with me. I figured we were young and had all the time in the world. But then I never came back. How long has it been? Anyway, it doesn't matter how long. I'm not going to waste any more time."

The bouquet of forget-me-nots was still lying on the table where they had dropped during Allison's transformation.

"The forget-me-nots!" Allison exclaimed joyfully. She jumped up with a smile and carefully took a beautiful square cobalt glass vase out of the cabinet, filled it half full of water, put the forget-me-nots in the vase and arranged them into a beautiful bouquet. Then she grabbed a bowl, filled it with water, and put it on the floor for Frost.

Watching Frost drink, she fully felt the joy that was hers to have. Allison felt so happy and alive she thought she might just float away. She was so overwhelmed to realize that it wasn't enough for God to bless her to be back in reality but to also discover that Jonathan had been taking care of her. She'd always been in love with Jonathan. It was something in the way he looked at her. He made her feel brilliant, loved, and most of all, free. She'd put her parents' expectations over everything. She realized now that Jonathan was the only person who had ever allowed her to feel free to be all she really was. She'd been close to her sister, but she'd felt an obligation to provide a good example for Maddie. But with Jonathan she had no obligations. They had just simply enjoyed one another.

"Jonathan! Let's go get Jonathan," she said and ran out the back door, her skirt flying back in her wake.

Chapter Forty-six

Jonathan put the finishing touches on the next day's orders and headed toward the shop to close up. Just then, a loud crackling sound made him stop and look toward the cottage. The electric sparking sound grew, and a light shone from the woods.

Iris came out of the shop, accompanied by a group of customers, to see what was happening.

Light like lightning began to swirl around the unseen cottage, rising above the trees. As the bolts twisted and crackled, they became a huge ball of light. Lightning bolts reached from the cottage up into the heavens and down again. With a sound of a deep explosion, the lightning plumed and raced into the sky. And with a flash, the light disappeared into a cloud.

"Oh!" Jonathan jumped in his nearby utility cart and sped full speed toward the cottage. *What is happening?* Jonathan was sweating in a panic. Saren was there too. "Oh, Lord, protect them."

As he came around the final bend near the house, he saw something he dared never to even dream.

Allison, in full color, looked almost exactly like she had the day they'd left her at college, apart from her snow-white locks streaming behind her. She ran toward him. Not only was she unhurt, but she was back and in color. He stopped the cart just short of meeting up with her and leaped out of the vehicle.

"Jonathan! Jonathan!" Allison ran to him and embraced him with an uninhibited hug.

"Allison!" He swung her around and around then set her down to look at her. "Alli, you're back."

"I'm back."

"What was that explosion?"

"This!" She fluffed out her white hair, and the curls bounced.

"Explosive hair dye?" He furrowed his brows and tilted his head. She laughed freely and joyfully.

Saren and Frost caught up with Allison to greet Jonathan.

"Are you guys okay, young one?"

"Better than okay, Uncle Jonathan. Look! She's normal. Well, maybe not exactly normal with miracle white hair, but she's with it and with us."

"So, what was all that lightning?"

"It was God fixing me. Oh, Jonathan, I remember everything. Thank you so much for watching over me all these years and taking care of me. I'm so grateful."

"It wasn't just me. Maddie and Luke were here too."

"Yes, I know. Where is she?" Allison peered straight into his eyes.

"She would be picking up J.D.," Saren said.

Allison let go of Jonathan. She put both hands on Saren's shoulders. "J.D.?"

"My little brother."

"Oh!" Allison clapped her hands in glee upon learning she had a nephew. "Let's call her!"

Jonathan put his arm around Saren. "So how did you get that white strand?"

"I was really close to the action. Some of God's power must have landed on me too."

Jonathan and Allison chuckled as he helped her into the utility cart. Saren hopped in, and they headed to the cottage.

Chapter Forty-seven

As soon as the cart came to a stop at the back of the cottage, Saren sprang out and ran straight for the only telephone in the cottage. The heavy black rotary phone sat on the table in the entryway. It was so old it belonged in a museum, but it worked. Saren was glad that her *dad* had answered the phone. "Dad, bring Mom to the cottage ASAP."

"You got it," Luke said, then Saren heard a click. Her dad was a man of few words.

Saren ran back to the kitchen, scratching Frost on the head as she passed. Frost and Jonathan were watching Allison make hot chocolate and arrange cookies on a platter. Frost's gaze never left Allison's movements. His ears and tail were in their happy position.

"They're on their way," Saren said.

Jonathan nodded and continued to stare at Allison with such intense longing that Saren decided to give them a moment. Besides, her mind raced with so much new information.

She'd already began compiling all the clues she'd gathered so far. She knew this was the end of the mystery, and she wanted to leave no stone unturned. She retrieved her journal out of her satchel and flipped to the page titled "Mystery of the Gray Lady and the Miracle Cottage," where she'd written a list of questions. She checked off the questions she'd answered, but she still wanted to know why all the flowers from different seasons bloomed together. Saren hadn't solved the mystery of the snake and how to get rid of it, and she also had to add some new mysteries.

1. What changed in Allison to allow her to come back?
2. How was she able to remember everything?

She was just finishing up jotting these down when she heard her dad's pickup drive up to the front of the house. Ol' Blue's tags jingled from the front of the house.

She had one more checkmark to make now, but it would have to wait. It was about to get really exciting around here. Saren dropped her journal into her satchel.

She could barely contain the excitement over the anticipation of Allison and her mom seeing each other for the first time. It would be hard, but she would try to remember to be quiet and let the adults have their moment.

The doorbell rang with an old-fashioned chime that seemed to come from all directions at once. Saren bounced up and jogged after Frost, whose self-designated job was to greet the ringer of any doorbell.

Saren opened the door for Madeleine and Luke. Ol' Blue swiftly ran in past Frost in a welcoming competition. Looking around for her little brother, she asked, "Where's J.D.?"

Just then he popped into the doorway from the darkness. "Here I am."

Luke casually gave Saren his usual fatherly welcome hug. Luke touched Saren's white streak. "You're okay?"

"Yeah, wait until you see Auntie Allison."

"She didn't become Allison the White, did she?"

"Wait! How did you know?" Her dad had a special intuition for knowing what was happening. Saren always took comfort because she believed that her dad knew everything.

Madeleine, on the other hand, looked worried and hurried past Saren. "Where is she?"

"She's in the kitchen, Mom." Before she got it out, her mom took off toward the kitchen. Without a glance to her dad, she followed after her mother in quick step.

The lights were on in the kitchen, which glowed with warmth. Saren was proud of her self-discipline and kept her tongue. She wanted to tell her mom everything, but she knew this stage belonged to Allison. It had taken Allison a long time to learn that she deserved this.

Madeleine breezed quickly into the kitchen, and everyone followed. Even J.D. and the dogs seemed to understand something important was happening and that they shouldn't interrupt.

Seeing the rest of the family enter, Allison flowed over to meet Madeleine.

"Maddie!" Allison hugged her little sister and squeezed her tight. Madeleine was bawling huge tears of relief and joy.

Jonathan made jokes about flash flood warnings because there were so many tears. Luke, too relieved to make jokes just yet, shook his head and gave a Jonathan a look that said, "Really?"

Allison didn't cry, but she beamed happiness and love all over her little sister.

"Allison, are you really back?" Madeleine asked in between sobs. "Are you here?"

"I'm here, Maddie. I'm cured." She pulled back in her embrace to face Madeleine. "I'm forgiven, redeemed, restored, and have a lot of piled-up love to distribute."

"Yes, you are, and yes, you do. I missed you. You sound like yourself too, always thorough and in charge." Madeleine smiled knowingly at her sister.

"Luke," Allison said. She released her sister and gave her brother-in-law a hug. "Thank you, Luke, for everything." She looked at her sister, niece, and nephew.

Luke nodded quietly and smiled at Allison.

The two sisters, arm in arm, sat down next to each other at the table and bid the others to sit as well. Saren pulled a chair up in between her mom and her auntie. She didn't want to interrupt, but she didn't want to miss anything either.

Madeleine began, "I don't even know where to start, Allison. How... Actually, I'm going to let Saren ask. She has certainly earned her answers."

Saren knew she'd witnessed a great miracle, and the presence of God was so strong that they had glowed. Still, she wanted to hear it from Allison's point of view. Something in Allison's prayers were so strong—she wanted to understand that kind of faith.

"So, Auntie Allison, what happened between you and God to make you go from your tormented expression to the joy we see now?"

Chapter Forty-eight

Allison looked around the table, taking inventory of the faces she loved most. Little Maddie had become so mature and motherly. Luke was the way he always had been, minus a few locks of hair on top. Saren, her joyful niece, was wise beyond her years. Little J.D. had been surprisingly quiet, but Allison could see mischief in his eyes. Jonathan put his warm hand on top of hers. She longed for him in a way that was new to her, strong and powerful.

"Yes, Allison, what changed?" Jonathan's voice was soft yet masculine.

"I am forgiven. It is the biggest miracle, and I am so grateful." Allison's smile beamed freedom and unburdened lightness.

"But, Auntie Allison, why were you able to see it now and not thirteen years ago?" Saren eyes were wide with bewilderment.

Allison smiled sweetly and calmly at Saren. "You see, guilt is meant to redirect us back to God. But unchecked, it can drive a wedge *between* us and God. Then, I didn't know that perfection for God was unattainable. But now I understand that Jesus shares *His* righteousness with us."

"Auntie Allison, what happened to you back then?"

"Blaming myself, I was horrified by the judgments of men and terrified of the wrath of God. I judged myself so harshly over too much disgrace that I lost myself. I couldn't face that I'd put myself in that position in the first place. I couldn't acknowledge that someone I trusted had taken my virginity from me."

Jonathan suddenly sat up straight and squeezed Allison's hand tighter.

"Jonathan?" Allison put her other hand on Jonathan's shoulder to comfort him.

"Allison," Jonathan said softly. "We've found Mort, finally."

Madeleine forced both hands down on the table. "What? Where?"

"They're extraditing him to America from Spain as we speak," Jonathan said.

"He was wanted on other charges too. We helped them find him," Saren said.

"Wow, Allison gets justice on the same day she's back." Luke shook his head and put his arm around his wife. Maddie put her hand to her heart.

"I'm glad he can't hurt anyone anymore." Allison took a deep breath of relief. "But I've wasted too much time dwelling on the past."

Madeleine had been listening patiently to Allison. However, years of abandonment and hurt still disfigured Madeleine's expression. She could no longer hold back. "Why now, Allison? Why today?" Torrential tears rolled down her checks.

Allison released Jonathan's hand and took her sister's face in her hands. She wiped Maddie's tears from her cheeks. "Madeleine, it wasn't your fault. This was all part of God's plan for our lives. What matters isn't what came before—our sins, our guilt, our tragedy—but what happens *between* thorns and glory. Jesus wore thorns, but he didn't stay in them. Instead, he defeated death and rose to receive His glory. I was trapped in the gray shame of my thorns. I forgot all about His glory and righteousness that Jesus chose to share with us. Maddie, you understood this all the time. That's why you left our parents' church and went to church with Grandma Emma."

With tears still streaming down her face, Maddie nodded.

"Jonathan, you and Grandpa, too, but I couldn't see it then. I was blinded to the truth. But now I get it."

"Yes, Allison. I wish I had tried harder to make you see," Madeleine said.

"We all do," Jonathan said.

Releasing her sister's face, she took Jonathan's hand once again. "You can't make someone see what they don't have eyes for. This morning, I woke up for the first time in my life with no guilt, only a deep and satisfying love floating in and around me. When Saren brought the forget-me-nots, I remembered you, Jonathan. I remembered the day I left for college, and how I hated leaving you."

"I hated it too. I've regretted not making you stay or sucking it up and going to college with you every day," Jonathan said.

Frost shook out his coat, making his tags jingle.

"You both did what you thought was right at the time," Saren said.

"Yes, thank you, Jonathan, for never giving up on me." She held up her arms and twirled them around. "I'm overwhelmed that God put these angels around me to protect me, even from myself." She bent down and patted Frost's fluffy hindquarters. "I'm grateful for Frost's example of pure bliss." She put her arm around Saren. "And for Saren's persistence. And you, Luke, and Maddie for your faith. My only challenge will be to not regret wasting so much time listening to that snake's lies. But I'm committed to forgetting the past and pressing forward with joy and love. It's obvious that God has a plan for my life."

"Wow!" Saren said, leaning back in her chair quietly. They all sat in silence for a few moments, soaking it in.

Then she suddenly sat up. "Auntie Allison, I still have a mystery to solve. Why did God give you a garden where all the flowers of different seasons bloomed at the same time?"

"He was trying to show me that all the seasons of myself must bloom together in harmony. I can't abandon myself because something happened in my spring, because I still have summer, fall, and winter blossoms to nurture."

"Whoa!" Saren said, her eyes like saucers.

Luke cleared his throat. "So, Allison, do all your selves talk to each other? Because those flowers loved to talk."

They all laughed.

"Yes, actually, they do." Allison gave them all a beaming smile.

"Just make sure they're all sweet to each other!" Saren said.

"Definitely!" Allison smiled and put her arm around Saren.

"Wow..." Maddie leaned across Saren to hug her sister, squishing Saren in between them. "I'm so glad to have you back." Maddie released Allison and looked down at her daughter. "Are there any more questions in that little notebook of yours?"

"Well, most of them are solved. The last one is how to get rid of the evil snake, but maybe he's already vanished. I do have a new question, Auntie Allison—you said *between* thorns and glory. I get that the thorns are the sin, guilt, or troubles of some kind and glory is what we get from Jesus, but what's between them?"

"Oh, all the good stuff of life! We fulfill the plans God has for us between thorns and glory. Each of us picks up our own cross, our own purpose, and we must grow past the thorns and joyfully look forward to the glory that He shares with us."

"Cool!," Saren said.

Suddenly, J.D. could take no more being still. He hopped off his chair, ran around the table, and jumped up into Allison's lap to give her a big hug. "Welcome back, Auntie Allison!"

Everyone chuckled.

"Thank you, sweetie. I am back... and *hungry*. Jonathan, how long has it been since I had ice cream?"

"At least thirteen years." He faked defensiveness. "Hey, I fed you healthy." He looked around at everyone. "We're riding with you, Luke. I only have the ATV here."

"Let's go," Luke said.

They all got up to go.

Allison paused to look around. "I've always loved this kitchen, but somehow, it looks different from when we were kids."

"Yeah, the blessing that was over this place has disappeared on everything except for the counter tile. That, some angel made." Jonathan pointed to the porcelain mosaic on the counter.

"Wow, that looks like me," Allison said, "and that angel looks like you."

Jonathan came around to look at it more closely. "Hm, I never noticed that before."

They both paused in a sudden mutual understanding that the mosaic was showing an allegory of when he had rescued Allison in the snowy mountains. He was not an angel, but it was clear beyond doubt that an angel had guided him.

J.D. pretended to fly around the room like an angel.

Jonathan let out a holler of happiness. "Whooo hooo!"

Allison turned quickly to meet his embrace.

"Thank you, Jesus!" Allison yelled.

Chapter Forty-nine

S aren marveled at the moonlight so bright that it cast tiny rainbows around the foyer. Luke opened the door. Everyone waited
for Allison to take her first step out into the world. The moist night
air washed over them like a healing salve. The full moon beamed
through the forest and glistened on the beads of dew. Gone was the
fairytale beauty of the garden beyond the front porch. The regular,
natural beauty of God's Earth had been restored to the cottage garden.

The six of them, plus two canines, made their way down the
front porch steps. All the miracle flowers from every season were
replaced by natural California forest wildflowers in bloom, Indian
paintbrushes, daisies, aster, and mustard plants as tall as Jonathan. A
meadow of red-orange poppies spiced the lawn.

They passed to the right of the grove of small pines and manzanita trees. In the middle of the poppies stood a solitary wild rosebush—the one Allison had been trimming every day for the past
thirteen years. It was no longer perfectly manicured. The stems were
wild and tangled. However uncultivated, it still flourished with massive, lush red roses with white spots on them. It was the only plant in
the garden that retained any of its supernatural characteristics.

Saren eyed the bush suspiciously.

"Wow, what beautiful roses." Madeleine took a step toward the
bush.

Saren blocked her mother from getting any closer.

"These are the flowers I was telling you about. They grew back like this today. Aren't they amazing? Maddie, do you mind if we take some of them to your house for the table?"

"I would love that." Madeleine smiled.

Jonathan retrieved a pair of gardening shears from the loop on his cargo pants and handed them to Allison. She waded through the tall grass and wildflowers surrounding the bush. She took the shears with one hand and held her other hand up to carefully grab the stem, watching out for the thorns.

Luke shouted, "Allison, watch out. There's a snake in that bush."

Allison smiled. "Oh, that old snake can't hurt me. Not anymore." She reached her right arm deep into the rosebush. Even though it was pitch-black in there, her hand was guided by the need to snip out an evil spirit.

They heard a clean swoosh of the shears, and the black head of the snake rolled out of the bush and onto the tall grass at her feet. The yellow eyes stared without seeing.

"Yeah! That was the last mystery. You did it! You got rid of the snake! You did it!"

She winked at Saren. "Don't just watch out for snakes. Don't talk to 'em either, and get rid of the poisonous ones as fast as you can."

Jonathan took off his hat and wiped his forehead.

Allison flicked the snake blood off the shears. "Okay, back to business." She snipped the prettiest red-and-white rose and pulled it from the bush.

The rest of the red drained from the rose, leaving it as pure white as snow. Then the entire bush of crimson-and-white roses turned to flawless pearly white.

Allison shook her head. "See what God did to show me one more time so I would remember and never be able to forget?"

"What do you mean?" Madeleine asked.

"The red of roses were like the blood of Jesus, and once it was spilled, those of us who believe were all turned white like snow, pure. Like me, these roses are now free from the sin of the snake and the guilt and shame of misdirected teachings. They too are redeemed and pure. Wow! God is good."

Saren added, "Plus, you have only to look at your hair in the mirror. Your hair is white as snow too. You're clean, pure, and washed with bleach."

Everybody laughed.

"You have a reminder of God's purity too, Saren." Allison picked up Saren's white strand.

For the first time, Madeleine focused on her daughter. She took the white strand of Saren's hair from Allison's hand. "You experienced this too, didn't you?"

Saren could see that her mom was astounded. Her expression was of pure pride and gratitude. Saren smiled at her mom and nodded. She had so much to tell her mom. She was glad all the secrecy was at an end.

When Allison had cut enough white roses from the bush, Frost sacrificed his blue ribbon for Jonathan to tie the roses together into a bouquet. All done gathering flowers, they headed toward the rock wall. Even though the vegetation had grown over with wild red roses, the section that had cleared for Saren and Frost to pass over the wall was still clear. But there was no need to climb over the wall. As they approached it, the rock wall receded, and the wooden gate rebuilt itself as when Allison had arrived. The half circle of wooden lattice came down on each side to meet the gate, creating a perfect circle. The red roses shifted and covered the archway. When the circle was complete, the red drained from the roses, leaving them sparkling white.

"Wow!" Allison, Saren, and Madeleine said in unison.

Saren wanted to stay and marvel at the archway and gate awhile, but Allison was ready to get on with her life. She held out her hand to Jonathan. As she took her first step, the gate opened itself as if to welcome Allison back into the world. Without hesitation, she passed through the gated archway.

Jonathan followed her lead without letting go of her hand. He looked down at Allison with eyes full of meaning. Jonathan grabbed up Allison by the waist, and arm in arm, they started toward Luke's vehicle.

Once they had all passed through the rose-covered archway, a great mass hit the ground with a thud. They quickly turned to see a long coil of shiny black scales reflecting the moonlight. The headless body of the snake lay dead in the grass beneath the tall rosebush.

Allison and Saren looked at each other with satisfaction, having the physical confirmation that the purity of the light overcomes all that is darkness.

Saren looked around, gathering the last bit of data for the day, then jogged ahead, chasing J.D. to the vehicle. From the position of the pickup, she could see the archway and open gateway welcoming them to come and go freely.

As the adults made their way to the truck, Saren realized that this was near the area that she'd first observed the cottage. She examined the scene, taking mental notes of things that had changed.

"Hey, that's you guys." Saren pointed to the main stained-glass window that she'd admired on her very first encounter at the cottage. "Look, you even have the same clothes on in the picture as you're wearing now."

"Whoa, you're right," Jonathan said.

"How long has that been there?" Allison asked.

"Since the transformation of Grandma Emma's cottage that first night we brought you here. I guess the angels decided to let it stay,"

Madeleine answered. "I often wondered if it was a prophecy or just a hope."

Saren simultaneously stretched both her arms overhead into a V and hollered, "Prophecy!"

They all smiled at Saren in agreement.

Jonathan shouted at the top of his voice, "Amen and hallelujah!" He picked up Allison and swung her around.

She kissed him and held him tightly. Back on the ground, Allison turned around and held her palm up to Luke. He tossed her the pick-up keys. She bounced up into the driver's seat. While she pulled the seat forward so she could reach the gas pedal, everyone else piled in. Frost positioned himself on the center armrest right next to Allison.

"Is everyone buckled up?" Allison asked.

"We're buckled up and ready for our next adventure!" Saren said. Frost barked twice in agreement.

"Yep, this one is a wrap," Jonathan said.

With a smile on her face and her light shining from within her clear eyes, Allison drove everyone out of the forest, unimpeded by vegetation, memories, or condemnation. She passed out of the darkness into the well-lit street to go out for ice cream—and to live free with peace, forgiveness, love, and joy ever after.

Discussion Questions

for book clubs, Sunday school, or Bible study groups

Have you or someone you knew had a traumatic experience like Allison?

What did you do about it?

How did those you told react to it?

How would you react to moving vegetation? Would you go back again?

Why is Saren not afraid?

Have you ever known a place that was mysterious and you wondered who lived there?

Would you seek out an adventure?

Is it surprising that Luke allows Saren to investigate? Why did he?

Why do you think the Gray Lady is gray? What is the significance?

Why do you think Jonathan is so loyal?

Were the birds Jonathan saw real?

Would you be scared after the teen boys revealed the danger of the cottage? Would you return?

Why do you think the Gray Lady is cutting off the blossoms and leaving them on the ground?

Have you ever had something happen and the authorities did not help you? What did you do? What could you do?

What would you do if you were in a situation like Megan? Did Jonathan make the right decision keeping Donny?

Jonathan takes the route of helping boys to protect girls from being abused by the boys. Do you think that is a feasible solution?

What would you do if you discovered a bridesmaid of your mother's was someone you'd never heard of?

What keeps Jonathan going?

Who and what does the snake represent?

Who do the cardinals represent? Why did the author choose cardinals to represent them?

Why did Allison respond to the Frostie Dog and then Saren?

How would you feel if you were Jonathan after Saren spoke with Allison?

Have you asked yourself, "What do I want?"

What do you think the author is trying to show with the enchanted cottage welcoming Allison?

What was the significance of Allison turning gray? Have you ever felt like you were in a gray state? Why?

What was the purpose of the wall closing up after Allison entered the enchanted garden?

Would you have kept Allison in the cottage?

Do you think the enchanted cottage is evil or good?

Do you relate best to Saren, Allison, Maddie, or Busy Bea?

How would you approach a sad or depressed person? Or would you?

Why did Busy Bea do what she did? Was it her fault? Does she take responsibility for her role in what happened?

Why do you think Allison remembered the song?

What was most surprising about the flower-arranging scene?

Do you ever hear accusations in your mind, like Allison?

When did you first realize that God was faithful? What is an example of His faithfulness in your life?

Why do you think the painter painted the words backward only to be understood in the mirror's reflection?

What is an example of appropriate sin-driven guilt versus ongoing chronic guilt? What is the solution to each?

Have you ever been told that you could not seek and hear from God directly?

Have you ever abandoned yourself like Allison?

Do you have something you need forgiveness about that you have never asked for? Why haven't you?

Do you think Busy Bea was justified to hide what happened to Allison?

Have you ever experienced physical torment brought on by mental or emotional pain?

Have you ever felt so much joy you thought you would light up?

Do you ever feel guilt over things that were not your fault? Do you know someone who has the bad habit of misplaced guilt?

What is between thorns and glory?

What surprised you most in the last chapter?

If you could ask the author a question, what would it be?

Scripture References

Chapter 25

Romans 4:5 [5]However, to the one who does not work but trusts God who justifies the ungodly, their faith is credited as righteousness. NIV

Ephesians 2: 8-9 [8]For it is by grace you have been saved, through faith — and this is not from yourselves, it is the gift of God — [9]not by works, so that no one can boast. NIV

Chapter 30

Philippians 2:12-13 [12]Therefore, my dear friends, as you have always obeyed — not only in my presence, but now much more in my absence — continue to work out your salvation with fear and trembling, [13] for it is God who works in you to will and to act in order to fulfill his good purpose. NIV

Chapter 34

Philippians 4:8 [8]Finally, brothers and sisters, whatever is true, whatever is noble, whatever is right, whatever is pure, whatever is lovely, whatever is admirable—if anything is excellent or praiseworthy—think about such things. [9]Whatever you have learned or received or heard from me or seen in me — put it into practice. And the God of peace will be with you. NIV

John 10:7-10 [7]Therefore Jesus said again, "Very truly I tell you, I am the gate for the sheep. [8]All who have come before me are thieves and robbers, but the sheep have not listened to them. [9]I am the gate; whoever enters through me will be saved. They will come in and go out and find pasture. [10]The thief comes only to steal and kill and destroy; I have come that they may have life and have it to the full." NIV

Romans 1:20 For since the creation of the world God's invisible qualities — his eternal power and divine nature — have been clearly seen, being understood from what has been made, so that people are without excuse. NIV

John 3:16-17 [16]For God so loved the world that he gave his one and only Son, that whoever believes in him shall not perish but have eternal life. [17] For God did not send his Son into the world to condemn the world but to save the world through him. NIV

Ephesians 2:8 God saved you by his grace when you believed. And you can't take credit for this; it is a gift from God. [9]Salvation is not a reward for the good things we have done, so none of us can boast about it. [10]For we are God's masterpiece. He has created us anew in Christ Jesus, so we can do the good things he planned for us long ago. ESV

Philippians 3:3 For we who worship by the Spirit of God are the ones who are truly circumcised. We rely on what Christ Jesus has done for us. We put no confidence in human effort. NLT

Philippians 4:4-7 [4]Always be full of joy in the Lord. I say it again — rejoice! [5]Let everyone see that you are considerate in all you do. Remember, the Lord is coming soon. [6]Don't worry about anything; instead, pray about everything. Tell God what you need, and thank him for all he has done. [7]Then you will experience God's peace, which exceeds anything we can understand. His peace will guard your hearts and minds as you live in Christ Jesus. NLT

Chapter 35

Genesis 9:12-13 And God said, "This is the sign of the covenant I am making between me and you and every living creature with you, a covenant for all generations to come: [13]I have set my rainbow in the clouds, and it will be the sign of the covenant between me and the earth." NIV

Psalms 119:89-90 [89]Your word, Lord, is eternal; it stands firm in the heavens. [90]Your faithfulness continues through all generations; you established the earth, and it endures. NIV

Psalms 119:105 Your word is a lamp to guide my feet and a light for my path. NLT

Chapter 36

Matthew 6:12 And forgive us our debts, as we also have forgiven our debtors. NIV

Genesis 3:4 "You will not certainly die," the serpent said to the woman. "For God knows that when you eat from it, your eyes will be opened, and you will be like God, knowing good and evil." NIV

Chapter 39

Isaiah 1:18 Come now, let us settle the matter," says the Lord. "Though your sins are like scarlet, they shall be as white as snow; though they are as red as crimson, they shall be like wool. NIV

John 3:17 For God did not send his Son into the world to condemn the world, but to save the world through him. NIV

Genesis 4:4 And Abel also brought an offering — fat portions from some of the firstborn of his flock. The Lord looked with favor on Abel and his offering. NIV

1 John 4:8 Anyone who does not love does not know God, because God is love. ESV

1 Timothy 1:15-17 [15]This is a trustworthy saying, and everyone should accept it: Christ Jesus came into the world to save sinners

—and I (Apostle Paul) am the worst of them all. [16]But God had mercy on me so that Christ Jesus could use me as a prime example of his great patience with even the worst sinners. Then others will realize that they, too, can believe in him and receive eternal life. [17]All honor and glory to God forever and ever! He is the eternal King, the unseen one who never dies; he alone is God. Amen. NLT

Matthew 27:45 From noon until three in the afternoon, darkness came over all the land. NIV

Romans 8:26 In the same way, the Spirit helps us in our weakness. We do not know what we ought to pray for, but the Spirit himself intercedes for us through wordless groans. NIV

Mark 3:28-29 [28]Truly I tell you, people can be forgiven all their sins and every slander they utter, [29]but whoever blasphemes against the Holy Spirit will never be forgiven; they are guilty of an eternal sin. NIV

Lamentations 3:22-23 [22]Because of the Lord's great love, we are not consumed, for his compassions never fail. [23]They are new every morning; great is your faithfulness. NIV

1 Corinthians 1:9 God is faithful, who has called you into fellowship with his Son, Jesus Christ our Lord. NIV

1 Thessalonians 5:24 The one who calls you is faithful, and he will do it. NIV

2 Thessalonians 3:3 But the Lord is faithful, and he will strengthen you and protect you from the evil one. NIV

Hebrews 11:11 And by faith even Sarah, who was past childbearing age, was enabled to bear children because she considered him faithful who had made the promise. NIV

Psalms 119:90 Your faithfulness continues through all generations: you established the earth, and it endures. NIV

Psalm 119:105 Your word is a lamp for my feet, a light on my path. NIV

Mathew 7:7-8 [7]Ask, and it will be given to you; seek, and you will find; knock, and the door will be opened to you. [8]For everyone who asks receives; the one who seeks finds; and to the one who knocks, the door will be opened. NIV

Chapter 40

1 John 1:9 But if we confess our sins, he is faithful and righteous, forgiving us our sins and cleansing us from all unrighteousness. NET Bible

Chapter 41

Ephesians 1:7 He is so rich in kindness and grace that he purchased our freedom with the blood of his Son and forgave our sins. NLT

Matthew 6:9-13 [9]After this manner therefore pray ye: Our Father, which art in heaven, hallowed be thy name. [10]Thy kingdom come, Thy will be done in earth, as it is in heaven. [11]Give us this day our daily bread. [12]And forgive us our debts, as we forgive our debtors. [13]And lead us not into temptation, but deliver us from evil; For thine is the kingdom and the power and the glory forever. Amen. KJV

Chapter 43

1 Timothy 1:15-17 [15]This is a trustworthy saying, and everyone should accept it: 'Christ Jesus came into the world to save sinners'—and I'm (Paul) the worst of them all. [16]But God had mercy on me so that Christ Jesus could use me as a prime example of his great patience with even the worst sinners. Then others will realize that they, too, can believe in him and receive eternal life. [17]All honor and glory to God forever and ever! He is the eternal King, the unseen one who never dies; he alone is God. Amen. NLT

Chapter 44

John 8:42-44 [42]Jesus said to them, "If God were your Father, you would love me, for I have come here from God. I have not come on my own; God sent me. [43]Why is my language not clear to you? Because you are unable to hear what I say. [44]You belong to your father, the devil, and you want to carry out your father's desires. He was a murderer from the beginning, not holding to the truth, for there is no truth in him. When he lies, he speaks his native language, for he is a liar and the father of lies. NIV

Chapter 45

Romans 10:11 As Scripture says, "Anyone who believes in him will never be put to shame. NIV

1 Corinthians 11:31 For if we would judge ourselves, we would not be judged. NKJV

Matthew 7:2 For in the same way you judge others, you will be judged, and with the measure you use, it will be measured to you. NIV

Philippians 3:13 No, dear brothers and sisters, I have not achieved it, but I focus on this one thing: Forgetting the past and looking forward to what lies ahead. NLT

Chapter 48

Romans 5:2 Because of our faith, Christ has brought us into this place of undeserved privilege where we now stand, and we confidently and joyfully look forward to sharing God's glory. NLT

Romans 4:23-25 [23]The words "it was credited to him" (referring to Abraham) were written not for him alone, [24]but also for us, to whom God will credit righteousness — for us who believe in him who raised Jesus our Lord from the dead. [24]He was delivered over death for our sins and was raised to life for our justification. NIV

Romans 8:17And since we are his children, we are his heirs. In fact, together with Christ, we are heirs of God's glory. But if we are to share his glory, we must also share his suffering. NLT

2 Corinthians 5:21 God made him who had no sin to be sinfor us, so that in him we might become the righteousness of God. NIV

Galatians 1:10 Am I now trying to win the approval of human beings or of God? Or am I trying to please people? If I were still trying to please people, I would not be a servant of Christ. NIV

Philippians 3:13-14 [13]Brothers and sisters, I do not consider myself yet to have taken hold of it. But one thing I do: Forgetting what is behind and straining toward what is ahead, [14]I press on toward the goal to win the prize for which God has called me heavenward in Christ Jesus. NIV

Isaiah 43:18-19 [18]Forget the former things; do not dwell on the past. [19]See, I am doing a new thing! Now it springs up; do you not perceive it? I am making a way in the wilderness and streams in the wasteland. NIV

Jeramiah 29:11 For I know the plans I have for you, says the Lord. They are plans for good and not for disaster, to give you a future and a hope. NLT

Isaiah 6:9 He said, "Go and tell this people: 'Be ever hearing but never understanding; be ever seeing but never perceiving. NIV

Romans 8:28And we know that God causes everything to work together for the good of those who love God and are called according to his purpose for them. NLT

Romans 8:38-39 [38]For I am convinced that neither death nor life, neither angels nor demons, neither the present nor the future, nor any powers, [39]neither height nor depth, nor anything else in all creation will ever be able to separate us from the love of God that is revealed in Christ Jesus our Lord. NLT

Romans 8:31 What shall we say about such wonderful things as these? If God is for us, who can ever be against us? NLT

2 Corinthians 4:16-17 [16]That is why we never give up. Though our bodies are dying, our spirits are being renewed every day. [17]For our present troubles are small and won't last very long. Yet they produce for us a glory that vastly outweighs them and will last forever! NLT

Acknowledgements

Ann Therese Ruelas

Anne Therese Ruelas was my friend from 2002 until her untimely passing in 2019. Ann Therese was that friend who, no matter how long it had been since we had seen each other, we picked right up where we left off. She was gifted in keeping a conversation on track without losing any threads that went off on a tangent. She always made everyone in the conversation feel important and that their thoughts were being heard. She had generously given up her life as the personal assistant to Janet Jackson to travel the country with her husband and three small children, spreading the Gospel as evangelists. Although we were not frequently in the same location, Ann Therese was always supportive of my writing. She granted me my first interview and encouraged me through the writing of *Between Thorns and Glory*. I wish she had gotten to read it. She showed me by example how to have joy and not feel sorry for yourself in the middle of great suffering. She thought of others before herself even in her last days. I am grateful for the true Christlike example of Ann Therese.

Marlene Barrett

I met Marlene Barrett walking my dog, the real Frostie Dog, on the beach in Del Mar, California. She was visiting from England and struck up a conversation with me that spanned four hours. She told me about her life in England, and I shared with her that I wanted to be a writer. She said that I was already an author. This was a revelation to me. From that point on, I believed I was an author, and so

I am. We have stayed in touch all these years. Thank you, Marlene, from across the pond.

Connie Anderson, Words and Deeds, Inc.

Connie was my first editor and became my friend. She is a founder of a writer's group for women called Women of Words in Minneapolis, Minnesota. During the pandemic, they zoomed the meeting and graciously included me. She helped me overcome my hesitation to show my work to anyone. She taught me the basics of novel writing and has been a supporter and advocate for *Between Thorns and Glory* as well as my blog, kimfrostpinkney.com You are much appreciated, Connie.

Lynn McNamee, Owner, Red Adept Editing

Lynn took on my project at a challenging time. The pandemic still roared on, and in the middle of my editing deadlines, my house burned down to the ground. Her professionalism, exceptional competence, promptness, and patience has been invaluable to me. I am truly grateful for you and your staff.

Alyssa Hall, Content Editor, Red Adept Editing

Alyssa opened my mind to greater possibilities. Her attention to detail and curiosity guided my story to heights that it would never have found without her. She was thorough and professional, using delicate precision in telling to me to cut entire characters from the book. Her insight into the themes and purpose of my book brought it to life in a new way. From her coaching, *Between Thorns and Glory* grew from a long novella of under sixty thousand words to a full novel of over one hundred thousand words. Alyssa, you are amazing. Thank you so much for bringing the painful chapters that needed to go into this book out of me.

Stephanie Spangler Buswell, Line Editor, Red Adept Editing

Stephanie is amazingly gifted at cutting half the words out and saying what I meant to say even better. She must have a magic wand. She was delightful and patient throughout the painstaking process of changing long blocks of conversation into lively discourse. *Between Thorns and Glory* is a smooth read thanks to Stephanie. Your professionalism made making the edits not feel like criticisms. I hope I get you again on the next book. You will always have my gratitude.

Irene Steiger, Proofreader, Red Adept Editing

Irene was quick and thorough. I appreciate her hard work on my project.

Ashley Peltier, Beta Reader

As an up-and-coming young novelist, Ashley brought insights and comments from her own unique perspective to make *Between Thorns and Glory* a better and more relevant read. I can't wait to read the end of your book, Ashley.

Anja Mila Marsalis, Beta Reader

Anja Mila's feedback showed me that my message was indeed getting across. This encouragement saw me through to the end of the writing and editing process.

About the Author

Since her birth was considered a miracle, Kimberly Frost Pinkney has always had a sense of purpose and thirst for spiritual truth. Raised in the boondocks of New Mexico, pegged "Loco Hills" because the hills were on one side of the road one day and the other side the next day, she had a vivid imagination that blossomed from listening to the tall tales of her dad, who influenced her love of public speaking and reading. He also gave her his entrepreneur spirit, which guided her in starting, growing, and selling her own small businesses, including starting her own financial consulting practice.

Kimberly shot professional photography and video for musical acts, corporations, and churches for television broadcast. She dreamed up and ran CrunchTime Popcorn in the Gas Lamp District of San Diego, two Major League Baseball stadiums, and several concert venues, where she mentored young adults from all over the world. There, she made a smoothie for Major League Baseball MVP Ryan Braum, who broke his record and Petco Park's with three homeruns and a triple that same day. Yes, he came back the next day for another one.

Buying and restoring abandoned properties, Kimberly made it possible for young people to become homeowners. Her quest for truth, a good story, and cooler weather led her on great adventures.

Kimberly has lived in the Rocky Mountains, in a loft overlooking Boston Commons, and on a yacht. She studied Greek and Latin at Harvard, stand-up paddle boarded the San Diego bay, invested in a mansion in the California mountains to turn it into a homeless shelter and resting place for traveling missionaries. She circumnavigated America in a forty-foot motorcoach, visiting churches of all kinds.

Kimberly has hiked many trails to settle down with her husband, David, in the Blue Ridge Mountains of Virginia to write, draw, hike, garden, and feed hummingbirds. Her goal is to inspire others to seek and find peace, freedom, and joy.

Read more at https://kimfrostpinkney.com/.

 The Way Publishing

About the Publisher

Be bold, be brave, be what you are — an author!

The Apostle Paul and his contemporaries called their life and calling The Way. The Way was a sect that was dedicated to believe and teach the Good News that Jesus Christ rose from the dead for all of our sins so that we may have eternal life. In Paul's day as well as our own many different groups have formed calling themselves all sorts of different names all following The Way. We walk, talk, work, sleep, live and write in The Way. Here at The Way Publishing we hope to give a home to all those who wish to follow The Way and labor in the building of the Kingdom of Heaven through their inspired writings both fiction and non-fiction, poetry and prose.

Our mission is to make it possible for our authors to write and publish what they believe that Jesus has laid on their hearts in a professional and cost-effective way.

We are dedicated to bringing inspirational stories to life through books, art, video and photography.

TheWayPublishing.com

Made in the USA
Columbia, SC
16 November 2022

71045827R00233